The Snake..... Of Sneyd End

By Ray Burston

© 2018

12910380

By the summer of 1969 the 'Swinging Sixties' has barely touched Sneyd End in the English Midlands.

Instead, while Neil Armstrong is walking on the Moon and The Beatles are recording *'Abbey Road'*, the good folk of this grimy, industrial town are trying to make sense of a series of unexplained disappearances amongst the pupils of the local high school.

One man declares he has the answer: Brian Danks is an eccentric zoologist who has made a name for himself on account of his dogged campaign to save the town's railway from closure. It's been an obsession that has won him few friends, and one or two powerful enemies.

So who will listen now when he tries to warn the people of Sneyd End about the monstrous killer in their midst?

'Vox clamantis in deserto.'

Dedicated to all those 'voices in the wilderness' who – by their willingness to uphold lonely and unpopular causes – have eventually made the world a better place.

… And to their spouses – who also bear the scars of having made it so.

"If you look into the eyes of any snake you will see that it knows all and more of the mystery of man's fall, and that it feels all the contempt that the Devil felt when Adam was evicted from Eden."

Rudyard Kipling

1

Everything was deathly quiet, aside from the obligatory cough from up the back of the church. The bride and groom had turned to stare nervously into the other's eyes. The vicar calling for him to go first, through his black-rimmed 'Buddy Holly' spectacles the groom caught the twinkle of a smile from behind the veil of his bride that also fired him up to plight his troth.

"I, B-b-brian M-m-matthew D-d-danks," he stumbled at first, "take you, Ruby Elizabeth Leadbetter, to be my wife; to have and to hold from this day forward; for better, for worse; for richer, for poorer; in sickness and in health; to have and to hold till death us do part, according to God's holy law. In the presence of God, I make this vow."

He'd done it! Not only had Brian Danks overcome his innate clumsiness in such matters to ask out one of the better-looking girls at university, but three years on here they were being joined in matrimony. All that remained to convince him he wasn't dreaming was to hear those words tripping from her lips too.

"I, Ruby Elizabeth Leadbetter," her dulcet voice affirmed, "take you, Brian Matthew Danks, to be my husband; to have and to hold from this day forward; for better, for worse; for richer, for poorer; in sickness and in health; to have and to hold, till death us do part, according to God's holy law. In the presence of God, I make this vow."

Along the front row the groom's mother gazed on proudly – though, alas, pride mixed with regret that Brian's father hadn't lived to witness this moment. Meanwhile, across the aisle the more judicious expression upon the face of Mrs Leadbetter spoke of resignation that, in the end, her bright and personable daughter had not changed her mind. Far from it. As the concluding benediction was spoken, Ruby was demonstrably chuffed that she and her bumbling, if endearing fiancé were finally man and wife. Well, except for the 'to have and to hold' bit – which the happy couple would no doubt be attending to later! For now, Brian contented himself with lifting the veil to plant a tender kiss upon Ruby's soft, receptive lips

And so, arm-in-arm, the newly-weds turned to lead the procession of family and friends out into the warm, spring sunshine. Following behind her daughter, Mrs Leadbetter donned a faux smile for the rejoicing guests. What was done was done – for better or for worse.

* * * * *

One advantage of having booked a two o'clock wedding was that by the time the photographs had been taken, everyone had been sat down in the church hall, and the speeches and toasts had been made, there was a handy window of opportunity to attend to the other important event that Brian Danks had pencilled in for Saturday, June 6th 1964. He stared down at his watch. Observing him, his best man studied his own watch too. Ruby also looked at hers and wondered whether they might be cutting it a bit fine. There would certainly be no time for her to change out of that elegant white wedding dress.

"Really! Must you do this? And on today, of all days?" her mother protested as her daughter explained again. Her father too looked askance, shaking his head upon being reminded.

"We won't be away long. It will be his last chance and Brian desperately doesn't want to miss it. Just chat to the guests while we're away. Introduce yourself to the vicar too. Father Allen's a really nice man. He's made me so welcome at the church."

As with much else about her new son-in-law and his seeming hold upon her daughter, Mrs Leadbetter knew it was pointless to reason with her. With a sigh of resignation, she looked on as the couple temporarily made themselves scarce. They say love is blind. Sooner or later, she feared, the scales would fall from her daughter's eyes.

"Right, let's go, Jonathan. And don't spare the horses!" Brian hollered as he and his new wife plonked themselves onto the back seat of his best man's beige Ford Prefect. Off the car sped, leaving Sneyd End church hall behind as it wound its way along the town's busy shopping street, where the shopkeepers were packing away their wares and winding in their awnings.

"Thank you for your speech, Jonathan. And for the kind words you said about Ruby and me. Oh, and thank you, of course, for being my best man," Brian twittered.

Jonathan looked up into his rear-view mirror and offered him a wry smile. "You're welcome. Besides, somebody had to do it. I get the feeling Ruby wouldn't have trusted *you* to take care of the rings without losing them!" he chuckled.

Ruby emitted a wry smile too. Brian Danks and Jonathan Hunt had been friends since they'd been in short trousers. Indeed, she suspected there had been times when Jonathan had been his *only* friend, such was her husband's knack of enchanting and repelling people in equal measure. Yet, forthright and opinionated though he undoubtedly could be, there had always been an appealing sincerity about her quirky new spouse. His heart was indisputably in the right place. Perhaps it was this side of his mercurial nature that had won Ruby's heart when, during their final year at university – and after two years spent watching in frustration while she'd dated a succession of other boys – he'd finally plucked up the courage to ask her out.

On and on, the car hurried past the Town Hall, where many of her husband's forthright opinions had been expressed during the time they'd been engaged. She stared up at the proud Victorian edifice. Love was not so blind that the sight of its flanks and columns darkened by the grime that pervaded this unsung corner of the Black Country didn't remind her that (as her mother had periodically reminded her too!) there *had* been other choices for a mate. And other more salubrious corners of England for her to have been found setting out upon a marital journey.

Eventually, Jonathan steered the car down a driveway on the outskirts of town to draw it to a halt outside a shabby station building. The railway had first arrived in Sneyd End one-hundred-and-twenty years ago during the heyday of Victorian 'railway mania'. However, since the war it had progressively been run down to the point where the town's station had become an unmanned halt, its booking office boarded up and the paint flaking from the saw-edged valances of its platform canopies.

The bride, groom, and best man leapt from the car and raced onto the weed-strewn platform just in time to catch the Gloucester RC&W diesel railcar that had been working what few passenger trains had been calling at Sneyd End of late. A lazy trail of grey fumes was rising from its twin, upward-facing exhaust pipes.

To be sure, British Railways had planned no great ceremony for the final departure of a train from this station. However, a press photographer was on hand to capture the moment for posterity. Suffice to say, the sight of a comely young lady attired in a wedding dress immediately caught his eye. Neither could the accompanying reporter believe his eyes when he spotted the groom who was about to usher her aboard the waiting train. This was certainly going to be a railway story with a difference.

"Mr Danks, are you disappointed that trains will no longer call at Sneyd End?" he buttonholed the couple, notebook in hand.

"Disappointed, yes. But this is not the end of our fight," Brian insisted, halting with the handle of the carriage door in his hand.

"But the Beeching Report made clear this line is barely used and hopelessly unprofitable," the newshound pointed out. "Surely closure is the only sensible option."

"Sensible only to the bean counters in the Ministry of Transport who have no understanding of how railways are part of the fabric of our national life," he sniffed. "Besides, just look over there," he then pointed to a cluster of rooftops off yonder. "The new Sneyd Park development is nearing completion: over eight hundred new houses. How will all the professional types who will soon live on this modern estate commute to their offices if this railway is no longer here?"

"By car presumably," the scribbler had the audacity to suggest.

His photographer briefly looked up from behind his camera before sizing up another shot of Ruby in her nuptial finery. She forced a nervous smile – even as she knew such a flippant remark was like a red rag to a bull to her indignant husband.

"You mean the same motor cars that are choking our towns and cities? The same motor cars that are the reason our politicians destroy beautiful old buildings so that they can cover those towns and cities in concrete and tarmac? The same motor cars that threaten to turn them into soulless, polluted wildernesses – as has already happened in the United States?"

If nothing else, this outspoken twenty-four-year-old was always good for a provocative quote. Not for nothing had he become the rallying point for the small, but vocal campaign that had sought to save the Sneyd End line from closure.

Alas, as the local hack had alluded, not even the terrier-like tenacity of Brian Danks had been able to stave off the inevitable. In March 1963, Dr Richard Beeching – appointed Chairman of the British Railways Board by transport minister, Ernest Marples – had published a study into how Britain's tired and underperforming railway network could be made to pay its way. As well as recommending a programme of modernisation for the most profitable parts of the business (bulk freight, London commuter lines, and inter-city passenger services), the Beeching Report (as *'The Reshaping of British Railways'* had become known) had controversially proposed that over two thousand stations and over five thousand miles of track should be closed – a third of the country's railway network. Though occasioning an outcry from those communities that would thereby lose their railways, the Conservative government of Harold MacMillan had largely rubber-stamped the closure programme (aware that three thousand miles of similarly loss-making routes had already been closed on the quiet during the 1950s).

"Anyway, gentleman. If you don't mind, my new wife and I have a train to catch," Dr Beeching's most vocal critic in the Midlands reminded them, Jonathan urging bride and groom inside the carriage and pulling the door shut.

"Mr Danks, what do you say to those who…"

It was too late. The guard pressed the buzzer that instructed the driver to depart. The malachite-green 'Bubble Car' revved its motor and – amidst more clouds of swirling exhaust – the last ever passenger train to depart Sneyd End station began to pick up speed for its final twenty-minute dash to Birmingham.

"We only just made it," Jonathan noted with relief. "And though I hate to point it out, we wouldn't have done so had it not been thanks to the services of a 'motor car'!"

His ironic observation was lost on his friend – as such attempts at irony frequently were. Instead, Brian was on his feet, peering out of the window he'd drawn down – desperate to catch a final glimpse of the town as it could be viewed from a train. As if to rub in the fact that modernity had already relentlessly intruded into that view, he gazed up at the afternoon sun glinting upon the windows of the Tiger Street flats – a newly-completed municipal housing estate that had swept away the old Victorian back-to-back terraces where he'd been born and grown up.

In due course, he sat down: for there was one familiar piece of the town's railway heritage that it was best not to experience with one's head hanging out of the window. A blast of the train's twin horns signalled its imminent approach. Then suddenly all was darkness save for the dull illumination afforded by the light bulbs of the carriage, the rattling of the railcar magnified as it plunged into Sneyd End Tunnel.

"Of course, Beeching is wrong," Brian shook his head, sufficiently immersed in mourning that he failed to notice his wife brushing off annoying traces of soot that had swirled in through the open window to dust her immaculate gown – the legacy of over a century or more of steam locomotives passing through the tunnel. "Okay, this line's been losing money," he conceded.

"Hand over fist," Jonathan sighed.

"However, with a bit of investment it could have been turned around. Instead, they've closed it. It's sheer lunacy. Neither is it any coincidence that Ernest Marples has made his money out of building motorways. Perhaps that's why our transport minister is no fan of Britain's railways."

The railcar re-emerged into daylight, permitting them on one side to view the promontory on which was sat the new secondary school where Ruby taught; and on the other the cooling ponds of Fens Bank that serviced the giant Alcock & Robbins steel works in the distance. Tethered horses were grazing upon the expanses of wasteland that surrounded these green-hewed, man-made lakes. Symbolic of the industrial revolution that had once transformed Britain into a pre-eminent economic and military power, its production had been despatched the length and breadth of the globe in the time that this colossal works had been rolling steel – aided by the railways (the tangible evidence of which was the sprawling network of sidings that hove into view as the train clickety-clacked past them.

Meanwhile, modernity kept on relentlessly intruding. Before the train arrived in Wednesbury (where it would join the Birmingham Snow Hill-Wolverhampton main line) in the distance it was possible to make out construction proceeding apace on the new M6 motorway that would soon connect the West Midlands to Ernie Marples' fast expanding motorway network. Meanwhile, upon a bridge that the little train rattled beneath, a line of cars and a double-deck Midland Red bus waiting at traffic lights likewise provided the symbolism of how Sneyd End would henceforth be connected to the outside world.

* * * * *

"Good grief, Ruby. Where on Earth have you been? Look at the state of your dress!"

Mrs Leadbetter's clucking questions were very much rhetorical. She could guess from where her daughter had acquired the traces of soot that had dusted it. It was yet one more reason for her to despise the new son-in-law who was always dragging her off on these ridiculous railway jaunts. And another good reason why (regardless of Brian's nostalgic ramblings) the sooner British Railways replaced steam with cleaner diesel and electric trains the better.

In like manner, Ruby vicariously explaining how the train she had just ridden had been the very last one that would ever serve her adopted town failed to iron out her mother's censorious glower. Neither did she have the heart to tell her mother that it looked like it would be her pretty face – wedding gown and all – that would be gracing the accompanying news story that would be appearing in Monday evening's 'Sneyd End Gazette'. The things one does for love!

Indeed, now that the bride and groom were back in their midst, love was very much in the air again. On cue, the disc jockey dropped Cilla Black's 'You're My World' onto his turntable and the lights were dimmed so that Brian and Ruby Danks could take to the floor to savour their first dance as man and wife, watched over by their friends and families. And by Brian's mother too – who again glanced heavenwards to sniffle thankfully that the Almighty had caused her oddball son to stumble upon this wonderful woman who would love and look after him.

* * * * *

Whatever was going on at Sneyd End church hall tonight, its patrons were clearly having a whale of a time. Darkness having meantime fallen, it was while they were dancing the night away to the likes of Cliff Richard & The Shadows, Gerry & The Pacemakers, and The Dave Clark Five that an anonymous-looking Bedford van drew up unnoticed in a quiet lane across the way. Extinguishing the engine, its driver lit up a cigarette. In due course, he stepped outside to check if anyone was about. As if to steel himself for whatever wrongdoing he was about to get up to, he began whistling along to Millie's upbeat *'My Boy Lollipop'* that was drifting from the hall on the warm breeze. Otherwise, the preoccupation of its shuffling partygoers would hopefully enable this furtive character to do what he'd come here to do before scarpering. Gripping the ash-tipped fag between his teeth, to this end he opened the rear doors of the van and scrambled inside.

Grabbing hold of a large canvas sack, he dragged it in stages to the lip of the loading floor. He was about to lift it to his chest to carry in his arms – only to be rudely reminded just how big and heavy Betty had become. Therefore, he turned about and threw the old girl over his shoulder instead – in the manner of how he'd seen the coalman delivering the nutty slack. Even so, lugging her was hard work – even for a bloke of his muscular build.

Truth to tell, this exotic lady had thrived during the time she'd been a guest under his roof. Indeed, she'd thrived rather too well. As such, a tinge of sadness came over him that it was time for them to part. Put simply, Betty had outgrown her welcome. Therefore, he now staggered over to a convenient gap in the wooden fence that ran alongside the railway embankment, bearing the sack in which he'd tied her up. This lonely spot would be Betty's final resting place. Unlike the deceased denizens of the adjacent cemetery, she would not be receiving a Christian burial.

Dumping the sack on the ground and pausing from his exertions, her assailant was suddenly startled by the door to the church hall bursting open. Hastily, he ducked below the chest-high brick boundary wall of the cemetery. Peering over it, he could observe that, as well as Martha & The Vandellas' *'Heatwave'* escaping to disturb the balmy, nocturnal stillness, an excited posse of partygoers was racing about in merriment.

"Promise me you'll forget all about railways while you're away on honeymoon," someone ordered a guy who was sporting a pair of thick, dark-rimmed spectacles, and who was ushering a pretty girl with bobbed hair into the back of a Ford Prefect.

"Yes, for one week at least Ruby deserves your wholehearted attention. Otherwise, you'll come back from train-spotting to find she's been wooed by some strapping Jock in a kilt!" another cautioned, prompting mirth on the part of the crowd now gathering around the car.

"Brian forget about trains? More like he'll take her off gallivanting on all those West Highland lines that Dr Beeching wants to close," a further wry comment surmised.

"Come on, chaps, out of the way. I need to step on it if I'm to whisk the happy couple to Wolverhampton in time to board the overnight sleeper service to Scotland."

The geezer who'd uttered this timely admonition dived into the driver's seat and started the car up, its passage off the car park attended by a forest of waving hands bidding the happy couple *bon voyage* (as well as by the clanking of the tin cans that some wag had sneakily tied to its rear bumper).

The ne'er-do-well still skulking behind the wall looked on while the well-wishers wandered back inside to enjoy the party. Thereupon, the old graveyard returned to a semblance of tranquillity disturbed only by the dreamy, muffled refrains of The Everly Brothers that were drifting from the hall.

Returning to the matter in hand, with all his might he lifted his erstwhile female housemate and hurled the sack in which she was sealed down the embankment, looking on as it tumbled through the undergrowth. Straining in the darkness, he spotted that it had come to rest beside the track.

"Sorry, Betty. No hard feelings, like. But it's better this way," he puffed as he leant against the fence post to gather his breath.

Job done, he climbed back into the van, lit up another cigarette, and slumped over the steering wheel – as if gripped by a final fit of remorse. However, lest his skulduggery risk being uncovered by some other unexpected troop of late-night revellers, he promptly pushed it from his thoughts and fired up the engine, crunching the van into gear to make his getaway.

However, no sooner he'd departed than something began to stir beside the now abandoned Sneyd End railway line. There was movement inside the sack he'd dumped alongside it: a desperate shuffling and twisting that was starting to force the knot that held it shut. The man who had callously abandoned the unloved Betty was confident the world had seen the last of her. Betty, however, had other ideas.

2

Outside No. 14 Churchill Avenue it was dark and it was raining. From the main road at the end of the Sneyd Park estate, the first stirrings of the morning commute to work could be discerned in the distance. Inside – and with the central heating humming away – all was warm and cosy.

Too cosy. One of its occupants was also stirring. Soon enough, the recipient of the surreptitious fumbling going on beneath the sheets awoke and felt a snake-like hand sneak under her nightie. Warming to the sensation of it scooping up her bosom and thumbing the nipple that was firming up, eventually she rolled over to spy the suggestive glint in his eyes. She permitted him to gently kiss her – a kiss that soon blossomed into something more. In no time at all, he'd moved to conjoin with her. Soon those bed sheets were billowing. Brian and Ruby Danks were unashamedly celebrating their marriage in the most tangible way that two people in love possibly can.

The celebration had not long reached its breathless consummation when the alarm clock on the bedside table rudely reminded them that their own morning commutes beckoned. Reluctantly, the happy couple unravelled themselves from each other's embrace and began the chore of trooping to the bathroom and to the kitchen in preparation for their working days.

Brian had already washed, dressed, made tea and prepared breakfast by the time Ruby breezed into the kitchen, humming along to The Beatles' ubiquitous *'She Loves You'* single that was playing on the transistor radio on the work surface. Dressed smartly in a grey woollen jumper and pleated skirt – and with her silky brown hair swept back in a headband – she slipped into the chair opposite her husband and selected a slice of warm toast from the rack. While she was buttering it, the radio counted down six evenly-spaced beeps and a final, more emphatic one, upon which a brisk voice replaced the music.

"Good morning. It's seven o'clock on Thursday, October 15th and here is the news. Polling stations across Britain have opened on what promises to be a closely-fought General Election…"

"You know, I shall be so glad when this election is over," said Ruby, her lips eventually emerging from sipping the cup of steaming tea she was holding with her delicate fingers. "All these horrid things being said about 'if you want a nigger for a neighbour, vote Labour'! I certainly won't be voting for anyone who talks about coloured people that way. Black, white, yellow or brown, we're all God's children."

Brian smiled. The product of her strong Christian faith, his wife's perpetually charitable view of humanity had always been one of her more commendable traits – even if, in this instance, it was at odds with the more atavistic opinions of many people in the Midlands, for whom immigration from Britain's former colonies was another aspect of post-war modernity that the country could have done without.

To be sure, it was a tired Conservative Party that had entered this election after thirteen years in power, having lately been rocked by the revelation that war minister John Profumo had been sharing a call girl with a Russian spy. In addition, in the era of classless meritocracy that the 1960s had ushered in there was dismay in some quarters over the controversial elevation of Sir Alec Douglas Home to the premiership (an Etonian and an aristocrat, Labour leader Harold Wilson had dubbed him the 'Fourteenth Earl of Home') – to say nothing of an openly racist campaign mounted by one of its candidates. Meanwhile – having likewise succeeded to his party's leadership the previous year after the death of the popular and principled Hugh Gaitskell – the wilier Wilson had papered over Labour's own divisions to present himself as a 'man of the people' ('the fourteenth Mr Wilson', as Home had wittily riposted!), someone willing to lead Britain into this new era forged in what he'd termed 'the white heat' of a technological revolution.

"I intend to cast my vote on the way to work. If you want to as well, I can give you a lift to the polling station," Ruby offered, buttering some more toast.

Her husband had always possessed an emotional transparency that made it difficult for him to disguise the thought processes going on inside his head. He'd never make a poker player! Just then this curious trait alerted her to the possibility that he'd taken offence at something she'd just said. Did he think she was hinting at how she wanted him to vote? Then she realised what was troubling him.

"I know you have this thing about public transport, Brian. But my little car is not your mortal enemy. Besides, it's raining outside," she fired him a warm grin.

Aware that he'd offered her his considered opinions about the importance of people using buses and trains on many diverse occasions, the folds of apprehension cleared from his brow.

"Thank you. That would be nice," he nodded.

"Anyway, I thought you'd be eager to get down there and vote. After all, Mr Wilson has promised to reverse the Beeching cuts if Labour is elected!" she said, shamelessly playing to his prejudices. "What's more, the Labour candidate here is even promising to reopen the line through Sneyd End."

* * * * *

With breakfast out of the way and the washing up done, while he was waiting for Ruby to gather her things together Brian took a moment to drift into the living room. There he lingered to admire the other stunning female occupant of 14 Churchill Avenue.

Lazing in her big glass tank beneath the powerful glow of a sun lamp, Lizzie was a California kingsnake. Brian would have happily filled their house with other exotic snakes and lizards had Ruby (like his mother before her) not put her foot down and drawn the line at him keeping just one token representative of the reptiles that were her husband's other abiding passion. The model train set in the spare room his wife could live with (even if it did mean he frequently deserted her in the evening to go tinker with it). A house full of slithering beasts was another! Ruby Danks might be a biology teacher at the local secondary school. However, even her professional interest in the animal kingdom had limits!

Brian gazed on, marvelling at how the black-and-white striped serpent was probing its habitat, reaching up the glass front of the tank to show off its three-foot length.

"Come on, you. Time to attend to your other cold-blooded friends," said Ruby, having spotted her husband doting upon the snake while she was donning her coat and beret in the hallway.

Once outside – and in a reverse act of chivalry – Ruby opened the door so that he could jump into the red Austin Mini that had taken up residence on the drive of their new detached house. Checking her reflection in the driver's mirror, Ruby tucked away an odd strand of loose hair before starting it up.

"You're quite proud of your new car, aren't you?" her passenger noted, observing the deftness with which she was soon slotting it up and down the gears.

"It's shaved valuable time off my journey to work. And it's handy for shopping. I suspect that kind of convenience is why more and more people are buying one nowadays. You can't tell me you don't get fed up of waiting for buses – especially on a day like today," she glanced at him and probed.

Brian said nothing – as if for him to concede that public transport was not always the most practical travel option was akin to having to renounce his own Christian faith. Otherwise, the analogy reminded him of something he'd forgotten to mention.

"Father Allen asked me the other day if I'd like to become a lay reader. I think he must have been impressed by all those speeches I made during the campaign to save the railway," he chortled with more than a hint of self-satisfaction.

"Good for you," his wife cheered, glancing at him again.

She knew Brian was capable of summoning boundless energy and enthusiasm when he set his mind to something – qualities which were not always appreciated by those on the receiving end of them. With the fight to retain the town's railway effectively over, it would be good for him to set his mind instead to this new (and more spiritually-uplifting) challenge.

Ruby parked the car outside the nearby primary school that had been closed for the day to serve as their polling station. The couple were about to head inside when who should they bump into keeping watch outside the main door? It was none other than Jonathan Hunt, attired smartly and professionally in the uniform of a police constable.

"Gosh! Don't you just look the part," Ruby ribbed him from beneath the shelter of her umbrella.

"He does indeed. If I was a villain he'd certainly put the fear of God into me!" Brian added, likewise teasing his old friend.

Not only had Jonathan finally fulfilled his ambition to pursue a career as a police officer, but during the few weeks since he'd passed out from training college he'd also learned how to mimic the phlegmatic demeanour of one too. Gone was the frivolity that often attended their get-togethers and in its place was the diligent sobriety of one sworn to uphold the Queen's Peace.

"Yes, well. Someone has to ensure that the people of Sneyd End can exercise their right to vote without let or hindrance," he muttered from beneath his bulbous blue helmet, around the rim of which the rain was dripping.

"Not expecting any trouble then, are we?" Ruby wondered.

Jonathan did not respond. Instead, he eyed her up and down charily, unsure whether she was pulling his leg again.

"Anyway, talking of exercising the right to vote, we need to get on with exercising ours right now – before I'm late for work," Brian beamed his wife a cheesy grin.

Upon which, she followed him inside the polling station, leaving their stolid police officer friend to perform his boring vigil. Jonathan took a moment out to stare up at the leaden skies in the hope it might stop raining.

Voting complete, on their way back to the car the couple bumped into another by-now familiar face: their new next-door neighbour heading in through the school gate. Clutching a brolly with one hand, an excitable Labrador was straining at the lead she was gripping with the other.

"Hello, Ruby. Hello, Brian. Good to see the younger generation doing their civic duty. 'Vote early, vote often', as they say," she enthused, her canine companion panting and wagging its tail, eager instead to recommence its morning walk.

"Hello, Mrs Channon. Good to see Bertie is on fine form," Ruby joked when his owner rebuked him for attempting to deposit his wet paws on Brian's mackintosh.

"Yes, sorry. He is a bit of a handful sometimes. Still, you're just a great big softie really, aren't your Bertie," she cooed fondly, glancing up to assure her that "He wouldn't hurt a fly."

Brian patted Bertie on the head, mindful that the cats the mischievous mutt was forever chasing over the garden fence might beg to differ.

"You know, we're really lucky to have nice, friendly neighbours like Mr and Mrs Channon," Ruby opined once they were back in the car and out of the rain. "So many of these modern, new estates they're building nowadays are full of stuck-up, self-regarding people who are wrapped up in their own acquisitive social climbing."

"You mean like your mother?" Brian couldn't resist quipping.

Ruby shot him another sideways glance, this time a longer one that informed him she was only vaguely amused.

"She just wants the best for herself and her family, that's all," she sought to strike a more generous note (though the sigh that preceded her defence of her mother suggested she couldn't entirely gainsay Brian's blunt observation).

"She doesn't like me, you know. She's never liked me. Ever since that day you first introduced me to her and I accidentally knocked a coffee table full of drinks all over her brand new carpet. I swear she thinks I'm not good enough for you."

Ruby reached across to squeeze his hand.

"I'm sure she likes you really, dear. She knows that you love me and that you care about me," she sighed again. "It's just that, well... sometimes you can be a bit too..."

"...Clumsy? And wrapped up in my own obsessions?" he completed her sentence for her.

She didn't demur. He hung his head in remorse.

"Brian, I know you like trains. And I know you like reptiles. And I'm happy to indulge your passions, because I love you and want to spend the rest of my life with you. All I ask in return is that you never forget that I have needs too."

As they neared the bus stop from where her husband could catch the service to Dudley, she turned to observe that he'd meantime donned a huge smirk.

"And not just *those* needs!" she castigated him playfully.

Drawing to a halt alongside the stop, she yanked on the handbrake and leant across to grasp his neck and haul him in close for a parting kiss – much to the bemusement of the passengers already waiting there.

"This morning was nice though!" she assured him upon releasing her grasp. "Now have a nice day at the zoo."

"You too – in the classroom," he smiled.

Leaning over to grab the duffle bag containing his lunch from the back seat, he planted a final quick peck on her cheek before hauling his gangling frame out of the tiny car. Closing the door behind him, he poked his spectacles back onto his nose and offered her a parting wave, spotting her gorgeous brown eyes glancing up into the rear-view mirror to offer him one too as she drove off. Yes, Brian Danks did love his wife. And he cared about her too. She was the best thing that had ever happened to him.

* * * * *

To be sure, that final railcar journey to Birmingham had not been the last train to pass through Sneyd End. That dubious honour had fallen to the engineering train that – seven months later during the week of Winston Churchill's lavish state funeral – began the invidious task of lifting the track. Like many of the fine steam locomotives that were also being withdrawn – many of which had once hauled the most prestigious trains on Britain's railways – the town's permanent way was to be cut up and melted down. Perhaps it would end up being refashioned into panels for the cars that were rolling off the production lines of Midlands motor factories in ever-increasing numbers now that more families were sharing in the rising post-war affluence. All that was to remain of the Sneyd End line would be a short section from Wednesbury to the sidings of the Alcock & Robbins steel works.

Braving a biting wind, from an embankment over-looking it a downcast character in a tan duffle coat had come to watch the stretch of track being removed from the north end of the Sneyd End Tunnel. Below him, a work gang was methodically unbolting the rails to permit the crane that a diesel locomotive was hauling to lift them onto accompanying flatbed trucks.

For Brian Danks, it was an unedifying sight. In fact, it was more than just the bleak chill of winter that had sharpened his countenance. He had failed. Despite spear-heading a year-long campaign that had occasioned packed public meetings and petitions to Parliament – and thereby made him something of a celebrity in his home town – he'd been unable to prevent the closure of Sneyd End station and the withdrawal of its passenger services. Neither had he been able to prevent the abandonment of the line itself – which was proceeding apace before his very eyes.

3

Word had spread. The sense of anticipation – trepidation even – was palpable. Having spent a very wet April morning wandering around this zoo sat atop a hill from which the entire Black Country could be viewed, they were off to see 'The Snakeman'!

Having peered down at the tigers and the polar bears in their Tecton pits and giggled at the comic capers of the occupants of the ape house, this troop of soggy, but excitable nine-year-olds had finally escaped the rain to huddle up in the presence of this boyish, bespectacled character who everyone called by that name. The hum of nervous chatter was promptly stilled by their teacher summoning their attention.

"Boys and girls, this is Mr Danks and he's the keeper of the reptile house," the flame-haired and freckled young woman proffered Brian his more formal title – as well as that of the dim and spooky lair in which he laboured.

"Good morning, Mr Danks," came the well-drilled collective reply, the gloom of the place leavened by their inquisitive smiles. Meanwhile, a mist was swirling in response to two dozen damp capes, caps and mackintoshes warming in the enervating heat.

"Now do you remember what kinds of animals we said are reptiles?" the teacher enquired of them. Here and there rigid arms could be spotted being thrust aloft.

"Crocodiles, Miss," one eager lad replied.

"Lithzards, Misth," a ginger-haired girl with cute pigtails lisped through her missing front tooth.

"And horrible, slimy snakes, Miss!" a snotty-nosed nipper at the head of the ensemble cackled to general amusement. Like their teacher, Brian summoned up an indulgent grin. There's always one in every class!

"That's right. Well, I'm sure Mr Danks here is going to tell us all about crocodiles, lizards and snakes. And if you're good, he might even have a surprise for you."

Pairs of wide young eyes glanced at each other excitedly as Brian stepped forward to address them, immediately injecting into the proceedings an enthusiasm about his vocation that was positively infectious – especially to these awestruck youngsters.

"Yes, as your teacher has explained, I don't just want you to go away from here having *seen* reptiles. I want to welcome you into their world too! And while your parents might have told you that snakes are 'horrible', I hope to show you that they're actually fascinating animals that have adapted incredibly well to the places where they live."

As with his love affair with trains, Brian Danks sometimes struggled to pinpoint the precise moment as a child when a passing interest in reptiles was ignited into an abiding passion for them. Was it seeing snakes slithering about in *'The Speckled Band'*, *'The Mask Of Fu Manchu'*, and *'King Solomon's Mines'* during matinee screenings at Sneyd End's Essoldo cinema? Or was it that memorable day when, as an impressionable nine-year-old himself, his mother had brought him to this place too? Either way, by the time he'd left school he'd resolved that he would pursue a vocation as a herpetologist – someone who studies snakes. Having won a place to read biology at the University of Birmingham, thus it had transpired that, at a relatively young age, he'd come to be managing this important collection of their kind – as well as educating the next generation of children from the Midlands about the wonders of reptiles and amphibians.

"… So, if you'll follow me, I'm going to take you on a journey into that world. But do remember to be quiet, won't you, children," he beseeched them, lowering his voice to a whisper for dramatic effect, "because, although they don't have ears to detect sound, snakes, in particular, are very sensitive to the noises we make, and can pick up the vibrations through their bodies."

And with that admonition the troop followed him down the humid, dimly-lit corridors – reinforced by their teacher drawing a finger to her lips to shush another burst of chatter.

First off, Brian halted them in front of an illuminated glass tank where all that struck the eye at first was a small pond surrounded by verdant vegetation. However, eager eyes were soon spying out tiny, vivid shapes. Cue pointed fingers and more excited chatter (as well as another shushing from their teacher).

"Those fwogs are weally pwetty colours," the little girl with the lisp looked up at Brian and marvelled.

"Yes," he concurred with avuncular charm, "pretty – but also deadly. These are poison-dart frogs. Those pretty colours you see – yellows and reds and blues – are intended to warn predators not to eat them. That's because their skin secretes toxic substances. They're called poison-dart frogs because some Indian tribes in the forests of South America – where they come from – dip their arrows and darts in their poison in order to paralyse animals that they shoot down from the trees to eat."

Next stop: another glass-fronted enclosure where, beneath the glow of a sun lamp, the swivelling eye of an otherwise motionless veiled chameleon had trained itself upon a cricket that was minding its own business. Suddenly, a huge tongue shot out and seized the insect, reeling it in to be crunched and devoured – much to the horror or amusement of its young onlookers.

Further down the corridor, Brian could tell them all about the red-eared slider terrapins that were swimming around in their enclosure or basking on rocks – what they eat, how long they live, how big they can grow, and where they can be found.

"Yer' can find 'em over Fens Bank too, mate," the cocky kid with the snotty nose crowed.

"No, seriously, Miss," he insisted upon being presented with his teacher's beady (and suitably sceptical) eye. "Me an' our bruvva' often see 'em when we'm fishin' over there," he was adamant. "Big uns' too!" he extended his palms to demonstrate.

"I suppose it's possible," Brian rode to his rescue. "Although terrapins prefer warm wetlands like those of the southern United States – from where they originate – hardier ones could survive the British climate. If you have seen any, then they'll be ones that have been kept in captivity and then released into the wild – as sometimes happens when they grow too big to keep in a tank.

"It's another good reason to think long and hard before buying a reptile as a pet," the Snakeman then cautioned the class, who looked up at him attentively. "They might look cute when they're babies. But sometimes they can grow very big indeed."

As if to demonstrate, the next enclosure he escorted the school party to contained baby crocodiles – most no bigger than a school ruler – and which were bobbing about in the water with just their snouts and their bulbous eyes exposed.

"Wow! Look!" there was a sudden collective gasp on the part of the children when Brian urged them to shuffle along and meet their mother.

With just a partial glass barrier separating nervous children from the motionless eight-foot crocodilian, this enclosure really did offer them the authentic feel of the African lakes and rivers it inhabited. There was even a water cascade that chuckled its way down through the foliage to tumble into the large, artificially-fabricated pool, further adding to the stifling humidity.

"Boys and girls, meet Hannah. Hannah is a Nile crocodile. They usually hunt by waiting unseen at the water's edge. When zebras or antelopes come down to drink, quick as a flash the croc will strike," Brian pounced on a startled little girl, snapping his hands together like so, "grabbing one and hauling it under the water to drown it. Then, because crocodiles and alligators can't chew, they will eat their prey by biting it and spinning around in the water to rip pieces of flesh off to swallow whole."

Some of the other girls made their squeamishness apparent. However, for the boys this was all gripping stuff – literally so as they peered into Hannah's gaping mouth to observe the dozens of sharp teeth that it was intended would do the gripping.

"Doh' crocodiles eat people too?" one of them asked.

"They do indeed. Every year people in Africa, Asia and Australia are attacked and killed by crocodiles – often when fishing beside lakes and rivers," Brian added, offering the lad with the snotty nose a wicked wink. Perhaps it might make him think twice about what else might be lurking in those cooling ponds that serviced the steel works (and which had always been a haunt of anglers seeking somewhere peaceful to dip their rods, as well as youngsters up to mischief – despite the warning signs advising trespassers to 'keep out').

"Crocodiles and alligators are truly amazing animals too. In fact, what you're staring at right now is a real, live descendant of the dinosaurs that once roamed the Earth."

Warming to his subject, Brian was in his element, both the children and their teacher impressed as he waxed lyrical about how "they have one of the most powerful bites of any animal. That massive jaw you see can snap down with *four thousand pounds* per square inch of force," he enthused. And, lest he blind his prepubescent audience with facts and figures, he elaborated that "by comparison, when you bite into a chocolate bar you'll be doing so with barely a hundred pounds per square inch. However, the muscles that hold a crocodile's jaw shut are quite weak. It means that when I'm handling Hannah I can hold her mouth shut with just my two hands."

"Wot'? You mean you have to get inside there with that big crocodile?" one of the girls expressed shock.

"Oh, yes. Someone has to clean the enclosure out. After all, just like you, Hannah does poos too!"

"Urgh!" the class shuddered in unison, prompting one of the lads to point out what looked like one of Hannah's turds floating by. Even their teacher grinned: the Snakeman certainly had a way of making reptiles sound interesting… and funny!

Thereafter, he led them down another corridor of glass-fronted enclosures – this time containing the zoo's extensive collection of serpents. From the tiny, wormlike Brahminy blind snake (at four inches long, the world's smallest snake) to a mighty king cobra that fixed its lurid gaze upon them (at over ten foot long, the world's largest venomous snake) – and with all sorts of adders, vipers and rattlesnakes in between – the youngsters jostling to catch sight of them listened spellbound to their proud keeper reeling off more facts and figures about these weird and wonderful creatures.

Finally, the time had arrived for The Snakeman to live up to his name. Beckoning them towards his office, he announced to them, "Children, I want you to meet Julie."

"Julie? Who's Julie? Is she an alligator or somefink'?" that cocky youngster with the snotty nose wondered aloud.

"No, silly! Julie is my assistant," Brian chuckled, introducing a chubby young lady whose tomboyish comportment the zoo's functional uniform of brown slacks and a tan shirt exaggerated (and upon the collar of which her shoulder-length chestnut hair was dancing as she corralled the youngsters in a circle around the cluster of boxes that she'd prepared ready).

When the Snakeman was confident he had their wholehearted attention, Julie lifted the lid of the first crate. Taking hold of the mottled red-and-black serpent, she drew it up for them to behold.

"There – isn't she a beauty!" Brian beamed, his audience unsure whether to back away or move in closer for a better look. Once again, a certain waggish lad was eager to demonstrate an absence of fear, stepping forward to gaze up at the snake.

"Careful," a female classmate warned him. "It might bite you."

"This is a corn snake – from the United States. And though they can bite, they're usually docile," said Brian, putting her at ease. "It's why they're the most common snake to be kept as pets. Unlike those other snakes you just saw, corn snakes are constrictors. That means they don't kill their prey by injecting it with venom. Instead, they grab it and curl their bodies around it. Usually a snake this size will feed on small rodents – like mice and rats. They wrap themselves around their victim so that every time it breathes out the snake will coil a little tighter until it can no longer breathe at all. Then they swallow it whole."

"So how do they do that then?" that curious kid demanded to know of a beast with such a small, pointed head.

"Well, their jaws are capable of opening wide enough to close around it. Then, once they've swallowed it, over the next few days powerful acids in the snake's stomach will dissolve the animal – bones and all."

"Cor! That's amazin'," he marvelled, lifting his cap out of his eyes to better study it.

"Snakes are amazing animals. Anyway, tell me: what's *your* name?" Brian enquired of the intrepid youngster.

"Wot? Me? Ar'm Robin – Robin Jukes," he snuffled.

"Well, Robin, you know you said snakes are horrible and slimy. Well, here: just feel – this one's not slimy at all, is it."

At first wary, with a smile and a nod of encouragement from Julie, he tentatively raised his hand and ran his fingers down the animal's scaly back.

"Nah. It ay'," he turned to his classmates and concurred. "And it's warm too."

Observing how his daring act had broken the spell of fear, Julie passed the snake around for the other children to take turns stroking it or being the recipient of its flicking tongue upon their coats – the means (or so the Snakeman enlightened them) by which the animal was able to sniff out its surroundings.

"Now, snakes might feel warm, but they're what we call 'cold-blooded' animals," Brian meanwhile explained. "That means that – unlike us humans and other mammals – they can't generate their own body heat. To become active, they either live in hot climates; or have to find somewhere to lie in the sun to warm up. That's why there are only two species of snakes that live in Britain – the grass snake and the adder – neither of which grows very big. Adders are venomous; but their venom is not very toxic – unlike that Eastern brown snake from Australia that I showed you, which can deliver enough venom in one bite to kill every single one of you," he swept his finger about the class, "… plus your teacher as well!" he added, jabbing at the comely young pedagogue observing proceedings from behind them. Julie offered her the chance to stroke the snake, which she politely declined.

Brian waited for a murmur to subside before noting that "Adders in Britain are quite shy, so it's unlikely you'll ever come across one. But if you do, just leave it alone – and certainly don't go poking it with sticks; not just because it might bite you, but because snakes are quite delicate creatures and it's easy to injure them," he explained, conscious that the two dozen paws mobbing the one curling around Julie's hand were in danger of stressing it.

Therefore, Brian signalled her to place the corn snake back in its crate before motioning for her to lift the lid on a larger box. This time there really was an audible gasp – accompanied by the startled school party stepping back a pace or two. For out of this box the Snakeman himself now hauled the huge, chunky yellow-and-white coils of an altogether much bigger constrictor.

"This, boys and girls, is Maisie," he introduced her, draping the snake across his shoulders. "She's an albino ball python from West Africa. She measures just short of six feet in length – which is about as large as these snakes grow."

Sure enough, one audacious soul was affecting a nonchalance that suggested he was unfazed by her. Glancing down at him,

Brian had a brainwave. Lifting the serpent from his shoulders, he flashed his eyes to suggest it was an opportune moment for someone else to play host to Maisie's hefty trunk. Thus it was that another gasp greeted the spectacle of this colourful beast being lowered onto a different pair of shoulders.

"Blimey, mate! 'Er' ay' arf' 'eavy!" Robin puffed, watching anxiously as the snake and its flicking tongue probed here and there about his person.

"No, Maisie's a tiddler really. Other species of python can grow much bigger and heavier than this. For example, South American anacondas can grow to over twenty feet in length and weigh more than you and I put together."

"Gosh, children! Over twenty feet! That's almost as long as the coach on which we travelled to the zoo today!" their teacher interjected.

"That's right. It can take several people to handle a huge snake like that. Big constrictors like those are capable of catching and swallowing pigs, deer, and even crocodiles. There are even stories of them swallowing people!"

His words prompted another audible gasp. At last, Robin's faltering smirk hinted that he was not as unfazed as he'd led his classmates to believe. It was with relief that he allowed Maisie to be lifted from his shoulders by her keeper.

"Normally in the wild, these pythons are dark in colour so that they're camouflaged when hunting. However, Maisie here has been bred in captivity. In fact, we rescued her from an owner who was no longer able to look after her."

Soon enough, it was time to bid goodbye to Maisie, who Brian lowered back into her box, Julie obliging by placing the lid back on it. Otherwise, there was still time for the class to stroll around the reptile house by themselves and marvel again at the lizards, snakes and other miscellaneous creepy-crawlies on display.

"Thank you, Mr Sthnakeman," the cute little girl with the pigtails thought to express her gratitude on the way out, bodging one of his hips to catch his attention. "Now I can tell my mommy that sthnakes aren't sthcary at all."

"You're welcome," he smiled down at her.

"Yes, thank you," her teacher concurred, sidling up to Brian as her pupils were jostling to file back out into the rain. "The children really enjoyed seeing all your reptiles. It's been the highlight of their day out so far."

"My pleasure. It's important that they learn to treat snakes with respect; and to not always be frightened by them."

"I'm sure you're right. Me? I think I still prefer looking at them from behind a glass panel," she dipped her eyes apologetically.

Brian was tempted to chide such residual fear and loathing, but then remembered what his wife was always telling him – about not being too overbearing with his adult listeners.

"Ah, well," she sighed as they dallied in the doorway to stare up at the leaden skies still doing their worst, "the final stop on our itinerary today is to watch the sea lion show. It's such a shame the weather's been so miserable."

"I wouldn't worry," he joked. "Of all the animals around here, I'm sure the sea lions won't be deterred by a drop of rain!"

"I'm sure you're right about that too," she chuckled, opening out her umbrella. "Still – rain or shine – it's always nice to be able to get ones charges out of the classroom for a change."

"I know. My wife's a teacher too," he said, recognising that world-weary expression she offered him.

"Then she'll know exactly what I mean. Anyway, goodbye Mr Danks. And once again, thank you for your really informative presentation."

"Er, g-g-goodbye, M-m-miss… Er?" he bumbled, realising they hadn't got around to properly introducing themselves.

"Trotter. Pauline Trotter," she called out, turning to offer him a coy, parting grin.

He lingered to savour the compliments she'd paid him, as well as to admire the firmness and resolve with which she commenced the task of rounding up her pupils. Yes, teaching can be a challenging job at times.

4

From their flagging expressions, it must have seemed as if the four o'clock bell was never going to ring. When it finally did it was as much as Ruby Danks could do to avoid being flattened by the stampede of fourth-formers rushing for the door. For sure, no one was paying attention to her hollered parting instruction about completing the homework she'd set them.

Within the space of ten seconds her entire class of thirty students had vanished, leaving her alone in the ensuing silence to gather up her papers and to ponder whether they'd been paying attention to anything she'd taught about enzymes and proteins during the last fifty minutes. Maybe some of them had – the bright ones who could appreciate that a good education (including a grasp of animal biology) – would be the key to getting on in a world that was going to be increasingly dependent upon science and technology. For most of the boys, however, the only 'animals' she'd overheard them enthusing about were the ones who sang about *'The House Of The Rising Sun'*; while, sadly for the girls, the 'biology' lessons that looked set to have most pertinence for them would be the ones she'd given on human reproduction – or rather its practical application in filling the prams that most of them would spend the best years of their lives shunting about town.

Once again, the academic idyll of her varsity days seemed a million miles removed from the mean, unaspiring classrooms of the industrial Black Country where she'd felt called to put her own expensive education to good use.

* * * * *

"Grief, you look like you're carrying the world on your shoulders," someone remarked upon spotting Ruby barge through the staff room door. Clutching her folders of work to her bosom, she made a bee-line for the kitchenette to place them down and flick the electric kettle back on the boil.

"Ever wondered why you chose a career in teaching?" she huffed while mixing some sugar, milk and coffee. Picking her folders up again, she then wandered over to lay both them and a steaming mug of coffee upon a low table around which her fellow teachers were sat, slumping into an easy chair.

"Cheer up, Ruby, love. We all ask ourselves that question from time to time – in my case, I'd say about three or four times a day; maybe less often during school holidays!" joked a colleague from behind her who had meanwhile strode over to the kettle to brew another one for himself.

"Anyway," one of the women around the table observed, "it's unlike you to sound a note of despair. You've always been one of the more idealistic souls around here: like you really did come into the profession to change the world."

She forced a grin of acknowledgement that her convictions about the power of education to open minds and stir hearts – especially in youngsters who'd not enjoyed her own privileged upbringing – had not gone entirely unnoticed. Whereupon she felt a pair of warm, powerful hands alight upon her shoulders. She looked up to observe the seductive smile of their owner, who'd breezed up behind her unnoticed.

"I hope we *all* came into the profession smitten by that noble ambition," he said, those eyes glancing around at the others present, "even if 'changing the world' is sometimes an arduous calling. Fortunately, however, a calling made bearable by the knowledge that one is changing it in the company of like-minded colleagues," he added, looking down at Ruby and smirking.

The bemused and quasi-envious stares of the other female staff suggested it was not the first time they'd spotted the lush, cobalt blue eyes of Graham Weston – the school's handsome and eloquent new headmaster – alight upon this attractive young teacher. Therefore, she politely slipped free of the unsolicited massage he was treating her to and leant forward to take a sip of her coffee, hoping to thereby dispel any notion that the feeling might be mutual. In this respect, she was aided by the interjection of one of the older male teachers, who – talking around the pipe he was puffing on – couldn't resist an opportunity to gainsay all this talk about 'changing the world'.

"Uh!" he grunted. "Perhaps she's realised that there's only so much erudition you can cram into the heads of kids who are counting down the days until they're out of here – no doubt to spend the rest of their lives beavering away in a foundry or a typing pool. And now there's talk of keeping the little oiks in school until they're sixteen, there is! God help us!"

Cledwyn Davies was the school's frustrated head of history – frustration that derived from the fact that Sneyd End High School was the spawn of a controversial decision by the local council to merge the distinguished Sneyd End Grammar School (where he'd been teaching) with the markedly less eminent Sneyd End Secondary Modern School (where Ruby had commenced her teaching career upon moving to the town). In the process it had created a new, one-thousand place 'comprehensive school' that would cater for children of all academic abilities.

Several such schools had been established over the last decade or so, challenging Britain's 'tripartite' secondary education system. That system – put in place by the landmark 1944 Education Act – comprised 'grammar schools' (often renowned and longstanding centres of academic excellence that selected their pupils by means of a competitive 'eleven-plus' entrance exam); 'technical schools' (intended to churn out engineers and other skilled manual workers – but which, due to shortages of money and suitably-qualified teachers, had never taken off); and 'secondary modern schools' (which had by default ended up becoming repositories for the great rump of less able children destined to toil in low-paid, dead-end occupations).

"Meanwhile, that misbegotten merger two years ago destroyed an outstanding grammar school that had propelled many of its alumni into the country's finest universities," he continued in his fulsome Welsh accent. "Ordinary men and women like your husband, Ruby," he namedropped one of the school's better-known alumni. "A brilliant boy, he was," he crowed, puffing pensively on his pipe. "A bit of an eccentric young man, I grant you – but undeniably gifted. I should know. I taught him."

"Oh, come on, Cled," a colleague rebuked him on her behalf, observing Ruby blanch at the mention of her 'eccentric' spouse. "You know how crushing it is for an eleven-year-old child to be told that, henceforth, he or she will receive a second-rate education in second-rate school with second-rate staff morale to match – and all because he or she failed a solitary exam!"

"So the big solution they came up with is one massive, mediocre school where the brightest pupils are forced to proceed at the pace of the dimmest. They've even tried to sugar the pill by calling it a 'high school'. So bloody American, it is!" the history teacher from the Valleys scoffed.

"No, I tell you: the victims of this madness will be the Brian Danks' of this world: talented working-class kids who will lose their opportunities to excel thanks to the great levelling down of standards that'll be the legacy of these so-called 'comprehensive schools'. Meanwhile, wealthy and well-connected parents," he sucked on his pipe and noted – meaning her own, Ruby deduced – "they'll still be able to pay privately for the kind of education that will enable *their* children to excel."

"Whoah! Ladies, gentleman!" Graham cried, the brushing of his hand through his wavy, grey-black mane adding to the sardonic melodrama of his interjection, "Let's not spend our passion fighting yesterday's battles when we have work to do."

Still on his feet, once more his hands alighted upon Ruby's shoulders, this time to use as a prop for his contention that "Rather let us be inspired by this young lady's commendable determination that *all* our students – the talented and not-so-talented alike – should have the opportunity to 'excel', each in their own inimitable way. I assure you: while I'm in charge this new school of ours will never be 'mediocre'."

Cledwyn looked suitably unconvinced. Meanwhile, humbled and abashed by his kind words (yet relieved too that his hands had lifted from her shoulders again), Ruby watched Graham Weston stride purposefully around her chair to stand erect in their midst and remind them of another pertinent fact.

"And anyway, regardless of our personal opinions, I suspect the upshot of this 'Circular 10/65' that Mr Crosland, our new education secretary, has issued is that every education authority in

England and Wales will sooner or later find itself having to implement fully comprehensive secondary schooling."

"God help us!" the Welshman grunted again under his breath.

Ruby looked up and offered the debonair headmaster an awkward smile of affirmation – even though the price of her innocent gesture was to elicit from him a doting stare that could only further fuel gossip about his interest in her.

* * * * *

For all her pedagogic idealism, Ruby Danks was relieved when Friday afternoon finally came around. Hopping into her Mini for the journey home, as she was pulling off the school car park she spotted her head teacher's little red Austin Healey sports car parked in his reserved bay.

Both the car and the garish colour attested that Graham Weston was a larger-than-life character. For example, though he'd only been in post since September rumours had preceded him that in his previous roles the forty-year-old had acquired a reputation for being something of a 'lady's man'. With his film star good looks, it wasn't difficult to see why. Indeed, during the few weeks this charmer had been wandering the corridors of Sneyd End High Ruby had noticed how female students would also manifest an awe bordering on coquettishness upon being confronted with the presence of their dashing new headmaster.

Preceding him too – and of greater import to the school's older, more traditional teachers – had been a reputation for being an innovator given to bold and revolutionary thinking. The growling, open-top sports car hinted that he was too much of a *bon viveur* to ever cut it as a political revolutionary. However, their new head was very much a convert to the so-called 'progressive' theory of education: that schools should be places where young people were encouraged to discover their true inner selves; and not just production lines for the passing of exams (and thence for slotting into 'careers'). As such, Ruby suspected he viewed his latest appointment as very much a vehicle for 'changing the world' through how and what its pupils were taught: revolution by subtle, if no less profound means. As if to confirm the worst fears of members of staff like Cledwyn Davies (as well as to lay down a marker for the direction of the school on his watch), one of the first decisions he'd announced was that henceforth corporal punishment (caning, or 'six of the best', in layman's parlance) was no longer to be administered to the school's more wayward and wilful 'little oiks'.

Pondering these things during the drive home, as she approached the old railway bridge Ruby spotted a familiar figure wandering the pavement and peering over its parapet. It was Mrs Channon. She was clearly looking for something; or someone. From the lead she was anxiously clutching in her hand it was most likely Bertie. The mischievous mutt had presumably run off again – as he had a habit of doing whenever she let him off the lead over the park.

Ruby would have liked to have stopped to help. However, when the queue of traffic moved she was impelled to follow the car in front. With the autumnal dusk advancing, she just hoped her neighbour came across Bertie before darkness closed in.

* * * * *

"Welcome home, love. Tell me how your day's been," Brian greeted her as she trudged through the front door, having spotted the car pull up on the drive.

Ruby was certainly in need of an opportunity to unburden herself of the woes of being at the 'chalk front'. However, touched by his concern, for now she contented herself with weary platitudes, asking after his day-off from work instead.

"Oh, I've managed to get loads of things done. For instance, I've cleaned out Lizzie's tank. And I've finished the sermon that Father Allen has asked me to give on Sunday. I'll read it to you, if you like," he offered, waving the reams of hand-written notes he had in his hand. "I think you'll be impressed."

Like a child's clockwork toy, once wound up and let loose to reel off chapter-and-verse about some 'project' he'd tasked himself with there was no stopping him. Barely surfacing for air, her husband now commenced reeling off chapter-and-verse (literally!) of what he intended to preach about St Paul's Epistle to the Romans. Politely, but firmly Ruby steered the conversation back onto a more pressing need: to prepare the evening meal.

"Always remember, Brian," she reminded him once dinner was served, grace was said, and they could both sit down, "the essence of a good sermon isn't just the research you put into it, or the passion with which you deliver it. This is the Word of God you'll be bringing to the congregation. Therefore, the most important ingredient of all is prayer. You need to ask the Lord what *He* wants you to say to them through that sermon."

From the guilty look he offered her across the dining table she could tell he hadn't been as conscientious about the input of prayer into his assignment as he had about his 'research'. But then, habitually self-absorbed as always, she knew it had not been purposely overlooked. Its oversight was just Brian being Brian.

Brian being Brian too was the need to keep her posted about the latest developments in his ongoing battle to save what was left of a certain disused railway line.

"You know, I've heard that British Railways are thinking of selling off the track bed for redevelopment. The local council may even be interested in buying some of it for that new swimming baths they're talking about building. Yet if that happens, hope of one day seeing trains serving Sneyd End again will be dashed forever. Ruby, I cannot stand by and let that happen."

"I have to say, dear, on past form, the likelihood of you being able to stop it is not good," she said, though loathed to pop his bubble. "People have been talking for a long time about the need to replace the crumbling Vicar Street baths."

Yet – Brian being Brian again – he appeared not to be listening. Instead, off he veered into another monologue, debating with himself what was needed to get the campaign to save the Sneyd End line back on track (as it were), as well as bitterly recounting the perfidy of those politicians who, by their inertia or their mealy-mouthed rhetoric, had betrayed that campaign.

"It would appear those votes we cast for Labour haven't done much good. Already the Prime Minister is reneging on the promises he made about the railways during the election. He might have sacked Beeching; but he hasn't reversed any of the closures that the previous government agreed – except for those that just happen to run through the marginal constituencies his party holds in Wales and Scotland," he sniffed cynically. "No wonder people say there are only two things to dislike about Harold Wilson: his face!"

"No small consideration though for a prime minister sitting on a razor-thin majority of just four seats in the House of Commons!" Ruby observed in between mouthfuls.

Having been in good measure responsible for persuading him which way to cast those votes, she glanced up to proffer her husband a guilty look. However, very soon her pricked conscience gave way to regret that she hadn't seized the opportunity of his earlier invitation to talk about her own day – in particular, about the upheavals that Graham Weston's appointment as head teacher had set in train.

"… As for our own Member of Parliament, that's the last time I vote for him! He's a Judas," Brian hissed, venting his frustration by stabbing at a potato on his plate. "He's totally reneged on all those promises he made during the election about restoring trains to Sneyd End…"

Trains, trains, trains! Once again, the chance of having a fulsome *tête-a-tête* about things of more immediate import to their marriage had been lost to this airing of her husband's obsession with the fate of that old railway line. Picking at her own meal with dwindling enthusiasm, she smiled obligingly, continuing to periodically nod her concurrence when Brian made plain that – if only for the benefit of future generations – preventing its track bed being sold off was a fight he simply had to wage. Meanwhile, Ruby wondered when the turn would come to talk frankly about things that were on *her* heart – such as when the time would be right for them to contemplate making a contribution of their own to that 'future' generation that her husband was busy rambling on about.

* * * * *

If Brian Danks could at times be irritatingly self-absorbed, it was offset at other times by the considerate side of his nature. Guessing that a week of trying to inculcate knowledge in truculent fifteen-year-olds had taken its toll, he shooed Ruby out of the kitchen and instructed her to go switch on the television, put her feet up on the sofa, and relax to the comic capers of Harry Worth on BBC1. Ever the comedian himself, he pressed his nose up to the edge of the kitchen door and raised his one leg to demonstrate like so in the reflection of its glass panel, eliciting a heart-warming giggle from his wife.

Thereafter, his duties in the kitchen accomplished, it was while Brian was stepping outside to put the rubbish out that he noticed a distraught-looking Mrs Channon come trudging up the drive, Bertie's lead hanging limply from her hand. Had the wilful Labrador run off again?

"I was walking him down by the old railway line when he must have spotted a squirrel or something and took off after it," she explained through watering eyes. "I've been searching for him since four o'clock this afternoon. I do hope he turns up. Do you think I should call the police?" she snuffled, explaining that her husband (who was a travelling salesman) was away on another of his expeditions around the country.

"There's never any harm in letting them know," Brian replied.

However, the considerate side of his nature surfaced again in the suggestion that "Why don't I ask Ruby to give them a call. Then, if you like, I'll grab some torches and this time we can take up the search together. I doubt Bertie's strayed very far. And now that it's dark and well past his supper time he'll probably be more amenable to coming when he's called."

On that optimistic note, he nipped back inside to ask Ruby to do just that, his wife resigned to having to postpone yet another opportunity to sit down and discuss when the time might be right to try for a baby. Meanwhile, armed with a chunky Eveready torch, her husband set off with Mrs Channon' to resume the search of that old railway line.

* * * * *

It was a fifteen-minute walk to the park – and to the gap in the fence where the flaxen-coated canine had made its latest bid for freedom. Torch in hand, Brian cocked his leg over the splintery cross member and shone it down the gently-sloping embankment on the other side.

"Are you sure it's safe?" Mrs Channon fretted as she too poked her head through the gap to behold the deserted railway line.

"Trust me, we'll be okay. There's certainly no danger of being run over by a train!" he quipped sardonically. "Just watch out for the brambles though. It might be a bit muddy at the bottom too."

With that meagre reassurance, he steadied her while she cocked her own leg over the fence. Anxiously gripping his hand, they made their way down past old prams, mattresses and other fly-tipped detritus until they reached the relative safety of the track bed itself. While Mrs Channon lost no time shining her torch up and down its length, Brian took a moment to breathe in a lungful of cold night air and to come over all wistful.

"Ah, Mrs Channon, I can hear the whistle of those trains even now; and smell the smoke billowing from them. You know, I used to spend hours as a boy watching them come and go along this line. That was in the good old days of steam. In fact, steam locomotives were hauling goods trains through Sneyd End right up until its closure."

With a choice of two directions in which to commence their search, Brian suggested they head south in the first instance. Thereupon, after walking for several minutes without sight of Bertie, they came upon the ghostly silhouette of the abandoned Tipton Road signal box – forlornly standing watch beside points and semaphore signals that were no longer there. Brian was unable to resist the urge to clamber up the stairwell and shine a light over what remained of it. Gripping the frayed handrail, Mrs Channon nervously followed him up the steps.

Inside all was destruction and dereliction. Anything that the lifting gangs had deemed not worth salvaging had since been trashed or strewn about by vandals. Meanwhile, not a pane of glass remained of the panoramic, full-length window out of which the signalman had once surveyed passing trains (and through which a faint evening breeze was soughing). On the floor, were strewn the pages of yellowing newspapers, along with discarded traffic schedules that attested to the last occasion he'd worked its missing signal levers. On the floor too, the cup in which the signalman had once brewed his char lay stained and chipped.

"Sad, isn't it," Brian mourned. "To think, we're the nation that invented railways; and gave them to the rest of the world. And now so many of our own have come to this."

After a moment spent contemplating this wanton vandalism – in both the literal and the political sense – he turned to her with a lift in his voice to announce that "But I still haven't given up hope that one day this particular line will rise again; and maybe others like it too. If only we had politicians who possessed the foresight to see that Britain will one day need its railways again – including the one through Sneyd End."

Fascinating as her next-door neighbour's musing about them could be, at that moment Mrs Channon was more concerned for the whereabouts of her missing family pet. Brian took the hint. With neither sight nor sound of Bertie at this end of the line, they descended back down the ladder and set off in the other direction.

"Bertie... Bertie..." his owner cried out at intervals as, on and on, they trekked in the darkness.

Having become increasingly desperate to find him, imagine what music it was to her ears when, suddenly, she could make out his bark echoing somewhere up ahead in the distance.

"It seems to be coming from the old tunnel," she exclaimed.

"I think you're right," Brian confirmed, picking up the pace. "Come on, let's go see."

"I did wonder whether he might have disappeared inside," she said, endeavouring to keep up with her more spritely and sure-footed neighbour. "However, without a torch I had no hope of following after him – though I stood outside calling him."

Eventually, they arrived at the tunnel mouth, halting to pierce the gloom within with their torches. Nine hundred yards long and built to carry the Sneyd End line beneath the town itself, on a sunny day its other end could just about be discerned as a glimmer of light. On a night illuminated by just fleeting glimpses of a waning crescent moon it was impossible to make out anything beyond the range of those torch beams. However, in response to Bertie's increasingly anguished barking, they made their way inside. Tightening her headscarf, Mrs Channon sought to keep up with the intrepid herpetologist.

"Perhaps the poor thing's been injured; or has become trapped somewhere," she meanwhile gave voice to her worst fears.

"He's not squealing or yelping. I'd wager he's probably cornered some animal; most likely a rat. There are some real big ones in here, I can tell you," Brian quipped – a wisecrack that was unlikely to calm his neighbour's gnawing phobias.

"Phew! It's warm in here," Mrs Channon was surprised to discover, loosening both scarf and the buttons of her turquoise tweed coat as she progressed into the tunnel's confines. At the very least she'd expected it to be colder than it was above ground. Perhaps the strange heat might explain the giant rats.

"Yes, it's a curious feature of this tunnel," Brian enlightened her, calling upon his prodigious local knowledge. "On my train-spotting forays I remember getting into a conversation with the track repairmen who worked this line. They told me how they would strip to the waist whenever they had to labour inside here – and that's before they'd even started tapping the rails!

"They say it's on account of an old colliery working that runs beneath the tunnel. The Black Country is riddled with them, you know. In fact, it's because of the rich seam of coal that was once mined here that the Black Country acquired its name," he added, aware that Mrs Channon was not a native of the area.

"During the last century though, this particular working had to be abandoned following a catastrophic underground fire in which dozens of men lost their lives. Their bodies were never recovered. Apparently, the shaft in question is still burning. Some local people even say the tunnel is haunted by their ghosts."

Her ebullient young neighbour really did know how to spook a woman! Therefore, it was with relief that, a few hundred yards inside the tunnel – and with the beam of her torch having alighted upon his prone outline – they finally came upon Bertie baying at something he'd identified lurking up ahead.

Shining his own more powerful torch in the direction the dog was barking, for a split-second Brian thought he could make out the sparkle of a huge pair of eyes. However, whatever the mysterious creature was, when he flashed the beam at it again it had disappeared.

"What is it, Bertie? Show me," Mrs Channon rushed up to him, rubbing her hands up and down his coat.

However, if it had been a rat then it must have been sizeable enough to have spooked the bulky golden Labrador too. Instead of rushing to chase after it, Bertie was nervously whimpering in the embrace of his owner, suggesting that right then he was as glad to be found by her as she was to have caught up with him. Meanwhile, ever the curious zoologist, Brian was tempted to tiptoe amongst the debris of the lifted track to spy out that giant rodent for himself. However, having taken a few hesitant steps he thought better of it. Bertie was safe; Mrs Channon was rejoicing; and Ruby had been left at home on her own for long enough. Eventful evening over, it was time to head back.

As the search party retreated – their dog back on its lead – in the darkness a head surfaced unseen from the drain cavity into which the owner of that mysterious pair of eyes had slunk. Alas, the opportunity to make a kill had retreated too. However, Betty was nothing if not patient. She could wait. Soon or later, the opportunity to kill would present itself again.

5

"...Behold, there came up the champion, the Philistine of Gath, Goliath by name, out of the armies of the Philistines. And all the men of Israel, when they saw the man, fled from him, and were sore afraid..."

From the pew where she was sat a few rows back from the front, Ruby Danks could admire her husband pouring his heart and soul into the sermon he was delivering in his capacity as the lay reader at St Stephen's Parish Church – the little Anglican congregation that was their regular place of worship.

Although that congregation dotted about the pews reflected the waning of religious belief since the war (as well as the ageing profile of those who did attend each Sunday), they were clearly impressed by Brian's dramatic elucidation of this epic battle of old. Meanwhile, Father Allen – the hand-wringing parish priest of St Stephen's – was content to sit and listen from his own seat a few paces to the side of the elevated lectern from which Brian was regaling his fellow worshippers.

"...And when the Philistine looked about, and saw David, he disdained him: for he was but a youth, and ruddy, and of a fair countenance. And the Philistine said unto David, 'Am I a dog that thou comest to me with staves?' And the Philistine cursed David by his gods. And the Philistine said to David, 'Come to me, and I will give thy flesh unto the fowls of the air, and to the beasts of the field'. Then said David to the Philistine, 'Thou comest to me with a sword, and with a spear, and with a shield: but I come to thee in the name of the LORD of hosts, the God of the armies of Israel, whom thou hast defied'..."

To be sure, Ruby had noticed her husband had become agitated again of late about his own epic battle against the Goliath that was the British Railways Board. Determined to press on with its programme of 'modernisation', it had announced a further tranche of 'rationalisation' – including plans to close Birmingham's magnificent and much-loved Snow Hill station (the former Great Western Railways main line from London to Wolverhampton which it deemed a pointless duplication of routes now that electrification of the former London, Midland & Scottish line through Birmingham New Street was nearing completion).

> "*... And it came to pass, when the Philistine arose, and came, and drew nigh to meet David, that David hastened, and ran toward the army to meet the Philistine. And David put his hand in his bag, and took thence a stone, and slang it, and smote the Philistine in his forehead, that the stone sunk into his forehead; and he fell upon his face to the earth...*"

Ruby emitted a wry smile: was her husband sneakily inferring a parallel between those grey bureaucrats who'd been tasked with consulting on the closure and the zestful young zoologist who had come against them? Alas, there the parallel ended. While David had '*prevailed over the Philistine with a sling and with a stone, and smote the Philistine, and slew him,*' poor Brian had little to show for the time and energy he'd expended in his attempts to prevail over his enemies – for all that his commanding oratory and dogged tenacity had frequently put their noses out of joint.

"Bravo, Brian! A cracking sermon," the vicar congratulated him, shaking Ruby's hand too as they filed out of the church.

"My pleasure, Father. The Beatles might think they're more popular than Jesus, but Our Lord is still '*the Way, the Truth, and the Life*' – John's Gospel, Chapter Fourteen, Verse Six."

Father Allen's indulgent smile faltered just a little. Like many people down the years who'd availed themselves of the talent and enthusiasm of Brian Danks, those commendable qualities took some handling. His sermon on Luke Chapter Eighteen – in which he'd likened the self-righteous Pharisee and the repentant publican to a British government minister and a common prostitute – had certainly proved a thought-provoking analogy! That said, the forbearing and mild-mannered vicar had soon enough warmed to the congenial side of Brian's nature.

In the spirit of such forbearance he assured his headstrong lay reader that "I'm sure Mr Lennon didn't mean his comments to come out quite like people have interpreted them."

"Let's hope not," Brian guffawed. *"'Be not deceived; God is not mocked: for whatsoever a man soweth, that shall he also reap'* – Galatians Chapter Six, Verse Seven."

"You're really enjoying your lay reading, aren't you," Ruby remarked afterwards on the walk home. "Ever considered whether your true calling might be to minister the Gospel?"

To which her husband laughed.

"As you once said, I need to do more on the prayer front before I could ever be entrusted to do something like that," he confessed with a rare flash of self-deprecation. "But I'm working on it… the prayer, that is!"

"Should I take it then that you've finally come to terms with your country having a smaller, if more modern railway network?" she couldn't resist teasing him.

"'Modern', yes. But if 'smaller' means leaving my corner of the Black Country without rail connections to the outside world, then no. Never! I will not let that happen."

"But realistically, what can you do? Even voting for a different set of politicians hasn't halted the closure programme. Face it, Brian: you're just one man up against the machinery of government. And unless you, yourself, can pull those levers of power I fear you'll carry on getting nowhere."

There was a pregnant silence that eventually goaded Ruby to glance across at him. As she did, she beheld that aura of emotional transparency in her husband's eyes that told her his over-active imagination had been working on that too.

"Then seizing and pulling those 'levers of power' is what I will do. If I can't influence the 'machinery of government' from outside then I will just have to do it from within."

"What? You mean stand for Parliament?" she tittered at the absurdity of such a thing. Then a further brooding silence on the part of her husband caused her to stare his way again.

"No, Brian. Tell me you're not…" her mouth dropped open.

"Yes, I'm going to be your next MP. Well, at least I'm going to have a go at becoming one," he hummed, explaining that "By-elections have wiped out the Government's majority. Sooner or later the Prime Minister will be compelled to call another general election. And when he does I'm going to put my own name forward and fight the Sneyd End parliamentary constituency as an independent candidate."

"But that's crazy," she shook her head, desperate to dissuade him from this latest hare-brained scheme. "Britain has a first-past-the-post voting system that favours the two main parties. Only rarely does a third-party candidate – much less an independent one – achieve more than garner an odd mention in the newspapers."

"Ordinarily, you're right," he conceded. "However, David Wallace – our Labour MP – only had a majority of just over two thousand votes at the last election. What with all the new middle-class housing estates they've been putting up around here since, he must be worried whether that majority will still be there next time around. What better way of sending out a signal about the unpopularity of these railway closures than by beating him."

Ruby's countenance was drooping with each twist and turn of her husband's reasoning. For a second time, she glanced his way aghast and endeavoured to be the voice of reason.

"But David Wallace is also a minister in Harold Wilson's government. You must know that Labour will throw everything it has at this seat to prevent him losing it. And anyway, if all you do is steal enough votes from Labour to allow the Conservative candidate to win, what good will that do? After all, it was a Conservative government that appointed Dr Beeching in the first place; *and* instructed him to take an axe to the railways."

She could see her pleas were falling on deaf ears – or, more likely, ears that had been purposely closed to her arguments.

"What about your job?" she twittered. "You love your work at the zoo. And what about your mother? You know how she worries about you. And what about us?" she then beseeched him. "How will we ever find time to be together if you're off down Westminster all week? And what about the plans we discussed to try for a baby?"

By now, even a monomaniac like Brian Danks could sense that his wife was teetering in despair. Therefore, he reached across to drape an arm around her shoulder.

"Don't worry. If I know Mr Wilson he'll try and hang on into next year at least – especially with the figures for the economy not looking too good. At least that will give me time to plan my campaign. I promise you, Ruby. I will never do anything to hurt you; or put our marriage in jeopardy. I love you too much to ever do that – more than that railway line even!"

Once again, a sweet smile and a complete absence of guile on his part helped allay her concerns. Besides, if she was right about Britain's voting system favouring the 'big boys' then, if nothing else, her husband might make the town's incumbent MP sweat a little. Perhaps that would be no bad thing – a rebuke from the people of his constituency for his forked tongue about the fate of their railway.

* * * * *

Ruby Danks was quickly plunged back into despair. In the very week following their conversation Harold Wilson stood to his feet in the House of Commons to drop the bombshell that he'd met the Queen to request the dissolution of Parliament. A general election had been called for Thursday, March 31st 1966.

Suddenly, Brian's assurance that he would have plenty of time to plan his madcap attempt to win the Sneyd End parliamentary seat had gone out of the window. During the week or so that followed the announcement, he'd been compelled to race about filling out and submitting nomination papers, as well as withdrawing money from their joint savings account with the Midland Bank to stump up the deposit required to have his name added to the ballot paper.

Suddenly too, every time she'd answered the telephone it was another journalist on the line seeking a quote from her husband about this, that or the other matter of national or international concern. What was the 'Independent – Save Our Railways' candidate's views about Britain making another attempt at joining the Common Market? How did the 'Independent – Save Our Railways' candidate propose to deal with the breakaway white minority government in Rhodesia? Meanwhile – and with that certain inevitability upon recalling her husband's unusual occupation – the local hacks had taken to resurrecting the *nom-de-guerre* he'd been christened with during the consultation hearings into the Beeching Report three years earlier.

Sure enough, whatever copy they'd managed to wheedle out of the 'Snakeman' would always be appended by Brian Danks reminding them that he was the only candidate who had pledged to return trains to Sneyd End again – even as what was left of the line itself was decaying with each passing day. Vegetation had taken over much of the track bed; vandals were busy picking apart what remained of the old station building; meanwhile, youngsters from the local high school had taken to getting up to no good inside the abandoned Sneyd End Tunnel.

Ever the loyal wife, after venting her dismay Ruby had nonetheless promised to help Brian see through this latest chapter in his campaign to 'save' the railway. If nothing else, maybe getting all this nonsense out of his system would once and for all convince her husband that he should stick to his 'calling' as a herpetologist – a literal 'snakeman'.

* * * * *

If Brian Danks was a novice to the formidable task of a fighting and winning a parliamentary election – including the marshalling together of the army of foot soldiers necessary to successfully deliver and canvas in a constituency of over sixty thousand people – then the next rude shock would come when, having retired to bed at the end of another exhausting day on the campaign trail, he was awoken by the sound of the phone ringing in the hall.

"Who the blazes is that?" he wondered aloud, propping himself up on his elbows in a daze.

"It's probably another reporter from the newspapers," Ruby cursed, springing up in bed to flick on the bedside light and pick out the digits on the alarm clock.

"At ten-past-twelve in the morning! Grrr!" she growled, burying her head beneath the pillow and pressing it tight.

Expecting to have to field more questions about his campaign, Brian donned his slippers and trooped down the stairs to lift the receiver on the telephone.

"Sneyd End 4011," he burbled.

"Mr Danks? Is that Mr Brian Danks? Brian Danks the independent parliamentary candidate?" a well-heeled voice at the other end of the line enquired hopefully.

"Speaking."

"Ah, I'm so glad I've caught up with you – even if it is a little late," the voice apologised. *"It's Bill Patterson here."*

"Bill who?"

"Councillor Bill Patterson. I'm the agent for the Conservative candidate, Martin de Vere – your opponent. Well, I say 'opponent'. However, in truth, you and he share quite a few things in common – if you know what I mean."

It was late. Or early. Or certainly not a conducive hour to be trading riddles down the telephone line. However, with Brian's brain befogged by somnolence, it was left to his midnight caller to elaborate upon precisely what he *did* mean.

"Look, Mr de Vere's been reading those press releases you've been putting out. He can see you plainly hate this confounded Labour chap with a passion…"

"Look here, Mr Packington…"

"No, it's Patterson – Councillor Bill Patterson."

"Well, Mr Whoever-you-are. I'm a Christian. I don't hate anyone," Brian twittered naively.

"Well, let's just say Mr de Vere agrees with you that this socialist fellow is an absolute bounder: going about breaking all these promises he made in opposition. I can see why you're desperate to get the man out. But look here, Brian old chap – I can call you Brian, can't I," the Tory agent presumed, *"you must know that – as a respected local businessman – Martin de Vere is the only person who has a realistic chance of knocking David*

Wallace clean off his perch. However, by standing in this seat as a third candidate – as well as criticising my party's record over the railways – you are rather queering the pitch for him...."

"I'm not sure I get your drift."

"Then let's not beat about the bush, shall we. To oust David Wallace the people of Sneyd End need to rally behind the candidate who is best placed to defeat him. In a straight two-horse contest the Conservative Party can easily overturn the blighter's majority – especially with Edward Heath, our modern, forward-thinking leader, heading up our campaign. So how about you do the decent thing: withdraw your nomination and then publicly endorse Martin de Vere as the only man who can stop Labour. In return for your co-operation in this matter, Mr de Vere has asked me to convey to you his willingness to sit down with the Conservative Party's transport spokesman and see what can be done about some of the things you feel strongly about."

"You mean like re-opening the railway through Sneyd End?"

"Well, Mr de Vere can't make any promises, you understand. British Railways is losing a lot of money. And money will be in short supply for an incoming Conservative administration, what with these socialist chaps going about spending it like water."

It didn't exactly constitute a tempting offer. A 'willingness to see what can be done' was no guarantee that – like Harold Wilson before him – the new Conservative leader wouldn't just press on with closing more railways. The silence at the Churchill Avenue end of the line must have alerted the caller to this. Perhaps it was time for Martin de Vere's *consigliere* to up the offer.

"Look here, Brian. You're a smart young chap. You've made quite a name for yourself these last few years running rings around all those Ministry of Transport officials. In fact, you're just the kind of effective communicator my party needs to get its message across to voters. The local elections will be coming up soon. And we're still looking for candidates to fight them – including in our safe Sneyd Park ward. Between you and me, the councillor we have there at the moment is a bit of a useless old duffer. Perhaps it's time for an infusion of new blood, so to speak. So if you can see your way to helping Mr de Vere in this matter, as leader of the Conservative Group on the Council I will

personally ensure that the ward selects you *as its candidate. Just think: you will then have a guaranteed seat on the Council – along with the chance to exercise real power over real decisions affecting the people of Sneyd End. What say you to that?"*

It was indeed a more persuasive offer: a 'guaranteed' seat on the Council as opposed to the faint prospect of a seat in Parliament. However, Brian could do the arithmetic: the healthy majority that Labour boasted on Sneyd End Borough Council was unlikely to be overturned any time soon. If so, then what hope of exercising 'real power over real decisions'?

"I'm sorry, Mr Packington…"

"Patterson – Councillor Bill Patterson," the voice repeated with gathering impatience.

"… Patterson, I mean. You see, I'm very flattered by your kind offer. However, the Sneyd End railway means a lot to me. And I just don't think your party is committed to our railways..."

"Committed? Look here, old chap: I'll remind you that it was a Conservative government that approved the modernisation programme. Soon we'll have smart, one-hundred-mile-an-hour electric trains hurtling back and forth between London, Birmingham, Manchester and Liverpool.

"Besides, the motor car is how people want to get about nowadays. Added to which, lots of jobs here in the Midlands depend upon the motor industry; and Mr de Vere can't exactly be indifferent to the fate of those jobs, can he – as I'm sure you will find out should you choose to proceed with your fruitless intervention in this election. After all, even your wife owns a little car… which I'm told she's rather fond of."

It was an intriguing thing to say. How could he possibly know about his wife's love affair with her red Mini 850? Perhaps Brian Danks wasn't the only person who could boast about the diligence of his research! However, he was adamant he would not sell out his beliefs in return for the blandishments of his Tory rival.

"I'm sorry, Councillor Patterson. But the answer is no."

There ensured a long, purposeful silence before he heard a deep sigh at the other end of the line.

"As you wish, Mr Danks. If that's your final word then it only remains for me to wish you goodnight and 'may the best man win' – which, I assure you, Martin de Vere fully intends to do!"

And with that the caller put the phone down. More annoyed than perturbed, Brian trudged back up the stairs.

"Who was it then?" Ruby enquired, re-emerging from beneath the pillow.

"Someone who knows a lot about you and your little Mini," he grunted, planting his posterior on the bed.

However, before he could enquire to whom she might have gossiped about her 'love affair', the phone rang again.

"This is getting too much!" Ruby cursed, once more burrowing her throbbing head beneath the pillow. Once more, her husband resignedly trooped back down the stairs in his pyjamas.

"Hello!" he snapped, wondering what blandishments Martin de Vere was prepared to put on the table this time. The man was clearly desperate to have a rival removed from the ballot paper.

"Is that Brian Danks? Brian Danks the independent parliamentary candidate?" an earthier voice this time enquired.

"Yes, who's calling?"

"It's Horace Bissell here. Councillor Horace Bissell – the Leader of Sneyd End Council. You might remember me from the public enquiry into the closure of the Sneyd End line a few years back," the caller continued, attempting to jog his memory.

It seemed to work. Brian did indeed recall being introduced to a rather blunt and portly figure with a balding pate who went by that name: a forthright local politician who had also spoken out against the 'Beeching Axe' being taken to the town's railway.

"Yes, I do. It's good to hear from you again – even at this rather ungodly hour," Brian replied, not consciously seeking to remind this one-time ally that it was fast approaching one o'clock in the morning – and that his wife had to be up for work in just shy of six hours' time!

"Tell whoever it is to go away!" he heard her yell down the stairs, prompting him to shield the mouthpiece with his hand while he listened to what the caller had to say.

"Look, Brian, mate, I know you feel strongly about things, so I'm gonna' tell it like it is," he briskly got down to business.

"You've got to understand that, by putting up against Labour in this election, you're creating a situation where those bloody Tories might win this seat. I'm sure you don't need me to tell you what a disaster that would be."

"Be that as it may, Councillor. But didn't David Wallace sit on his hands in Cabinet when it came to reversing Dr Beeching's closures?" the 'independent' candidate in Sneyd End thought it moot to point out.

"Come on, Brian. We're both men of the world. You know how it is sometimes. Many of those closures were already well advanced when Labour came to power. Of course, had we had chance to do something about them earlier on then…"

"But neither does it look like David Wallace is going to oppose the closure of the Snow Hill line. Perhaps he fears for his job as a minister if he rocks the boat. It does rather make one question whether he's serious about protecting our railways," Brian thought it moot to also point out.

"Serious? Look here, young man. I should remind you that no one feels more strongly about these things than I do. Okay, I know Labour has reluctantly had to cut a bit of dead wood out of the rail network. And we might have to cut a bit more still," the councillor confessed. *"But my party remains absolutely committed to public transport – unlike those bloody Tories. They're all rich geezers who live in big houses and own big cars. No wonder they want to build more roads!"*

Perhaps Councillor Bissell could sense that Brian was underwhelmed by such party-political tribalism. Or maybe the aggrieved zoologist had taken umbrage that he'd changed his tune such that he was now dismissing the railway they'd once campaigned together to save as 'a bit of dead wood'!

"Look, I know you probably want to get back to your bed – and to that beautiful lady wife of yours." he acknowledged, softening his tone. *"She's a teacher, isn't she? At Sneyd End High School – the school I just happen to sit on… as the chairman of its governing body,"* he then added ominously.

Though picking up on the nuances of conversations was not Brian's strong point, he wondered if he detected a hint of menace in that curious aside. However, before he could speak up David

Wallace's *consigliere* had cut to the chase of why he was calling at this unusual hour.

"Let me get to the point, son. If you're prepared to knock on the head all this nonsense about 'winning' this constituency, and instead publicly endorse our sitting Labour MP, then – as Leader of the Council – I personally promise I'll find you a nice safe seat where you can stand as a Labour councillor. Okay, you might not get everything you want; but at least you'll get something. And, in politics – as you'll find out if you stick at this game long enough – half a loaf is better than no loaf at all.

"Maybe I can even find you a committee to chair. As it happens, I'm on the look-out for a new chairman of the Planning Committee. You see, I have big plans to transform Sneyd End; to sweep away many of its old dilapidated buildings and replace them with bold, modern ones – to turn Sneyd End into the 'Athens of the Midlands'," he boasted (rather fancifully, Brian thought – certainly if the ugly concrete monstrosities that were the Tiger Street flats were anything to go by).

"No, son, you do right by me and you can get to make a real difference to the lives of the people of Sneyd End. What say you to that?"

It was a much more tempting offer: real power to make real decisions. However – notwithstanding that Brian Danks didn't profess an affinity with either of Britain's main political parties – he pondered the fate of David Wallace. Here was a man who had campaigned vigorously against the 'Beeching Cuts' in 1963 while an opposition MP. And yet the price of receiving 'half a loaf' in the shape of a place at the top table of government – exercising real power to make real decisions – had been keeping quiet while some of Britain's best loved railway lines were being run down and closed. Likewise, Councillor Horace Bissell – who ever since he'd been elevated to the top job on Sneyd End Borough Council had, for some inexplicable reason, grown remarkably indifferent to the fate of the railway line through his own back yard.

Of course, there was a quaint unclubbability about Brian Danks that made him wary – resentful even – of attempts to invite him inside someone else's big tent; especially if the price was betraying a cause he held dear. He recalled how Christ's apostles had been willing to brave scorn, hardship and imprisonment – death even – to remain true to the Gospel. He recalled too the sermon he'd given a few Sundays ago about Judas Iscariot – and how Our Lord had been betrayed for thirty pieces of silver. No, he would remain true to what he'd increasingly come to see as his calling: to preserve the track bed of the Sneyd End railway – even if it meant he would have to brave scorn, hardship and… well, who could say what fate awaited him (and maybe his wife too!) if he persisted in putting the backs up of some very powerful and influential people.

"I'm sorry, Councillor Bissell. Your offer is very kind. But the answer is no," he said, juggling a lump in his throat.

There was an ominous silence at the other end of the line.

"You fool. You'll regret this," the reply eventually came. *"We could have achieved so much together – you and me. But if this is your final word, then one day you'll look back on this conversation as a moment of missed opportunity. Good night, Mr Danks. Or should that be good morning? Oh, and one final thing: do please convey to your good wife my best wishes for her progressing career at Sneyd End High School."*

"What did this one want?" Ruby groaned when her husband returned.

"Oh, nothing," said Brian, slipping back into bed alongside her. "It was just someone wondering if I might have reconsidered my decision to stand."

"And have you?" she shuffled onto her side and hauled the sheets over her head.

He paused before answering. In the soft glow of the bedside lamp he glanced across at the promontory beneath those sheets that was his wife's curvaceous hip. He recalled his promise never to do anything to hurt Ruby; or put their marriage in jeopardy.

"No," he confessed.

"I thought not. Now can we get some sleep!" she hissed, that hip shuffling out of reach the instant he pressed a conciliatory hand against it to caress it.

6

With Brian Danks having rebuffed all inducements to quit the contest in favour of his political rivals, his campaign to win the Sneyd End parliamentary seat had begun in earnest. As if to underscore this, Ruby had arrived home from the school this afternoon to discover that their new Ercol dining table had disappeared beneath a mountain of election address flyers that he'd had printed outlining his 'manifesto'.

In disbelief, Ruby stared at box after box piled high on the table, opening one to ascertain how many flyers might be inside. She extrapolated that there must be thousands of the things! How on Earth did her husband intend to deliver one of these to every address in the constituency in the three weeks of the campaign? Recalling her exhortation about the importance of prayer, she gazed up to Heaven. Roll on March 31st, she implored.

* * * * *

It was yet another murky winter's night – though at least the earlier rain had eased off, to be replaced instead by a light drizzle. Plodding the beat on such unsavoury evenings was one of a policeman's more thankless chores. However, whistling to himself and fortified by a hot toddy he'd downed in the late-night café on the High Street, PC Jonathan Hunt continued on his way – content in the knowledge that his regular circuiting of its streets was keeping the citizens of his home town safe (like 'Dixon Of Dock Green' in the popular television series, he amused himself with the analogy).

"Evening all!" he was suddenly startled by someone jumping out from a dimly-lit back alley to purloin him with the eponymous character's famous greeting. Only the japing familiarity of the voice stayed the hand Jonathan instinctively reached inside his cape to whip out his regulation issue truncheon.

"What the…!" he cursed. "D'you realise I could've throttled you just now!"

"What? And put a possibly fatal end to our long friendship?"

"Yes, well. If this had been America it would've been a Smith & Wesson .38 Special I'd have been stuffing up your nostrils. Just think about that!"

Jonathan tucked the truncheon back in its holster and heaved his shoulders to shore up his frayed nerves. As he did, Brian draped a fraternal arm around one of them to draw him in close.

"Look, Jonathan, you know how you always wanted to be a policeman; but how everyone else thought you were mad because the career in accountancy you'd taken up instead would prove more financially rewarding. And how they all tried to talk you out of it; but I was the only one who said right from the start that you'd make an excellent copper…"

"Yes," Jonathan screwed his eyes up, pausing from plodding to look his best friend up and down. There had to be some ulterior motive to all this gushing, late-night flattery.

"A favour, that's all I ask of you."

"Go on," the wary policeman bade him.

"You see, I've decided to stand for Parliament…"

"Yes, so I heard," the officer hummed, carrying on plodding.

"Well, as part of my campaign I've had these election flyers printed," he informed him, whipping one out of the pocket of his duffle coat to show him. "Rather a lot of them actually… Well, twenty thousand to be precise."

"How many?"

"Yes, I know. It is rather a lot to deliver in just a few weeks. But I've gathered together a small team of folk who are willing to help me. For instance, Mr and Mrs Channon – our next-door neighbours – have said they'll deliver Sneyd Park for me as a thank-you for foiling their pet wammel's latest escape attempt. Mom has offered to deliver some too. And I know Ruby is eager to help me."

"Uh! Did she have any choice?" Jonathan wondered. The guilty look on his friend's face spoke volumes.

"And you want me to help you get rid of them as well, I suppose," he continued, drawing on past experience.

"It would be appreciated. As many as you think you can. After all, as a police constable you've had plenty of practice walking these streets!"

The joke fell flat. The chary policeman had invariably been there for his old schoolmate during his previous campaigns: helping with public meetings; writing indignant letters to the *'Sneyd End Gazette'*; and waving placards outside the regional office of British Railways. However, the continued heaving of the shoulders by which the would-be MP was persuaded to loosen his embrace hinted that, for once – and to Brian's dismay – he was not going to be forthcoming.

"Well, I can't," he muttered bluntly.

"Why not?"

Jonathan took a deep breath. "A serving police officer is prohibited from taking part in politics; or being seen to take sides in a political campaign. It's rules and regulations."

"Oh... Not even a..."

"No," he was adamant.

"So I don't suppose there's any chance of you being my agent then?" Brian chanced his luck. If the invitation had been intended as a joke it too fell flat.

"Sorry, mate. I'd like to help. But this time it's different."

Brian drew a deep breath himself and patted his friend's shoulder with the hand that had been hovering over it expectantly.

"Ah, well. Never mind," he sighed. "But I meant what I said: you've made a fine copper!"

* * * * *

Ruby Danks was no stranger to politics. As a child, she'd helped her mother bake cakes for the Conservative ladies' branch in the Sussex constituency where she'd grown up; and held the ladder while her father had put up posters during the 1951 General Election. As a teenager, her parents had also persuaded her to join the Young Conservatives (though – for Ruby, as for other middle-class youngsters – its principal attraction was that it had been the best youth-club-cum-dating-agency in town). However, by the time she'd reached university her own political views had firmed up – and not always to her parents' liking. For example (and to their horror), she'd taken part in the CND march on London from the Aldermaston atomic weapons research centre in 1960.

That said, she'd never delivered leaflets door-to-door before – and certainly not in a tough, urban constituency in the Black Country. It was certainly gruelling work. Not only were there an awful lot of hills in Sneyd End, but the time of year meant she would have to undertake much of that delivering in the dark. What's more, on this particular council estate every house seemed to boast a rickety front gate for which one required a degree in mechanical engineering to figure out how it opened.

Aided by the glow from a lamp standard, she lifted the latch at last. Making her way up the front path, her attention was distracted by the swirling silhouette on the ceiling of a woman dancing to Sandie Shaw's *'Long Live Love'*, which was playing in an upstairs bedroom. As such, she failed to spot the enormous crossbreed dog that emerged from the back of the property. Racing to the front gate, there it stationed itself, barking and snarling and blocking any thought of escape. Ruby gulped and slowly backed herself up to the front door – the colossal hound pacing forward and eyeing her up in a manner that suggested she had the word 'dinner' written across her forehead.

Fortunately, the dog's barking had roused the occupant. That front door suddenly swung open to reveal a barefoot young woman staring in surprise at this visitor who almost stumbled inside. Moreover, a visitor that the young woman recognised.

"Oh. Hello, Mrs Danks. Fancy seeing you 'ere," the lass emitted a nervous titter, brushing a shock of her long, bushy brown hair over her forehead.

"Bad boy, Rex. Now gerrin' yer' kennel," she hollered at the huge dog, which hung its head in remorse and slunk back around the house. The visitor could breathe easy again.

"If it's about me' homework, Miss, I can explain."

Ruby grinned. Fifteen-year-old Emily Ashmore had always had a somewhat tenuous relationship with her biology homework, for which the teenager had frequently been the object of her teacher's ire. Even so, it was ire mitigated by the fact that Emily was one of the more cheerful pupils that 'Mrs Danks' taught.

"No, that's okay, Emily. I haven't come about your homework. I'm delivering these leaflets. They explain why my husband is standing in the General Election in this constituency; and asking people to vote for him. Perhaps you can pass it to your mother and father," she suggested, handing her one from the ream she was holding in her hand."

"Oh. Right," said the schoolgirl, relieved. "They 'ay in at the moment, Miss. Mom's down the bingo; and Dad's down the pub – as always. Not that they'm into all this politics stuff much, like. So they probably woh' read it anyway."

Ruby pursed her lips. Emily had often let slip little insights into her troubled home life – including her parents' fondness for their respective pastimes. Sadly, it was a fondness that precluded any interest in their eldest daughter's education; and which caused them to value her primarily as an unpaid babysitter for their two younger children (who Ruby could overhear squabbling in the front room). Such unpropitious domestic circumstances presumably explained why Emily's homework was suffering.

"Oy, yow' pair! Stop fightin', will ya'!" she yelled over her shoulder at them. "Sorry, Miss. They'm like cat an' dog at times," she apologised.

"Yes, I remember you saying. Well, like I said, just pass this to your parents if you would," Ruby moved to disengage from this unproductive and mutually embarrassing encounter, aware that Emily was anxious to separate her siblings – from the sound of things, before one of them or both sustained an injury.

"Yeah. I will," she again evinced that nervous titter, easing the door shut to leave Ruby by herself on the doorstep once more.

"Now no more scrappin', both on' ya'. Otherwise, Dad'll' kill ya' when he gets back… and me too!" she caught the screech of an involuntary teenage child-minder at her wit's end.

With half-an-eye cocked in case the fearsome Rex reappeared, the idealistic young teacher hurried back down the path to fiddle again with that awkward gate latch. Safely back on the pavement, she couldn't help thinking that the social and economic disadvantage that had denied opportunities in life to Emily Ashmore (and youngsters like her) might have been a more worthwhile call upon her husband's campaigning zeal than the fate of some crumbling old railway.

* * * * *

Jonathan Hunt was wandering the streets of Sneyd End again. Except tonight – rather than doing so as a police officer in uniform – he was flitting from house to house like some skulking fugitive. Indeed, the kind of skittish character that on any other dark night he'd have had no hesitation feeling the collar of.

Having taken pity upon his old friend and the slow pace at which Brian's election flyers were being distributed, the ever-charitable copper had reluctantly agreed to use his night off to help deliver some. Mindful of police regulations however, he was desperate that no one should spot him doing so. To this end – and with a balaclava over his napper and the collar of his coat drawn up around his neck – he moved swiftly to despatch a flyer through the letterboxes of each of the big, opulent houses on the Gainsborough Gardens estate.

It was while moving briskly up the long drive of one particular mansion that he was startled by the appearance of a car slowing to turn into the drive behind him. Panicking, just in time he flung himself behind a clump of rhododendron bushes to avoid the beams of its headlights picking him out – though at the cost of the wad of leaflets he'd been clutching flying out of his hand. He could only watch in horror as those headlight beams now illuminated them fluttering about the drive.

The car drew to a halt and the engine was extinguished – the monstrous 3.5 litre lump of a huge Rover P5 saloon from which the driver now stepped to behold this littering of his property.

"Look at the darn mess they've made!" the man cursed, collecting up some of the leaflets. It was while he was studying one that Jonathan peered around the bush to observe him. He promptly drew his head back in again. Yikes! It was Chief Superintendent Trotter – his new boss!

"What are they, Cyril?" his wife enquired as she too stepped out of the car.

"It looks like they're election flyers – from that confounded railway candidate who's standing in this seat."

"Oh, you mean Brian What's-His-Name. Yes, I've heard he's quite a character," said his wife, endeavouring to take the edge of her husband's indignant scowl. "He's certainly got the town talking. Our Pauline tells me she knows him from visits to the zoo, where he works with his impressive collection of snakes. I presume that's why everyone calls him 'The Snakeman of Sneyd End'. Apparently, he's as passionate about them as he is about this railway line he's fighting to re-open."

"Yes, well, that daughter of ours has always had a soft spot for clowns," her husband groaned. "But I don't care what they call him; I'm going to have words with the man tomorrow. We can't have his minions messing the place up by dropping these confounded things everywhere. This is a decent neighbourhood, Margaret. We don't want it ending up like those 'problem estates' that my officers have to patrol in panda cars!"

Jonathan remained hidden behind the rhododendron bushes all the time the gaze of his gruff, non-nonsense superior was roaming the drive, perchance to spy which minion might have dropped them. Therefore, it was with relief that the inspector eventually heeded his wife's call to hurry up and open the front door.

Once it had closed behind them, Jonathan leapt from out of the foliage to hastily gather up those flyers that were still scattered about the front garden. Making haste back to the street, the palpitating copper whipped off that sweaty balaclava and gave thanks that an encounter with the man who possessed the power to terminate his career with the police had been narrowly averted.

* * * * *

'Streets in the sky', they called them. Four low-rise blocks of flats connected by interweaving concrete walkways, towering over which were two huge, fifteen-storey high-rise blocks that dominated the Sneyd End skyline. Indeed, finally arriving at the topmost floor of one of them afforded Ruby Danks a magnificent view of her adopted town from the vented window at the end of its corridor – including the busy High Street, St Stephen's

Church, the deserted railway line, and the giant steel works in the distance. Why, you could even see the newly-opened section of the M6 motorway from up here! It made it the perfect place to pause and rest from posting Brian's flyers through the letterboxes of the flats she'd visited on her way up.

Conceived in the 1950s (when he'd been the ambitious chairman of the town's housing committee) and completed in 1963 (by which time he'd schemed to become leader of Sneyd End Borough Council), the Tiger Street flats had been Councillor Horace Bissell's opening bid to make Sneyd End the 'Athens of the Midlands'. Influenced by the brutalist style of controversial French urban planner Le Corbusier (who once insisted that "the design of cities is too important to be left to their citizens") and Hungarian-born architect Ernő Goldfinger (a cold, driven man who'd inspired the archetypal megalomaniacal villain in Ian Fleming's eponymous *'James Bond'* novels), they presented an image that was at once audacious and futuristic, and yet also worryingly dystopian and impersonal. Sneyd End High School had been constructed along the same lines and stirred up similar, contradictory emotions amongst both staff and pupils.

Initially popular with those of its tenants who'd been re-housed from the town's Victorian slum hovels, already there were rumours that all was not well with the flats – notwithstanding that the Civic Trust had awarded Councillor Bissell and the Borough Architect a prize for the 'boldness' of the project. Hasty construction using cheap materials (principally reinforced concrete that was standing up less well to the British climate than in those Mediterranean cities where Le Corbusier had first experimented with it) had prompted a steady stream of complaints about damp ingress and poor thermal efficiency. Similar shoddy workmanship and corner-cutting had left Sneyd End High School suffering from the exact same problems.

Just then, Ruby's musing was interrupted by the emergence from her flat of a housewife in curlers and slippers, The Walker Brothers' *'The Sun Ain't Gonna' Shine (Anymore)'* that was playing on the radio emerging with her. Bending down to collect the bottles that the milkman had left beside her front door, she glanced up and spotted this stranger in a Fair Isle sweater.

"It's a fantastic view from up here," Ruby turned from gazing out across the town, attempting to make small talk.

"About the only thing this place has goin' for it," the woman replied, underwhelmed. "From up 'ere though it's almost impossible for us mothers to keep an eye on our kids.

"It's summat' else the bloke who designed this place never thought about," she observed, having sidled up alongside her, clutching the milk bottles to her bosom. "Not that I let mine out much. It's gettin' rough around here, what with gangs of bored teenagers hanging around the play areas. Add to that having to lug yer' shoppin' up all them' stairs when the lifts keep breaking down, and this place can feel like a prison sometimes.

"Anyway, what you up 'ere for?" she enquired, noticing the flyers in Ruby's hand.

The candidate's wife smiled and handed her one.

"They're from Brian Danks – the Independent Save Our Railways candidate. He's looking to re-open Sneyd End station and make other improvements to the town. He'd really appreciate your support on polling day," she enthused.

The woman speed-read both the front and the back of the flyer before abruptly handing it back to her

"Nah, not really interested. These politicians am' all the bleedin' same," she grunted. "They promise you the world and end up giving you sweet Fanny Adams!"

Before Ruby could summon up the presence of mind to announce that her husband wasn't just another 'politician', the woman had returned to her flat and closed the door behind her.

However, their brief conversation prompted Ruby to recall that the Leader of the Council remained ebullient in the face of these 'minor teething problems'. Indeed, he'd unveiled optimistic plans to build more such tower block estates, as well as to construct a new shopping centre in the town and demolish Sneyd End's tired old Vicar Street swimming baths and replace them with a brand-new leisure complex – all to be constructed in the same grandiose, brutalist style, no doubt.

No wonder this man was determined that nothing should stand in the way of his visionary schemes for 'transforming' and 'modernising' Sneyd End – least of all a pesky 'independent' candidate who was threatening to up-end his party's hopes of being returned to government.

* * * * *

Even though television was increasingly pointing the way to how elections were going to be fought in future, in the backwoods of the Black Country the highlight of every candidate's election campaign remained the public meeting. Martin de Vere had already addressed a packed gathering in the Town Hall, where – to sporadic heckling – he'd outlined the Conservative vision for government. So too the following night had David Wallace for Labour (Tory hecklers returning the favour).

Now, on a wet and windy Monday evening in the final week of the campaign, the time had arrived for Brian Danks to rise to his feet, notes in hand, and address the good citizens of Sneyd End who'd gathered in St Stephen's church hall to hear the Save Our Railways candidate speak. All sixteen of them!

Ruby couldn't help thinking that the tiny gathering was a metaphor for her husband's disappointing campaign so far. For while many voters she'd spoken to had expressed fondness for their erstwhile local railway (as well admiring Brian's courage in fighting to save it), it was plain that there were issues of greater import weighing on their minds: the economy; industrial relations; even whether Britain would find itself sucked into the burgeoning American war in Vietnam.

Despite this, tonight her husband threw himself into his expatiation with no less passion than had he been addressing a gathering of sixteen *thousand*. He explained to them that – contrary to the prevailing *zeitgeist* at the Ministry of Transport – with a bit of imagination and investment many of those railways that were being closed could have a bright future. Indeed, rather than choking towns and cities with more roads, more cars, and more pollution, surely now was the time to launch a different kind of transport revolution. However, while his audience was polite and attentive (and applauded him as he sat down), sixteen enthused voters heading home with a warm glow inside was unlikely to propel 'The Snakeman of Sneyd End' into Parliament.

"How did I do?" he asked her once the hall had emptied and the only thing to disturb his childlike angling for reassurance was the sound of the caretaker stacking away the chairs.

She offered him that warm, loving smile she reserved for those moments when this campaigning visionary was in need of an encouraging word.

"You were very impressive – as you always are."

"Do you think I can win?" he asked, dipping his gaze.

She knew this was his coded way of admitting that, despite the platform his candidacy had afforded him, he remained an unheeded voice in the wilderness. Indeed, it was telling that people from neither of the other two parties had bothered to turn up and challenge him. As with his past campaigns, Brian Danks had failed to translate the undeniable respect in which many people held him into the kind of solid political support he needed to advance his transport revolution.

"Your time will come, my dear." she insisted, tenderly trailing the back of her hand along his cheek – her coded way of letting him know that the past few weeks of hard work and heartache might not have been entirely in vain.

* * * * *

The architect who'd planned this older, more traditional housing estate had certainly been no great friend of postmen. Every property was set atop a steep flight of steps that required the descent of those steps again in order to access the next house in the street – which was also sat atop a steep path. Added to which, it was raining. Barely half-an-hour into her delivery round, Brian's other half was dripping wet and puffing like Billy-ho.

One lesson Ruby had learned about delivering leaflets door-to-door was never to put your hand through a letterbox unless you could see what was lurking on the other side. On a previous evening she'd almost lost her fingers to a dog that had leapt at the flyer she posted. Tonight therefore, she'd come armed with a wooden spatula borrowed from the kitchen drawer.

It now proved its worth. Spatula in hand, she strode up a garden path and employed it to bodge another flyer through a letterbox. Though the dog on the other side gnashed at the leaflet, at least this handy little device had spared Ruby's delicate feminine digits from harm. Smirking with self-satisfaction, she therefore moved to extract the spatula from the letterbox.

Except that it wouldn't come. Tugging at it from the other end was a mutt that was determined to not let go. Ruby tugged again – but to no avail. Pressing a foot against the door, this time she tugged at the spatula with all her might. However, still the dog would not let go. A comical stand-off thus ensued.

Determined not to let the animal win, she was readying herself to tug at it again when the dog growled and wrenched it from her grasp completely, in the process causing Ruby's knuckles to impact hard against the letterbox. What's more, the lethal combination of a wet night and unseen green slime on the slab that she leapt backwards onto caused her to lose her footing. Leaflets suddenly flung into the air, she found herself tumbling through a flower bed to be deposited arse-first in the ornamental fish pond at the foot of it. If she wasn't soaked through before, she certainly was now.

"Ouch!" she hollered, clutching at a sore knee through the gaping hole that had been torn in her tights.

However, the wince of pain was as nothing to the scream of horror when, attempting to lift herself out of the pond, she spotted a large frog pounce from the lilies and land on the breast of her raincoat. This electioneering malarkey was a dangerous business and Ruby Danks had had enough of it!

* * * * *

This was it: the culmination of everything he'd been working towards these last few weeks. The polls had closed. The people had made their choice. In Sneyd End Town Hall the first ballot boxes were arriving from polling stations around the town, to be emptied and verified by the army of counting clerks who were sat around the tables that ringed the hall's cavernous interior.

Wandering about those tables, never in his wildest dreams had Brian Danks imagined that what had started out in this place a few years earlier as a public meeting to protest the closure of a railway would witness him one day standing for parliament in the town he loved – and with every chance that, even if he didn't win, he could at least unseat a minister in Her Majesty's Government.

Indeed, the last few days had witnessed both main parties pull out all the stops to win this seat. For the Conservatives, Edward Heath had put in a surprise appearance alongside his candidate in Sneyd End. Meanwhile, David Wallace must have hoped that a similar much-publicised visit by Harold Wilson the following day had shored up the Labour vote (and with it both his job and that of his Prime Minister!).

Then as now, the zealous young zoologist who had dared to challenge them was genuinely grateful that Ruby had remained by his side throughout. He now paused from surveying the count to behold her again looking svelte in the fashionable beige mini skirt she was wearing (even if beneath it she'd donned a pair of thick, woolly tights to disguise that grazed knee).

Moving along the tables, Brian was genuinely grateful to the other woman in his life too, who – in her own inimitable way – had also helped fortify his resolve. Arriving alongside the seat in the hall from where she was eagerly observing the count, he bent down to place a tender kiss upon her cheek.

"Hello, son. Not long now. Hello, Ruby. Are you looking forward to being the wife of a Member of Parliament?" Myrtle Danks warbled to her daughter-in-law excitedly.

"You bet, Mrs Danks," she smiled and enthused.

Yet both the smile and the enthusing were contrived. Brian's doting mother had always been his Number One fan and admirer. Broaching not a scintilla of doubt, she really did believe in her son in a way that left Ruby feeling terribly inadequate on that score. Perhaps it was just what mothers do. Maybe one day, when she finally got to suckle the child she was longing for, Ruby too would feel the same way about her offspring. Until then, continuing to stroll about the counting tables, hand-in-hand with her husband, she contrived again to offer onlookers the obligatory smiles expected of a loyal candidate's wife – even as the trays marked *'Wallace'* and *'De Vere'* began filling with hundreds of ballot slips (while, conversely, considerably fewer were being tossed into the trays marked *'Danks'*).

"Were you really expecting a different result?" her guilty introspection was interrupted by this sarcastic question. Both Brian and Ruby turned to be confronted by the looming presence of a man with a gaudy red rosette pinned to the breast of his suit.

"C-c-councillor B-b-bissell, what a pl-pl-pleasant surprise," said Brian, trying not to appear flustered by this bombastic giant of a man. "But then, as my sports teacher at school used to say: it is nobler to fail while trying than never to have tried at all,"

"Strange that," the corpulent councillor snorted. "I thought they taught you grammar school boys that winning was everything!" he grunted.

"I think what my husband is alluding to is that one should remain true to oneself and one's beliefs – even if doing so carries a price," Ruby looked up at the council leader, politely venting her frustration at the way both main parties had mocked and belittled Brian and his valiant, if amateurish campaign.

"I'm tempted to say 'one' is right," he mocked, though feigning politeness. "But what if the price of remaining 'true to oneself' is the election of a Tory government that will perpetuate an education system that favours their own children – inequality which I'm told you, like me, feel passionate about, Mrs Danks?"

Unsure what the Leader of the Council was driving at, but affronted by this attempt to denigrate his wife, before Brian could open his mouth to protest he was reminded anew that Ruby Danks was more than capable of fighting her own battles.

"You're right, Councillor Bissell, I do care – passionately. After all, it's why I chose a career in teaching. My husband cares passionately too – about other things he believes will make this town a better place. However, unlike certain politicians in Sneyd End, at least when this election is over he'll be able to sleep soundly at night with a clear conscience," she returned the councillor's stare of contempt.

"Then long may he slumber undisturbed," he feigned politeness again, adding "And while he does, this particular 'politician' will be getting on with the real business of making this town 'a better place'.

"I hate bullies!" Ruby hissed once this colossus of a man had brushed past and was out of earshot. "And they don't come much bigger than Horace Bissell – literally and metaphorically!"

"But he's chairman of governors at your school. He could... I mean..." Brian gabbled, appalled.

More than the sore feet (and a grazed knee) she'd acquired from tramping the campaign trail with him, it was the thought that Ruby might have laid her career on the line that jolted Brian into realising the 'price' his wife might have ultimately paid to demonstrate her loyalty to him.

* * * * *

Brian and Ruby Danks weren't the only people nursing sore feet tonight. At the end of a long shift plodding the beat, PC Jonathan Hunt caught the familiar sound of the town clock striking midnight. Out of uniform and attired in his pyjamas, after a long soak in the bath he now detoured to place an ear against the door of his parents' bedroom. With them soundly asleep, he drifted downstairs and switched on the television set in the sitting room, where he could linger to watch the election results coming in from around the country (and which made a change from the National Anthem rounding off the programme schedules at ten-thirty prompt).

As predicted, Labour appeared to be ahead from those results that had been announced so far, presenter Cliff Michelmore recapping the raft of big names on the Conservative side who had succumbed to the tide of red victories. Periodically going over 'live' to the more eagerly anticipated results, one contest was of particular interest to the somnolent copper. He craned in to stare intently at the flickering, black-and-white image of the three candidates lined up on the stage of Sneyd End Town Hall.

"... Being the Returning Officer for the said parliamentary constituency announce the results to be as follows: Danks, Brian Matthew..."

"Independent – Save Our Railways candidate," Michelmore interjected *sotto voce* for the benefit of viewers watching at home.

"... Four thousand, eight hundred and seven votes."

Crikey! Jonathan spluttered: if nowhere near enough to take this seat Brian had certainly done much better than expected. Perhaps the Snakeman still possessed the ability to strike a chord with the good people of his home town.

"De Vere, Martin Heydon Romaine…"

"Conservative Party candidate."

"…Sixteen thousand, three hundred and eight votes."

"Wallace, David Lionel…"

"Labour Party candidate."

"…Eighteen thousand, eight hundred and eighty votes."

An almighty cheer went up from the Labour supporters in the Town Hall as David Wallace thrust his hands into the air, returned to Parliament again for another four years – notwithstanding that the Snakeman's 4,807 votes had robbed him of the kind of sizeable majority that his comrades elsewhere in Britain's urban working-class constituencies were clocking up.

One thing was for sure. The body language of both the Labour and Conservative supporters in the Town Hall – and especially that of the waspish Councillor Horace Bissell – suggested that Brian Danks would be neither forgiven nor forgotten in a hurry.

7

It had been a gruelling eight-hour trip. One day the bits of the new M5 motorway that had been constructed so far would be joined up to form one continuous fast route that promised to halve the time it took to journey from the Midlands to the beaches of the Devon Riviera. Today though – at 5.30pm on the dot – Brian and Ruby Danks could finally clamber out of her little red Mini and give thanks that they'd arrived to glorious sunny weather. What better start to their annual holiday!

"Of course, we could have caught the train!" Brian teased his wife as he lugged their cases up the front steps of the hotel.

She turned to curl an eyebrow at him – the same one she'd curled upon discovering that he'd craftily chosen both a hotel and a room that conveniently overlooked the main railway line as it hugged the coast at this point.

Just then their attention – like that of the patrons chatting over their drinks on the sun terrace outside – was taken by an almighty roar emanating from the bar that fronted it (and which completely drowned out the melodic Herb Alpert brass instrumental that had been softly playing in the background). Everyone looked round to observe grown men jumping up and down and hugging each other.

"Geoff Hurst has scored… in the seventy-eighth minute," someone raced out to enlighten them. "It could be the goal that takes us into the semi-final!"

Maybe not though: on the little television set that everyone had gathered around players from the opposing side could already be spotted hurrying over to the referee to gesticulate that the English striker had been offside.

"It's the Argentina match," the portly man on reception enlightened the bemused arrivals as they strode up to him to check in. "It's been a right dirty game too. Antonio Rattin, their captain, ended up having to be escorted from the pitch by police after a foul against Bobby Charlton!" he snorted in contempt.

A sentiment shared by the guys in the bar, it appeared. Goal allowed – and while Brian was filling out their particulars and paying for their room – Ruby drifted over to hang in the entrance and observe this sensational World Cup fixture draw to a close with a 1-0 victory over the South American side (notwithstanding that indignant manager Alf Ramsey had seen fit to race onto the pitch to prevent his players swapping shirts with the unsporting Argentine team).

"Rule Britannia, Britannia rules the waves. England never, never, ever shall be slaves…" the bar wallahs were crowing in an outburst of atavistic, drink-fuelled patriotism. God forbid that these two nations should ever come to blows in a real conflict!

"I didn't know you were into football," said Brian, joining his wife in the bar once the formalities had been completed.

"I'm not," she replied.

"Good. That makes two of us."

It was heartening to know. Mercifully, after the travails of the year so far, Ruby could look forward to enjoying her husband's wholehearted attention during their fortnight away – unlike those soccer widows whose other halves were still volubly debating the match over their beers.

Ascending to their room – and too weary to do much beyond pack away their belonging – Brian threw open the window to briefly admire both the sea view and a passing train before crashing out alongside his wife on the sumptuous double bed. After what seemed like an age spent in somnolent reflection, Ruby eventually propped herself up on her elbows to reach across and remove his spectacles. Beholding the dreamy look in her husband's eyes, she initiated the kiss he was clearly angling for. Then the fingers at the end of the arm of embrace that had drawn her in close alighted upon the zip of her dress. After unsuccessfully fumbling with it, they were supplemented by Ruby's own, more expert hands.

The garment peeled from her shoulders, a slow, yet determined undressing took place until they were both sufficiently naked to be able to remind each other again that this often seemingly mismatched couple had some truly wondrous things in common (of which a shared disinterest in football was just one!).

* * * * *

With a gathering roar and a loud blast of its two-tone horn the majestic, maroon-liveried locomotive thundered past within feet of the awestruck train-spotter, who noted down its number: sixty-six thousand pounds of tractive effort pulling behind it a rake of rattling carriages from which small children were waving. Brian looked up and waved back at them wistfully.

"D1009 – *'Western Invader'*. And that was *'The Cornishman'* to Penzance that she was hauling," he enlightened his wife, having hopped down from the sea wall that ran alongside the main line to amble back to the spot on the beach where Ruby had spread out their towels.

"It's one of those powerful 'Western' class diesels. They work most of the important passenger trains on this line now that steam has been withdrawn from the south-west," he elaborated.

Ruby looked up at him, squinting in the sun as she did. She was happy to indulge her husband's boyish interest in trains now that it was once again confined to the model lay-out in the spare room, as well as (like this afternoon) the occasional foray to spot the real thing.

"I remember catching that train in the summer of 1952," he continued, plonking himself down to accept the sandwich Ruby offered him from their picnic basket. "It was headed up by a 'King' class 4-6-0 locomotive. Or was it a 'Castle' class?" he interrogated his recollection. "We boarded it at Birmingham Snow Hill station. How sad to think that soon steam trains will be gone from Britain's railways. And that soon trains will be gone altogether from one of Britain's most iconic city centre railway stations too."

Ruby squeezed his shoulder with an empathetic hand. The General Election landslide that had swept Harold Wilson back to power with a ninety-eight-seat majority had done nothing to halt the remorseless 'rationalisation' of Britain's railways. Alas, it would now be left to posterity to judge whether the headlong rush to close both lines and stations had been misconceived and myopic – as her husband was still maintaining.

"Yes, that memorable week in Torquay was one of the rare holidays Mom was able to afford on her war widow's pension," he continued his reminiscence between mouthfuls.

"It's a shame your father never lived to witness you grow up. I can't even begin to imagine what it must be like to have never known one's father," Ruby opined, gazing out to sea and recalling the awe and affection in which she held her own.

"There was a war on. It was just one of those things that happen," Brian sought to put a brave face on what his wife, looking on, knew had left an indelible scar upon him.

Private Arthur Danks had never got to hold his new-born child, conceived before he'd been packed off to France in 1939. Within weeks of Brian's birth, the Germans had attacked and overrun the Low Countries, pushing the British Expeditionary Force back to Dunkirk, where the hastily-promoted Corporal Danks had been killed during the fraught evacuation of its beaches.

Thereafter, it had been left to Brian's mother to raise the boy alone as best she could. A quirky, yet studious child who the other boys at school had alternately mocked or shunned, Ruby wondered if the over-compensating love and encouragement that Myrtle Danks had lavished upon her only son might have contributed to that righteously-indignant monomania that so readily afflicted him. Commendable in many ways, it was even so a character flaw that repelled some as surely as it impressed others; and would surely one day – Ruby feared – impel her husband to waltz blasé into a situation replete with danger, of which a worrying paucity of modesty or self-doubt would render him oblivious to, or dismissive of.

"Still, Mom brought me up as best she could," he meanwhile glossed over his inauspicious life story. "It's thanks to her unerring belief in me that I made it into grammar school, where I was consistently the top of my school year; then to university and a first-class honours degree in animal biology; thereafter to become one of the foremost authorities on herpetology in the country – and certainly in the Midlands."

Ruby flashed him a touching smile. A 'worrying absence of modesty or self-doubt' indeed!

"With a little help from my old form tutor, of course," he thought to add, attempting to interpret that smile. "For all his fustiness, Cledwyn Davies was a superb and dedicated teacher. I'll always be indebted to him."

Ruby broke from dissecting her husband's psyche to assure him that "He would have been so proud of you."

"Who? Mr Davies?"

"No, silly. Your father."

"I do hope so. I often wonder if he's up there looking down on me. Maybe one day God will place an angel across my path to tell me, on his behalf, that he is indeed proud of me," Brian chuckled, briefly glancing heavenwards. "Then again, maybe he's ashamed of me: that I've turned out to be such an oddball figure – someone who nobody likes; and everybody shuns."

"Don't be daft, Brian. People don't dislike you; or shun you. You're just different, that's all. And it's not a sin to be different," she attempted to console him.

"I know he would have been proud of *you*, Ruby; to have had you as his daughter-in-law; and to have witnessed how you have loved me and believed in me."

She masked her unease by dipping into the picnic basket to trawl up another sandwich for her 'oddball' spouse. Thereupon, there ensued an awkward hiatus in the conversation.

Brilliant, yet so maddeningly obsessive, her husband's self-pitying observation had more than a grain of truth about it. Few people had ever possessed the patience to get to know the real Brian Danks – the teenage misfit with the cheap NHS spectacles who could be found most days after school standing alone on Sneyd End station, spotting trains as they passed. However, it was on that same station one afternoon that he'd discovered a soul mate of sorts: Jonathan Hunt – himself mocked and shunned for the way teenage acne was disfiguring him – also shared Brian's love of trains. Thus the two boys had become firm friends. Indeed, far better than Ruby herself, Jonathan seemed to be the one person in this world so far who'd been able to act as a brake upon her husband's more fanciful delusions.

"You know, I'll never really understand what it is *you* see in me," he turned to Ruby – almost as if he'd discerned what she was thinking at that moment. "I mean, you could have had the choice of any boy you wanted at university," he winced with another self-pitying glint in his eyes. "And yet you chose me."

"Even back then I could tell you were special," she replied, having asked herself that question a thousand times since. "There was something about you that I warmed to. Yes, you *were* different to the other boys. Yet it was almost as if there was an aura about you that was imploring some girl somewhere to love you and to believe in you. I guess it was God's will that that girl be me!" she looked him in the eye.

"*'Ye have not chosen me, but I have chosen you'* – John's Gospel, Chapter Fifteen, Verse Sixteen," he chuckled in humility. "And there was me thinking it was *me* who fell for you!

"And do you *still* love me – and believe in me?" he asked after a suitable pause in which to reflect upon whether that strange, intangible aura that had first attracted her to him still glowed.

Ruby offered him that tender smile again.

"Yes, I do," she affirmed.

* * * * *

England's successes in the World Cup so far, along with the fact that the team was playing on home turf, had provided a welcome diversion from an especially egregious story that had dominated the news headlines in the run-up to the tournament.

On May 6th 1966 – after a two week trial at Chester Assizes during which accounts of their cruelty and depravity had shocked the nation – a psychopathic hoodlum called Ian Brady and his blonde-mopped girlfriend and accomplice, Myra Hindley, had been sentenced to life imprisonment for the abduction, rape, sadistic torture and murder of several children in and around Manchester, whose bodies had been discovered in shallow graves on the bleak Pennine moors to the east of the city.

Appalling too was the revelation that it had been Hindley who had lured the youngsters to their deaths – as well as performing some of the murders. Was the female of the species really capable of such a thing? Too bad, many people seethed, that capital punishment for such crimes had been abolished in Britain just a few months earlier!

However, on this beautiful warm July morning the possibility of being lured to one's death never entered the thoughts of a young, wilful canine that had seized the opportunity to run and frolic in the sun – and in a strange new playground too that his owner had taken to exercising him in. After weeks of otherwise exemplary behaviour, Bertie the golden Labrador had availed himself of a session off the lead to ignore his owner's frantic pleas and prolong this moment of freedom.

The fields and copses of Fens Bank certainly offered a dog the chance to explore. Pacing along the shoreline of one of its large, man-made cooling ponds, Bertie eventually halted to press his twitching nose to the ground and savour an interesting scent. Truly a veritable haven for wildlife, perhaps it might herald something worth chasing. A rabbit maybe; or even one of Fens Bank's big juicy rats.

By-and-by – and still oblivious to Mr Channon periodically calling him in the distance – the cooling ponds proved irresistible for another reason too. Wading amongst the bulrushes at the lake's edge, Bertie dipped his tongue to lap up the warm, pea-green water – the perfect tonic for a hot, panting Labrador.

Thirst sated, the dog looked up and spotted that a peculiar scaly object had meanwhile surfaced further out in the pond. Floating amidst the plant life, it appeared to possess eyes that were trained upon him. Unsure what it was, he let out the playful yap of the habitually curious. Tempted to wade in a little deeper, he ventured to prod at it warily with his shiny black nose.

It was at that moment that a head reared up and sank a gaping mouthful of sharp, backward-facing teeth into Bertie's neck. Dragged beneath the water, the flailing dog resurfaced just long enough to emit a pathetic, anguished yelp before it was pulled under again.

So it was that, barely a minute into a one-sided struggle, this most fearsome of assailants had coiled itself around the hapless hound and throttled the life out of it. Who said the female of the species was incapable of pitiless killing?

* * * * *

One week into Brian and Ruby's fortnight by the sea and it had already proved an invaluable aid to rejuvenating their marriage. It had been good for Brian to be able to step back from his indefatigable crusade (and Ruby from the tribulations of classroom life) and just enjoy the sea, the sun and the sights.

However, fortified by the assurance that his wife was still on his side, it wasn't long before Brian was subtly testing the water in anticipation of the next instalment in that crusade. Yet Ruby was neither so naive (nor her husband so subtle) that she couldn't deduce what cogs and gears were crunching away inside that restless mind of his.

"Last week, British Railways agreed to sell off the station site to the Council," he contrived to mention in passing as they strolled along the sea front, both of them licking from the ice cream cones they'd purchased. "So it looks very much like that's where they're going to build it."

"But you can't deny the town needs a new swimming baths," Ruby noted, aware of the public clamour that had been mounting to replace the worn-out Victorian-era baths on Vicar Street.

"I understand that, Ruby. But if these plans are approved and construction goes ahead, then Sneyd End station will be gone for all time – and the railway through the town with it."

"Perhaps, in the larger scheme of things, people value a new swimming baths more than they do a railway that few people ever used – at least towards its end. After all, Horace Bissell has made a personal pledge to voters that he will build one. And what makes the old station so attractive is that – if you include the adjacent sidings too – there's plenty of land upon which to build the baths, an accompanying sports hall, and a large car park too. There's no other site in town where the Council could do all those things."

"Once again, everything has to revolve around the needs of the motor car!" Brian screwed his face up indignantly.

Upon which Ruby offered him the kind of stern expression that sought to jog his memory about how handy their little car had been this past week for exploring the coves and cliffs of south

Devon, along with the wild uplands of Dartmoor aback them. So wasn't it about time he swallowed both his pride and his principles and learned to drive the thing too?

"I guess you're right. You have done rather a lot of driving this holiday. I'll have to book a course of lessons when we get back," he chuntered. "That's after I've written another long letter to Councillor Bissell," he remained defiant concerning the substantive matter they'd been discussing.

"I would imagine Councillor Bissell has a drawer full of your letters by now," she teased him, "As does every other politician in Sneyd End, for that matter!"

The self-appointed defender of the town's railway failed to spot the pun. However, for all that he now railed against the perfidy of a corpulent council leader who had turned his back on the railway he'd once promised to save, surely even the Snakeman wasn't so obtuse as to be unaware that this time – unlike in his previous campaigns – the sympathies of the voters were likely to be elsewhere. It had been over two years since a train had last called at Sneyd End station. During that time the buses had mopped up what few passengers had ever waited there, while the masonry of the tired old Vicar Street baths had continued to flake – a source (as she'd reminded him) of other angry letters to Councillor Bissell. It was a truism that one can't stand in the way of progress. However, Ruby worried that this time it really could be her husband against the rest of the world.

* * * * *

"Come on, England! Come on, England!"

Brian and Ruby returned to their hotel to once again find the bar – and the sun terrace onto which watching guests had spilled out – alive to the thrill of another titanic struggle being played out. Ninety-six thousand people had gathered at Wembley Stadium to witness England face West Germany in the Final of the 1966 World Cup.

While Brian went to retrieve the key to their room, Ruby found herself sufficiently smitten by the 'beautiful game' to once again wander into the bar and gaze on. She was in good company too:

even the hotel's 'soccer widows' had gathered about their menfolk and were willing the home team on.

"Who's winning?" she sidled up to one couple, attempting to peer through the sea of heads to catch glimpses of the black-and-white television in the corner.

"Neither side at the moment," the husband glanced away to apprise her in a voice replete with nervous tension. "Geoff Hurst scored in the first half with a goal that was challenged, but which the ref allowed. Then the Germans went two up. And now Martin Peters has equalised. So there's still everything to play for."

His flitting gaze quickly returned to the screen, leaving Ruby having to crane on tiptoes if she wanted to follow the action. Soon enough, the supporters in the front rows became hopeful enough to rise again from their seats – to the exasperation of those behind them also jostling for a view.

"Yes… come on, my son!" the cry went up as the spritely form of Geoff Hurst could again be picked out racing up to the German goalie.

"YEEESSSS!!!"

The entire room erupted in a deafening holler. Beer was slopped, sun hats were thrown into the air, and grown men were dancing and skipping about with abandon. Returning from his detour, Brian was dismayed to observe that Ruby had been lifted bodily from the floor and was being swung around and kissed by some complete stranger.

"We've won, I gather," he grunted to the man, who apologised and lowered the comely teacher to her feet.

"Not yet, mate," he quivered as debate ensued on the pitch about whether the ball had crossed the goal line.

However, the Swiss referee allowed it. And so, with the Germans desperate to equalise, the anxious crowd in the bar hurriedly re-trained it collective gaze on the television set.

"…The referee's looking at his watch… Any second now…" the commentator meanwhile assured them. *"It's all over… I think… No, here comes Hurst…"* his voice rose again.

The disbelieving troop of fans were quickly on their feet once more, their heads obscuring Ruby's view of a fourth and final goal that was hammered into the back of the German net.

"They've got people on the pitch… They think it's all over…
IT IS NOW!"

The final whistle had been blown. It was indeed 'all over'. For several minutes the delirious hotel guests continued to dance about in joy, eventually wiping the tears from their eyes to behold Bobby Moore mount the stand and receive that glittering cup from Her Majesty, the Queen. The England captain then turned to face the roaring Wembley crowd and lift it high in triumph.

"We won the Cup. We won the Cup. Ee-ay-allio, we won the Cup!" the jubilation in Torbay continued.

* * * * *

"Land of hope and glory, mother of the free…"

Britain might have lost her empire (coincidentally – yet symbolically – the Colonial Office would finally be wound up the day after England's World Cup victory); but it was heartening to know that she'd regained her prowess on the football field (or at least that portion of Britain south of the Tweed had!).

Down at the 'Pig & Whistle' public house on Sneyd End High Street the victory celebrations had been underway for several hours. Much beer had been downed and many patriotic songs had been bawled. Yet still the barman was working flat out to keep his regulars victualled.

"There'll always be an England,
And England shall be free…"

Talking of patriotic fervour, forty-six-year-old Ernie Baxter hadn't witnessed scenes like this since VE Day. Neither had he toped as much Banks' Bitter either! So elated had he been by England's stunning victory that he'd even ventured onto a whisky or two as well. However, if the booze and the spirits didn't finish him off then his missus surely would when he finally elected to stagger home to face her. Swigging back the dram, he therefore decided to chance his luck with another one before departing to confront the old dragon. Standing uneasily to his feet, he managed to arrive at the bar without stumbling, placing the glass down on the counter in expectation.

"I doh' think so, Ernie, ol' mate. Ar'd say yow've 'ad enough by the look of it. Time to 'ead hoom' and give the fire a good poke. That's if yer' poker's still up to it, eh!" the barman tapped his nose suggestively, guffawing above the din.

Ah well, it was worth a try. Blinking exaggeratedly, Ernie staggered past the blokes still singing and supping in the smoke room to be greeted outside by a delightful summer evening on which the sun was setting. It was the kind of glorious sunset that was able to make even a grimy, industrial town like Sneyd End appear enchanting.

> *"… And did those feet in ancient times,*
> *Walk upon England's mountains green…!"*

Sure enough, the other pubs on the High Street were still heaving with beer-fuelled celebration too. Ernie paused, minded to try his luck in the 'Miner's Arms' instead. However, still blinking exaggeratedly, he teetered on – abetted by a succession of handy lamp standards that he could grip for support.

The sobering up process would normally have been aided by a twilight walk home. However, at some point while staggering along the Wednesbury Road the intrepid drunk decided he was neither intrepid enough nor sober enough to want to face his wife just yet. Therefore, he decided to head off down the lane that meandered through Fens Bank – shielding his eyes from the sun that was caressing the horizon ahead of him – the better to pluck up the courage to finally face her.

As he did, he was once again mumbling to himself about how he could have been someone had he not rather stupidly (and bibulously) 'poked the fire' while home on leave from Arctic convoys; and (as a result) got Daisy Skidmore from Plant Street in 'the family way'. Meanwhile, staggering past one of Fens Bank's cooling ponds in this sozzled state, the setting of the sun reflecting romantically on the stillness of its leafy-green surface suddenly drew him towards it. Something that was lurking in the bulrushes had caught his attention: some big, mottled, scaly thing.

His vision still blurred, he staggered right up to the water's edge to take a closer look.

Now he knew he really had imbibed far too much. For there in front of his swivelling eyes an enormous snake lay motionless – larger than anything he'd ever seen before (and certainly way bigger than the occasional grass snake he used to come across when playing over these parts as a nipper). What's more, the creature must have recently feasted. For there, midway down the length of its colossal trunk, he spied a bulge that he presumed to be the last meal the snake had consumed.

Ernie Baxter had seen enough. He turned to leg it as fast as his unsteady limbs would transport him – which was not very far. Tripping over his feet, he tumbled down the embankment to land in the water with a loud splash.

Wailing and flailing in the shallows, mercifully he was able to take advantage of the animal's postprandial torpor to rise again, hurriedly wading back to the shore. Staggering away, he resolved that having his ear chewed by the missus was preferable to having his whole being devoured by this monstrous serpent.

At last, he could lunge through a gap in the chain-link fence and stumble back onto the main road, dripping wet and jabbering to himself like a total idiot as he rehearsed in his head how he might explain this bizarre encounter to his wife. However, warily watching over his shoulder lest the creature was somehow stalking him, as he lurched in the direction of home he suddenly slammed into another huge, fearsome creature instead.

"Evening, sir. Taking a short cut, were we?" enquired a tall, looming policeman who glared down at him.

It was all Ernie could do to keep from swooning.

"Snake!" the miscreant tried to make himself understood, "Giant un'…! This big…!" he then spanned out his arms as wide as they would stretch, pointing in the direction of the cooling ponds still visible in the twilight.

"Really, sir?" the constable feigned to marvel. "And was sir perchance endeavouring to converse with this giant snake when he fell in the water?" he stooped to eyeball the pitiful little man.

"Snake...! Big un'!" Ernie continued to protest, a hiccup surfacing to waft unsavoury, alcohol-marinated breath in the officer's pockmarked face.

"Of course, sir. And I'm Nobby Stiles!" the bobby straightened himself up, unimpressed.

It was no use. If the 'long arm of the law' wouldn't credit the truth of what Ernie had just seen with his own two (admittedly rather glazed) eyes, then what hope was there of convincing the eternally-sceptical Daisy Baxter!

"Snake... Big un'!" he wept dispiritedly.

"Look, you can read these signs," the officer bodged his shoulder, using his free hand to rotate Ernie's head about to observe that finger then point to the one affixed to the fence behind him. "*'KEEP OUT – no trespassing'.* Therefore, might I suggest sir keeps to the main road in future – especially after he's had one too many down his local!"

Ernie Baxter nodded, blinked exaggeratedly, and then saluted (some navy habits die hard!). Then off he teetered in the direction of home and to the fearsome tongue-lashing he'd been seeking to postpone, depositing a sopping wet trail behind him as he went.

"Giant snake, my arse!" the officer meanwhile shook his head as he observed this catatonic little man pause to avail himself of another lamp standard for support.

PC Jonathan Hunt had been fed some likely stories during his time on the beat; but that one took the biscuit! His friend Brian Danks would certainly have found it amusing.

8

"I told you he would be no good for you. But did you listen to me? No, you've never listened to me, Ruby. Yet you know I love you and only have your best interests at heart."

There is often a wilful blindness that will cause a spouse to deny or rationalise the glaring faults of their other half – standing in solidarity with them, as it were, despite mounting evidence that the naysayers might be right. Once upon a time, Ruby Danks would have vigorously argued back against her mother. Instead, seated on the swing in the garden of her parent's opulent Sussex home upon which she used to play as a child (and upon which she'd not given up hope that children of her own might one day play too), she rocked herself lazily in the late summer sunshine and said nothing. Meanwhile, Mrs Leadbetter carried on lecturing her daughter about how unwise she'd been, at the same time as pruning the hydrangeas with the secateurs she was wielding briskly with gloved hands.

"You're such a pretty girl, Ruby. When I look back on some of the boys you could have chosen… Take that Timothy Forbes, for instance. He absolutely adored you. I thought you two were made for each other... In fact, that was another instance of where you didn't listen to me," she clucked – the furious snipping of those secateurs the conduit for her evident frustration.

"And look how well he's done for himself since," she added, suddenly halting to lecture her with them. "He's a stockbroker now, you know. He married Julia Makin, who you went to school with. They own this beautiful, big house on the other side of Lewes. And they have three children – with another on the way."

In a similar vein, Ruby didn't have the heart to point out to her mother that Timothy Forbes was an arrogant and ill-mannered brat whose gods were his bank balance and his social standing. Nor that he treated the hapless Julia as little more than an adornment to be wheeled out and paraded at social functions (that's when he wasn't availing himself of her womb to populate that 'beautiful, big house' with his equally arrogant and ill-mannered children). It was a fate that could so easily have befallen Ruby too had she been partial to the persistent and unsubtle advances of her mother's preferred choice of suitor.

For all Brian's flaws, at least he possessed true moral character – a quality that had drawn Ruby to him at university; and that had nursed the flame of love and devotion through the crazy ups-and-downs of their relationship ever since. And besides, beneath those Hank Marvin spectacles he remained a considerably more handsome chap than the porcine-faced Timothy Forbes! So why was Ruby once again doubting the wisdom of her choice of mate?

"Pray tell me what hare-brained scheme he's dreaming up now," her mother sneered upon returning to her gardening duties, oblivious to her daughter's gathering self-doubt.

"He's bought a steam locomotive," Ruby drew breath and announced.

Mrs Leadbetter thought she'd misheard. Then – eyes wide and mouth agape – she turned to stare at her daughter.

"He's done what!"

"Well, Brian and some other train buffs," Ruby explained, returning the look of askance disbelief her mother was sporting with an apologetic shrug of her bare shoulders. "Apparently there's this big scrap yard in South Wales where these engines are waiting to be cut up. They've raised a pot of money and have managed to rescue one from there. They intend to restore it and run it on a disused section of line that some other railway enthusiasts have clubbed together to buy."

Mrs Leadbetter's gaze lingered before she turned away to vent her dismay upon a few more rogue flower heads.

"One of these days he'll realise that he's a married man with responsibilities," she continued to cluck. "Probably not though. On past form, he'll disappear every weekend to tinker with it. Soon enough, the only time you'll ever see this supposed 'husband' of yours is if you trail after him and tinker with it too."

She didn't have the heart to tell her mother that Brian was still campaigning too (this time his restless mind exercised by the forthcoming public hearing into the closure of Birmingham's Snow Hill station). And now this other 'tinkering' pastime had turned up, threatening to drive a further wedge between the couple. Sometimes the fate of being Mrs Ruby Danks was a terribly lonely one.

"I suppose he's also still scribbling sermons that no one ever listens to – rather like the vicar in that new *'Eleanor Rigby'* song" her mother scorned, rolling her eyes as she did. "In fact, is there no end to the pies your husband will insist on sticking his fingers in? And no doubt you're going to tell me he's filled the house with yet more of those horrible snakes too," she shuddered.

"No, still only the one, Mummy," Ruby idly riposted, unsure whether to be impressed by her mother's awareness of pop music; or disappointed that the façade of respectability that was her own lukewarm Sunday observance inhibited Muriel Leadbetter from looking more charitably upon her son-in-law's sincere profession of Christian faith.

Otherwise, revenge was to summon a wry, if unseen smile of her own. For if nothing else, that irrational fear of snakes had spared Brian from more frequent visitations by his remonstrative mother-in-law.

"You mark my words, Ruby dear. You'll come to bitterly regret the day you ignored your mother's advice and hitched your star with that man. When I think of all the dashing and handsome young men you could have married instead," her mother carried on sniping and snipping.

Yes, to think, Ruby pondered to herself as she rocked herself lazily upon that swing.

* * * * *

All too soon the summer holiday was over and Ruby Danks found herself back in front of a blackboard once more.

Among this year's motley ensemble of new pupils who were staring up at her as she wandered down the lines of desks introducing herself – and bidding them introduce themselves in turn – there stood out a diminutive little girl with long, jet-black hair that was knotted in two pig-tails (and who was clearly self-conscious that two dozen pairs of eyes had meanwhile been burrowing into her with a mixture of fascination and suspicion).

"And what's your name?" Ruby enquired as the turn came to alight upon her.

"Parminder, Miss. Parminder Kaur," she replied, looking up to address her through unstylish spectacles that made her effulgent brown eyes appear even bigger than they actually were.

Ruby was pleasantly surprised. Her quiet, yet eloquent command of the English language stood in marked contrast to the gabble of coarse local dialects with which the young teacher had been greeted so far. Otherwise, an audible muttering coursed around the class that was immediately stilled when Ruby fired off a censorious glance.

To be sure, Parminder was not the first black or brown-skinned pupil to attend the school. However, while certain neighbourhoods in Birmingham, West Bromwich and Wolverhampton were by now home to significant numbers of immigrants from the Caribbean and the Indian subcontinent, dark faces remained a comparative novelty in the backwater that was Sneyd End. Perhaps it explained the interest that was being shown in the solitary one that had somehow wound up in Class 1H of the town's large comprehensive school.

"And where are you from, Parminder?" she probed, returning the smile that the respectful youngster offered her.

"From Mafeking Street, Miss – behind the gas works."

Ruby evinced a hint of amusement before her gaze retrained itself on Parminder's classmates, aware that this unwittingly banal revelation had occasioned further tittering.

"No," Ruby chose her words tactfully, "what I mean is: where is your family from originally?"

"Oh, I see, Miss," the little Asian lass beamed graciously. "My parents were born in the Punjab – in a small village that is today in Pakistan."

"'Ere, Miss. Does that mean she's a Paki?" some wise-cracking young lad raised his hand and piped up from the back of the class.

Again, the voluble tittering that broke out was deftly stilled by another censorious stare on the part of their new teacher. That stare then lingered on the culprit. Ruby wondered whether the blonde-mopped youngster was fully *au fait* with how derogatory that bandied-about expression had become. However, before she could summon a response, Parminder had turned to face the boy and address him politely in her dulcet tones.

"No, I am *not* a Pakistani. I was born in Amritsar – on the Indian side of the Punjab. It's where my parents fled following the partition of my country when it became independent. Before we moved to England my father was a locomotive engineer on the railways. He drove many famous passenger trains."

"Gosh! That's interesting," said Ruby, remorseful that her clumsiness had compelled the little girl to be so frank about her family's turbulent past. "You see, my husband's mad about trains. I'm sure he'd loved to meet your father some time,"

"'Ere, Miss. Your husband's that Snakeman bloke, ay' 'e?" the lad at the back raised his hand, piping up again with that same air of ribaldry masquerading as innocent curiosity.

Ruby looked up stone-faced. Slowly and purposefully – in her stout heels and chequered pencil skirt (and with her white cardigan draped across her shoulders) – she strode up the line of flanking desks to halt in front of this cocky little joker (whose tie and blazer were tellingly skewwhiff).

"And what's your name?" she looked him in the eye – aware that there's always one in every class (and that this particular one needed reminding who was in charge of it).

Wot? Me? Ar'm Robin – Robin Jukes, Miss" he snuffled.

"And where are *you* from, Robin?" she folded her arms and entreated him to the same line of questioning.

"From the Potter Street maisonettes, Miss. Me' parents fled there from West Bromwich when Dad lost his job, like. Yer' see, 'e's been on the Panel lately cuz' 'e did 'is back in liftin' fings' at the foundry in Oldbury where 'e worked. He used to pack the parts they used to mek' famous British trains, like."

The expressions on the faces of the pubescent onlookers all around suggested they were just itching to roar with laughter – whether at Robin's candid tale of family misfortune; or more likely because they (like their new teacher) could detect the undercurrent of satire in his confession – as well as at whom that satire was directed. Locomotive engineer indeed. Who'd ever heard of a 'Paki' holding down such a responsible job!

"I see," Ruby feigned to accept his story at face value. "So tell me then, Robin: how come you know about my husband?" she continued, wondering if the lad might have spotted Brian's face on television or in the newspapers.

"Ar' went to the zoo one day, Miss – on a school trip, like. That's when Ar' sid' him. He showed his snake off ter' me. And he let me hold it too. A real big 'un, it wuz', Miss."

Cue another fit of giggles. Indeed, she suspected this cocksure eleven-year-old was not totally unaware of the *double entendre* in his ostensibly artless tale. And that maybe he wasn't totally unaware either of the purposes for which the term 'Paki' was nowadays being employed.

"Then I trust your interest in snakes will stand you in good stead when it comes to my biology classes," Ruby suggested.

"Yeah, Miss. He's a good bloke, your old man. He certainly knows a fing' or two about 'em," Robin insisted.

The mellowing of his voice and the warm glow in his grey-blue eyes suggested that the compliment was sincere. Ruby looked Robin up and down one final time before turning to stride purposefully back to the blackboard, niftily confiscating a crumpled copy of the *'Beano'* from some lad who'd been covertly browsing it through the lifted lid of his desk.

Introductions complete, Ruby got down to the business of introducing her specialist subject too. Periodically chalking notes and illustrations on the board, during most of this first lesson she was observing her new class: looking and listening – as teachers often do – to discern who was paying attention and who was not.

Sure enough, Parminder was eagerly scribbling notes in her exercise book with her scratchy fountain pen – and in a manner that suggested she was transcribing the lesson verbatim, despite her flow being interrupted by a paper aeroplane that landed on her desk. As often as not too, her hand was to be found held aloft in the hope of answering those questions that Ruby would pose to test whether her new class had grasped what she was expounding.

Sure enough too, whenever Robin caught her eye up the back of the classroom it was for less commendable reasons. Indeed, Ruby suspected it was his engineering talents that were responsible for that paper aeroplane, which she bent down to retrieve from beside Parminder's feet, demonstratively screwing it up and tossing it into the bin. Feigning to search out who might have launched it, it was Robin's impish face that was gamely grinning back at her, as if butter wouldn't melt in his mouth.

Two different youngsters from two different continents – alas, possessed as well (Ruby feared) of two differing work ethics. This certainly promised to be an interesting class.

* * * * *

WALLOP!

Ruby Danks's hand impacting hard upon the varnished wooden surface of the workbench certainly re-engaged the teenager's faltering attention.

"Deborah Watson, for the final time will you stop turning around and talking and pay attention!"

Fast running out of patience with her class, she angrily stared the girl out. With the object of her wrath once more facing the front, the tetchy young teacher returned to the blackboard at the front of the laboratory to gesture at the illustration she'd chalked on it. As she did, the incorrigibly-loquacious Deborah proceeded to prop her elbows sullenly upon that workbench (and her chin likewise in the trough her hands had formed). While Ruby was chalking up some more notes, she then removed one of those hands and employed two of its fingers to offer Mrs Danks a gesture of her own – such insolence accompanied by the subdued snickering of those of her mates who spotted it.

"Now the pancreas plays an important role in the human body. Do any of you remember what we said that role was?"

If teaching the eleven-year-olds of Class 1H was proving to be an 'interesting' experience, then trying to inculcate knowledge in the surly fourteen-year-olds of Class 4S was a challenge of an altogether different magnitude. The sea of blank faces staring back at their biology tutor suggested they were either wilfully declining to answer her simple question; or that what she'd taught them the other day really had gone in one ear and out the other. Once again, it was left to the class swot – a studious and smartly-attired girl who was sat at the front – to raise her hand and enlighten her classmates.

"The pancreas converts food into fuel for the body, Miss. It also assists digestion and regulates blood sugar."

"That's right, Susan," said Ruby, loathed as she was that – by indulging her star pupil – she was letting the others of the hook again, as it were.

Though relieved to be able to crack on with the lesson in hand, Ruby couldn't help thinking that the commendable standard of work that Susan Pritchard consistently put in owed less to the professionalism of her teacher and more to the girl's sheer determination to learn – in spite of being surrounded by a cohort of stroppy or bone-headed peers for whom biology lessons were just one more big yawn.

Indeed, she'd noticed over the last year how discipline at Sneyd End High appeared to be taking a turn for the worse. Colleagues like Cledwyn Davies were muttering that it was all the fault of the 'progressive' regime that the school's head teacher had put in place (including his decision to abolish caning).

"Six of the best never did a lad any harm," the Welshman had insisted during another of those tense staff room exchanges during which he'd regaled them with the tale of how one boy he'd once 'thrashed' had not only gone on to become a don at Oxford University, but still sent him a Christmas card every year!

Ruby's mother meanwhile had insisted that it was all down to a general slackening of 'moral standards' as the decade was progressing – the so-called 'permissive society' whose champions were busily seeking to overturn the country's legal prohibitions on drugs, pornography, homosexuality, and easy divorce. Thank God, she'd exclaimed, that into the breach to defend traditional virtues had stepped a tenacious, bespectacled Shropshire school teacher and 'clean-up television' campaigner called Mary Whitehouse, who'd made herself a gadfly at the BBC through a letter-writing campaign in which she'd condemned the drift towards obscenity and bad language in its programmes.

That said, Ruby herself wondered whether there might be some correlation between the increased prevalence of expletives and profanities she was overhearing around the school and the

Corporation having broadcast the first episode that summer of a popular television comedy series called *'Till Death Us Do Part'* (in which a bigoted, working-class anti-hero called Alf Garnett had peppered the airwaves with them).

At last, the lunchtime bell rang and Class 4S filed noisily out of the laboratory. Rubbing the blackboard clean of notes and illustrations, Ruby pondered anew whether there might be a more rewarding calling in life than the peripatetic one she'd chosen.

"Thank you, Miss."

Suddenly startled to hear the voice call out behind her, she turned to behold Susan Pritchard standing there alone, her satchel hooked over her shoulder and a warm smile on her face.

"… For the kind comments you wrote on my homework. There was me, worrying all weekend about whether I'd misunderstood the assignment you set us."

Ruby's shoulders visibly relaxed as she evinced a smile of her own of almost palpable disbelief.

"You understood perfectly, Susan. And your homework is always a pleasure to mark. I just wish I could say the same about some of your classmates," she sighed. If only there were more Susan Pritchards in this school, she was tempted to add.

"I really want to do well in biology, Miss. You see, I'm hoping to go to university; and thereafter to medical school to train to be a doctor," the teenager elaborated, explaining that "My mother was a nurse during the war – though she always wanted to be a doctor too. But not many girls from Sneyd End went to university and became doctors when she was young."

Ruby stared into Susan's doleful green eyes and thought she detected belated embarrassment on her part – perhaps at having lingered behind to pay a teacher a rare compliment in this way.

"I'm sure you will, Susan. And that you'll make an excellent doctor too. All I ask in return is that one day, when you look back on your schooldays, you'll perhaps remember my modest part in that successful career," she joked.

Susan's smile widened as she nodded. Then she exited the biology lab to join the other pupils volubly making their way to the school's cavernous dining room. Ruby meanwhile gathered up the last of her things – heartened to know that teaching was still a rewarding career choice after all.

Or at least that was the warm feeling she was basking in when she found herself passing the boys' toilets on her way back to the staff room. As she did, she thought she could make out the animated hollers of some sort of fracas taking place within. Halting, it was indeed the sound of testosterone-fuelled young males laying into each other that was filling her ears.

With no male staff about to turn to, Ruby took the impulsive decision to intervene herself. Brushing aside the nervous look-out who'd been posted outside, she marched into the boys' bogs bearing her most determined, no-nonsense demeanour.

"What the hell is going on in here?" she thundered at the top of her voice.

The brawl's dozen or so onlookers were sufficiently startled by this unexpected female intervention to desist from their excited cries (the lad who was huddled over a urinal up the corner also hastily zipping up his fly). However, that still left the two protagonists aiming fists at each other, hoping to land the killer punch. Indeed, one of them had already acquired a bloody nose.

"I said what is going on in here?" Ruby repeated, interposing herself between them – a brave (nay, reckless) act that witnessed her swerve aside just in time to narrowly avoid one of those punches impacting upon her own cute little nose).

However, again the shock of observing Mrs Danks suddenly emerge in their midst – and with a countenance (if not a nose) that could have chiselled granite – prompted these two burly teenagers to lower their fists and take a step back.

"Well?" she dug her own fists into her hips and demanded an answer. Instead there ensued a chastened silence.

"It's Randall, Miss," one of the onlookers eventually called out. "He's bin' sniffin' around Cooper's bird."

"Yeah, and if Ar' catch him at it again Ar'll friggin' deck 'him!" the more aggressive of the two pugilists snarled at his opponent, who'd availed himself of Ruby's intervention to dab his vermilion-dappled snout with a handkerchief from his pocket.

"Hoy! Language!" she hissed, seizing Cooper's clenched fist and lowering it.

For one terrifying moment the venom in his eyes brought home to the intrepid teacher just what peril she'd foolishly placed herself in. Was this stocky kid so incensed that he would really contemplate hitting a member of staff? And a woman at that! However, Ruby's own iron stare caused the aggrieved fifteen-year-old to think better of it.

"Wot' yer' gunna' do, eh, Miss? Thrash me? Oh, Ar' forgot: yer' cor' do that anymore, can yer'!" he sneered instead.

She didn't reply. However, before her lack of a response could rebound on her everyone had turned to catch the echoing of a masculine voice of authority arriving to defuse the aggro.

"Now, Now, Cooper. You weren't about to lay hands on a member of the fairer sex, were you?" Graham Weston boomed as he strode in to take charge of the situation. "And one of my teaching staff at that," he added, moving Ruby aside to go eyeball-to-eyeball with the truculent fourth-former.

With the tall, unyielding head teacher now staring down at him (unlike his more diminutive female colleague, who'd been staring up), Cooper shuffled in a manner that spoke or ardour giving way to the need to retreat. With one party neutralised, Graham Weston then turned to train his searching gaze upon Randall, who was still clutching at that scarlet-speckled handkerchief.

"And did I hear someone suggest you'd come to blows over a member of that fairer sex? Pray tell me, who is this lucky lady?" he snorted.

"Deborah Watson, sir," Randall proffered an adenoidal mumble.

"Deborah Watson!" Weston roared. "Oh, lads! For pity's sake! You're prepared to be expelled from this fine institution over the trifling affections of Deborah Watson?"

He completed his *coup de théâtre* by turning to address them vicariously through Ruby, scoffing to her that "For a moment I thought you were going to tell me your mortal struggle was intended to impress the likes of Brigitte Bardot; or maybe Catherine Deneuve. You know, *une touche tres classe*," he exhorted them, employing the Gallic turns-of-phrase that this French teacher-by-training often took great pleasure in showering upon both staff and students. "*Mais non!* Deborah Watson!" he scoffed again, throwing up his hands in faux despair.

Ruby folded her arms and tried not to let slip how impressed she was that – by sheer force of personality (and a dint of thespian panache) – the school's flamboyant head teacher had completely taken the wind out of the two boys' sails.

"Ne pleurez pas," he fired off another scornful stare at both combatants in turn. "Translate!" he then ordered.

Ruby looked on bemused as the lads wracked their brains to recall those French verbs that – like her biology lessons – had probably long since entered one ear and exited the other.

"Don't cry," Randall – the more cerebral of the two – eventually burbled.

"Exactly. Don't cry; and certainly not over a vapid wench like Deborah Watson!" he pleaded. "Why, blink and that girl will have you roped into marrying her! Before she does though, to my office. Both of you. Now!"

Both Cooper and Randall duly skulked off to their appointment with whatever chastisement Mr Weston had planned for them in the absence of a rod across their buttocks.

"The rest of you: be on your way," he then turned to instruct the others, cynically quipping in parting that "And if any of you have been paying attention in Mr Dixon's RE classes you'll know that the medieval church preached the doctrine of Purgatory. However, remember: in these more impious times we live in we still have Marriage – which fulfils a not dissimilar function!"

Shuffling away, the spectators made themselves scarce and – in this Kafkaesque *mise en scène* of gurgling urinals and odorous male ablutions – Ruby found herself alone in the presence of her more experienced colleague (in rank, as well as in years, linguistic flair, and venturesome sensuality).

"Thank you – for being on hand to sort that out," she mumbled, dipping her gaze.

To which he shrugged, as if it was no big deal.

"The male of any species – fifteen-year-old *homo sapiens* included – never takes kindly to a female being poached. But then to poach is the impulse of every full-blooded male," he noted, those libidinous qualifying words oozing from his lips.

She resisted the impulse to stare up into the searching blue eyes that she sensed were roaming across her face. However, Weston drew his fingers up to her smooth chin and ever-so-gently lifted it so that she might behold her rescuer.

"So, it would appear, I guess you now owe *me* a good turn," he suggested, withdrawing those fingers and allowing both her face and her own beautiful brown eyes to sink again lest they betray that she was blushing.

However, before she could enquire in trepidation how or when or where he intended that she should redeem that debt (or even whether his risqué, soft-spoken admonition was intended to be taken seriously) – as swiftly and purposefully as he had marched into the toilets Graham Weston now strode back out of them again.

Thus, while the trip on the cistern cleansed those urinals with another gurgling flush, Ruby suddenly found herself alone and incongruously out of place – as well as more confused than ever about her feelings towards her dashing colleague.

9

"...Lead us not into temptation; but deliver us from evil: For thine is the kingdom, and the power, and the glory, for ever. Amen."

Though there were others whose heads were also bowed as the priest recited the Lord's Prayer, Ruby Danks felt herself alone and incongruously out of place. As out of place, in fact, as Birmingham's majestic eighteenth-century St Philip's Cathedral, set as it was upon a quadrangle of greenery surrounded by a city in which famous old streets and buildings were being remorselessly bulldozed to make way for modern new flyovers, underpasses and office developments.

Having tired of being dragged around station platforms on this chilly afternoon, she'd come to seek repose within the walls of this august place of worship. Thereupon, she reflected upon the kind of temptation she was wrestling with that, if indulged, would shatter her marriage and make a mockery of her faith. Forcing herself to lift her head to gaze about at the images of her Lord and Saviour amongst its Burne-Jones stained glass windows, she felt desperately unworthy of the forgiveness being celebrated at this Saturday afternoon Eucharist service.

She lowered her head again and stared at her hands hanging limply in her lap. Amidst such introspections she found herself meditating again upon those Bible verses that had been searing her heart: *"Watch and pray, that ye enter not into temptation: the spirit indeed is willing, but the flesh is weak....";* *"Blessed is the man that endureth temptation: for when he is tried, he shall receive the crown of life, which the Lord hath promised to them that love him...";* *"Submit yourselves therefore to God. Resist the devil, and he will flee from you..."*

When the time came to step up to the altar and receive the symbolic body and blood of Christ, Ruby remained stubbornly in her pew. She felt unworthy. For even though no physical act of sin had taken place that might render her so in the eyes of the congregation now rising around her, the knowledge that she'd fantasised about such sin was enough in her eyes – and, she knew, in those of an all-seeing, all-knowing God: *"But I say unto you, that whosoever looketh on a man to lust after him hath committed adultery with him already in her heart,"* she paraphrased another Gospel verse. Reflecting upon which, tears began to moisten those hands still resting in her lap.

* * * * *

"Sorry I took my time, dear. But it was a very emotional moment. I was in tears, I can tell you."

Ruby looked up to observe that the cathedral had emptied. Brian had sidled up alongside her in the pew, his breathless apology echoing in the stillness of the building.

"7029 *'Clun Castle'* was there – hauling her final Paddington-Birkenhead express. I've taken plenty of pictures," he said, lifting up the little Pentax camera that was hanging on its strap around his neck. "The driver invited me onto the footplate too! Oh, how I shall miss the excitement of steam trains when they're gone. Another reason to get '6418' working again, eh!" he nudged her before allowing a veil of melancholy to descend that momentarily tempered his excitement.

"It's been a sad day too though – Saturday, March 4th 1967: the last day of main line operation at Snow Hill Station. From now on the only trains to call there will be a handful of local commuter services; and most of those are being run down ready for the station's closure. Hey, you look like you've been crying."

At last he'd come up for air; at last he'd noticed *her* tears. Ruby sniffed, dabbed a knuckle at whatever streaks might have lingered, and shrugged her shoulders.

"I've been praying," was her excuse.

"Yes, I've noticed you praying a lot lately. Is something on your mind, Ruby? Is it about that baby we're…?"

What could she say? How could she explain to him the other reason for the turmoil in her heart? No, *that* torment was *her* cross

– and hers alone. Maybe the Lord would grant her the strength to resist the temptation.

"Oh, lots of things," she babbled instead. "For instance, I've been praying for the families of all those children who were killed at Aberfan last year."

If her reference to the Welsh slagheap disaster was intended to be an analogy for matters closer to home, it was far too cryptic for Brian to grasp. He took her words at face value – as he invariably did all Ruby's cryptic inferences about the state of their marriage.

"Yes, we'll never know why God allows such tragedies to happen. Perhaps bad things happen to remind us of those things that should matter to us. I intend to preach about that very subject in the next sermon Father Allen has asked me to present."

Still he didn't get it. Maybe he never would. Maybe such obtuseness was just Brian being Brian. Maybe Ruby was tiring of Brian being Brian.

"Anyway, come on," he nudged her again, this time with more tenderness. "Enough train-spotting for today. And praying, eh!"

Ruby stepped out into the aisle to permit her husband to drape an arm around her shoulders and escort her out into the Cathedral grounds, where dusk was descending on Birmingham's famous 'Pigeon Park' – though instead it was the trilling of the flocks of starlings returning to roost in the eaves of surrounding buildings that greeted them on this dank and dismal evening.

By-and-by they returned to where Brian had parked the car. For not only had he taken up her advice and learned to drive; but only a few days ago he'd passed his driving test first time. What's more, gone was the little red Mini that Ruby had been so in love with and in its place the couple had purchased a beige Austin 1100 saloon – as befitted a 'family man' and his wife who were still trying for their first baby.

"Yes, I grant you it's much roomier," Ruby commented as they set off home – even if the car's new-fangled Hydrolastic liquid suspension made for a livelier ride.

"Excellent little motor!" exclaimed her husband, seeming to have unexpectedly commenced a love affair of his own with the joys of motoring. Even so, he couldn't resist reminding her that

"Of course, we could've come into Birmingham this afternoon on the train…"

"… Had Dr Beeching not closed the line to Sneyd End!" Ruby completed the sentence with him. They both glanced at the other and chuckled, Brian mournfully so.

It was a welcome moment of accord. Soon enough, their eyes returned to the road ahead. Of late, the demands of their respective careers (as well as Brian's plethora of campaigns and pastimes) had meant they seemed to be spending less and less time together. Meanwhile, the baby they'd been trying for in those other moments when they'd been of one accord was taking its time coming. Maybe it was why Ruby seemed to be spending more of her time at the school, he wondered: sublimating her frustrated maternal instinct into her career instead.

Just then, his wife spotted something as the car crawled in the traffic.

"Pull over," she tapped Brian's arm and instructed him.

"Why? What is it?"

"I think I know that person."

Brian duly indicated and stopped, thereby permitting Ruby to better study some young girl in an overcoat who was trudging along the pavement bearing a distant look on her face, as well as a knapsack on her back and arms that were straining under the weight of the two shopping bags she was carrying.

"I thought it was," Ruby announced.

"Thought it was who?"

"It's Emily Ashmore: a pupil from my school. Well, she was up until last year," she added, quickly alighting from the car to bound over and halt the girl's languid peregrination.

"Hello, Emily. Long time, no see," she introduced herself. "And no, I'm not here to berate you about your homework!"

The joke was lost on the downcast young lass. At first it was as if she didn't recognise her erstwhile biology teacher. Then finally she emitted a nervous titter, downing a shopping bag to brush a shock of her long, bushy brown hair over her forehead.

"Oh... Hello, Mrs Danks. Fancy seeing you 'ere."

It was a moment replete with *déjà vu*. Emily Ashmore – the attractive, music-and-fashion-loving teenager that Ruby remembered appeared to be once again conveying on her youthful shoulders cares that were every bit as burdensome as the contents of that bulky knapsack – to say nothing of whatever it was she was carrying around in those two shopping bags. Ruby wondered if those 'cares' might also explain the bruise she could make out on Emily's face.

"Where are you off to?" she enquired, her voice laden with concern. "It's a bit of a rotten night to be tramping the streets of Birmingham on your own."

Brian was looking on intrigued while this sudden and unexpected re-acquaintance was taking place. This was certainly not a nice quarter of the city for a teenage girl to be found by herself at night – even if this 'Emily' appeared older than the sixteen years that Ruby's brief explanation had intimated. Their conversation continued for several minutes, Brian eventually extinguishing the engine in the hope it might chivvy his wife to wrap it up. He would be kept waiting a while longer before Emily eventually allowed Ruby to take those bags from her and wander over to place them in the boot of their car. In the wing mirror he observed Emily unhook the knapsack from her shoulders and do likewise. Then Ruby flung open the back door and this girl plonked herself down on the bench seat behind him.

"Emily, meet Brian – my husband. Brian, meet Emily – our new house guest," Ruby announced, returning to the passenger seat alongside him.

"Our w-w-what?" he stuttered in surprise.

"She's coming to stay with us," Ruby elaborated with a smile of presumption. "If that's okay."

"Er… Yes. I sup-p-pose," he replied, lost for words. Dutifully, he restarted the car and tucked back into the traffic.

Whatever plan had his wife cooked up now? Brian Danks glanced at their new 'guest' in the rear-view mirror and became conscious of those many times when he himself had burst through the front door to boldly announce some fancy scheme or other that he had assumed his wife would dutifully fall in line with. He listened in chastened silence as she filled him in on what had been agreed while he'd been waiting in the car.

"Emily was on her way to New Street Station – or so she's told me. You see, she and her father have had a bit of a falling out. So she'd decided to leave home, head for London, and maybe see if she could find herself a job and a flat there. However, I've persuaded her that, while 'Swinging London' looks glamorous on television – all those boutiques on Carnaby Street and fancy night spots where one can hob-knob with the likes of Twiggy, Jean Shrimpton, and Michael Caine – in reality, the capital's not a very nice place for a young girl like her. Neither are the 'jobs' that she's likely to end up doing; nor the 'flats' she might find herself working from; nor the men she could end up working for."

Brian glanced through the rear-view mirror again. He tried to visualise how this diffident, working-class teenager might have fared once lured into the kind of sordid *demi-monde* that had snared the likes of Christine Keeler and Mandy Rice-Davies a few years earlier. Emily, meanwhile, was self-consciously trying to avoid staring back at the reflection of those inquisitive brown eyes surveying her in the mirror.

"Not that Emily is likely to have made it to London with what meagre change she has in her purse," Ruby continued, "well, not without a spot of begging on the station forecourt beforehand! Therefore, she's agreed to come and stay with us instead – for a while at least; until she can sort out the issues she has at home."

Yes, Brian mused, taking a final look at her in the mirror: this girl clearly had 'issues'. For instance, the bruise on Emily's face that he thought he could make out in the glow of passing street lamps led him to think there might be a bit more to this 'falling out' with her father than Ruby was letting on.

Spotting the look of consternation rippling across her husband's face, Ruby decided it was time to play the ace card she'd been holding in reserve throughout this bizarre pronouncement. She glanced across at him and ever so matter-of-factly reminded him that "I thought it would chime quite nicely with that sermon you gave the other day about the Good Samaritan. You know, the man who helped the traveller in distress. What were those words of Jesus that you quoted? *'I was a stranger, and ye took me in'*. And did Jesus not say of such acts of hospitality that *'inasmuch as ye have done it unto one of the least of these My brethren, ye have done it unto Me"*? Well, for 'brethren' read 'sister',," she then turned to gaze at their backseat passenger with a crafty smile – her nifty paraphrasing of Scripture eliciting from Emily a doleful wince of gratitude.

Brian had the sense that Ruby had hoisted him on his own petard, so to speak. Blinking exaggeratedly, he guessed he'd better reconcile himself to his wife's new calling as a social worker – and his new calling as a landlord! The Danks household had suddenly acquired a rather different new member of the family to the one that they'd been trying for.

* * * * *

"I want you to know I'm ever so grateful, Mrs Danks," Emily repeated for what seemed like the umpteenth time this evening. For the umpteenth time too, Ruby reminded her that the first condition she would be expected to observe during her stay with them was to address her hosts by their Christian names!

Having been fed a hearty meal, offered plenty of cups of tea, and been encouraged to avail herself of a hot bath (as well as the lady-of-the-house's slippers and favourite fluffy bathrobe), Ruby escorted their new guest to the second bedroom, which she'd made a start transforming into a nursery.

"No, Mrs Danks. It's lovely," Emily cooed in response to Ruby apologising for the clutter. She stared about at the light, airy décor, as well as fondling the bed's pressed white sheets and pillow cases and its cosy, pure-wool blankets. Why, this house even boasted luxuries like an indoor toilet and central heating. No having to nip outside to spend a penny or refill the coal scuttle!

"I ay' ever slept in a room by myself before. You see, I share mine at home with my little brother and sister. Mom keeps on to the Council to find us a bigger house, but... well, nothing's come of it since Dad threatened to thump the rent man."

"Yes, your father likes thumping people," Ruby observed, sensing Emily's shame and embarrassment. "However, I hope you'll enjoy staying with us," she said, placing a delicate, reassuring hand upon the youngster's shoulder. "Feel free to use the kitchen, the living room, and the bathroom any time. And do please call me Ruby!"

"Of course, you really should call your mother," she insisted after a brief lacuna during which Emily's winsome brown eyes had beamed their gratitude again. "I'm sure she must be worried about you. Or if you prefer, Brian and I will pop round and tell her that you're okay and that you're staying with us."

The silence and the sudden avoidance of eye contact informed Ruby that she was going to have to work on that particular sore subject. She wandered across the room to draw the curtains.

"Oh, they're nice," Emily's engaging countenance returned. She drew up alongside Ruby to admire the cute little cartoons of ducks and fishes embossed on the drapes.

"Yes, I chose them. Like the wallpaper, I've tried to furnish the room in gender-neutral décor. Of course, Brian wanted ones with pictures of trains on them. But as I said to him: what if our first child is a little girl…?"

"Oh," the teenager suddenly looked askance. "Are you expecting a baby too then?"

Ruby glanced away to mask *her* shame and embarrassment.

"Not exactly. But we've been trying for a while now. It's just that these things come easier to some couples than they do to others. Sometimes, I guess, they don't come at all."

It was a fear that had been the subject of Ruby's other fervent prayers in that cathedral: the prospect that either she or her husband might have a spot of 'dicky plumbing' down below, as her mother had rather indelicately put it – convinced that (if so) it simply had to be on Brian's side. It was yet another reason that Muriel Leadbetter had reproached her daughter for not requiting instead the conspicuously fecund Timothy Forbes.

"I see," Emily lowered her gaze – anguished that she was imposing upon this kindly Christian couple in the manner that she was. Perhaps she should have persuaded Ruby to just lend her the train fare instead.

"Never mind my problems. Right now, we need to think about how to address yours," Ruby insisted, her gaze subconsciously flitting over Emily's abdomen. "Does the father know?"

Emily glanced past her swollen bosom to see if she was indeed showing. She looked up at Ruby for a moment before glancing away in further shame and foreboding. She shook her head.

"Does your husband know that I'm…?"

"Not yet," Ruby admitted. "However, I will tell him; maybe tomorrow. I think he's had enough shocks for one evening!"

"I'm sorry, Mrs Danks, I really am… I mean, Ruby."

It was time for that reassuring hand to alight upon Emily's shoulder again. However, noticing the tears escaping down her rosy cheeks, Ruby dispensed with any lingering formality, instead drawing Emily tight into her embrace. As she did so, those escaping tears became a torrent.

"I've done an awful thing. I'm wicked, I really am," she sobbed. "That's what Mom told me; it's why Dad hit me too."

"You're not wicked, Emily. You were just young; and foolish. Just like I was when I was your age – only in different ways. Besides, no man has the right to beat his daughter," her host clenched her teeth indignantly.

Ruby rocked her gently in her arms, her own 'problems' seeming to pale into insignificance. Emily Ashmore was at her wit's end – as young girls in her predicament frequently are. However, if ever there was a time that, in place of condemnation, she instead needed to know compassion, forgiveness and hope then it was now. Perhaps the Lord had elected to answer Ruby's prayers about the patter of tiny feet after all – albeit in a surprising and altogether more unselfish way.

* * * * *

She'd been staring at Lizzie in her glass tank for what seemed like an age – observing the serpent probing hither and thither with its flicking tongue. Brian glanced up from penning his latest sermon, heartened: unlike his ophidiophobic mother-in-law, there was wonder and fascination in Emily Ashmore's eyes as she stooped to study his pet snake. So much so that he couldn't resist waxing lyrical about this other great passion of his life.

"That tongue is packed with sense glands. She's using it to pick up clues about her surroundings," he explained.

"What does she eat?" Emily broke from staring to enquire.

"Mice. Rats. Other snakes too."

"Really?" she was amazed.

"Absolutely. Unlike us, a snake can't chew food. Instead it has to swallow its prey whole. If you think about it therefore, one of the easiest things for a snake to swallow is another snake."

"Does she have to poison them first?"

Brian smiled at her innocence.

"No, not Lizzie. She's not venomous. California kingsnakes are constrictors. They kill their prey by coiling around it and asphyxiating it. I keep some dead mice in the fridge that I coax her to eat. But snakes can be very temperamental eaters. Sometimes I have to drop a live mouse in there and let Lizzie kill it herself. It's not a very edifying thing to watch – especially if you're squeamish."

He was right on that score. The revelation prompted a grimace on the part of his young listener. Drawing back from the glass, she wandered back to the sofa to sit down, picking up and leafing through the copy of *'Jackie'* magazine that Ruby had rather thoughtfully purchased for her.

Neither rugged nor rakish, Brian was far from being a 'lady's man' (though his awkwardness with women owed more to incomprehension than timidity). As such, Ruby knew having another female around the house was always going to occasion a certain unease – if not outright anxiety. When that female was a naïve, pregnant sixteen-year-old girl from a dysfunctional home – for whom coming to terms with being a guest in someone else's house was itself a cause of unease – then it certainly made for an interesting study of human interaction.

That said, during the week so far that Emily had been sharing their abode the bumbling, bespectacled snake keeper and the elfin teenager with the dark, flowing locks appeared to have established a tentative rapport. Perhaps Ruby wasn't the only person in whom this mannerly young lady had evoked quasi-parental concern.

"There's some sort of snake rumoured to lurk over Fens Bank," Emily opined. "A massive python or summat' – or so some bloke that Dad knows has been tellin' everyone."

Brian glanced up again. He recalled Julie, his assistant, mentioning a similar tall story doing the rounds in the local pubs. Mrs Channon had even been tempted to blub whether such a fantastical creature might have devoured Bertie. Her boisterous pet Labrador had been missing for almost a year now.

"I suspect it's just a yarn," he replied, offering Emily the same reasoned rebuttal he'd employed to placate his distraught next-door neighbour, "a bit like the story of Sneyd End Tunnel being haunted. It may even have been put about by the management of British Steel to frighten you youngsters from wagging off school over there," he chuckled, recalling how he and Jonathan used to sneak off to its virescent, man-made cooling ponds to trawl for the frogs and newts that inhabited them.

"Or some boozer's excuse for rollin' in late after pissin' the housekeepin' money up the wall!" Emily joked.

Brian looked up again from the Bible he was perusing.

"Oh… Sorry," she twittered.

"Pythons aren't native to Britain," he assured her, overlooking her earthy colloquialism. "And while ones that have been kept as pets sometimes survive after escaping into the wild, it's usually only for a short time. The climate in Britain is simply too cold. There's certainly no way one could have survived that long, bitterly cold winter of 1963," he noted, recalling the time a few years back when Fens Bank's cooling ponds had frozen over for weeks on end (and it had been skating, rather than fishing, that had tempted truanting teenagers through those convenient gaps in the perimeter fence).

"You and Ruby are quite into this Christianity thing, aren't you," Emily changed the subject, observing her host still transcribing Bible verses for his sermon.

Brian glanced up a third time.

"Both Ruby and I believe that Jesus Christ died to forgive us our sins. And that He rose again so we can one day enjoy everlasting life with Him in Heaven," he explained.

"Yeah. Mr Dixon – our RE teacher – he used to tell us stories about Jesus and how we should forgive people, like. I enjoyed listening to them. But you and Ruby are good people. You've been kind to me. Surely you don't need forgiveness for anything."

Where to start! The Snakeman laid aside the pen in his hand and sat back in his chair, interlocking his hands behind his head.

"We *all* need forgiveness, Emily. We are *all* sinners. Sometimes too we need forgiveness for the things we *don't* do as much as the things we do. I'm sure I must need a lot of forgiveness on that score," he intimated, perhaps conscious of his own manifold omissions (of which Ruby had been reminding him more and more of late).

"In the Bible Jesus tells us that the shepherd rejoices when he finds the 'lost sheep' that has gone astray. Because of our sins, we are *all* lost sheep in God's eyes. That said, Emily, there is nothing we've done that can ever put us beyond the love and forgiveness of Our Lord and Saviour. *"For whosoever shall call upon the name of the Lord shall be saved"* – Romans Chapter Ten, Verse Thirteen."

"Really? Even me?" she probed again, dipping her eyes upon recalling her own 'wicked' sin.

"Even you," he smiled and assured her.

Just then, this momentous realisation was cut short by the distinctive whine of an Austin 1100 pulling onto the drive. In due course, Ruby burst in through the front door, her arms loaded with marking-up work from school, as well as a bag of groceries she'd purchased on the journey home.

"Hi, Brian. Hi, Emily. Good day?"

"Yes, I've almost finished the sermon I intend to give. Meanwhile, I've been telling Emily here all about snakes – what they eat and how they survive. We've also been discussing love and forgiveness. I've been explaining to her that Jesus died and rose again to redeem each one of us from our sins."

"Sounds like you've had an interesting conversation," Ruby smiled, heartened to know that their new lodger had settled in sufficiently to be able to discuss such things. She just hoped Brian had been mindful that RE lessons at Sneyd End High School had probably not readied this jejune young lady for the kind of erudite theological disquisitions he treated the congregation of St Stephen's Parish Church to every other Sunday. And above all, that he hadn't been boring her with talk about trains!

* * * * *

Preparing the evening meal was usually a joint husband-and-wife task in the Danks household. However, with Emily eager to help (not least to assuage lingering guilt about the way she was 'imposing' upon the couple), the two women were again nattering away together in the kitchen. Finding himself to all intents and purposes excluded from their feminine deliberations, at least Brian could attend to finishing off his sermon.

Once his missive was complete, in the time that remained he wandered over to stare at Lizzie still probing about her tank. Meanwhile, from the squeals and giggles emanating from the kitchen, it was difficult to believe that barely a year ago these two women had been teacher and pupil; the one impatiently berating the other about the tardiness and sloppiness of her homework.

In due course, the squeals and giggles abated. Maybe it was Ruby's turn to chat with Emily about her eternal salvation. She certainly seemed to be partaking of an earnest discussion of some sort with her newfound female friend. Perhaps Emily just felt more at-ease opening her heart up to a woman.

Eventually, the girl emerged into the dining room to lay the table in readiness. As well as showing her how to prepare food on the kitchen's modern, Formica work tops, and teaching her to operate her new Kenwood food mixer, setting a table was another useful 'life skill' that Ruby had imparted to the teenager during her stay (by all accounts, mealtimes in the Ashmore house were invariably a case of perching a plate of greasy egg-and-chips on one's lap while gathered around the television). The task complete, Emily smiled at Brian and returned to the kitchen.

Joining the two women at the dining table, he was unsure what to make of this symbiotic bond that had developed between them; or whether to instead feel peeved by his exclusion from it. Emily glanced his way again – this time offering him a curious, hangdog smile. Otherwise, she was about to tuck into the meal she'd helped prepare when Ruby looked up and fired a look of faux dismay across the table. Dutifully, Emily placed the knife and fork back beside the plate, closed her eyes, and bowed her head.

"Dear Lord," Ruby petitioned the Almighty, "thank you for this food and for Your goodness to us this day. Make us ever mindful of Your grace and Your mercy to us. Give Brian the wisdom and the eloquence to deliver his sermon on Sunday. Give me the wisdom and the patience to survive yet another week in the classroom," she sighed, Brian and Emily cocking open a crafty eye to smirk at each other. "And we trust and believe too that You will provide a way whereby *together* we can help Emily deal with *her* situation. Amen."

"Amen," Brian affirmed, this time cocking an eye in his wife's direction while hers were still closed.

In particular, he was intrigued by the more resolute edge to that petition that his wife had been repeating in her prayers all week. To be sure, the self-absorbed train buff had never been much good at picking up on nuance and body language. However, even he couldn't fail to notice that the words 'trust and believe' had suddenly replaced 'hope and pray'. Nor the tone of Ruby's voice that complimented this newfound affirmation of certainty.

"Amen," Emily meanwhile went through the motions, her own body language hinting that she too was aware that the nature of her relationship with her hosts had suddenly changed.

* * * * *

"It won't work."

"How do you know it won't?"

"Because… I just do," Brian struggled to articulate his doubts. "Think of Hagar and Ishmael in the Book of Genesis. Look what trouble it ended up causing when Abraham and Sarah tried to short-circuit God's promise about giving them a child."

"Goodness me, Brian. I'm not asking you to sleep with the girl!" Ruby rolled her eyes in the half light.

Snuggled up next to him in bed and whispering in case the occupant of the next room might still be awake, Ruby had finally revealed to her husband what she had been discussing in the kitchen with Emily: a proposition so hare-brained that it ranked alongside the many crazy adventures he'd roped Ruby into over the years. What's more, she was deadly serious about it!

"But what's the alternative? Emily couldn't possibly cope with raising a child. She's barely out of school; she has no job and no home; her father beats her up; her mother has washed her hands of her; and the father of her baby – whoever he might be – is evidently in no hurry to come forward and make an honest woman of her. Even now, I'm not so sure she won't just 'short-circuit' matters – as you put it – by taking herself off to one of those backstreet places to end her pregnancy."

"Don't be silly. Emily would never do that," Brian scoffed, desperate to disabuse his wife of the drastic solution that had been concocted instead: namely, that she and Brian step up and adopt Emily's child themselves.

However, he knew his assurance about what Emily would or wouldn't do was little more than conjecture. Who could say what fears and doubts might assail her as time wore on and her pregnancy could no longer be kept under wraps. Or (assuming she did see it through) that Social Services wouldn't just snatch her child from her – like they had in that controversial *'Cathy Come Home'* TV play that they'd watched a while back.

However, Brian's scepticism about the wheeze that Ruby was mapping out was tempered by the knowledge that his wife was by now desperate to conceive. All their 'trying' to date had come to nought. What's more, his wife was increasingly taking that frustration out upon *him* (and which further inhibited her willingness to surrender herself totally to him on those occasions when they had 'tried'). However, he was not the arrant emotional dullard that Ruby had often accused him of being. It broke his heart to see her struggling with the self-condemnation that haunts any woman who finds she's unable to bear a child of her own. Maybe (just maybe) nursing and loving a baby – even someone else's baby – might render her fulfilled at last. Maybe too it might remove a salient point of resentment from their marriage.

"Look, Emily is willing to give it a go. We can't say fairer than that. She knows and accepts that we can give the child a better quality of life than she ever can," she reminded him.

"And what if she changes her mind? Girls often do when they finally get to hold their babies in their arms. Then if she does you'll just end up even more anguished and disappointed than you are now. So why don't we just trust in God and wait for a child of our own."

The possibility that Emily might back out of any agreement had certainly crossed Ruby's mind. However, in another poignant instance of how she'd learned – and learned well – from observing (and being a grudging accessory to) her husband's relentless railway monomania, she tightened her mouth, shook her head, and refused to be fazed by such doubts.

"I'm confident she won't. I really do believe that God has caused this vulnerable young lady's path to cross our own for just this eventuality: that we might demonstrate love and compassion to her; but, more importantly, to the precious little child that she has growing inside her."

10

"Item Five: the erection of a swimming baths, sports hall, and car park on the site of the former Sneyd End railway station. Borough Architect to report."

This was it: the most contentious item on the agenda of Sneyd End Borough Council's Planning Committee was about to be debated; contentious if only because the most infamous critic of the local authority's proposal was present in the room to argue his case in person. Brian Danks stared through his bulky, black-rimmed glasses at the assortment of councillors who were about to deliberate upon the fate of the railway line that he had devoted four long years of his life fighting to reopen.

Present in the room too to observe the Committee's deliberations (and to maybe intimidate any of its majority Labour members who might be tempted to step out of line) was none other than the corpulent leader of the Council, Horace Bissell, who was spread across one-and-a-half chairs on the far end of a row of them that had been set aside for members of the public.

To be sure, the local elections were just a week away and the Labour leader was desperate to obtain approval for his bold and imaginative scheme to drag recreation provision in the town into the modern age. It was a manifesto pledge that his Conservative opponents would no doubt take great pleasure rubbing his nose in should these plans fail.

Aware of what was riding on the outcome of this meeting, the press too had turned up in force to report it, their pencils poised over their notepads in readiness for the verbal fireworks that this item was almost certain to generate.

"… And so, Mr Chairman, it is the recommendation of your officers that the said plans be approved, subject to the conditions detailed in items 7.a and 7.b of the report."

Upon which the Chairman, Councillor Clement Burt, thanked the officer, and glanced around the table to see if any of the

Committee's members wished to speak. The smattering of raised hands indicated they would.

Much to Brian's patent disappointment (though not to his surprise) not one of them sought to question the wisdom of choosing this particular site for the town's new leisure centre. Instead, the Labour members who spoke couldn't praise this ambitious scheme enough, while the minority Conservative members were content to chide the Council (and by implication, the unsmiling Councillor Bissell) for dragging its feet over the matter and submitting a scheme that was not ambitious enough!

"If members have no further comments to make then I'll ask the Borough Architect to report any objections to this proposal," Councillor Burt moved.

The officer swallowed hard and sighed. "Only one, Chairman. Mr Brian Danks has submitted an objection – as well as a petition signed by two hundred and forty residents of Sneyd End. The nature of his objection is summarised in Item 4.c of the report. Mr Chairman, Mr Danks has indicated that he would like to speak in person regarding his objection."

An audible mumble coursed around the room and which goaded the press to recommence scribbling.

And so it was that 'The Snakeman of Sneyd End' rose to his feet to once more do battle on behalf of a railway line upon which trains had ceased running, and which (as far as most people were concerned) was just a weed-strewn relic of a golden age of branch lines that had passed into history. Meanwhile, surveying the leery stares of the councillors gathered around the grand oak committee table in front of him (as well as the reminder that, in the end, only a relative handful of townsfolk had seen fit to join Brian in condemning the scheme) suddenly brought home to this maverick campaigner just how isolated he'd become in his quest to preserve it. Neither could Councillor Bissell (who was eyeing the Snakeman gruffly) have failed to notice that, for once, Brian's graceful and ever-loyal wife was absent from his side (Ruby having pleaded the need to attend an important parent-teacher meeting at school). Clearing his throat and glancing at the notes in his hand, Brian Danks drew up to the table.

"Mr Chairman, while I endorse the Council's aspiration to modernise leisure provision in Sneyd End, it is my contention that should you choose to approve this scheme *on this particular site* then you will be committing an act of transport vandalism that the people you represent will one day bitterly regret."

"A mere two hundred and forty objectors? I think not!" Councillor Bissell murmured under his breath, his arms folded and draped contemptuously upon his expansive stomach.

Just then, Brian's flow was halted when the door to the committee room burst open, and in waltzed a stout, balding figure in a crumpled tweed jacket with leather patches on its elbows.

"Oh! Sorry I'm late, I am," Brian caught wind of a familiar Cambrian lilt from behind him.

He turned to observe a clerk ushering Cledwyn Davies into a spare seat at the back of the room.

"He's a former pupil of mine, he is," the Welsh pedagogue proudly pointed out Brian to the man he was placed next to – only to be hushed by the clerk for his troubles. Otherwise, the history teacher fired off a demonstrative wink at his one-time protégé. The Snakeman was not alone in the lions' den after all.

"Please continue, Mr Danks," Councillor Burt instructed him.

"And I should remind you that three minutes is all you are allowed in which to state your objection," he then glanced at his watch and lectured him sternly.

"As I was saying, Mr Chairman, this is the wrong scheme in the wrong place. I will refer members to the Council's Ways-And-Means Committee meeting of March 2nd 1965, which resolved to – and I quote – *'identify options for improving public transport provision, including working with the Birmingham & Midland Motor Omnibus Company to enhance connections to the surrounding towns'*.

"Mr Chairman, I would further refer members to the evidence from this Council's Transportation Working Group's own traffic surveys – presented at its meeting of September 1st 1966, and which I have summarised on page six of my objection – showing how road congestion in the West Midlands has reached a point where those bus services are struggling to keep to time.

"Mr Chairman, I believe that the currently disused Sneyd End branch line still has an important role to play in providing those links. For example, the present Midland Red bus service from Sneyd End to Birmingham is timetabled to take forty-five minutes," Brian reminded them, picking out the said timetable from his notes and holding it aloft, "though those traffic surveys state that the actual time taken to complete that journey can be anything up to sixty minutes during the rush hour. Even travelling by car, those surveys suggest you'll be lucky to reach Birmingham in less than forty minutes – and that's assuming, Mr Chairman, that you can find somewhere to park at the other end!"

There was a flash of amusement amongst the reporters observing the proceedings. Perhaps they'd tried that journey themselves. Councillor Bissell wasn't amused though, watching with mounting impatience as his most eloquent gadfly poked his spectacles back onto the bridge of his nose and drew out an item from his collection of railway memorabilia.

"In contrast, according to British Rail's London Midland Region timetable book for May 1964," he continued, holding the said document up (and at the page in question), "the 'Sneyd End Shuttle' enabled commuters to complete that journey in just twenty minutes. It's a similar story for journeys to Dudley, Walsall and Wolverhampton."

"Mr Danks, this is all very interesting. But can I remind you that the Committee can only consider relevant planning matters. The time the Number 125 bus takes to get to Birmingham is neither here nor there!" Councillor Burt interjected curtly.

"I'm coming to that," said Brian, drawing out the next nugget of evidence from his notes and refusing to be flustered.

"Mr Chairman, I would draw the Committee's attention to a resolution this Council passed at its meeting of July 1st 1963 – at a time when the attitudes of certain councillors to the Sneyd End branch line were very different to today," a feline grin swept across the face of this seasoned debater (a curling of the eyebrows conversely striating Councillor Bissell's).

"Three minutes, Mr Danks. That's all," the Chairman trawled up his pocket watch from his waistcoat again to remind him.

Thank God there was only a minute of this contemptible buffoon's invective left to endure, spoke the restive glancing of Councillor Bissell at his own watch. Meanwhile, his nemesis was again reading aloud from a document he'd brought with him.

"*That this Council lobby the Minister of Transport and the British Railways Board to rescind the closure of the Sneyd End branch railway owing to its importance to the transport of goods and people in the Borough. Furthermore, should such representations prove unsuccessful, that this Council take all measures in its power'* – *all* measures!" Brian broke to emphasise, "*'to preserve the track bed of the said railway, and to prevent development that would be prejudicial to the re-opening of the line in the future.'*

"Mr Chairman, I charge that, by permitting this new baths and sports hall to be built on the station site, this Council will stand in breach of a resolution it has passed," he tapped his bony finger demonstratively against the page in question, "and that this be deemed a 'relevant planning matter' that mandates you and your fellow committee members to overrule your officers' recommendation and reject these plans."

Suddenly, there was uproar. As usual, the Snakeman had been thorough with his homework – such that, as he huddled in close to brief his chairman, the Borough Architect could only throw his hands up in despair at this embarrassing oversight. The Borough Solicitor – plainly a worried man too – also barged into the huddle to offer his thoughts regarding this new revelation. Who would have thought that an evanescent resolution passed four years previously – in the heat of the moment, when Dr Beeching's newly-published report was inflaming passions (and when a general election had also been in the offing) – would return to haunt the Council.

"He was my star pupil at grammar school," Cledwyn Davies was meanwhile crowing to those reporters sat nearby. "Bloody brilliant boy, he was!" he added, chewing on his pipe, and leaning back into his seat to beam smugly.

"Members of the Committee," Councillor Burt eventually emerged from his conflab, banging his gavel to announce above the furore that "The Borough Solicitor wishes to offer clarification about the matter Mr Danks has raised."

He was compelled to bang his gavel a few more times before finally gaining everyone's attention.

"Mr Chairman, Committee members," the officer stood to his feet, earnestly gripping the lapels of his jacket as he addressed them. "Given that the resolution in question has not been formally rescinded by the Council, it is my considered judgement that it proscribes members from approving this application on the basis that the construction of the baths on the station site could, in law, be deemed to be 'prejudicial' to the re-opening of the Sneyd End railway line."

"Mr Chairman," Councillor Bissell rose to counter, "that resolution cannot bind this Committee because *in law*," he gripped his own lapels in mockery of his legal officer's stiff, courtroom manner, "it is in the gift of the British Railways Board – and not this Council – whether or not the line ever reopens. And British Railways have made perfectly clear that they have absolutely no plans to do so – either now or in the future."

"But refusing planning permission to build on the line *is* in the gift of this Council, Councillor Bissell," Brian rose to point out. "So are you refusing to be bound by a resolution that this Council has passed – and upon which your name appears as seconder?"

The charge incensed the already volatile leader, who turned to confront his nemesis.

"Why you… you imbecilic busy-body!" he spat.

"Councillor Bissell, may I remind you that you are *not* a member of this committee and are present purely as an observer," the Chairman rebuked him.

"… You would scupper a vital improvement to the well-being of this Borough? And all for the sake of preserving a few miles of useless old railway?" the council leader continued to rant.

"Councillor Bissell. Will you sit down – *please!*"

"Gosh! You've certainly changed your tune!" Brian scoffed. "Whatever happened to *'its importance to the transport of goods and people in the Borough'*?" he waved the minutes of that now-distant meeting at him, also earning himself the Chairman's ire.

"No, Councillor Bissell, it is you who have scuppered your own scheme," a Conservative committee member meanwhile rose to interject, having spotted this sudden and gratifying open goal mouth. "Firstly, by not checking your facts before submitting these plans; and now, by daring to cast aspersions upon the more learned counsel of the Borough Solicitor."

"'Snakeman', eh? You're a bloody snake alright: a sneaky, snivelling little serpent!" Councillor Bissell hissed at Brian.

"Gentleman! Gentleman!" Councillor Burt hollered, banging his gavel so furiously that it risked shattering the plinth upon which it was being hammered. "Enough! Be seated! All of you!"

His forceful intervention at last goaded the protagonists to do as they were told, an expectant stillness settling upon the meeting. If nothing else, it gave the reporters present the chance to recover from their frenetic scribbling.

"Mindful of the advice of the Borough Solicitor, as Chairman I therefore consider it prudent to withdraw this application…"

"What!" Horace Bissell gripped what little hair he had over his ears and fumed.

"…Pending further clarification about the legality of approving it in the absence of the Council's resolution of July 1st 1963 being formally rescinded. Next business," Councillor Burt then banged his gavel again, directing his officers to move the meeting on.

And that was that! Round One to the Snakeman!

Brian gathered up his papers, barely able to conceal his glee that one man armed with little more than tenacity, conviction and a nose for meticulous research had brought one of the most prestigious construction projects in Sneyd End to a juddering halt (as, presumably, it had Councillor Bissell's hopes of waving it like a shroud in front of a grateful electorate).

"Bloody marvellous to behold, that was!" he meanwhile felt his shoulders being gripped by an exultant Cledwyn Davies, who had bounced out of his chair to offer Brian a boisterous backslap.

As both men hurriedly withdrew from the meeting, neither could the exuberant Welshman resist reminding his former pupil from whom he had acquired that talent for dissecting historical records to such devastating effect.

* * * * *

"You off out again, Emily?"

"Yeah. It's a nice night, so I thought I'd go for a walk. Meet up with some friends, like. I'll try not to be too late back."

Having caught up with her in the hallway (and reminding herself again that Emily Ashmore was no longer one of her pupils to be directed or cajoled), Ruby smiled benignly lest her enquiry come across as over-protectiveness (or worse, disapproval). After all, had she not assured their nubile lodger that she remained free to come and go as she pleased? Otherwise, Ruby was mindful that she remained as dependent upon Emily's co-operation and goodwill to see through the 'deal' they'd agreed as the teenager was upon the continuing generosity and forbearance of the couple under whose roof she was domiciling.

"I can offer you a lift to wherever you're going," she offered.

"No, it's' okay. I doh' mind walking, honest," a polite shake of the head informed her. "Like I said, it's a nice night."

The furtive youngster forced a grateful smile of her own and completed her passage down the stairs and out through the front door, leaving Ruby to fret that her frequent expressions of concern might be starting to jar on their guest.

Outside it was indeed a bright and most pleasant evening. Jauntily making her way along the decorous avenues of this modern, middle-class estate (and with the warm breeze caressing her face and trailing her locks), Emily was inclined to view such fussing in a forgiving light. After all, Mrs Danks had certainly taken a far keener interest in her well-being than her own mother ever had (notwithstanding the tacit self-interest that now underscored it).

Eight weeks had passed since Emily Ashmore had moved in with the Dankses. During that time relations between them had remained cordial, if sometimes a little forced. Ruby herself was still pulling out all the stops, as it were, to make the teenager feel welcome (protecting her investment, a cynic might have dubbed it). Her husband, meanwhile – though capable of great courtesy and thoughtfulness – was more and more of late allowing his discombobulation at having to share his home with a pregnant sixteen-year-old to show. The free-and-easy discourses about snakes and Christianity had given way to more perfunctory remarks about remembering to wash up empty cups; or to be mindful when playing The Byrds on the transistor radio in her room that both he and Ruby had to be up for work the next day.

Emily herself felt increasingly circumscribed by an unspoken obligation to talk and behave in a manner that deferred to her hosts' moral and religious sensibilities. She never thought she'd look back with fondness upon feckless parents who were unfazed by what their daughter got up to (carelessly landing herself in 'the family way' excepted).

By-and-by, the neat lawns and twitching curtains of Sneyd Park estate gave way to the shabbier Victorian terraced streets aback from Sneyd End town centre. It was upon rounding the corner into one of them that Emily finally alighted upon the friends she'd set out to meet. What's more, they were chatting to a group of older boys who she recognised too.

Suddenly, her heart was racing. A tall and roguishly handsome young man had looked up to behold her rooted to the spot in joyful anticipation. He stubbed out his cigarette, thrust himself away from the weathered brick wall he'd been leaning against, and stepped up to greet her.

"Warro', Em. Long time, no see, eh," he smiled down at her, an incongruous gentleness in his voice.

"Yeah, it's bin' a while. I thought you'd forgotten all about me," she simpered.

He curled his bare forearms around her and gathered up her delicate frame so that he might plant a kiss upon her lips – a kiss that soon mushroomed into a more torrid tongue-searching.

"I've missed you, Gary," she gazed up into his sharp blue eyes, waiting for him to utter those three magical words too. Instead, he ran a rough, if purposeful hand through her bushy mane. He smiled, but otherwise said nothing.

"Nice of yer' to join us, Em," one of his male companions meanwhile called out waggishly.

"'Er ay' come to see yow', Fisher," the object of her affection turned to sneer at his mate. His joshing aside teased a guffaw from the other lad who was stood around with them, smoking.

"Ar' bet her' ay' come to see her ol' man either," one of the two girls surmised. "He ay' still lampin' yer', 'is he, Em?"

It rankled to be reminded of such things. However, allowing herself to slip under the protective carapace of one of Gary's muscular arms she glanced across at her mate and replied "No, Shazz. I'm living with a couple who've kindly taken me in."

"Oh, arr'. An' who might they be then?" probed Fisher, puffing on his fag.

Emily pondered the question, aware that an explanation might just get complicated. However, the desire to unburden herself to her friends impelled her to be candid about her new domestic arrangements.

"Brian and Ruby Danks. They live in a nice new house on Sneyd Park estate," she replied.

"Sneyd Park, eh? Gone up in the world, ay' we," Gary was impressed. She smiled up at him again awkwardly.

"Wot'? Mrs Danks? Our old biology teacher?" Shazz meanwhile expressed disbelief.

"That's right."

"That posh bat who wuz' always gooin' on to us about our homework?" her mate expressed similar incredulity.

"Ar' tek' it yow've told 'em about the babby?" Shazz ventured to ask, observing how four months into her unwanted pregnancy her friend was starting to show beneath that rayon sweater dress she was wearing. What's more, somebody was evidently giving her money to buy such 'dolly bird' outfits.

Emily nodded guiltily.

"'Ere, an' that wouldn't be Danksie the Snakeman, would it'? Yer' know: that mon' with the funny specks who wuz' on telly the other day rantin' about the old railway line?" said Fisher, dragging on his fag one final time before flicking it aside.

Again, Emily nodded. Nowadays it seemed that everyone in Sneyd End had heard of the Snakeman – even thuggish, teenage thickos like Wayne Fisher.

"Why do they call him the Snakeman then," Fisher's mate piped up even so, and with a suitably dumb expression.

"It's because he looks after the snakes at the zoo, stupid!" Emily hissed, rolling her eyes. "He's got a snake himself that he keeps at home. He let me stroke it the other day – and hold it."

"Ar' bet 'e did!" Fisher smirked.

"Yeah, while his wife's bin' holdin' and strokin' the one that belongs to that creep of an' eadmaster who wuz' always sniffin' round 'er," Shazz surmised to further knowing laughter.

Alone amongst this gathering of Ruby Danks' ex-pupils, Emily failed to find such tawdry innuendoes amusing.

"Pack it in, will ya'. They'm good people. They've bin' really kind to me, like," she scowled.

"Looks like it," said Shazz, still admiring that pretty dress.

Indeed, who would have credited that this low-born wench who'd so carelessly got herself up the duff (and thereby ended up being ejected from her family home) would have wound up in the sway of that hectoring, middle-class school teacher and her eccentric, do-gooding husband. Still, so long as they were looking after her it obviated the need for the father of the child to take responsibility for his 'mistake'. The two girls took a moment to leer at Gary, who offered them a dismissive look in return.

"Anyway, what's with all the gear, like?" Emily was eager to deflect their snide comments, remarking instead upon the tough-wearing jeans, buttoned-down shirts, braces and boots in which Gary and his gang were attired. She'd noticed too that his neat blonde hair had been cropped closer to his scalp than usual.

"Blimey, Em. Where yer' bin'! It's the next big thing, ay' it: the 'Skinhead' look," Fisher presumed to answer on his behalf.

"Yeah. All that Mod stuff's old hat now," Gary added, notwithstanding that the familiar Vespa scooters the lads had been riding around on since their 'Mod' days were parked up on the pavement a short distance away.

"Yeah. Fisher 'ere 'as even bin' wearin' his Levis in the bath, tryin' to shrink 'em to fit!" the other lad mocked.

Emily grinned. Perhaps it explained why the turned-up hem of Fisher's trousers appeared to have fallen out with his boots!

"They'm into all this West Indian music too," said Shazz.

"It meks' a change from beatin' the poor buggers up," Emily proffered a wry observation.

Indeed, she was aware that none of the lads had much time for the 'wogs' and 'Pakis' (as they were given to taunting them) who'd been moving into the neighbourhood of late. Otherwise, as Gary now explained, the cropped hair offered one less item for their opponents to grab during the fights these aggressive eighteen-year-olds regularly picked on their dark-skinned rivals.

Gangs; fights; 'Paki-bashing': Emily wondered what the saintly Brian and Ruby Danks would make of the kind of hardened, streetwise characters their precious 'investment' was keeping company with behind their backs.

Suddenly, she feared they might be about to find out. For around the corner there spluttered a different sort of riding machine: the white, visor-topped Norton Atlas motorcycle that belonged to the local police patrol. Emily's heart skipped a beat when it drew to a halt alongside the youngsters.

The tall, pock-marked policeman switched off the ignition and dismounted. Lifting his goggles onto his helmet, he then propped his gauntlet-clad hands on his hips.

"Hello, hello, hello. What have we here then, gentlemen?" he chortled breezily.

"Uh! Look, lads: it's PC Plod – on his new Noddy bike!" Gary sneered, unlooping his arm from around Emily and squaring up to the inquisitive copper.

"It's PC Hunt to you, son. And less of your lip!" the policeman prodded a stern finger into his chest and eyeballed him.

"We ay' doin' nuffin'. Just talkin', that's all," Fisher meanwhile grunted.

"Yeah. An' chattin' up birds ay' a crime," Gary insisted.

"Impressing these young ladies with the breadth of your vocabulary isn't an offence," the constable acknowledged, wandering over to eye up the trio of Vespas resting on their stands. "But, under the provisions of the Road Traffic Act 1930, parking on the pavement is. You see, I've received complaints about groups of young lads riding their scooters on pavements around here. So I suggest you shift these things, sharpish!" he demanded, those gauntleted hands once more thrust into his hips.

Unyielding, he stood watch while the three lads drifted over to sullenly cock a leg over their respective 'hairdryers' and crank them up. The burping of the Vespas was then supplemented by the roar of the officer's own throaty 750cc machine as he remounted it and cranked it too in readiness to resume his patrol.

"Looks like we'm gunna' have ter' catch up with yer' some other time, girls," Gary called across to them, his insouciant gaze lingering upon Emily. "...When there ay' no coppers about to interrupt us, like," he then smirked for PC Hunt's benefit.

'That boy ay' no good fer' yer'', Mrs Ashmore had observed upon one of those rare occasions that she had bothered to take an interest in her daughter. Some nagging sixth sense told Emily that her mother was right – even as it clawed at her heart to see Gary tear off up the street in a plume of two-stroke exhaust smoke, his mates in tow. Once again, he'd left her hanging in mid-air, as it were; refusing to confirm what his true feelings towards her might be – as well as towards the child that was growing inside her.

* * * * *

"The man has no shame! No sooner the elections are out of the way, he calls an extraordinary meeting of the Council and whips his fellow Labour councillors into passing a new motion that rescinds the original one that forbade development along the line.

"Of course, making a mortal enemy out of the Chairman of the Planning Committee didn't exactly do Horace Bissell any favours – payback, I guess, for scheming to oust Clement Burt as leader of the council a few years back. In fact, it was probably why old Clem proved only too willing to stall the application for the new leisure centre under the pretence of heading off a legal challenge to it; though believe me, Ruby, I was ready to mount that challenge – even if it would have meant having to dip into my own pocket to fund it."

Read *our* joint pocket: Ruby looked up from the pillow into which she'd buried her head, thunderous reproach and disbelief etched into a face that was otherwise weary from another trying day at school. Over my dead body!

"I was going to read up on planning law and stand before the judge as my own counsel for the plaintiff," Brian meanwhile continued, brushing his teeth in the bathroom across the landing (or at least that's what he'd gone in there to do ten minutes ago – before his frothing mouth had started spewing damnation at the Leader of Sneyd End Borough Council).

And pigs will fly! Ruby sighed through her nose and clenched her teeth. Upon which, a welcome silence ensued. Thank God her husband had shut up at last! Well, almost.

"Now however, Horace Bissell has shamelessly side-stepped any such challenge. I really don't know how the fat, ignorant, two-faced, contemptible bully sleeps at night."

Presumably because he doesn't have Brian Danks squawking at him in bed! However, Ruby declined to point this out, instead submerging her head beneath the pillow – again.

Round Two to Sneyd End Borough Council – and the contest with it, Ruby didn't doubt. Having rectified the procedural upset by which her husband had delayed the application for the grand total of twenty-eight days, the new Sneyd End Leisure Centre had secured planning permission at last. Otherwise, its approval had been the cue for the Snakeman to unleash more paroxysms of invective in the local press about this 'travesty of democracy'. Ruby was accustomed to Brian's righteously-indignant monologues, but tonight's was in a different league. She feared her husband really had taken leave of his senses (as evidenced by all those ridiculous threats to 'fund' a court case; or act as his own legal counsel; or even his use of all those florid and unchristian adjectives to describe the portly Councillor Bissell).

"Look, Brian, will you please just come to bed!" her patience finally snapped. "The fight to save the Sneyd End railway line is over. It was over three years ago. The trains are *not* coming back; and all your bluster about doing this, that or the other to prevent the leisure centre being built is not going to make any difference. Face it: you've lost the war. So why don't you just retire from the field of battle with some semblance of grace and dignity!"

This sudden and unexpected rubbishing of everything he'd been fighting for during that time stopped Brian Danks in his tracks. He turned about from ramming the toothbrush in and out of his foaming mouth to glare at her in consternation, thereafter hurriedly ducking into the sink to rinse his mouth out.

"Oh, that's nice. Stab a man in the back, why don't you! If my own wife no longer believes in what I'm doing then I might just as well crawl under a stone right now!" he fumed in self-pity, extinguishing the bathroom light to storm into the bedroom.

Enough was enough! Incensed, his wife suddenly sprang up in bed, illumination instead provided by the bedside lamp she flicked on as she flung the sheets aside to confront him.

"Don't be so petulant and childish! In case you've forgotten we have a young lady living under our roof who is going to give birth to a child we're committed to adopting and raising as our own – although goodness knows what she's getting up to when she keeps staying out this late…" she hollered, grabbing the alarm clock and studying it with angry eyes.

"Well, we can't exactly imprison the poor girl – much as you'd like to! She's probably making the most of any opportunity to be away from *you*. Goodness me, Ruby, I thought your mother could be a suffocating and remonstrative old witch!"

"Well, at least I've tried to make Emily welcome," she raged, "Of late, all you've done is castigate the poor girl every time she leaves a light on. And Heaven forbid that she wanders into the spare room and disturbs that precious train set of yours!"

By now, Brian was as incandescent as his wife.

"You deliberately sent her in with the vacuum cleaner without asking me first, knowing she'd disturb what was in there," he jabbed a finger at her as she leapt to her feet to square up to him.

"I'm encouraging her to take turns with the housework. How was I to know she'd accidentally hoover up the contents of that tatty cardboard tray that's been lying on the floor for weeks?"

"That 'tatty cardboard tray' contained the sheep I was planning to glue onto the hillside overlooking the goods yard. I just needed to finish painting them first."

"Brian, they're little plastic animals, for crying out loud!"

"They might just be 'little plastic animals' to you, Ruby…"

"My God, you really can't see what you are doing to this marriage, can you! What with all these interminable shenanigans over that disused railway line; or that blessed model railway; and now that rusty old steam engine you seem to be spending every weekend of late tinkering with, deserting me in the process!"

"What *I'm* doing to it?" Brian hollered, marching back onto the landing with his hands thrown up in mock despair. "What about you? Frustrated maternal instinct has turned you demented: like some broody little kid who can't wait for Christmas…"

"That's unfair, Brian!"

* * * * *

One outcome of the spell of warm weather was that, with the bedroom windows left open at night, every little sound carried on the still night air. Invariably a light sleeper, the man at No. 19 Churchill Avenue rose from his bed to peer through the curtains at one such voluble disturbance emanating from across the road.

"I see the neighbours at No. 14 are arguing again, Hilda," he observed, glancing over his shoulder to address his wife (who was shuffling somnolently in bed, her curlers in her hair). "That's the second time this week they've been at it."

"Probably rowing over that young girl they've got staying with them," Hilda surmised, disapproval evident in her tone.

"Yes, bit of a funny going-on, it is," he replied, his head once more inserted through the gap in the drapes he'd fashioned.

"I was only talking about it to Mrs Cotton at No. 23 the other day," his wife continued. "She told me that strip-of-wind is one of the wife's former school pupils. Well, I say strip-of-wind: it looks to me like she's put on weight since she's been staying with them. In fact, if I'm not mistaken I'd say she was pregnant."

"Hmmn. Strange. You don't suppose the father is that skinhead on the moped who I saw her canoodling with in the front room the other day while they were out?"

"Very strange, if you ask me. Mind you, the husband is a bit of a strange character. Every time you bump into him all he ever does is gabble on about that railway line he's trying to re-open."

"Perhaps it's *him* who's got that girl pregnant. Perhaps that's what they're rowing about. Maybe that's why people call him the 'Snakeman' – the randy old goat!"

"George! Trust you!" his wife grunted in faux disgust.

* * * * *

Cripes! It was eleven o'clock – or so said the chiming of the clock on St Stephen's Church as it carried on the still night air. Conscious she was pushing her luck staying out this late, Emily Ashmore quickened the pace and hurried through the estate into Churchill Avenue. As she did, she looked up across the street and spotted that nosy old busybody from No. 19 spying on her again from behind the bedroom curtains.

Yet perhaps his attention had instead been drawn by the kerfuffle that was emanating from the Dankses front bedroom, where the light was on and Ruby was chewing her husband's ear again. Poor Brian! No wonder on those occasions when he was at home lately he preferred to be shut away in the box room with his model railway. Or failing that, to escape to that old steam engine he and his friends were restoring.

As stealthily as she could, Emily turned the key in the lock of the front door and crept inside, ready to apologise should Ruby ambush her on the way to her room. Instead, their bedroom door burst open and onto the landing emerged Brian in his pyjamas.

"What *I'm* doing to it?" he hollered at his wife. "What about you? Frustrated maternal instinct has turned you demented: like some broody little kid who can't wait for Christmas…"

"That's unfair, Brian!"

"Unfair? Huh! I'll tell you what's unfair: a conniving old nag who can't have children of her own and so prevails upon a vulnerable young mother to part with *her* kid instead!"

"Why, you bastard!" Ruby screamed, racing onto the landing to slap him hard around the face.

He countered by wrestling with her fists.

"That's it! I'm through with your crackpot idea! I want that girl out, you understand – first thing tomorrow morning!" he seethed, pushing her down the stairs in the ensuing tussle.

Having tumbled to a halt part way down them, Ruby looked up and spotted the trajectory of her husband's horror-struck eyes. Nursing her wounded shoulder, she stumbled to her feet to also behold the figure who was staring up in shock from the half-light at the foot of them.

"Emily!" she drew her hand to her mouth in similar horror.

"I'm sorry, Mrs Danks. I didn't mean to cause any trouble, honest," the teenager began to sob.

However, before Ruby could hobble down the remaining stairs, Emily was through the front door and was fleeing down Churchill Avenue as fast as her legs could carry her. Clad only in her nightdress (and with no shoes on her feet and her shoulder still throbbing), the tearful teacher could only call after her in vain from the end of the driveway.

Meanwhile, looking on from behind that twitching curtain, her nosy neighbour across the way was left to wonder what that oddball husband could have possibly done this time that had goaded him to beat up his wife and compel their distraught young lodger to depart in such haste.

11

"Peaceful, ay' it," he observed, chewing on a strand of grass and picking up another stone to toss into the water.

That it was. The expansive wilderness that was Fens Bank had always been an oasis of verdant tranquillity amidst the grim bustle of the surrounding metropolis. Likewise, the cooling ponds that collected run-off water from the huge steel works that dominated the horizon, the pea-green waters and lush reed beds of which remained a haven for aquatic wildlife.

More than anything after the furore of the previous evening, peace and tranquillity were what Emily Ashmore now sought. And who better to have found it with than the boy she adored – even if she was still no nearer to hearing him repeat those three words that she now dropped in his ear once more.

"I love you, Gary," she murmured, nestling beneath the powerful, protective arm he'd thrown around her. "I loved you the first day I glimpsed you through the window of Mr Turvey's geography class. I wondered then if such a handsome boy like you would ever notice me – the skinny little wench from Class 2S with the pimply face and the flat chest!"

He said nothing, gazing instead at a chest that was now ample enough to protrude nicely inside that dress she was still wearing from last night. Meanwhile, the arm that was draped around her shoulder drew her in a little tighter, flooding her heart with exhilarating memories of their courtship. However, the free hand that ceased throwing stones and clumsily sought to fondle one of those breasts she politely, but insistently steered away.

"So what will you do now?" he loosed her and sulked.

"I cor' go back to 'em. Well, I suppose I'll have to at some point. All my things are there. And I suppose I should at least say goodbye to them – properly, I mean. Brian and Ruby have been good to me. They deserve that, at least."

"'Er'll probably persuade yer' to stay, yer' know."

"I know that. But my mind is made up. I'd only be a source of trouble for them. Besides, the more I've thought about it, the more I've decided that I wanna' keep my baby after all."

Unseen, Gary's expression of caring concern faltered. It was not necessarily what he wanted to hear.

"But how will yer' cope? And where will yer' goo'?" he rephrased his original question, hoping she'd at least been working on a credible 'Plan B' now that handing over her kid to that irksome biology teacher was no longer an option.

Emily shrugged.

"Yer' con' always see if yer' old mon'll 'ave yer' back."

She shook her head at the thought of it. Instead she confided that 'Plan B' to him, pausing to ponder it again before she did.

"Maybe I'll find a hippy commune somewhere that I can join – you know, like them' you see on television in America. They'm springing up over here nowadays too: the 'Summer of Love' they'm calling it. Wouldn't it be great to live deep in a forest somewhere, and not to have to worry about money, or gettin' a job, or anything like that; to wear flowers in your hair and gather around a fire at night, singin' songs by Bob Dylan."

Again, unnoticed by the dreamy-eyed teenager, Gary sniffed. He somehow couldn't visualise this guileless girl who'd seldom ventured out of Sneyd End embracing a world of 'flower power', 'free love', and psychedelic substances that was a million miles removed from the one she was familiar with. And anyway, who amongst those effete, middle-class drop-outs would want to share their commune with an uneducated waif from the Black Country who was waddling about it with a 'bun-in-the-oven'!

"Why doh' yer' come with me, Gary," she petitioned him, gripping his arm and staring excitedly into his startled blue eyes.

"Wot'? Pack up me' weldin' job and leave behind all me' mates?" he grunted, the suggestion having caught him on the hop.

"Yeah. Why not? Then we can always be together. You, me... and *our* baby," she enthused, her soft, delicate paw drawing his own, more manly hand to her belly.

"Did you feel that – just?" she pressed it firm against her. "That was a kick. I've felt it once or twice this week. You know, I have this feeling I'm gonna' have a little girl."

"Yow' am?" he gaped incredulously. "How' d'ya know?"

"I just do. If so, then I'm gonna' call her Esther. It's a nice name, doh' yer' think. Esther was a character in the Bible – or so Brian told me. She was a mighty woman of God."

"Nah! No chance!" Gary recoiled, yanking the hand away and picking up some more stones to throw – a means of venting his alarm at both her proposition and all this yampy talk about babies and religion. "Yer' woh' catch me burnin' joss sticks wiv' a bunch of kaftan-wearin' poofters – chantin' 'peace' and 'love' and listenin' to all that weird Paki music. Ar'm Black Country an' working-class, I am – an' Ar'm proud of it! An' I ay' ready to be lumbered wiv' no babby either."

Her gaze sank. It was the answer Emily had feared. Perhaps she'd been foolish to ask. Or perhaps Gary was right: perhaps their world was a different world – one that the *bien-pensant* protest movements of the 1960s (as well as the intellectual currents that propelled them) had yet to stir. Yet to stir it too was the world of condoms and the Pill – new-fangled things that might have spared Emily the 'babby' that her boyfriend was so adamant he had no intention of being 'lumbered' with.

"What am' ya' tryin' to hit?" she enquired by-and-by, noticing how he seemed to be aiming at something in the pond.

He didn't answer. Instead, in his frustration at feeling cornered by the consequences of his night of passion, he carried on aiming stones from the escarpment they were sat upon (and which afforded him the opportunity to lob plunging shots at this strange object lurking in the reed beds below them). Then suddenly, the object submerged with an audible plop.

"Gorrit'!" he crowed with juvenile self-satisfaction.

"Was it a rat?" she cheered, having joined him tossing small pebbles at it that she too had scooped up – none of which had landed anywhere vaguely near it.

"Dunno! It's gone now anyway. Perhaps it wuz' that python that's s'posed to lurk over 'ere."

She looked up and spied Gary's lurid grin.

"Doh' say that!" she nudged him. "Brian told me it's all nonsense anyway. The weather in Britain is too cold for such an animal to survive in the wild. He reckons British Steel have put the story about to scare people from comin' over here."

"Probably have. I ay' never sid' one."

Upon her rebuke, a silence ensued that permitted Emily to wistfully recall those fond, if fleeting moments when her relationship with Ruby's husband had been more fulsome. She'd learned a lot about snakes from this kindly, if eccentric figure – and, having handled Lizzie, certainly not to be instinctively revolted by them. He'd taught her a lot about faith too – in particular, that she didn't need to keep beating herself up for having done a 'wicked' thing. There is a God in Heaven who forgives wayward 'sheep' who have 'gone astray' – anxious young single mothers included. It was this hope to which she'd clung during those times when she'd felt despised and worthless because of her predicament. Besides, as Brian had pointed out, the Virgin Mary had faced her share of scorn and ostracism upon being found mysteriously 'with child'.

It was a hope the teenager clung to again now the realisation was dawning that the boy in whom she'd invested her hopes and dreams was not going to requite her love. Meanwhile, the knowledge of that awesome forgiveness impelled her, in turn, to forgive Brian for those hurtful words he'd spoken in anger; but which – at heart, she knew – he didn't really mean.

* * * * *

Emily hadn't had much excitement in her life so far – of the kind that stirs the blood. However, tearing about on the back of Gary Willett's little scooter was as close as she'd come – more so as he revved it hard to assault the tracks that criss-crossed Fens Bank. Like a giddying roller-coaster ride, up one grassy hillock he would zoom, only to whizz down the other side – leaving her stomach (and her womb!) behind somewhere on the crest of it. For what seemed like an age on this hot, sunny afternoon, up and down they rode, Emily's bushy brown locks trailing from the spluttering Vespa as it churned up dust in its wake.

Eventually, she decided the time had come for her to face Brian and Ruby and explain her change of mind (as well as to face down their inevitable attempt to change it back again by pleading concern for her safety and well-being). She could then collect her things – as well as the jar of coins she'd amassed – and make a second stab at reaching a mainline railway station. She resolved that she'd spent her last night in that spare bedroom that Ruby had been busy transforming into a nursery.

Neither would she avail herself of Gary's offer that she could sleep in the shed on his uncle's allotment – beneath that same blanket and mattress on the floor that she'd shared that night she'd lost her virginity to the owner's footloose nephew (and thereby gotten herself into this predicament in the first place!).

So it was that she ordered Gary to steer his scooter back towards the main Wednesbury Road. However, crossing the track bed of the disued Sneyd End railway line on the way, he paused before tearing off instead in the direction of the cutting that led up to the mouth of the abandoned tunnel. There he halted and turned about to face his breathless pillion passenger.

"No. Tell me you ay' gunna'…?" she brushed the hair from her face to behold the impish grin he presented to her.

"Fastest way back to Sneyd Park," he insisted, turning and hunkering over the handlebars.

The noise of the revving two-stroke motor drowned out her attempt at protest. All she could do was cling to his solidly-built abdomen and pray he could handle his steed as deftly within the tenebrous confines of the tunnel as he had over the dusty pit bonks of Fens Bank. Once inside, all she could see – when she dared to open her eyes – was the bike's juddering headlamp picking out the assorted trail of fly-tipped debris around which Gary was steering. Stirring the blood indeed!

However, before they could reach the glimmer of light that was the other end of the tunnel, they were jolted by the scooter impacting upon an object that Gary hadn't spotted in time. Only those deft reflexes enabled him to keep the machine upright long enough to steer it to an abrupt halt.

He nudged her to cock her leg clear of the scooter – oblivious to the obvious discomfort that the jolt had caused her (to say nothing of her baby). Dismounting too, he then reached into his back pocket and trawled out his cigarette lighter. Thumbing the flint, with the flickering glow it afforded he was able to inspect the back wheel and confirm his worst fear.

"Bollocks!" he cursed.

"What's happened?" Emily fretted, clutching her stomach.

"Worreva' Ar' walloped back there has torn the back tyre."

"Can you fix it?"

"Norrin' 'ere Ar' cor'. Ar'll just have to push it out."

"Idiot!" she hissed – one of several uncomplimentary asides she'd muttered as the afternoon had worn on – indicative of her gathering disillusionment with her boyfriend and his immature antics. "That'll teach you to take shortcuts – especially through this place. It's supposed to be haunted, yer' know. It's certainly spooky. Maybe that's why it so hot in here too," she was surprised to discover.

"That's cuz' of the old mineshaft fire still burnin' under 'ere. It's got naff all to do wiv' ghosts, yer' stupid cow!"

That was likewise one of several pejorative comments by which he'd made plain his contempt for her too. Truly this had been a teenage crush that was destined for disappointment.

However, here they were – stranded in this eerie, disused railway tunnel, the darkness of which was only leavened by the glow of the Vespa's six-volt headlamp. For all Gary's annoyance about what had happened, even he could empathise with his girlfriend's skittishness as she traipsed after him. Therefore, he halted from angrily wheeling the scooter in the direction of daylight to turn and behold her in the dimness.

"Come on. Ar'm sorry. Ar' day' mean wot' Ar' said just now," he consoled her.

"It's just that it's so…. so scary in here."

"Nah! It ay' that bad. A few weeks back Fisher brought Tracy Price in 'ere and shagged her! Or so 'e's bin' braggin' to everyone ever since. Worreva' they got up to though, her' lived to tell the tale!" he attempted humour.

Emily was unamused – neither by his annoying mate's choice of venue in which to fornicate, nor by her boyfriend's follow-up quip that if she was stuck for somewhere to bed down tonight she could always do so in here. After all, she wouldn't be cold!

"Just get me outta' 'ere, will ya'," she chivvied him.

They recommenced walking – though Emily noticed that the headlamp on the Vespa had meanwhile grown markedly dimmer.

"Mind you, Tracy Price is a right slag. A kind word and a few fags and her'd have her knickers off for anyone – even a pig-ugly little runt like Fisher!" Gary chuntered.

"Shhh!" she thumped his upper arm.

"Sorry. Ar' wuz' only trying' to mek' you loff', like!"

"No, listen."

He turned about and in the ghostly stillness tried to make out whatever it was that had spooked her.

"Ar' cor' 'ear nuffin'," he was adamant. He motioned to carry on pushing.

"No, there's summat' in 'ere. I can sense it."

Desperate to pacify this whingeing tart, he spun the scooter around and pointed the fading beam of its headlamp back along the shaft of tunnel – even though that beam only gave out enough light to illuminate a few yards behind them.

"There ay' nuffin' there, Ar' tell ya'."

The certainty in Gary's voice had faltered. There was indeed something lurking in the blackness that they couldn't see. They turned to carry on walking, hurriedly picking up the pace. Then suddenly the glow from the scooter's lamp faded completely. Everything was pitch-black.

Emily screamed. Gary hurriedly rifled in his back pocket to dig out that cigarette lighter again, cursing when it slipped from his fingers and fell to the ground. While Emily was blubbering uncontrollably, he groped hither and thither to locate it, frantically sifting the dirt. At last he fingered it – though not before his hand brushed against something firm, substantial and scaly.

He stood to his feet and gulped audibly. In the light now provided by the lighter's flickering flame Emily looked up to behold the sheer terror in her boyfriend's eyes.

"Wh-wh-what is it?" she stuttered.

Suddenly, all hell broke loose. Gary let out a terrified wail as that thing sank its teeth into his jeans to puncture his leg. Pulled to the ground, he dropped the lighter. All was darkness again, Gary's frenzied wailing echoing in the tunnel.

"Gary!" Emily screamed, aware that something big – indescribably big – was wrestling with him in the blackness. However, the only thing she could make out was the tiny half-moon of light that was that elusive southern tunnel mouth.

Then she too felt the wrath of whatever it was. An object with the mass and feel of a human thigh slammed into her stomach, lashing her off her feet and winding her. Breathless, she lifted herself onto all fours.

Gary's cries were becoming indistinct – as if whatever this colossal creature might be was throttling the life out of him. All she could think to do was to rise to her feet and make for that shaft of daylight. She had to escape and summon help. However, the cramping of her stomach reduced her escape to an agonising limp.

Fortunately, whatever had assailed her boyfriend appeared uninterested in apprehending her. It had its prey securely in its embrace. On and on she staggered, not looking back – adrenalin and the horror of what she'd just witnessed impelling ever closer to the light at the end of the tunnel.

Then, at last, she emerged into it, the blinding rays of a blazing sun forcing her to cup her hand to her eyes. She'd escaped! Too terrified to tarry, she stumbled forward still clutching her belly.

* * * * *

Young Emily Ashmore never did say goodbye to Brian and Ruby Danks. Neither did she ever find that hippy commune she'd dreamed of joining. Instead, in early June 1967 – in the week that the world was talking about The Beatles' new *'Sgt Pepper's Lonely Hearts Club Band'* album, and Procol Harum's *'Whiter Shade of Pale'* was Number One on *'Top Of The Pops'*; the week that Israel launched a pre-emptive 'Six-Day War' against her Arab neighbours, and a brand new country called Biafra was born – Ruby arrived home to find two police officers waiting for her in their panda car. The body of a teenage girl had been discovered on the old Sneyd End railway line.

12

"You're going to have to tell us the truth some time. So I ask you again: what were you doing wandering in the vicinity of the Sneyd End Tunnel on the afternoon of Friday, June 2nd?"

Brian had been cleaning out the crocodile enclosure when the two detectives had turned up at the zoo to 'cuff' him, read him his rights, and bundle him into the back of a police car for the journey to Sneyd End 'Nick' – there to be photographed, fingerprinted, and banged up in a cell.

"My client has already told you. He was photographing the old railway line for the next stage of his campaign to prevent it being built upon," his lawyer interjected.

The detectives looked unconvinced.

"But when we searched your property and developed the reel of film in your camera we found no such photographs. Indeed, the film hadn't even been used. Can you explain that, Mr Danks?" one of them was eager to hear.

Brian looked up from staring at the table around which they were sat, still too shocked to formulate a response. However, with the beady eyes of both of his interrogators burning into him, he knew it was incumbent upon him to account for his movements.

"I n-n-never got r-r-round to t-t-taking any ph-ph-photographs," he burbled. "I often c-c-carry m-m-my c-c-camera with me j-j-just in case I sp-sp-spot s-s-something interesting."

Brian Danks had stuttered badly as a child. However, in time – and with his mothers' patient encouragement (as well as the growing confidence that came from excelling at grammar school) – his stammer had largely disappeared. Only rarely since had he stuttered to the point of incomprehension; once when he'd finally plucked up the courage to ask Ruby out; again when he'd gone down on one knee to ask her to marry him; and now, as the realisation sank in that these two gruff detectives really were fingering him as the prime suspect in Emily's murder.

"Do you often venture into the tunnel? I mean, you're familiar with the old railway. In fact, one could say that campaigning to re-open it has become an obsession almost."

Brian nodded his affirmation.

"Your neighbour told us that you and your wife had – and I quote – 'one almighty bust-up' the night before Miss Ashmore was last seen alive. Is that right, Mr Danks?" the other detective probed, having consulted his notes.

"We did," he confessed, ashamed that, as well as saying an awful lot of things that he didn't mean, its outcome had been that Emily had fled the house in tears – ultimately (he now knew) to her death, however it had occurred.

"Can you tell us what that argument was about?"

Brian blinked and shook himself out of his remorseful daydream.

"We've not always seen eye-to-eye lately. Ruby's concerned that I'm spending too much time on that campaign."

"It's also true, is it not, that Miss Ashmore had been living with you for several weeks prior to that argument?"

"Yes. She was. I m-m-mean, she had."

"We've also established that Miss Ashmore was expecting."

"That's right. She was."

"We have reason to believe that you might have been resentful towards her because of that; and that the reason that you and Mrs Danks had this 'bust-up' was because she had found out that *you* were the father of Miss Ashmore's unborn child."

"N-n-no. That's absolutely n-n-not the c-c-case. Emily had got herself pregnant by some boy she knew from school. Or so she told us. Her parents found out and disowned her. Ruby and I found her roaming the streets one night and offered her a place to stay. We offered to help take care of her and her baby too."

"Indeed. It would appear your wife has been quite generous towards Miss Ashmore."

"Ruby liked to buy Emily nice clothes, as well as magazines and pop records. You see, she comes from quite an impoverished background and has never had such things."

"Yes, I can see," his colleague chipped in, consulting his file of notes again. "Looking at some of these bank statements, it would appear that Mrs Danks' has also been putting aside a not inconsiderable pot of money – in a savings account at the Midland Bank in Sneyd End High Street – for what she termed *'Our Baby'*," he reminded him, turning a statement about to show it to the suspect and watch for his reaction. Brian recognised Ruby's hand-writing on the folder that contained them.

"Why *'Our Baby'*, Mr Danks?" he cocked a curious eye.

"It was an agreement we had," he nervously explained.

"Agreement?"

"Yes. Knowing that, with no home and no money, Emily would struggle to raise a baby, Ruby offered – and Emily agreed – that we would adopt her baby when the time came. Unfortunately, we're unable to have children of our own. The money was intended to help pay towards…"

"… To pay Emily Ashmore to hand over her child to you and Mrs Danks," the copper leaned forward to complete the sentence.

"Well, yes… and no... If you want to put it that way."

"What other way is there to put it, Mr Danks? You and your wife paid this 'impoverished' teenager to hand over the child she was carrying – *and* also to keep quiet about its paternity; because it was *your* child, as it turned out, wasn't it, Mr Danks."

"N-n-no. Absolutely n-n-not. I didn't … Look, there was never any impropriety between Emily and myself."

"Detective Sergeant, that is an aspersion for which you have presented absolutely no evidence," the lawyer angrily snapped.

To which, the burly copper sat back in his chair, folded his arms, and stared at the sheepish zoologist.

"As your lawyer has pointed out, we will have to wait and see what the pathologist reports when he's finished examining Miss Ashmore's dead foetus," he conceded.

A dead foetus! The description sounded so cold and cruel. This had once been a baby – a baby that was intended to be *their* baby. Was this what their well-intentioned endeavour to assist a desperate young girl and her unborn child had come to?

"Mr Danks, it remains my contention that *you* murdered Emily Ashmore – either because you feared she was about to renege on the deal that had been made to handover her child; or because she'd threatened to disclose by whom she'd conceived that child;

and that you wanted Miss Ashmore out of the way to prevent the resulting scandal from destroying your reputation as both a church lay reader and a vocal political campaigner."

"N-n-no. That's n-n-not true. I would never hurt Emily. Never, you understand!"

"Therefore, we intend to detain you in custody for the full forty-eight hours permitted by law so that we can undertake further enquiries into Miss Ashmore's death."

And with that, the two men rose from the table and signalled for the constable who'd been waiting outside to return and escort the suspect back downstairs to the confines of the cell block.

* * * * *

As is often a policeman's lot, an otherwise uneventful shift plodding the beat had transpired to witness PC 2988 Jonathan Hunt legging after some shoplifter he'd spotted emerging from Woolworth's. The pursuing plod had eventually apprehended the thief up a side street, cuffed him, and frog-marched him down the station – though not before he'd managed to elbow Jonathan in the face during the ensuing tussle on the pavement.

Unfortunately, the swelling to his right eye that had resulted was by now at its most pronounced – despite the best efforts of the cook in the station canteen to balm it with a packet of frozen peas.

However, that embarrassing black eye was of only minor concern to the brave copper. Of greater import was what he'd learned so far about the death a few days ago of young Emily Ashmore. Therefore – his conscience nagging him that something about the case didn't ring true – he strode up to the door of Chief Superintendent Trotter's office and knocked.

"Come in."

He grasped the handle and stepped into the office to stride crisply up to the desk where his boss was sitting.

"Ah, PC Hunt. Nifty bit of policework this morning? Pity about the eye though!" his boss glanced up at him and grimaced.

"Yes, sir. But that isn't what I've come to see you about," he replied, steeling himself to explain.

"Oh. And to what *do* I owe the pleasure of this unannounced visitation, Constable?" Trotter looked up again out of curiosity.

"It's about Brian Danks, sir. I'm right in assuming we intend to press charges against him for the murder of Emily Ashmore?"

"That's right. Although we don't yet have the conclusive evidence we need to prove it. So unless we can come up with it pretty soon, then I'm afraid we might have to let the swine go."

Jonathan swallowed hard and stared ahead respectfully.

"Sir, is it not possible that the blood-stained house brick that Forensics removed from the scene was not a murder weapon? That the injury to Emily's forehead could have been the result of her tripping and striking it, possibly while running?"

"But running from whom, Constable? And why?" his boss rose from his desk and interjected, intrigued why the officer was so concerned about a case in which, thus far, he'd had no involvement. "And what should we make of the pathologist's report that the victim had also suffered a blow to the stomach: one of sufficient force to occasion the placental abruption that caused her to miscarry her baby? I would suggest such an injury points to the suspect being so enraged that he kicked Miss Ashmore in the stomach before finishing her off with a blow to the head."

A particularly vicious and cowardly attack had indeed taken place. However, Jonathan paused for a moment before pointing to a more likely suspect in her murder.

"Sir, what about Gary Willetts – the lad whose scooter was recovered from inside the tunnel. Is it not possible that *he* might have had a hand in Emily's death? After all, she was his sometime girlfriend," the anxious copper reminded him – recalling that he'd interrupted them snogging on the corner of Jubilee Street a few weeks back.

"Furthermore, those two anglers who came forward reported seeing the two of them riding around Fens Bank on Friday afternoon – the last occasion Emily was seen alive."

Chief Superintendent Trotter was aware that this line of enquiry remained open – pending his officers catching up with the said suspect. Alternatively, had Brian Danks had a hand in Gary Willetts' death or disappearance too (and which might explain the wrecked scooter?).

"Constable, if you have observations to make about this case you might care to address them to Detective Inspector Sid Grayson, who's heading up this enquiry," he suggested impatiently.

The astute police chief then strode up to his underling and examined the worried look in his flitting blue eyes.

"Now tell me what's really on your mind, Hunt," he ordered.

Jonathan swallowed, those eyes observing his boss as he rested against the edge of the desk and waited for an answer.

"Sir, I've known Brian Danks for more years than I care to remember. We were at school together. I was best man at his wedding. I'm convinced he did not murder Emily Ashmore. I certainly can't visualise him kicking a pregnant young girl in the stomach! It's just not the Brian I know. In fact, I don't believe he had anything to do with her death. As for this talk about him seducing her and fathering her baby, well… to be honest, sir, the Brian Danks I know would have more likely bored the poor thing to death rabbiting on about snakes and steam trains."

"Be that as it may, Constable; but upon what irrefutable evidence do you base this 'conviction' you have? What unique investigative insight do you possess that has so far eluded DI Grayson and his merry men? That the suspect was your classmate?"

"Sir, the Brian Danks I know wouldn't hurt a fly…"

"But we know he's capable of hurting more than just flies, Hunt. He threw his wife down the stairs! The neighbours across the road witnessed it; and Ruby Danks admitted it herself during questioning."

"But, with respect, sir, we know too that Gary Willetts has a history of violence. After all, he's the ringleader of that gang of skinheads we're sure was responsible for roughing up Mr Patel outside his corner shop a few weeks back. We could have nicked him if only Mr Patel hadn't been too scared to testify.

"And now he appears to have done a runner; and all his mates can tell us is 'we doh' know where he is'. Maybe Emily Ashmore was carrying *his* child, sir. Maybe it was *him* who lured her into that tunnel and did something to her. Maybe that's why he's abandoned his scooter; and seems in no hurry to claim it back."

"Maybe, maybe, maybe, Constable," the Chief Super had heard enough. "'Maybe' will not convict someone in a court of law. So might I suggest you stick to pounding your beat and nabbing a few more shoplifters! After all, Constable, by your own admission you're not exactly the most objective and dispassionate observer of this case."

"No, sir."

And that was that. Or so Jonathan thought. Looking for a face-saving means of disengaging from this unproductive conversation, he was ready to back himself towards the door when he heard it being treated to another hearty knock.

"Come in," Chief Superintendent Trotter snorted.

Jonathan turned to observe the most important man on the case unexpectedly poke his head around the door before stepping from behind it and drawing up to them.

"Good grief, Constable! That's a shiner-and-a-half!" Detective Inspector Grayson remarked, wincing upon beholding that bruised eye. He then turned to address his boss.

"A word, sir – about the Emily Ashmore case," he requested, staring Jonathan up and down again as if to hint that it was a word he would prefer to have in private.

"You can have that word in PC Hunt's presence, Detective Inspector," Trotter insisted. "Why, the constable here has some thoughts of his own about the case that he would like to share with you," he sneered.

"Sir, we've finished interviewing those two girls – Miss Ashmore's former school friends. They've confirmed that Gary Willetts *was* the father of Miss Ashmore's child. And a few minutes ago Forensics came back to me. They can find no trace of Mr Danks's fingerprints on that bloodstained brick that we believe was used in her murder.

"And finally, sir, a guy has come forward who was walking his dog in the park that runs alongside the old railway. He's made a statement to the effect that, at approximately 2.30pm on Friday, he observed a man fitting Brian Danks' description – that Pentax camera around his neck and wearing those distinctive black spectacles – emerge through a gap in the fence to the old railway cutting and head off in the direction of Sneyd Park.

"Sir," the detective then pointed out, "in their statements the two blokes who'd been fishing over Fens Bank confirmed that Mr Willetts and Miss Ashmore were still riding around on his scooter at four o'clock, when they decided to pack away their tackle to head home."

There was a pause while the Chief Super folded his arms and pondered the implications of all this new evidence.

"So it would appear the Snakeman has an alibi," he noted, observing Jonathan's face flush with relief.

"Yes, sir," Grayson conceded. "In the light of what we now know, I would therefore recommend that we release Brian Danks and instead concentrate our enquiries on Gary Willetts."

"Of course, the only problem, Detective Inspector, is that no bugger out there seems to know where he is. Or, if they do, they're unwilling to tell us!"

"We've interviewed his parents, sir. We've interviewed all his mates too. They're adamant they *don't* know. Look, sir, I know there's no love lost between my men and these thuggish delinquents. However, on this occasion, my gut instinct is to believe they're actually telling the truth."

* * * * *

It was a battered old teddy bear – with an eye missing. However, it was not just any old bear. Having popped his head into the room, Brian noticed his wife sitting on the bed and recognised that it was *her* bear that she was studying: the one her mother had bought her as an infant; the one she'd cuddled all through her childhood; the one that had been her mascot at university (where Brian had first been introduced to it).

It had therefore been no surprise that this beloved old bear had assumed pride of place on the dresser in the room Ruby had been busy preparing as a nursery; the room that until little over a month ago had also been Emily's room. Yet now the child Ruby had been looking forward to holding and loving (and maybe to one day bequeathing that favourite teddy bear) was dead, along with its teenage mother.

He watched Ruby glance up from fondling it and stare about the room. She then briefly laid the bear aside on Emily's bed so that she could wander over and gaze at dusk now drawing in. Unlooping the ties, she drew the curtains, admiring too those cute little cartoons of ducks and fishes embossed on them. Then she returned to the bed and sat down on it. Picking the bear up again, she continued to gaze at it longingly, as if imagining all the wonderful things that might have been.

All this time, though aware that Brian was there, she'd elected to comport herself as if he wasn't. Finally, he could bear her feigned indifference no longer. Ever the conciliator in their marriage, he therefore lifted himself from the door on which he'd been hanging and quietly drifted over to seat himself down on the bed next to her.

Still she feigned not to notice him, instead stroking the bear and wistfully studying that missing eye. Gently he slid a hand across to place it upon her knee. Gently, but firmly, she broke from stroking her childhood toy to remove it.

* * * * *

With Ruby inconsolable over what had happened – and unwilling to forgive her husband for what she considered to be his part in it – there was nothing more to do except to keep out of her way. Therefore, Brian reluctantly wandered across the landing to retreat into the room that contained the impressive model railway lay-out he'd built.

Soon enough, he was changing signals here and switching points there. His fiddling permitted a little tank locomotive to come trundling out of the engine shed and hook itself up to a waiting train of goods wagons. He watched the locomotive then haul it out onto the main loop of track, there to snake in and out of tunnels, cuttings and stations, passing the majestic Tri-ang Blue Pullman diesel passenger train he'd recently bought.

Despite this diversion, still he found himself brooding again over the events of the last four tumultuous months. How had things ever come to this?

Brian Danks had always had trouble getting inside the mind of a woman. In fact, he struggled to get inside the minds of most people he met. Was there something hard-wired in his brain that rendered him singularly unable to empathise with his fellow human beings? To read their body language or facial nuances and thereby be spared misjudging their moods and intentions?

More than anything he'd badly misjudged his wife's deep yearning to be a mother – as well as the lengths to which she would go to make that happen. This fatal flaw in his make-up had also caused many people who'd initially been supportive of his campaign to save the town's railway to back away; or even to turn on him for being an 'obsessive' (or worse, a 'crank').

Meanwhile, the inability to make the small talk that might have enabled him to reach out and make allies of them, or even to recognise or offer a timely compromise (and thereby do deals with them), had reduced him to a lonely and increasingly isolated figure; someone to be pitied, as much as mocked or despised. Someone for whom the terms 'tenacious' and 'principled' were forever being coined; but which were also polite adjectives to describe a man devoid of the interpersonal skills that might have netted him more of what he'd set out to achieve. Indeed, so manic and pig-headed had the Snakeman proved that he'd failed to achieve *any* of it.

And now his wife had turned against him too – a terrible blow to bear for a man who boasted few firm friends, of which, to date, she'd been his most loyal (and to whom he feared he'd behaved most selfishly). Tweaking the transformer at his fingertips, he halted the Blue Pullman in the station.

The room fell silent. There he sat staring at his trains – symbolic of an *idée fixe* into which he had poured his boundless passion. As he did – and pondered these things anew – so his eyes began to moisten.

Unseen meanwhile, Ruby quietly closed the door to the nursery and wandered onto the landing. Through the door he'd left ajar she spotted her husband, his head in his hands – sobbing.

To be sure, Brian Danks was different to other men. However, for all that, he was also capable of being supremely kind and loving. For such a socially awkward figure, he'd also sincerely sought to demonstrate loving Christian kindness to Emily during her brief time with them. Despite her lingering resentment, Ruby was generous enough to acknowledge that. Therefore, she reasoned too, it must be unbearable for him to know that, even now (and despite the police removing him from their enquiries), there were people out there who remained convinced that this aberrant misfit must have had a hand in her death somehow. It was one more reason for them to despise him; one more reason too for all those tears that he was now shedding.

As she pushed gently against the door to step inside, he turned with a start to behold her standing there. Emotionally transparent to a fault, he was unable to conceal from her the depths of his remorse. She offered him one of her soft, indulgent smiles – of the sort that always pandered to the vulnerable little boy in him.

Drawing alongside him, she folded her arms around his head and cradled it to her bosom. It was the cue for him to sob again, this time without restraint. In response, Ruby tightened her embrace and rested her head on his, there to shed silent, contrite tears of her own.

13

*"...All you need is love.
All you need is love.
All you need is love, love.
Love is all you need..."*

"'Ere, boyo! Turn that bloody radio down, will you. I can't hear myself think with that racket playing, I can't."

Over in a corner of the cavernous engine shed a callow, long-haired student broke from painting the large, circular smoke box door that he'd propped up on a workbench. Observing the Welshman's disapproving scowl, he grudgingly reached up to tweak the volume knob as instructed. With peace restored, Cledwyn Davies could return to the succour of his pipe – and to polishing the weighty piston rod he was gripping in his hand.

Sat on a stool next to him, polishing up one of '6418's combination levers – and likewise clad in a pair of grimy blue overalls – Jonathan Hunt glanced up unseen and rolled his eyes.

"Don't be so hard on the lad," he chided his former history teacher. "A bit of music helps pass the time. Besides, we're going to need all the help we can get if this old lady's ever to get up steam again," he reminded him, staring up at the rusty, partially dismantled hulk of the 0-6-0 pannier engine alongside them.

"She might be getting it up a bit sooner, lad, if you show that lever some elbow grease," Cled removed the pipe from his mouth to berate his one-time pupil.

The former Great Western Railway had built thousands of these small, yet versatile locomotives at their Swindon works, the final ones being delivered to the by-then nationalised British Railways in 1956. '6418' was a Charles Collett-designed example that dated from 1932, and which had spent much of her life shunting ingot wagons to and from the Alcock & Robbins steel works. Jonathan had first fallen in love with her as a lad while watching her haul the autocoach through Sneyd End station. Alas, in 1962, she'd been despatched to join those of her peers waiting their turn to face the cutter's torch – yet one more casualty of British Railways' headlong rush to rid itself of steam.

Then one day he'd perchance spotted her at a sprawling scrap yard at Barry Island. With a head full of dreams and the support of some like-minded enthusiasts, they'd stumped up the cash to rescue her and transport her to this sleepy Shropshire town, where another group of railway buffs had meantime purchased a disused station, an engine shed, and a section of abandoned track.

However, four years of languishing forgotten by the seaside had taken its toll on the old girl. Hence why most weekends this small troop of volunteers could be found grinding, welding, painting and polishing the various bits of '6418' ready for the day when this 'preserved' railway eventually opened for passengers, and she could be found hauling trains again.

"Where's Brian?" Jonathan meanwhile thought to ask.

"I sent him up the town for the bacon butties almost an hour ago. Either the queue to be served is out the door or the lad's gone walkabout again. He seems to prefer his own company a lot lately," Cledwyn noted, his forehead striating with concern.

"Understandable, I suppose. That business with the girl has shaken him up badly. He won't even talk to me about it," it pained Jonathan to admit before adding "That's why I'm keen to get him working on '6418' again. Apart from the fact – as I said – that we need every pair of hands we can find to get her running, Brian needs something to take his mind off his problems.

"Mind you," he also thought to add, "Ruby wasn't exactly happy about me dragging him away. In fact, I suspect repairing his relationship with his wife is the most daunting issue he's yet to confront. It's so sad. Brian and Ruby were once devoted to each other. Maybe she thought adopting Emily Ashmore's baby would bring them closer together again."

"Bloody crazy idea, if you ask me. And look where it nearly landed the poor man," Cledwyn shook his head and grunted. Then he paused from polishing to relight his pipe and stare up pensively at the silent locomotive.

"Why can't a woman be more like a steam engine?" he mused. "Simple to understand; a doddle to work with; and responds well to the care you lavish upon her. Just the qualities a man needs in a woman. You know, there's a reason why men always refer to steam engines as 'she'," he snickered around his pipe.

"And yet thirty years now I've been married to my Edith and I still don't understand how *her* mind works," he confessed. "It's like you do your best for a woman; but it's never enough. They moan that you never talk to them or spend time with them. But Heaven forbid that you try and hold a conversation with them when *'Coronation Street's* on the bloody telly. Edith disappears down the bingo with their mates every Tuesday night without fail. Yet she nags me blind for coming here on Saturdays. Why, you'd think I was seeing another woman, you would!

"No, lad," he admonished the unmarried copper with his pipe, "you stay single. That way you'll never find out the hard way that a woman is always right; even when she's wrong. I must have spent half my bloody life apologising to my wife, I have; yet I can't recall a time that she has ever said 'sorry' to me."

Jonathan was grateful for the older man's unsolicited advice – even as he preferred to return to the matter in hand.

"In fairness, I get the feeling that what happened is not all Ruby's fault," he intimated. "Brian can't be the easiest person to live with; and he's got some peculiar ways. I should know: he's my best friend! But neither is he the Devil Incarnate, and people shouldn't treat him like he is."

Just then he looked up from his mitigating plea to observe that the marital sage from Maesteg had spotted something. Frowning and turning about, Jonathan also spotted the familiar bespectacled silhouette standing in the entrance to the grimy engine shed, bag in hand and bathed in the rays of a low, autumnal sun.

"I've got the butties," the figure held the bag aloft.

"Ah, Brian, lad. You took your time. We thought you'd been run over, we did," Cledwyn burbled awkwardly.

Without saying a word (though plainly aware that his name had cropped up in conversation), the Snakeman drifted into the shed to present the tiffin he'd been on the errand to fetch.

"We were just saying: there's still so many unanswered questions about..." Jonathan dissembled, unsure how much of that conversation his friend might have caught.

"Which is why the first thought of your mates down the cop shop was that I'd done it," Brian grunted angrily, drawing up an upturned packing crate to join them. Sitting down on it, he began munching on his own bacon butty.

"But you *didn't* do it," Jonathan consoled him. "It's just that we can't find the person who we think *did*; or at the very least is the only other witness to whatever it was that went on that day in the tunnel."

"That said," the policeman continued, "I'm of the opinion that Gary Willetts may not have intended to harm Emily Ashmore either. For example, from the tear in the back tyre of his scooter it's likely he'd stopped inside the tunnel because it had struck an object, not because he'd chosen to. We also found his cigarette lighter nearby – his mates identified it as his. However, there was no evidence that any fags had been smoked and discarded. If the battery on his moped had died, then that lighter may well have been his only means of finding his way about inside the tunnel – which is presumably why he'd taken it from his pocket. So why would he have abandoned it when the flint worked and it still had plenty of fuel in it? And why would he have abandoned his scooter too? By all accounts it was his pride and joy. Indeed, from the footprints and the punctured tyre tracks we examined it appeared he'd been attempting to push it out of the tunnel.

"So did Gary Willetts really take Emily Ashmore in there to do her in? Was that why she was fleeing from him? Or did they unexpectedly encounter someone else – or something else – inside that tunnel?"

"Something else?" Cledwyn was intrigued by his ex-pupil's choice of semantics.

"Yes, I wonder if some kind of struggle took place that Gary and Emily found themselves caught up in. You see, there were these other tracks too; grooves in the dust which the guys in Forensics weren't able to properly explain."

"What kind of tracks?" Brian chipped in.

"Almost like they'd been created by some... I know this is going to sound silly," he shook his head, "... some giant snake."

"Oh, come on, man. That's nonsense. Ask Brian here: we don't have snakes like that in Britain," the Welshman scoffed, looking to his star alumni to scotch such a ridiculous notion.

"No, I tell you: Gary Willetts was a right hoodlum at school, he was. Swaggering about the corridors, picking fights on other lads and mouthing off at us teachers. You mark my words: the despicable delinquent's done a runner knowing that you coppers are after him over what he did to that poor young girl."

"Hmmn," Jonathan mused. "The guys in CID are still working on that premise. To them it's an open-and-shut case of foul play in which, one way or another, Gary Willetts is the prime suspect. However, it's just that, well... last year I bumped into some bloke sneaking through the fence that runs alongside Fens Bank. I remember it well: it was the night we won the World Cup – which probably explained why I found him two sheets to the wind. In fact, he could barely stand up."

"Yes, I confess I got a bit merry that night too, I did. I'd have gotten merrier still if it had been Wales that had carried off the Cup!" Cled chipped in with a puckish grin.

"What's more, this guy was sopping wet. He'd probably fallen into one of those cooling ponds. But I couldn't get a coherent sentence out of him. Except that he mumbled something about having seen a 'giant snake'."

Glum taciturnity banished, Brian sat up straight on the packing crate, folded his arms in earnest, and welcomed this opportunity to offer a considered opinion about a subject upon which he was a renowned expert.

"Yes, Emily said something about some bloke her father knew spreading such a story; *and* of the man in question being rather fond of a few beers! However, even if – a very big if – such a snake could survive the British climate, it's unlikely it could have devoured Gary Willetts – if that's what you're implying."

"What? Even a really big one?" Jonathan pressed him.

His friend shook his head.

"Such 'man-eating' snakes are a myth. For a start, while a python's mouth is capable of distending to swallow quite sizeable prey, the broadness of the human shoulder blades would present the creature with quite a challenge when swallowing a man."

"Gary Willetts was certainly a big bloke," Cledwyn reminded them, recalling those occasions when he'd had to look the snarling teenager in the eye and rebuke his malevolence.

"For that snake to be capable of extending its gape around a man of his stature *and* devour him I'd estimate it would have to be *at least* thirty feet in length – with a girth to match. And while such beasts are reputed to exist in the wild, the largest ones that have ever been captured were nowhere near that big – and they were living in far more favourable climates than the dismal one we enjoy here in the Midlands!"

"But it could have tried. That massive snake you showed me at the zoo certainly looked capable of bringing down a man," Jonathan was still eagerly interrogating him.

"You mean Zoe – our Australian scrub python? Absolutely! That's why I have Julie, my assistant, with me whenever I handle her. However, Zoe's only fifteen feet long – which is about as big as those pythons grow in captivity. If a snake of that size *had* tried to swallow Gary Willetts, then it would probably have had to abandon the attempt. In which case, Constable, you would have discovered his body – albeit that it wouldn't have been a particularly pleasant sight," the erudite herpetologist assured him, poking his spectacles back up his nose.

The rippling upon Jonathan's pitted face belied the deflation of realising that that line of enquiry looked set to go nowhere. However, for once Brian read someone's emotions correctly. Therefore, his smug grin dissipated, and he offered his friend a more considered demeanour instead.

"Of course, there are stories of people being eaten by large snakes," he conceded. "However, these have mostly involved children – or smaller adults from pygmy tribes. Like I said, if it did exist – and to get its jaws around the likes of Gary Willetts – this 'man-eating' serpent would have to be a real whopper; and probably a female too, because they grow larger than the males. I'd certainly like to meet her," he enthused.

Cledwyn flashed his eyebrows and puffed on his pipe.

"Rather you than me, boyo!"

* * * * *

Most of the pop stars of the 1960s had put in an appearance tonight – at least in spirit: from anodyne melodies by The Supremes, Stevie Wonder, The Beach Boys, The Seekers, Lulu, and Tom Jones (as requested by the staff); to edgier stuff by The Spencer Davis Group, The Yardbirds, The Doors, The Who, The Small Faces, and James Brown (as requested by the pupils). Toss in the inevitable Beatles and Rolling Stones hits and the resulting eclectic mix had ensured there was something for everybody to dance to at Sneyd End High School's third annual Parents' & Teachers' Association Christmas Disco.

Moreover, if Brian Danks could be awkward in social gatherings, no sooner had a spirited Motown track been dropped onto the turntable he was up on the dance floor, gawkily gyrating alongside Ruby's pupils. With many of them fondly remembering the zany Snakeman from childhood visits to the zoo, he'd proved a popular and much-valued participant at each of the PTA's previous Christmas bashes; someone who could be relied upon to get the party going.

"Yes, he's quite a mover is your husband."

Loitering on the sidelines while sipping on a beaker of lemonade, Ruby turned to observe that, unseen, a familiar figure had meanwhile sidled up to her – the better to chat her up under the guise of remarking upon her husband's coltish interpretation of Marvin Gaye's *'Ain't That Peculiar'*.

"Brian likes to let his hair down," she half-apologised, though otherwise affecting to be unfazed.

The school disco had been one of Graham Weston's more inspired fund-raising brainwaves – and certainly his most successful. Perhaps this risqué, forty-two-year-old charmer was out to prove he was 'with it' – able to empathise with an up-and-coming generation for whom the avant-garde jazz he preferred was as passé as that black polo-neck jumper he was wearing.

"I've asked the disc jockey if he has something slower with which to round off the evening: The Righteous Brothers, maybe; or Dusty Springfield. That said, I fear your husband will be fagged out well before then," he sniggered, marvelling at Brian's gangling pirouettes. "In which case, perhaps I could have the honour of accompanying the most beautiful woman in the room onto the dance floor? After all, you still owe me," he reminded her with that suggestive glimmer in his alluring blue eyes.

Ruby masked both her cherry-red lips and her trepidation by taking another nervous sip from the beaker, purposely declining to make eye contact with him.

"Then you underestimate the resilience of my husband," she replied calmly, but firmly.

To which Weston smirked. *Reculer pour mieux sauter*: archly sipping from his own soft drink as a means of making a face-saving retreat, instead he feigned to continue observing the action on the floor of the school's assembly hall.

Ruby breathed a momentary sigh of relief. This man was nothing if not persistent! That said, Graham Weston was also everything that Brian Danks wasn't. Suave and unctuous – yet also patient and supremely calculating – it was as if this shameless skirt-chaser knew perfectly which buttons to press to infuriate her, and yet retreat at just the right moment to leave her heart once more aflutter (and the ratchet of his slow, purposeful seduction perhaps one notch tighter around its intended victim).

Of course, it helped that Graham Weston was neither obsessed with restoring old steam engines nor re-opening old railway lines. Instead, the conversations he invariably manoeuvred Ruby into striking up were intended to demonstrate how – unlike her husband's inanimate infatuations – he shared many of *her* burning ideals. For example, he'd spoken eloquently of his revulsion over the apartheid government in South Africa; of the cruel and costly war that the Americans were waging in Vietnam; and of the cynicism of the Wilson government turning its back on (and even arming opponents of) Biafra and its brave bid for freedom. But more than anything, Graham Weston and Ruby Danks shared a passionate striving for social justice in Britain's education system: the belief that every child – no matter its background or the financial means of its parents – had the right to receive a quality education at a state school.

"Phew! That was good!" puffed Brian, having meanwhile returned from the dance floor and from his frenetic take on Aretha

Franklin's *'R-E-S-P-E-C-T'*. "You should have joined me, Ruby. You loved to dance at university," he reminded her.

"But I was never able to keep up with you," she ribbed him, welcoming his return with a smile and a peck on the lips.

Weston's eyebrows meanwhile arched upon observing this curious, mismatched couple, eager to discern what Ruby might have intended to signal with that demonstrative kiss.

"Nobody can keep up with you, Brian," he shot her husband a sardonic smirk. "You certainly put my students to shame."

"Well, you know what they say, Graham: you're only as old as you feel," Brian chortled, oblivious to the hint of derision.

"In which case, you should join the fifth formers in my French class next term!" he suggested, damning him a second time with faint praise. As he did, he glanced across at Ruby – who was plainly discomfited by his mockery and conceit.

"Love to, "Brian meanwhile puffed again, oblivious. "Unfortunately though, I'm going to be out of the country for a few weeks in the New Year."

"Oh really?" Weston expressed surprise (as well as perhaps sniffing an opportunity). "Off anywhere exciting?"

Just then (and, maddeningly, before the Snakeman could venture further details about this absence overseas), the disc jockey struck up the *andante* opening piano bars of Englebert Humperdinck's *'Last Waltz'*. It prompted Brian to stare into his wife's eyes and – without a word being spoken – implore her again to this time join him on the dance floor.

However, it was not without a quick (and almost plaintive) glance at the lustful head teacher – unseen by her husband – that Ruby permitted herself to be led away. Locating a spare portion of dance floor, Brian then locked one hand in hers and placed the other in the small of her back (and she a hand upon his shoulder). Thereupon, they could be observed gliding in time with the other parents, teachers, their wives and husbands – as well as with the odd fifth form lovers willing to be seen similarly shuffling about to this most 'square' and serene of chart hits.

It was neither the song nor the scenario that the cunning head teacher had hoped for. Momentarily assuaging his frustration with another swig from his glass, consolation came every now and then when the happy couple revolved full circle – and the wife he'd sought to prise away proved unable to resist the temptation of returning his wistful stare from over her husband's shoulder.

Perhaps the ratchet had been successfully cranked up another notch after all.

* * * * *

It was one of those bleak winter's days when the lot of a beat officer was an invidious one. Though the snow that had briefly flurried had abated (having deposited a sprinkling of the stuff), the mercury in the thermometer that hung in the yard of Sneyd End Police Station remained stubbornly below freezing.

Having repaired there to thaw out his limbs, PC Jonathan Hunt was downing a mug of cocoa when the call came in: an officer was required to attend to a report of children trespassing over Fens Bank – again!

"They're probably pupils from the high school," the duty sergeant rolled his eyes as he handed him the assignment. "They were sent home this morning because of burst pipes in the building. Looks like some of them have decided to make the most of their day off to go skating on the cooling ponds."

"In which case, I'll take the bike, Sarge. That way I might get there before one of the dopey little tykes falls through the ice."

Patrolling on the Norton Atlas in sub-zero temperatures was only marginally more bearable than being on foot. However, as Jonathan had rightly pointed out, it at least enabled him to reach the scene more quickly. What's more, once he'd turned down the lane and negotiated the broken-down gate that led onto this broad wilderness the ground was solid enough to be able to ride upon it without churning up mud.

Truth to tell, Fens Bank looked very different to how the constable imagined it must have done on that warm spring day when Emily Ashmore had last been spotted similarly traversing it on the back of her boyfriend's scooter. The trees were bare of leaves, the bramble beds had died down, and the horses that could be seen tethered here and there were snorting steamy breaths as they huddled together to stay warm. Meanwhile, the ponds that made this spot such a magnet for kids were glazed with a crust of ice. Definitely not the weather for snakes, the policeman mused as he cruised past the largest of the ponds – even though the surface hadn't completely frozen over in the middle of it (the result of the constant feed of warm water from the neighbouring steel works that was pumped here for cooling and recycling).

He hadn't been riding long before he came across what he'd been despatched to investigate. Sure enough, on one of the smaller ponds that *had* frozen over a group of pubescent lads were taking turns to run along the ice, careering as far as the momentum would propel them. Hearing the bike approach, and spotting its rider, their first instinct was to leg it back up the bank – an escape route that Jonathan deftly blocked by straddling it with his motorcycle. He switched off the ignition and lifted his goggles onto his helmet, the better to offer a suitably irate scowl.

"Here, you know you're not supposed to be over here," he called down at them.

"But we wuz' only playin'," one of them pleaded – a lad whose scraggly blonde locks were poking out the sides of his West Bromwich Albion woolly hat.

"That doesn't alter the fact that this land is private property – and that you should not be trespassing on it."

"Yer'll be tellin' us next there's a giant snake lurkin' over 'ere," he replied, to the nervous tittering of his pals.

"No, but I *am* telling you that this is *not* the North Pole. That ice is not very thick; and you could easily end up falling through it. Now be on your way, all of you – before I have words with your parents," the copper instructed them.

"But loads of people come over 'ere. I bet you even came over 'ere yerself' when you were a nipper," the blonde kid suggested.

"Hop it, I said!" Jonathan repeated, raising his voice.

The cheeky youngster finally accepted *force majeure* and turned to skulk away with his mates. Upon which Jonathan motioned to restart his motorbike. However – whether from a guilty conscience that he had indeed played over here when he was their age; or curiosity about a forward youngster who'd dared to question the authority of a police officer – he stayed his hand.

"Oye, you," he called after him. "What's your name?"

The lad turned about and faced him, hands in his pockets.

"Wot? Me? Ar'm Robin – Robin Jukes," he snuffled.

"Yes, well. Like I said, don't let me catch you over here again," Jonathan repeated, having memorised the face – for that strange policeman's intuition told him that this 'Robin' kid would sooner or later be in trouble over these parts again.

* * * * *

The squelching beneath his feet was unnerving. Treading gingerly across the lush reed beds Brian Danks sensed that the serpent was very close indeed (though as yet he couldn't see it). What's more, it was a big one too – just as the locals had warned. It was at times like this that he wished he had Julie alongside him. His ever-faithful assistant would instinctively know what to do.

Suddenly he spotted the tell-tale green-and-yellow coloration, despite the coating of glutinous mud that had mostly concealed it. It was the tail. But, crucially, where was the head? This was always the most heart-stopping moment. However, casting fear aside, he slowly stooped down and grasped hold of it with both hands. Yet no sooner had he yanked on that tail than out of the water the rest of huge beast writhed.

"Over here!" Brian hollered for all he was worth, gripping the massive snake and summoning help, the others racing over to join him as fast as the boggy ground permitted.

"Esto es una muy grande!" one of them exclaimed.

The first instinct of any cornered snake is invariably to seek out a hole to slither into. This one was desperately attempting to lunge back into the safety of the floating vegetation beneath which it had been lurking. Too large and heavy for the Snakeman from the Black Country to possibly handle on his own, it was only once half-a-dozen other burly *hombres* had grabbed hold of its enormous trunk that it could be prised into the open again. Even so, the snake's head was still flailing about.

With his reflexes attuned by eight years spent handling reptiles professionally, Brian manoeuvred to nab it with both hands, narrowly dodging a swipe by jaws that were agape to reveal a rake of needle-sharp, backward-facing teeth. At last though, the snake gave up resistance and permitted the expedition team to catch their breaths. Straightening the animal out as best as its tensing muscles would permit, it appeared to be *at least* twenty-foot long, maybe more.

A fellow of the Royal Geographical Society, one of the perks of Brian's job was that it granted him welcome opportunities to travel: speaking engagements; exchange visits to zoos around the world; and – like this unforgettable adventure – field trips to observe snakes up close in the wild. Working alongside local zoologists, this year he'd been invited to tour the extensive Llanos plains of Venezuela on a mission to capture and study the legendary green anaconda – the world's largest snake.

An impenetrable swamp during the wet season (and a soggy grassland – as now – during the dry), the Llanos drained into the Orinoco, one of South America's great rivers. Suffice to say, it was a wonderland for wildlife – including turtles, iguanas, howler monkeys and all manner of exotic birds. Colonies of capybaras could also be observed grazing serenely in the shallow lakes that had formed now the rains had abated. These curious, dog-sized rodents provided prey not only for the jaguars and caimans that prowled this wilderness, but also for its anacondas too.

At last, the train of humans that had seized the huge snake was able to walk it back to *terra firma*, where Brian ordered it to be set down so that he could measure it and take out his trusty Pentax camera to photograph it. While not the longest snake on the planet, green anacondas are certainly the bulkiest. He estimated this beauty must weigh close to two hundred pounds, with a trunk that was the girth of a railway sleeper.

Yes, this specimen was a whopper alright – although smaller than the thirty foot he'd estimated one would need to be to have swallowed Gary Willetts. However, marvelling again at the lumbering beast slithering in the dust, he was suddenly not so sure. If any species of snake could have done it, then had he been a gambling man his money would be on this one. Sure – and unlike more aggressive species of pythons found in Africa and Asia – there were no documented cases of these snakes actively seeking out human prey. However, a snake that was able to exert enough crushing force to swallow a deer (antlers and all) should theoretically be able to tackle a human being (even if crushing its shoulder blades would probably stress the animal to the point of exhaustion).

Could such a beast really have swallowed a grown man? At the very least, what Brian had witnessed today – manhandling the largest snake he had ever come across – had left him with an open mind.

* * * * *

Mission accomplished, PC Jonathan Hunt steered his motorbike back towards the main Wednesbury Road in anticipation of other incidents to attend before his shift was complete. However, crossing the course of the disued Sneyd End railway line on the way, he paused to gaze down at the snow-dusted track bed.

Then a strange urge suddenly gripped him. Pointing his steed in its direction, he gingerly made his way down into the cutting that led up to the abandoned Sneyd End Tunnel. There, he paused again to raise his goggles and study the graffiti-daubed brickwork of the tunnel mouth, as well as to spy out the pinprick of light that marked the far end of the nine hundred-yard passage. He put the bike in low gear and, slowly and warily, entered in – passing more graffiti inside, as well as the trickles of water that were here and there seeping through its roof and sides.

Having successfully dodged around the obstacles in his path, the ambient heat was overpowering by the time he was halfway inside – in stark contrast to the frigid air outside that had found its way in through every chink in his winter overcoat. He halted the bike and removed his helmet, brushing the perspiration from his brow and marvelling how – over eighty years after the event – that underground pit fire was still making its presence felt above ground. Meanwhile, the motorcycle's headlamp illuminated the rats that were scurrying to hide from this visitor and his noisy machine. One of them – a sizeable one, seemingly more fearless than the others – lingered to stare back at him, its beady red eyes aglow in that penetrating beam. Then it too scurried down the drainage shaft into which its rodent pals had sought sanctuary.

Suddenly the thought struck the inquisitive bobby: was Sneyd End really such a hostile habitat for a large, cold-blooded reptile (for example, a pet that had maybe grown too large and been dumped)? Thanks to that still broiling underground fire, even in the depths of winter this tunnel was an oasis of tropical heat and humidity. There was a ready source of prey too, in the form of those legendary big, juicy rats that also thrived in this pitch-black hothouse. Meanwhile, as he carried on slowly making his way towards the opposite end, inspecting the tunnel as he progressed, who could say where those drainage shafts led that periodically lined the route? Too narrow for a human to possibly squeeze through (which is presumably why the officers investigating Emily's death had made only a cursory inspection of them), they would even so prove no obstacle to something as ductile as... a snake? What's more, maybe some of them even afforded subterranean access to the cooling ponds of Fens Bank, he imagined (recalling something Brian had said about pythons being excellent swimmers).

Reaching the southern mouth of the tunnel at last, he halted in the chill to remove his helmet from the handlebars and drop it back onto his head. However, before riding off he availed himself of one final glance back down the shaft of the tunnel. Was it conceivable that an inebriated and terror-struck Ernie Baxter had not been imagining things after all?

14

It was Saturday, April 20th 1968; and Brian Danks wasn't the only person mourning the loss four years earlier of that handy rail connection from Sneyd End to Birmingham. Arriving in the nick of time after struggling to find somewhere to park, the audience was already seated by the time Bill Patterson hurried inside the city's Midland Hotel. Discreetly slipping into the packed meeting room, the dapper, white-haired Conservative councillor spotted a spare seat and hurried down the aisle to the row of chairs near the front, where its occupants were forced to tuck their knees in as he squeezed past to claim it. Nodding apologetically, once he'd sat down he gazed about to observe that the press and television people had also turned up to cover this afternoon's event.

With an air of solemnity that added to the drama of the occasion, their guest speaker rose to address them, his piercing grey-blue eyes scanning the notes in his hands before he lifted and trained them in earnest upon his listeners.

"Mr Chairman, the supreme function of statesmanship is to provide against preventable evils. In seeking to do so, it encounters obstacles which are deeply rooted in human nature. One is that, by the very order of things, such evils are not demonstrable until they have occurred. At each stage in their onset there is room for doubt and for dispute whether they be real or imaginary. Above all, people are disposed to mistake predicting troubles for causing troubles – and even for desiring troubles. 'If only,' they love to think, 'if only people wouldn't talk about it, it probably wouldn't happen'."

Enoch Powell was the Conservative Party's fifty-five-year-old parliamentary spokesman for defence. The intense and erudite only child of a Birmingham schoolmaster, he'd won a scholarship first to Kings Norton Grammar School and thence to Cambridge University to study classics. Indeed, so profound was his grasp of the subject that he'd been appointed professor of Greek at the University of Sydney at the tender age of just twenty-five.

He'd returned from Australia in 1939 to enlist as a humble private in the Royal Warwickshire Regiment. However, war's end would find him serving in India, having been promoted to become one of the youngest brigadiers in the British army. Ever the polymath, it was while stationed there that he would nurture a love affair with the British Raj that not only sharpened his innate patriotism but impelled him to become fluent in Urdu and conversant in other native languages too.

His political career had proved as meteoric as his military one. Elected Conservative Member of Parliament for Wolverhampton South-West in 1950, soon after he was invited to become a treasury minister in Harold MacMillan's government, famously resigning in 1958 after accusing his prime minister of being too profligate with public spending! Returning to government in 1960 as health minister, three years later he would famously resign for a second time after refusing to serve under Alec Douglas Home.

An increasingly quixotic figure who'd expressed misgivings about his country's nuclear deterrent, its military presence 'East of Suez', and its close alliance with the United States, this maverick statesman had given little hint to party colleagues about the bombshell he was about to drop.

"A week or two ago," he informed his audience, "I fell into conversation with a constituent – a middle-aged, quite ordinary working man employed in one of our nationalised industries. After a sentence or two about the weather, he suddenly said: 'If I had the money to go, I wouldn't stay in this country'.

"I made some deprecatory reply to the effect that even this government wouldn't last for ever," he explained, to amusement amongst those present in the room who were gleeful that Harold Wilson's devaluation of the pound six months earlier, as well as controversy about the recent influx of Asian immigrants from Kenya, had sent Labour's poll ratings into a nose-dive.

"But he took no notice and continued: 'I have three children; all of them have been through grammar school; and two of them are married now, with families. I shan't be satisfied till I have seen them all settled overseas. In this country, in fifteen-or-twenty years' time, the black man will have the whip hand over the white man'."

Suddenly, listeners here and there who'd been nodding politely looked up. The reporters present looked up too, otherwise scribbling a little faster.

"I can already hear the chorus of execration," Powell exclaimed. "How dare I say such a horrible thing? How dare I stir up trouble and inflame feelings by repeating such a conversation? The answer is that I do not have the right not to do so."

This was meaty stuff – even as most of the party members present (Bill Patterson included) seemed visibly relieved that, at last, someone senior in their party was articulating something that had been on many people's minds for an awful long time. It made up for the fact that Powell's semantic precision and remorseless logic could frequently overwhelm the senses – in much the same way that Brian Danks's could too, Councillor Patterson smiled to himself. However, just as that relentless Snakeman was the bane of councillors in Sneyd End, so there was no disputing too the resolve with which this other voice in the wilderness was now nailing his colours firmly to the mast, as it were.

"Those whom the gods wish to destroy, they first make mad. We must be mad – literally mad," Powell thundered, "to be permitting the annual inflow of some fifty thousand dependants, who are for the most part the material of the future growth of the immigrant-descended population. It is like watching a nation busily engaged in heaping up its own funeral pyre."

By now, the local politicians present – many of whom had witnessed their own Midlands towns filling with black and brown faces too – were giving voice to their concurrence, urging their new champion on as he demanded a halt to further immigration, as well as that measures be put in place to encourage these newcomers to return to their countries of origin.

Powell also took the opportunity to lay into the Government's forthcoming Race Relations Bill (which it was intended would outlaw racial discrimination), charging that it threatened to 'throw a match onto gunpowder' by rendering the host population 'strangers in their own country'. He referred to an elderly lady in his own Midlands constituency – the last white person residing in her street, he noted – who was being intimidated into selling her home to immigrants on pain of having her 'windows broken', or 'excreta pushed through her letterbox', or 'wide-grinning piccaninnies' chanting 'racialist' at her in the street.

Powell rounded off his address by returning to the classics he'd once taught, translating Virgil's *'Aeneid'* to gloomily contend that "as I look ahead, I am filled with foreboding. Like the Roman, I seem to see *'the River Tiber foaming with much blood'*. Only resolute and urgent action will avert it even now. Whether there will be the public will to demand and obtain that action, I do not know. All I know is that to see – and not to speak – would be the great betrayal."

* * * * *

One minute she'd been minding her own business, chatting on the walk home from school with one of the friends she'd made since starting. The next she suddenly felt a hefty tug on the pony-tail in which her jet-black hair was tied.

Upon its release, Parminder Kaur turned to observe a menacing phalanx of tough-looking white girls glaring at her, who she recognised from Class 2S.

"Who'm yow' starin' at, Paki?" the ringleader spat. Then she lunged forward to shove the diminutive Sikh to the ground. Upon which, the books and pencils in Parminder's satchel spilled across the pavement – along with her spectacles.

"Dirty, smelly, little piccaninny!" one of her mates joined in. "Goo' back ter' where yer' come from – like Enoch sez'!"

"Leave her alone. Her' ay' done nuffink' ter' yow'!" Parminder's friend rebuked them, motioning to shield her.

"Shut yer' cake-hole, Marion Clarke. Or we'll duff yow' too!" another girl stepped up and cautioned.

While Parminder was still scrambling to locate her glasses, her assailant pushed past, raised her heel and stamped on them. The little Indian lass whimpered in horror.

"Hoy! Pick on someone yer' own size, yer' bullies!"

The ringleader and her mates turned to spy that this unfledged male voice belonged to some puny little blonde-mopped kid, who came striding over to stare up at her defiantly.

"Well, Ar' never! If it ay' Robin Jukes – the five-foot-nuffink' pipsqueak from Class 2H!" the girl scorned, prompting a burst of derision from her mates.

"I ay' afraid of yow', Gillian Hickman!" he snuffled, this unexpected knight-in-shining-armour drawing himself up as tall as he could muster (though cursing that, at this stage of puberty, the girls in school were almost all bigger than he was).

"Well, yer' should be; cuz' her's gooin' out wiv' Patrick Smith from Class 3S," her mate interjected, adding for good measure that "He doh' like wog-lovers, like wot' yow' am', either."

However, like the mongoose before the cobra, the plucky little second-former was determined to show no fear, standing his ground and staring out his classmate's gum-chewing tormentor.

"Come on, girls. 'E ay' wuth' it. An' neither is the Paki," she eventually sneered and nudged past him, her troop of snarling female ruffians trailing after her.

"Phew! That's told her!" Robin crowed to his mates, who'd been looking on with a different sort of incredulity.

"But Patrick Smith's built like a brick shithouse!" one of them gasped. "He'll kill ya'!"

However, the warning went unheeded. Instead, some innate sense of chivalry goaded Robin to offer his hand to the little Indian girl still sobbing on the pavement, lifting her to her feet. Locating the mangled frame of her spectacles – along with its one intact lens that had come to rest in the gutter – he spent a moment trying and failing to piece the two together. Sorrowful at his impotence, he shrugged and handed them back to her.

"Thank you," she snuffled, returning his regretful smile through the trail of tears that had moistened her russet cheeks.

* * * * *

"Your father did the right thing coming to see me, Parminder," Ruby assured her.

Her pocket-sized pupil glanced up from staring at the floor of the school office to offer her form tutor an uncertain smile. Her doleful gaze then turned to her father as Ruby addressed him.

"I can only apologise, Mr Singh. Unfortunately, incidents like these have been happening a lot – despite the best endeavours of Mr Weston and the staff to stamp them out. Of course, I'm bound to say that the situation hasn't been helped by certain other developments of late."

Inderjit Singh knew exactly what she was alluding to. The forty-two-year-old Punjabi had read the newspapers and seen the television news. Like his daughter, he too had been made to feel the palpable hubris amongst his white work colleagues that, at last, the boil had been lanced and the pus of their festering resentment could ooze unexpurgated. After all – as Mr Powell had pointed out – why should a Sikh like Inderjit be permitted to ride his moped wearing his turban when everyone else was being badgered to wear a crash helmet?

After promising to keep an eye on his daughter, Ruby's voice lifted to finish the meeting on a positive note.

"While you're here, can I tell you how pleased I am with the progress Parminder is making in class. She is a very intelligent and hard-working girl, Mr Singh. You must be so proud of her."

"I fear it is her intellect and her industry – and not just her skin colour or her religion – that is the reason that these other girls resent her," Inderjit pondered aloud. "Perhaps they don't think an Indian girl should do well at school."

Ruby could have concurred. However, her apologetic frown did it for her. Anyone in Sneyd End High School who evinced 'intellect' or 'industry' was almost destined to be regarded with suspicion, if not outright hostility. She recalled Susan Pritchard, who'd also endured her share of snide comments for being a 'swot'. For a moment, she was tempted to believe Cledwyn Davies had been right after all to mourn the loss of Sneyd End's superlative grammar school, where the town's 'swots' had previously been funnelled and mentored.

"But she is not alone, Mrs Danks. I have trodden in her shoes too, as your saying goes. For many years I was a locomotive engineer. I drove the finest trains in India – as I'm sure my daughter has told you. However, when I came to England looking to make a better life for my family, I was told by your British Railways that there were no jobs for train drivers.

"Of course, what they really meant was that there were no jobs for train drivers with brown skin – even though it was you British who taught me how to drive a train! Perhaps – like these young girls – white train drivers feared *my* intellect and industry; that I would perhaps put them out of their jobs. So instead I had to accept a different job with British Railways – cleaning the toilets at Wolverhampton station. Perhaps I have even brushed the toilet that Mr Powell has visited!"

Ruby spotted Parminder gazing down at the floor again. It was an addition to her father's *curriculum vitae* that this bright young lady had been too ashamed to mention to her teacher.

"Mrs Danks, I am not ungrateful to your country for offering my family the chance to contribute to its prosperity," he continued. "However, I am saddened that my own contribution is so modest when I know there is more that I could give. But then I believe that God can see my dejection. I pray that one day He will grant me my wish to be driving a railway locomotive again."

* * * * *

> *"I dismissed Mr Powell because I believed his speech was inflammatory and liable to damage race relations. I am determined to do everything I can to prevent racial problems developing into civil strife. I don't believe the great majority of the British people share Mr Powell's way of putting his views...."*

As he sank back into the sofa to watch the television news – arms folded and feet propped up on the pouffe – Brian was tempted to believe it was the leader of the Conservative Party, Edward Heath, who was deluded. More so when replay of the fall-out from this 'Rivers of Blood' speech switched to London's East End, where a thousand dockers stopped work to march on Parliament, carrying placards declaring *'Back Britain, not Black Britain'* and *'We want Enoch Powell'*. Conversely – and in a startling reversal of political fortunes – Labour MPs who'd come out to parley with them were heckled and assaulted. Meanwhile, the organiser of the march announced to journalists that…

"I've just met Enoch Powell and it made me feel proud to be an Englishman. He told me that he felt that if this matter was swept under the rug he would lift the rug and do the same again. We are representatives of the working man. We are not racialists."

Similar sympathy strikes were reported amongst other dock workers, as well as amongst the meat porters of Smithfield market. And although vocal protests had been staged demanding Powell's arrest for incitement, they'd been drowned out by the tidal wave of support for the Tory MP elsewhere. For example, the *'Express & Star'* newspaper in his constituency had reported receiving forty thousand postcards and eight thousand letters so far – ninety-five percent of them supporting Powell's remarks.

Just then, Brian's viewing was interrupted by the sound of the latch on the front door being twiddled. Hastily sitting up, Ruby had burst into the living room before he had time to fluff up the cushions. He looked up to behold her face aglow.

"Uh! Not that despicable man again!" she shook her head in dismay upon spotting the black quiff atop a receding hairline, along with Powell's familiar austere, moustachioed mien.

"He's certainly got people talking," Brian replied, adding for what it was worth that "Some of what he said is undoubtedly right too. With immigration, as with much else in life, you can have too much of a good thing. Maybe we have let too many in."

"What?" Ruby exclaimed. "You agree with him?"

"Like I said, much of what he said is…"

"Brian, I have just spent the best part of an hour counselling one of my pupils – a gentle, inoffensive Indian girl who some other girls set about while repeating the antipathy their parents have no doubt been muttering since last Saturday. And I've had to explain to her father that such hostility is the price one pays for having dark skin nowadays – a man who, thanks to that same racialism, was forced to take a job far below his skills."

"Sorry! I was only saying," he threw up his hands and feigned offence. "Or am I a 'racialist' too for daring to express an opinion – like Enoch said?"

"Oh, it's 'Enoch' now, is it?" his wife glowered, slamming her folders of work down hard on the dining table and planting her fists firmly on her hips. "Best mates, are we? I suppose you also want them 'sent back' – these 'wide-grinning piccaninnies'!"

"Ruby!" Brian exhaled, slack-jawed. This was getting silly. Was it that time of the month already?

However, before he could work the old conciliatory magic upon her, she spun about in the doorway and fired him a searing glare, the likes of which he'd never seen before.

"You know, sometimes I think my mother was right: I don't know why I ever married you. We have absolutely nothing in common. Not satisfied with having spent the last four years boring the pants off me with your bloody trains, now you extol an ambitious Tory politician who has made it respectable to pour bile and hatred upon a twelve-year-old girl!"

"Ruby!" he tried again.

However, she would have none of it. Snatching the car keys from the phone table in the hall, she was out the front door before he could seize her and pacify her.

"Where are you going?" he begged.

"Somewhere. Anywhere to get away from you!" she proffered, unlocking the car, jumping inside, and starting it up. Crunching into reverse gear, in an instant it was off the drive and disappearing down the street – taking Ruby with it.

"I bet your mother supports him!" Brian couldn't resist calling after her – which, though far too demure to phrase her disdain for people of colour in such terms, he strongly suspected she did.

* * * * *

"I'm really grateful to you...for what you did for me... the other day," she found it difficult to articulate, her eyes dipping behind her new and more stylish spectacles.

"Nah, doh' worry about it," Robin beamed. "The girls in 'School' house am' mostly from the rougher side of town. Anyway, they ay' bothered you since, have they."

Parminder smiled. It was true that, aside from occasional leers of disdain, Gillian Hickman and her mates had left her alone since that day she'd had her other spectacles broken.

It was nice to know that she had a protector-of-sorts watching out for her – even if (as Robin's mates had pleaded) the brawny Patrick Smith was not to be trifled with. Perhaps that was why Robin – like Parminder – had these past few weeks found himself a pariah-of-sorts amongst classmates wary of aggro. In return, the brainy Sikh girl had obliged by assisting her less academically-inclined classmate with his biology homework, praying that Mrs Danks wouldn't remark upon this sudden grasp Robin had acquired of the mechanics of plant photosynthesis!

As if to cement their newfound friendship, today he'd offered to walk Parminder home from school along the peaceful trails that meandered across Fens Bank. He'd even offered to carry that bulky school satchel for her (a touching and gentlemanly act that she'd politely declined). However, she had permitted him to repair the strap when it broke.

"Should we be over here?" she fretted. "I noticed it said *'Keep Out'* on the signs."

"We'll be okay. I've bin' comin' over 'ere since I was in junior school," he assured her. "Lots of us lads play over 'ere."

"And I really shouldn't, well... my parents wouldn't approve of me walking home alone with a boy," she explained, again dipping her eyes. "It's our culture, you understand."

"Yeah, well. Talking of 'culture', I'm sorry too," he also fumbled to articulate something that was on his mind as they strolled in the sunshine.

"Sorry?"

"Yeah, for... you know... callin' you a 'Paki', like."

Parminder was visibly heartened.

"But when you said it, you genuinely didn't know," she graciously insisted. "You thought I was from Pakistan – even though I was born in India. But when those girls called me that name, it was different. It meant... something nastier."

"So what's the difference then? Between India and Pakistan, like? You both eat curries, doh' you. And you both worship a different god to the one we English people do."

Where to start! How could she begin to explain to her wide-eyed young classmate about the violent communal strife that had brought so much suffering to her family (and which had played its part in her winding up thousands of miles from the land of her birth)? How could she explain to him that her family had a very different concept of who God was to her Hindu or Muslim peers – to say nothing of this curious figure hanging on a cross that people in her adopted country supposedly venerated?

She was spared when the shallowness of Robin's intellectual curiosity got the better of him. As they drifted past one of Fens Bank's cooling ponds, the thirteen-year-old couldn't resist the urge to gather up a handful of stones from the path and demonstrate his proficiency at targeting a discarded pop bottle that was floating neck-up on the surface.

"You know, they say there's supposed to be some massive snake over here," he casually remarked. "I doh' believe it though. I mean, whoever heard of such a thing livin' in Britain?" he scoffed, having acquired the range and the trajectory.

"We have many different snakes in India. Some of them are highly venomous. They kill many thousands of people every year," Parminder enlightened him.

"I held a snake once, yer' know," Robin reminded her. "It was a big 'un too: a python. It wuz' when I wuz' at junior school and we went to the zoo where Mrs Danks's old man works. It wuz' him who told me such snakes cor' survive over 'ere cuz' it's too cold, like. That's why everyone calls him the Snakeman. It's cuz' he knows lots of fings' about snakes, he does."

Parminder was tempted to lay down her satchel and join the expert marksman throwing pebbles. However, as she was doing so, the sound of glass shattering put an end to the fun. Robin had scored a direct hit on the pop bottle.

"Oh no!" he turned about to witness his companion cry.

"Wozzup?"

"My pen has leaked – in my bag. When the strap broke and it fell to the ground, the impact must have damaged it."

Robin stared down at the stain on the exercise book she'd pulled from her satchel – as well as the inky blue smears on her fingertips. Wandering over, he gingerly lifted the offending fountain pen by the clean end and held it up to examine.

"Yeah, that's bust!" he affirmed and tossed it skywards to join the pop bottle in a watery grave.

"What shall I do about my hands?" she fretted, staring at them.

"Just dip 'em in the water. You might be able to gerrit' off."

It seemed an odd solution – unladylike even. However, in the absence of a better idea she ambled down to the water's edge to crouch down and swish her fingers in the pond.

"Is it workin'?" he called down.

"Yes… It's coming off," she replied, swishing some more.

Unseen by Parminder, this disturbance on the surface had meanwhile alerted another visitor to the pond. From the adjacent reed bed, a pair of beady eyes had spied the diminutive schoolgirl. The animal now weaved its way silently and stealthily through the reeds, anxious not to be spotted.

"KER-SPLOSH!"

Parminder instinctively leapt backwards and screamed.

"Gorrit!" Robin crowed, punching his fist in the air in triumph.

Well, not quite. The half house brick he'd lobbed had sent the chunky rat paddling away for all it was worth, clambering up the opposite bank, dripping wet, to disappear into the undergrowth.

"Idiot! You scared the life out of me doing that!" Robin's palpitating playmate stamped her feet and yelled up at him.

"Sorry," he apologised. "Mind you, if our bruvva' had bin' 'ere he'd have shot that rat dead with his air rifle," he added.

"Look, I've had enough of being over here. Please take me home," Parminder instructed him.

Gathering up their school bags these two unlikely friends wandered a little further. It was as they were approaching the canal bridge that they suddenly heard a commotion going on. Robin and Parminder ducked behind the foliage to observe it.

"Oh, come on, Gill. It day' mean nuffin'."

"Oh, it day', did it! Well, that ay' wot' Karen Hadley's bin' tellin' everybody! How could yer', Patrick? An' wiv' the biggest scrubber in the whole school?"

It was Patrick Smith – the stocky, knuckle-dragging kid from Class 3S. What's more, the distraught young lady who was haranguing him was none other than Gillian Hickman – his bird (and Parminder's tormentor). Or at least it appeared she'd been his bird until a few minutes ago. Now it was payback time for him being caught dallying with the notoriously concupiscent Karen Hadley from Class 3V. 'School' house might contain the town's young ruffians; but the girls in 'Vale' house were without rivals when it came to sexual precocity!

"Well, that's it. We'm finished!" Gillian screeched at him one final time before storming off.

"Gill!" he hurried after her. Were girls always this hysterical? Was it that time of the month already?

However, she thrust his chunky palms aside, stomping off along the towpath in the direction of the old canal basin.

"Well, at least Karen Hadley knows how to snog a bloke!"

In response to his observation, Gillian briefly turned and stuck two fingers up at him. Thereafter, she tearfully hauled a transistor radio from her school satchel, twiddling with the volume so that tinny strains of Love Affair's *'Everlasting Love'* playing at full blast would drown out any further parting sneers.

Reasoned argument having failed (and insulting his two-timed girlfriend likewise), there was nothing for the sullen third-former to do except trudge off in the opposite direction, angrily kicking a discarded beer can that he encountered along the way.

"Oh, well," Robin turned to Parminder and whispered, "I guess I woh' have to worry about Patrick Smith anymore!"

* * * * *

THE SNEYD END GAZETTE
Friday, August 9th 1968

MISSING GIRL – THE MYSTERY REMAINS
Despite conducting the town's largest ever man-hunt, Chief Superintendent Cyril Trotter of Sneyd End Police admitted today that his officers are still no nearer to finding Gillian Hickman, the missing thirteen-year-old schoolgirl who was last seen walking

along the Sneyd End Canal seven weeks ago. Yesterday, in an appeal to members of the public for information about her daughter, Gillian's mother described her as 'a delightful girl with a warm smile, who'd never done harm to anyone'...

NEW LEISURE CENTRE – WORK TO BEGIN AT LAST

Sneyd End Council today announced that construction will commence on the town's new leisure centre in the autumn. Work was due to start on the quarter-of-a-million-pound scheme last year, having been delayed due to the need to undertake essential ground stabilisation works. The old station site it is to be built on is known to sit on top of disused mine workings...

THE END OF THE LINE FOR STEAM

This weekend will mark the end of steam on Britain's rail network. Enthusiasts are expected to turn out in force on Sunday to ride the final train to be hauled by steam locomotives – a 'Fifteen-Guinea Special' passenger excursion that will take in Liverpool, Manchester and Carlisle. It will be worked in relays by Class 5 ex-LMS 4-6-0 engines, as well as by the BR 'Britannia' Class 4-6-2 locomotive '70013 Oliver Cromwell'...

15

Commentators were already calling it the Year of Revolution. Throughout 1968 young people had been taking their anger to the streets – protests fuelled by a surge of 'baby boomers' born after the war who had entered university systems that had been expanded on the back of growing affluence.

In April, the United States had been rocked by the assassination of non-violent civil rights leader Dr Martin Luther King, prompting riots in several US cities as Black Americans despaired of ever overcoming their country's entrenched racism. In June, it had been further traumatised by the assassination of Senator Robert Kennedy – one of the leading contenders for the White House following President Lyndon Johnson's announcement that he would not seek re-election, broken by his failure to achieve victory in Vietnam. Indeed, opposition to this costly war had torn the nation asunder, culminating in August with violent anti-war protests outside the Democratic National Convention in Chicago.

Across Europe too, opposition to the war had brought people onto the streets, protests that frequently ended in confrontation with the authorities. In France, student demonstrations had dovetailed with strikes by workers to paralyse the country. For a tumultuous few days in May it really did appear that revolution would topple the government of President Charles de Gaulle. Meanwhile, on the other side of the 'Iron Curtain', tens of thousands had taken to the streets of Prague to voice support for the reforms of Czech president, Alexander Dubček, who was offering them 'communism with a human face'. However, on August 20th Soviet tanks had rolled across the border to crush the 'Prague Spring' and install a more compliant regime.

Neither had Britain been immune to this spirit of revolution. In March, police and anti-war demonstrators had clashed outside the United States Embassy in London. Throughout the summer, counter-cultural discontent continued to simmer. For many idealistic young people who'd become dissatisfied with the soulless consumerism of the affluent 1960s, the revolution to usher in a better world was only just beginning.

* * * * *

It was clean and it was quiet – like no other train Ruby Danks had ever ridden. The sleek electric locomotive and its plush, spacious carriages slid effortlessly out of Birmingham's New Street Station. In no time at all, the 08.10 departure for London Euston had worked up to speed, the autumnal countryside flitting past with barely a murmur. The contrast with noisy, belching steam trains – the passing of which her husband had mourned – was both pronounced and symbolic.

"Are you sure Brian doesn't mind you joining us today?" the woman sat opposite enquired, noting the abashed hue in Ruby's guileless brown eyes.

The pretty teacher declined to answer. Instead, she offered her three travel companions one of those pained, apologetic smiles that she'd often found herself donning during her four-year marriage. The kind that spoke of a woman who had grown tired of playing dutiful wife to a man whose implacable passions were no longer her own – if indeed, they ever had been.

Instead, today Ruby Danks was determined that she was going to make a stand for something *she* had come to feel passionate about. If it meant forsaking another weekend passed amidst the loneliness and sterility of her anodyne, middle-class existence, then so be it. Today she would be seeking to reprise the idealism of her youth; to 'change the world', as Graham Weston had once proclaimed – and in the company of like-minded people.

"I hear he might be planning his own protest," the man himself ventured, tapping his wife's hand as it rested on the table across from Ruby. "You have to hand it to him: he's nothing if not passionate. In fact, it's a shame he's not joining us today. I admire people who are passionate. Maybe it's because I'm passionate myself," he insisted, offering Ruby an ambiguous grin.

Again, she proffered no comment. Perhaps it was a sore subject, Weston surmised – for speculation in the press about what the latest instalment of Brian Danks's long-running campaign to save the Sneyd End railway line might portend was plainly needling her. Otherwise, the better-looking half of this intriguing marriage had become sufficiently appalled by a matter of far greater substance that she'd read about in the papers and watched night after night on TV to want to do something about it too. A convert to the cause, Weston rejoiced. Another notch clicking on the ratchet, he pondered slyly.

"Gosh! This thing flies," the young woman sat next to Ruby meanwhile remarked, staring out of the window at villages and stations that were whizzing past in the blink of an eye.

Pauline Trotter was a twenty-seven-year-old primary school teacher with whom Ruby had become friends through their involvement in the local branch of the teacher's union. It was through that involvement that she'd discovered that Pauline's father headed up the local police in Sneyd End; and that – owing to field trips to the zoo that she'd headed up in the company of her pupils – she already knew Brian in a personal capacity too. It made Ruby perhaps wonder whether Jonathan Hunt hadn't been the only voice cautioning Chief Superintendent Trotter that his men had risked barking up the wrong tree by rushing to judgement about her husband.

Yet if Pauline's father (like Ruby's) was a pillar of the traditional establishment, then both women must also have proved a disappointment to them. As time went by, Pauline (like Ruby) had come to hold increasingly progressive views about the great issues of their time. Both women were committed to education as a vehicle for advancing opportunity and fairness; and both women had felt compelled to respond in some tangible way to *the* great issue of the moment: the ongoing war in Vietnam.

Step forward one Graham Weston: left-leaning head teacher of a large comprehensive school also given to eloquently opining upon the futility of this appalling conflict. He had put it to the two women that they give voice to their anger by joining him on the huge protest rally that was taking place today in London.

Even more outspoken in her views about the imperative of political agitation was his wife – the willowy, middle-aged woman of sallow complexion sat opposite. Indeed, this was the first time Ruby had met Virginia Weston (though she knew Graham had a wife, who he would occasionally allude to with a detachment that bordered on bathos). With her beads and her bangles and her dark, flowing hair funnelled through a tie-dyed purple-and-green bandana, it was tempting to wonder whether this vampish and sanctimonious college lecturer wasn't Graham Weston's alter ego. Or even his svengali? She certainly had a lot to say for herself, spouting forth during the ninety-minute journey about matters as diverse as the civil rights movement in Northern Ireland, the betrayal of the British Left by Harold Wilson's government, and the importance of a woman experiencing multiple orgasms during love-making.

By this time on a Sunday morning Ruby would normally have been sat in church. Instead, she prayed she'd made a wise choice in joining Weston and his exotic wife on this protest. It certainly promised to be an interesting day out. Thank God she would at least have her good friend Pauline by her side.

* * * * *

"... I have fought a good fight. I have finished my course. I have kept the faith. Henceforth there is laid up for me a crown of righteousness, which the Lord, the righteous judge, shall give me at that day..."

Father Allen was impressed. Brian Danks invariably poured his heart and soul into his lay readings, but this morning's sermon was a masterpiece of heart-felt oratory – even by his standards!

However, as Brian vacated the pulpit and sat down the perceptive priest could discern from the look of sorrow in his eyes that the verses he'd closed with (from St Paul's Second Epistle to Timothy) portended something more than just an exhortation to the congregation to persevere in the faith. And where was Ruby this morning? He made a mental note to have a quiet word with this troubled member of his flock after the service.

Meanwhile, the Snakeman was in despair at the way he and his wife seemed to be drifting further apart with each passing day. Indeed, this morning there had been the delicious irony that for once it had been Brian desperately imploring Ruby *not* to board a train! His plea had gone unheeded. He'd learned of late that when Ruby resolved to do something, she could not be dissuaded. There was a delicious irony there too.

More ominously, it gnawed at him, she would be doing so in the company of that smooth-talking headmaster – a man he'd never particularly liked (and who, once or twice, he'd caught flirting with his wife). If there really was a serpent at large in Sneyd End that he should have been looking out for, then he suspected it wasn't of the genus *eunectes murinus*! Thank God Ruby would at least have his good friend Pauline by her side.

He glanced at his watch and hoped Father Allen wouldn't detain him on his way out of church. Otherwise, he accepted that what he was about to do today would be a lonely and probably futile gesture – in contrast to the protest his wife was at that very moment about to take part in (and which the organisers were hoping would help put an end to a war). Be that as it may, he took a moment to stare down at the bulging duffle bag by his feet, into which he'd crammed the things he would need. Then he looked up to marvel again at the magnificent stained-glass windows behind the altar from which Father Allen was offering the congregation the parting benediction.

To be sure, Christ had faced Calvary alone as he'd borne the sins of the world – scorned by the masses and deserted even by His friends. Brian knew the feeling. He closed his eyes in a moment of silent prayer that he might follow that example: to make a sacrifice for a forgotten railway line that one day someone in Sneyd End might thank him for saving.

* * * * *

By the time the four teachers from Sneyd End had joined it there were upwards of fifteen thousand placard-waving demonstrators packed into Trafalgar Square. Dressed starkly in a bright orange cape and sporting a white crepe headband that the communist newspaper *'Morning Star'* informed readers was 'the Vietnamese symbol of mourning', actress Vanessa Redgrave gave an impassioned address to the crowd, reading out messages of support from film directors Sidney Lumet, Michelangelo Antonioni, Alain Resnais and Richard Attenborough, as well as the philosopher and veteran peace campaigner Bertrand Russell. Somewhere in the crowd, Ruby spotted Mick Jagger.

In due course, Redgrave led the assembled rally off along Oxford Street, armed with a letter of protest that she intended to hand into the United States Embassy in Grosvenor Square.

* * * * *

All was peaceful and still – exactly as Brian had hoped. Being a Sunday, there was only the watchman on duty, relaxing in his hut over a mug of tea. Neither were there any guard dogs roaming the compound – despite the signs on the fence warning of them. Or at least none that Brian could see!

This was it! Now or never! With the site levelled and the construction machinery assembled, tomorrow morning the contractors would begin cutting the first sods to lay the foundations of the new Sneyd End Leisure Centre. It was hoped it would be completed by the time next year's all-important local elections came around. At last, Councillor Horace Bissell would be able to point to something tangible that might persuade the town's voters to rally to his beleaguered administration (which was clinging on with a majority of just one seat following Labour's disastrous showing in more recent local elections). Thereafter, the huge, brutalist monstrosity that he intended to be his political legacy would stand in the way (literally!) of ever re-laying the tracks on the town's disused railway line.

Casting an eye about, Brian took the wire cutters from his duffle bag and fashioned a hole in the compound's chain link fence that would be big enough for him to sneak inside.

* * * * *

Somehow things weren't going to plan. Aware that any confrontation between the more hot-headed, red flag-waving protesters and the phalanx of police guarding the Embassy had the potential to turn nasty, Tariq Ali – the Vietnam Solidarity

Campaign's moustachioed young Pakistani organiser – decided the letter of protest should instead be handed in at Downing Street, the march thereafter decamping to Hyde Park to listen to further speeches.

However, a small group of demonstrators had broken away from the main march, determined to head for Grosvenor Square anyway. Somewhere in the confusion, Graham Weston and his party found themselves keeping company with these more militant elements. Tension was in the air when this detachment then turned down North Audley Street into the path of the heavy police presence. Suddenly, the pushing and shoving began.

* * * * *

The cab of the tall, lattice-work crane had been conveniently left unsecured. Therefore, before the watchman had time to spot him (much less realise what was going on), Brian had padlocked the trap door behind him and was scaling the ladder that would enable him to ascend right to the top.

"Hoy! You! Come down from there!" the guy raced out of his hut and yelled, cursing and rattling the trap door in impotence.

However, it was no use. The intruder briefly halted to apologise to him before continuing up to the cab, there to tip-toe Houdini-like along the jib of the crane and tie one end of the large, home-made banner he plucked from his duffle bag. The building site hovering perilously below him, he then tiptoed back again, unfurling the banner as he did: 'SAVE OUR RAILWAY – NO LEISURE CENTRE HERE', it announced.

Meanwhile, having been tipped off by the Snakeman that something big was in the offing, a bronze-coloured Ford Cortina pulled up outside the main gate of the site. Only a consummate showman and self-publicist like Brian Danks could have tempted the reporter from the 'Sneyd End Gazette' out of bed on a Sunday morning – along with his photographer, who now leapt from the car to excitedly train his lens on the spectacle taking place in the air seventy foot above them.

* * * * *

"He's done what!"

Councillor Horace Bissell had been washing the car when his wife had rushed out from preparing the Sunday dinner to announce that there was a reporter on the telephone.

The frown of foreboding he'd worn while storming back into the house – chammy-leather in hand – quickly gave way to one of utter disbelief when he picked up the receiver, quickly morphing into fury when he was asked if he'd like to comment.

* * * * *

"HEY, HEY, LBJ! HOW MANY KIDS HAVE YOU KILLED TODAY?"

Suddenly, Ruby and Pauline were on the front line of a very different war to the one they had come intending to protest. Corralled between a hedge and the police cordon, the other demonstrators were chanting all around them.

"Fascist scum!" someone with an untidy beard hollered at the line of officers who'd linked arms to block the way.

"Defy the pigs!" some other long-haired guy grimaced.

"Imperialist lackeys! Down with capitalism!" cried Virginia Weston, rising to the fight like a latter-day Joan of Arc – a fist thrust in the air and her face contorting with righteous fury.

Meanwhile, a bottle emerged from the crowd to land within the police ranks. An officer stumbled, nursing a blooded head.

"HO-HO-HO CHI MINH! HO-HO-HO CHI MINH!"

"This is not a good place to be," said Ruby, glancing up at Graham – who for once eschewed his penchant for sweet-talking his attractive (and increasingly jittery) member of staff.

Indeed, surveying the scenes of affray that were growing uglier by the minute (and possessed of a shrewder head than his radical and impulsive wife), he agreed they needed to get out of here – and fast! However, each time they tried either the police or the surging crowd had them hemmed in on all sides.

"WHAT DO WE WANT?"

"REVOLUTION!"

"WHEN DO WE WANT IT?"

"NOW!"

* * * * *

Quite a crowd had gathered by the time PC Jonathan Hunt arrived, having been summoned over his walkie-talkie to attend to reports of some sort of protest taking place on the old station site. His helmet shielding his eyes from the low, autumnal sun, he peered up at the figure hanging out of the cab of the crane.

"Stop the building work now! It's time for our politicians to accept they're wrong – before this town regrets forever the loss of its railway!" the protester was calling down.

Jonathan's heart sank. What on Earth was Brian Danks up to now? Why, the fool was risking his life swinging about up there!

"'Ere, that's the Snakeman, ay' it?"

The anxious policeman turned to behold that a pubescent youngster on a bike had skidded to a halt alongside him. It was Robin Jukes, whose face he'd memorised. Like the other bemused onlookers, he'd turned up with his mates to see what all the fuss was about on this otherwise uneventful afternoon.

"Snakeman? He's looks more like King Kong, if you ask me!" a woman from behind piped up wittily, staring up at him with a fag dangling from her gob and her hair still in curlers.

Jonathan wasn't laughing. His friend's little escapade might be occasioning something of a carnival atmosphere down here on the ground. However, he had to get Brian down from there fast, before the joker did himself an injury – or worse!

* * * * *

Like the English archers at the Battle of Crecy, hostilities in Grosvenor Square commenced in earnest with volleys of those red flags and angry placards being launched like arrows into the police lines, felling several more officers. Then the demonstrators too linked arms and surged at their blue-uniformed adversaries.

In response, police on horseback waded into the crowd, wielding their batons. Suddenly, it was the turn of the protesters to stumble about nursing blooded heads.

* * * * *

Unable to remove the padlock that Brian had snapped on the trapdoor, the arrival on site of the foreman at last presented Jonathan with a plan of action. Starting up the digger, the foreman drove it up to the base of the crane, where he lowered the shovel so that the policeman could step inside. Then, raising it up to its maximum elevation, it was just high enough to permit the gallant copper to grab hold of the ladder and place a foot on a rung that was on the cab side of the trapdoor.

Thereupon, Jonathan commenced the task of scaling that ladder all the way to the top – no mean feat for an officer who was nervous of heights. Steeling himself not to look down at a crowd of onlookers that had by now swelled to include both the leader of the council and the chief of police, eventually he reached the cab at its summit, out of breath and nerves fraying.

"Right, what's all this then?" he panted, locking his indignant blue eyes on his best friend hunched over the controls inside.

* * * * *

More punches were thrown; and more truncheons were flailing.

At times it really did seem as if the demonstrators would pierce the police cordon and storm inside the embassy – in like manner to how Viet Cong guerrillas had stormed inside another American embassy barely nine months earlier. However, with more police reinforcements arriving, the outcome could only be the same – even if, now as then, it would be the symbolism that the forces of revolution hoped would accord them a striking victory.

* * * * *

"No, I'm not coming down. I'm staying up here until this whole ridiculous project is scrapped."

"Don't be silly," Jonathan tried reasoning. "You know that's not going to happen. You've made your point. So why don't you follow me down before we both end up getting ourselves killed."

"Not a chance. And if the Council won't listen and stop the work then I intend to go on hunger strike up here!"

Jonathan feared his best friend really had flipped this time. Maybe his judgement was addled by the parlous state of his marriage. Perhaps Brian Danks really had convinced himself that he had nothing left to lose.

Back down on the ground meanwhile, Horace Bissell was watching proceedings with mounting impatience, the butt of overheard asides about his tardy and over-budget pet project (as well as similar uncomplimentary asides from disgruntled tenants of his other brutalist legacy to the town – the abysmal, damp-streaked Tiger Street flats). And now construction was once again under threat from his most persistent gadfly – that lunatic snake handler with an axe to grind.

"Why the blazes isn't your man talking the idiot down?" he harangued Chief Superintendent Trotter again.

"I assure you, Councillor, PC Hunt is one of my best constables. That's exactly what he *is* doing. These things take time, man," the police chief rebuked him.

"Too much time!" the paunchy civic leader fumed, having meanwhile spotted reporters from the *'Express & Star'* and the *'Birmingham Evening Mail'* also rolling up to make mischief out of his humiliation.

* * * * *

Having endured the barrage of makeshift missiles that had been hurled at them, the police were in no mood to be charitable. Suddenly caught in the wrong place at the wrong moment, Pauline squealed as a burly male officer seized her with the intent of yanking her out of the crowd.

Ruby turned and instinctively grabbed hold of her friend. What's more, in the ensuing melee righteous anger gripped her and she lashed out to kick the officer in the shin. Howling with pain, he let go of Pauline, enabling Ruby to pull her back into the ranks of brawling demonstrators.

Elsewhere, having rather quixotically sat herself down in the street, Virginia Weston found herself being hastily scooped up by a pair of officers and hauled away to a waiting police van.

"Here we see an example of the brutality of the reactionary, fascist, British state!" she screamed, going through the motions of resisting arrest for the benefit of the television cameras.

"Look at the way they're mistreating me!" she cried as the two officers plonked her in the back of the van.

* * * * *

"Come on, Brian, this has gone on long enough now. I want my tea tonight!" said Jonathan, abandoning reasoning with him and attempting moral blackmail instead.

However, the protester was unmoved. Finally, the policeman's patience snapped. He lunged inside the cab, attempting to yank Brian from it. However, the Snakeman's reflexes were sharp. He leapt out onto the platform of the crane to deftly evade arrest.

In the process though, not only had the lever been jolted that caused the jib of the crane to start revolving, but Jonathan's helmet was knocked from his head, rolling off the platform to bounce with a thud on the ground below.

A sharp and voluble intake of breath hurried through the crowds watching aghast from behind the perimeter fence

* * * * *

Ruby's act of defiance in shielding her colleague had enraged the police officer, who waded in to grab her instead. Catching her by the lapels of her coat, he attempted to haul her out and make an arrest. However, he failed to spot the fist that emerged from the crowd to sock him square on the nose. That fist then grabbed Ruby and pulled her back into the safety of the throng; a fist that belonged to Graham Weston, who hurried the terrified teacher into his embrace and hugged her tight.

However, he was unable to similarly redeem Pauline, who found herself accosted by two policemen and hauled away to a waiting police van – this time with considerably less finesse than his comically histrionic wife had been treated.

* * * * *

"Stop this leisure centre! Re-open the Sneyd End railway now!" Brian's voice was hoarse from crying.

"Look, don't make me do this... please," Jonathan begged his friend, who was fulminating from the furthest point of the jib as the crane continued to slowly revolve around.

The acrophobic constable had meanwhile shinned as far along the jib as he dared. All that stood between him and certain death was seventy feet of looming fresh air.

"Leave him alone, copper. He ay' hurtin' nobody," he looked down to spot Robin Jukes catcalling him.

The motion of the revolving crane was making Jonathan giddy and causing his panoramic view of the town to shimmer in and out focus. Brian, meanwhile, was also availing himself of that vista to survey the crowds below him – some of whom were cheering him (Robin and his juvenile pals); one or two of whom were rebuking him (an embarrassed Chief Superintendent Trotter and a visibly incandescent Councillor Bissell). However, most had congregated for no better reason than to witness the most exciting thing to have happened around here since Jeff Astles had scored the winning goal in West Bromwich Albion's FA Cup victory over Everton a few months earlier – the Baggies' fifth successive win at Wembley!

16

"Kiss me."

"You what!"

"Kiss me, I said!"

Before Ruby could protest that she would do no such thing, Graham Weston had hauled her in close and was pressing his mouth to hers.

However, before she could wriggle free and slap him about the face, out of the corner of her eye she spotted a pair of bobbies making their way down Oxford Street. Twigging the nature of his expedient plan, all thought of resistance ceased. Instead she settled into the swapping of tongues. By the time the officers had drawn level, she felt guilty that she was enjoying it!

"Oh. Sorry, officers. Honeymoon," Weston chuckled, holding up the fingers of Ruby's left hand that bore the evidence.

The two policemen stared at the wedding ring, grinning at the couple in mock censure as they passed by. After all the aggro they'd put up with this afternoon, the oral peregrinations of a pair of amorous, newly-wed tourists was the least of their worries.

"Phew!" Weston breathed easy. Maybe the older man's *savoir faire* – as well as Ruby's conservative dress sense – lent them the appearance of an unlikely pair of agitprop thugs.

"Yes, well. Don't make a habit of it!" she chided him, unruffling her scrunched-up conservative outfit.

"Anyway, what are we going to do about Pauline? And your wife?" she anguished. "We need to find out which police station they've been carted off to."

"Are you kidding? And be arrested for assaulting a police officer? Both of us? That's a serious charge, you know. The worst thing they can throw at Pauline and Virginia is resisting arrest. In Pauline's case, she'd have a strong case for claiming police brutality. That's assuming her father doesn't pull strings to have any charges against her dropped!"

Callous and cowardly though his advice sounded, Graham had a point. Did Ruby really want to spend six months in prison? And forfeit her job and her reputation in the process? The day had certainly turned out to be an interesting one alright. So what was the plan of action now?

"Hopefully, they'll release them on bail after a night in the cells. In the meantime, we need to lie low for the next few hours. With luck, the TV cameras were too busy filming Virginia's arrest to capture you and me accosting that copper."

"But our return train departs soon," she glanced at her watch. "And then there's school tomorrow," she reminded him.

"I'd steer clear of railway stations right now. They'll probably be crawling with police. As for lessons tomorrow, you'll just have to phone in sick. I guess I will too. I do hope it doesn't set tongues wagging," he said with sly cheerfulness.

Ruby looked away, crestfallen. How had it ever come to this? A fugitive from justice; her best friend and chaperone in a police cell; and now she was facing the prospect of having to pass the night in the company of the lustful superior from whom Pauline was supposed to be chaperoning her. What price now skipping church to protest against that ridiculous Asian war!

"I suggest we hop on a bus. Maybe head out west and find a lodging house somewhere, where we can lie low. The most important thing is that we avoid encounters with policemen – especially ones nursing bruised shins and flattened noses!"

* * * * *

This place had a disturbing familiarity about it: the tiny window; the four bare walls; the plain table and four wooden chairs; the lawyer to his left; the two interviewing officers across the table from him. What on Earth would Ruby make of her husband being hauled down the local nick again for – of all things – assaulting a police officer?

In the end however, Jonathan had requested that the charge be dropped, explaining that the loss of his helmet over the side of the crane had been an accident. Besides which – finally moved by his friend's mounting vertiginous terror – it had been Brian who had talked and guided his pursuer down from the crane!

Enquiries complete, for now he was free to go, bailed to appear before Sneyd End magistrates in a few weeks' time on a charge of causing criminal damage to a chain link fence.

It was already late by the time Brian arrived back home. Turning the key in the lock, he entered and peered into the living room: no sign of Ruby there. No sign of Ruby elsewhere in the house either. Perhaps they were returning on a later train.

Fatigued and despondent, he slumped on the sofa, having switched the television on in time to catch news coverage of the US embassy in Grosvenor Square – where people had been brawling with police and burning American flags.

"Here we see an example of the brutality of the reactionary, fascist, British state!" some achingly-trendy, middle-aged woman in a tie-dyed bandana was screaming, clearly going through the motions of resisting arrest for the benefit of the television cameras. He gave thanks that Ruby was far too sensible to have gotten involved in such mayhem.

Instead, he craned forward and tried to spy her face amongst the main body of the march, the peaceful, law-abiding majority of the thirty thousand protesters having continued to Hyde Park to listen to speeches condemning a war that they – like Ruby – felt so strongly about.

Finally, the home secretary appeared in front of the cameras, the bluff, avuncular Jim Callaghan touring the serried police ranks, thanking officers for their discipline and restraint.

"I doubt if this kind of demonstration could have taken place so peacefully in any other part of the world," he commented upon the self-control shown by the protesters.

On that comforting note – and having himself experienced more than enough excitement for one day – Brian Danks retired to bed to await the return home of his wife.

* * * * *

She was growing more fricative with each spirited insertion that he made. Such boisterous sex was rendered more voluble by a bed that had squeaked incessantly throughout their frenetic conjugation; and the whole experience more voluble still by someone in the room across the hall playing Cream's *'White Room'* at full volume!

Soon enough it was Jimi Hendrix's *'Voodoo Child'* that was cranking out corybantic guitar solos to serenade his involuntary grunting and her ecstatic wailing. Mutual release accomplished, their sweaty exertions ceased. Silence descended upon the room (the hard rock aficionado in the other room having also put his record collection away for the night).

Peace at last! Removing the pillow from around her ears, Ruby Danks sat up to place one of them against the wall. Whoever the woman in the adjoining room had invited into her bed plainly didn't believe in post-coital affection. In its place, Ruby discerned the door to their room open, followed by footsteps that thudded across the landing. A few seconds later she caught the sound of this young man aiming a powerful jet of piddle into the toilet bowl before rounding off his relief with a loud fart and a flush of the chain! Whatever happened to the 'love' in all this 'free love' business? Did intelligent young women really allow themselves to be used in this way?

Instead of slipping away by bus out west of the city, there had been a drastic change of plan. It was while taking five in a bar amidst the neon-lit fleshpots of Soho that Graham and Ruby had perchance bumped into some sympathetic students from the nearby LSE with whom they'd shared their tale. Thus, in an act of revolutionary solidarity, the youngsters had kindly offered to put the two teachers up for the night at their communal digs, which were located up a back street on the far side of Pentonville Road.

Imagine the students' surprise then when these two 'cool cats' requested to be permitted to sleep in separate rooms; or at least the younger and primmer 'cat' had! Perhaps the sexual revolution had yet to reach this strange place called 'the Black Country'.

Thus it was that Ruby had successfully secured a room of her own in which to sleep – though, in the event, sleep had proved impossible with all that copulating and freaking out going on in the adjacent rooms. She clicked on the light and sat up in bed to study her watch. It was one o'clock in the morning.

Just then there was a faint knock on the door.

"Come in," she nervously acknowledged, clutching at the bed sheet and gathering it to her bosom.

Around the door there appeared a head of dark hair and a familiar handsome face – the bare hirsute torso to which they were attached emerging with them. In his hands, Graham Weston was bearing two mugs of steaming coffee.

"I presumed you might be having trouble sleeping too," he smiled, placing one of the mugs on the chipped bedside table. "Therefore, I had a root around and discovered some milk and coffee in the kitchen. You take two sugars, don't you?"

Though affecting to be chary of this semi-naked nocturnal visitation, Ruby nodded – though masking the forbidden thrill of being semi-naked herself beneath that sheet.

"Alors regardez! Je me suis souvenu!" he beamed with the usual mien of self-satisfaction he paraded when waxing Gallic.

"How can anyone possibly sleep amidst the things that go on in this place!" she cussed in response.

He took the liberty of seating himself down upon the bed and taking a sip from the coffee he'd brewed. She shuffled her legs out of the way, feigning umbrage and gripping the sheet a little tighter as he answered her rhetorical question.

"I'm afraid that by insisting on having your own room you've rather upset our hosts' domestic arrangements. And forced the usual occupant of the bed you're in to relocate to someone else's bed instead. Not that I think she minded. And, by the sound of things, neither did the guy whose bed she's relocated to!"

Unwilling to dwell on promiscuous behaviour that was alien to her, Ruby reached over to take hold of the other mug, her free hand still nursing that sheet to her bare chest.

"You don't have to be quite so prudish, you know," Weston found her precaution amusing.

The affronted glint in her eyes told him she was still wrestling with the knowledge that he fancied her – and that (though she'd yet to admit it) the feeling was mutual. Perhaps clinging to that sheet was one last token act of resistance before she finally surrendered to him. Otherwise, her determination to play hard to get had only whetted his appetite even more.

"I'm a married woman," she fell back upon a stubborn mantra, alarmed by the priapic glint in *his* eyes. No less perturbing was his seeming indifference to the fate of his wife, who was still banged up in a police cell somewhere. It prompted Ruby to add for good measure, "And you're a married man!"

Despite the rebuff, he remained optimistic.

"What's marriage?" he shrugged dismissively. "According to Virginia and her feminist friends, it's a bourgeois construct – a euphemism for what is essentially legalised prostitution."

"And is that your view? Is your marriage just 'legalised prostitution'?" she put him on the spot, appalled.

He thought for a moment.

"Being married has its benefits. After all, school governing bodies can be a bit leery about appointing head teachers who co-habit with their 'partners'!" he noted cynically. "Joking aside though, Virginia and I do love each other – although it's not a soppy, fairy tale kind of love: all that silliness about there being 'someone out there for each of us' when what one is really doing is projecting one's hopes and expectations onto another person – and in the process setting oneself up for disappointment. Alas, if only real life was that simple!" he chuckled sadly.

"That said, sometimes two people who share a sexual chemistry will also be fortunate to discover that they share other things in common too – like an interest in art, or jazz, or politics. I guess that describes Virginia and me. However, our love isn't a possessive thing. That's another repressive bourgeois notion. After all, doesn't the New Testament say of the early disciples that 'none of them regarded his possessions as his own; but they had all things in common'?"

It was an interesting misinterpretation of Scripture, Ruby sniffed, though hearing this *flâneur* out as he elaborated further.

"Besides, does anybody really 'love' anyone anyway? Or are each of us, at heart, sojourning with the people we 'love' for the benefits we derive from being with them – socially, sexually or financially? If so, isn't 'love' just another transaction we undertake to get through life? Like servicing the car? Or paying the rent? Otherwise, and in answer to your question, Virginia and I have what might nowadays be called an 'open marriage'. She does her thing; I do mine – if you get my drift. So long as no one gets hurt, where's the problem?"

She got his drift alright. It left her more appalled still.

"So, having been candid about my marriage, Ruby, how about you be candid about yours. For a start, it plainly isn't working, is it. I sense the heartache is outweighing the benefit," he asserted.

"For that reason, I'd hazard a guess that you're no longer in 'love' with Brian, are you. Understandable, I guess. It sounds like he's not an easy chap to live with."

"Maybe he isn't," she admitted, clutching that sheet in her fist. "But he is still my husband. Besides, love is more than a feeling. Love is an act of will; an act of self-sacrifice. You might not get to choose who you fall in love with – that 'soppy, fairy tale kind of love', as you dismiss it; but you *do* make a choice to carry on loving them – even when it hurts; even when it seems hopeless. 'For better, for worse; for richer, for poorer; in sickness and in health', she defiantly repeated the vows she'd taken.

However, to her relentless pursuer it was just one more valiant attempt to rationalise her disillusionment; one more act of self-flagellation for the sake of those vows; and for her faith too – for Christians had this thing about love being self-sacrificial.

"That's very noble," Weston conceded. "However, are you 'carrying on' because you really believe in all that 'till death us do part' crap? Or is it because you can conceive of no way out of your situation? Don't get me wrong, Ruby: it breaks my heart to observe your pain and your frustration. How the idealism of your own 'fairy tale' marriage – no doubt in the beginning leavened with electrifying sex – has given way to soul-crushing emptiness. Yet you owe it to yourself to break free, my pretty one. After all, as Nietsche once observed – and as your husband would surely attest – 'the snake that cannot cast its skin perishes'."

The cunning head teacher had masterfully decrypted her thoughts. He stared her out until she dipped her gaze in shame, following up his observation with its corollary.

"So why don't you let me slip into that bed and remind you how electrifying it can be to have sex with someone you desire."

She looked up to present him with a lump bobbing guiltily in her throat. This was the first time during his patient three-year wooing of her that he'd been this direct. Neither could she disguise that he was right: like many young women – in her case, fuelled by a faith that lauded marriage as the noblest expression of sexual love – she'd entered into hers with enough idealism and commitment to offset the misgivings she'd harboured about Brian's more bizarre idiosyncrasies. Yet how much longer was she willing to contend for that marriage when it was indeed assailing her with feelings of 'soul-crushing emptiness'?

"Ye adulterers and adulteresses, know ye not that the friendship of the world is enmity with God? Whosoever therefore will be a friend of the world is the enemy of God," she clung to the Scriptures, as well as to that sheet. To be sure, her weekend in the capital had been a fiasco; but it need not be an irreparable one. Was she willing to just meekly submit to the advances of this man who represented everything that was worldly and exciting; yet almost certainly dangerous and destructive?

"God is faithful, who will not suffer you to be tempted above that ye are able; but will with the temptation also make a way to escape, that ye may be able to bear it," she further recalled the words of the Apostle Paul in First Corinthians. The way of escape was still within her gift: it was time to politely, but firmly tell Graham Weston to rise from her bed and depart her room – as she realised she should have done at the outset. All she had to do was say the word. Inexplicably, it was a word she shied from uttering.

Hastening to make her mind up for her, he placed his coffee on the table and leant forward to tenderly offer her a reprise of the kiss they'd exchanged the previous evening. Now, as then, once the initial astonishment had passed, she settled into it without demurring. In fact, it felt liberating – as she feared it would.

Eyes closed – and without breaking from that probing kiss – she laid her own mug aside to place one hand upon his shoulder. With the other hand, she then ran her delicate fingers through his luxuriant grey-black mane. With a hand no longer free to grip that sheet it slipped. Whereupon a more rugged hand moved in to cup one of her pert little breasts and caress it.

The ratchet clicked again and locked tight. The seduction of Ruby Elizabeth Danks was complete.

17

As well as being fined ten pounds for the damage to the fence of the construction site, Sneyd End magistrates ordered Brian Danks bound over from interfering with the building of the new leisure centre. Meanwhile, lest he try his luck at some similar stunt on the remaining land it owned (and mindful of the other unfortunate things that had gone on in there), British Rail had taken the precaution of installing sturdy metal gates across the entrances to the Sneyd End Tunnel. There would be no more using it as a short cut beneath the town; nor for any other illicit purpose.

Or so they'd thought. However, it was just too convenient a facility for all those things for those railings to remain in place for long. Soon enough, gaps had appeared in them just big enough for a man to slip through. After all, that extensive perimeter fence had never yet kept people from trespassing over Fens Bank!

In amongst all the swathes of pre-cast concrete that were going into construction of the new leisure centre, there were still bricks to be laid here and there. Therefore, on this cold day in early November, another lorry load of the things had just arrived on the old station site. As it was his first week on the job, it fell to young Kevin Wood to undertake the ball-breaking job of unloading it, stacking the bricks in piles so that they were to hand for the older guys to cement in place. If he was up to tasks like this, then the foreman of the gang had promised that the lads would teach the school leaver the tricks of their trade. Then one day he too could become a master bricklayer like them. In the meantime, the new boy took a few moments to rest from his labour, leaning on his hod to survey what had been built so far.

"Come on, Woody, put some muscle into it, like," the foreman spotted him slacking and badgered him.

"Arr'. Otherwise we'm gunna' brick yow' up inside the old tunnel with the giant snake," said one of the other guys, pointing to its southern entrance visible in the distance. He winked at the other brickies as they glanced up.

"Wot' snake?" Woody puzzled anxiously, wide eyes flitting about the gang of grinning brickies.

"Nah, there ay' no snake in there. Yow'm havin' me on! Everyone knows that's just a story put about to scare kids," he shook his head, relieved.

Ah, well. It had been worth it just to wind the youngster up. Woody accepted that, as the new boy, he was going to have to put up with a certain amount of japing as the price of being accepted by his workmates. It didn't help that, being only five feet three inches and thin as a rake, some of them remained sceptical about whether he possessed the necessary brawn to be a builder. He guessed he'd just have to work harder to prove himself. This he now did, balancing a few more bricks in his hod and teetering over to where the lads were busily at work.

Having earned their lunch break, come twelve o'clock nothing was going to keep them from the daily detour to the pub. Being unmistakably underage though, Woody wouldn't be joining them. Instead, he was left to huddle up alone in the site hut – there to munch on the spam sandwiches his mom had made him. He consoled himself that, by the time his eighteenth birthday came around, as well as being a master bricklayer he would also be able to join his mates downing a refreshing pint in the 'Pig & Whistle'.

Sandwiches consumed, having fed sustenance in one end Woody now felt the pressing need to expel it from the other. Therefore, in need of somewhere private and peaceful where he could 'turn his bike around' – and with the Portaloo once again rancid and overflowing – he grabbed a Tilley lamp from the site hut and trekked off towards that tunnel entrance, just a few hundred yards up the old track bed.

Like most youngsters of his age, Woody had gotten up to things inside the Sneyd End Tunnel too. Indeed, a popular rite of passage at school had been to dare friends to walk its entire length alone, armed with just a torch, hoping that the batteries would last; and that (as older boys took delight in regaling hesitant new initiates) one wouldn't encounter either the 'giant snake' or the ghosts of those dead miners along the way. Having completed this rite himself – and dared others – the tunnel therefore held no particular fear for the young Kevin Wood.

Or so he thought. Squeezing through the gap in the railings (British Rail should have employed the lads to *brick* it up instead, he chuckled), it was as eerie as it had ever been. He stared up at the glow the Tilley lamp cast across a tunnel roof that was still lined with soot from the trains that had once traversed it. Here and there water could be seen trickling down the sides. And though he couldn't see them, he could hear those legendary giant rats scurrying about in the darkness.

Of course, it was warm in here too – a humid, enervating heat that (along with his churning bowels) bade Woody remove his hefty donkey jacket. Laying it aside on a convenient sleeper, he lowered his trousers and squatted down to get on with the job he'd wandered in here to do.

* * * * *

Sneyd End High School was in shock. This was the third time that one of its pupils or recent ex-pupils had mysteriously gone missing. Gary Willetts; Gillian Hickman; and now Kevin Wood had all vanished, and no one – least of all Sneyd End Police – had the faintest idea what had happened to them. And then there remained the still unexplained death of Emily Ashmore.

Dismissing silly stories doing the rounds in class about them having been consumed by a 'giant snake', Ruby and her fellow teaching staff had redoubled their efforts to caution pupils about the perils of trespassing over Fens Bank or messing about in that old railway tunnel. Knowing the unspeakable things those Moors Murderers had done to their young victims in Manchester, there was every temptation to fear the worst.

Then, on November 16th, there came a breakthrough: Raymond Morris – a thirty-nine-year-old factory worker from Walsall – was arrested for the attempted abduction of one schoolgirl and the murder of another. Though he refused to confess, Morris remained the prime suspect in the murders of several other youngsters from the Black Country whose bodies had been discovered buried on the moors of nearby Cannock Chase. Suddenly, there was relief amongst Sneyd End Police that their colleagues in Walsall had apprehended someone who might be linked to the disappearance of their youngsters too.

Meanwhile, it was requiring every ounce of professionalism she possessed for Ruby to deal with a more personal rumour doing the rounds in the school. Though nothing was ever said, she could tell that other members of staff suspected she'd been carrying on with its head teacher. Likewise, though Brian could never bring himself to mention it, he too surely suspected she'd strayed during that eventful weekend in London. Perhaps it was written all over her face – in the way that she declined to go forward and take Sunday communion, spending most of the church service staring at the floor; or in the guilt she felt each time she was in the same room with her husband (but which, paradoxically, at least made her more forgiving of his own shortcomings). Perhaps saying nothing was a way of stringing out her mental torture. Or perhaps Brian Danks really couldn't deal with the thought that his wife might have dallied with another man, preferring instead to just blank it from his mind.

However, in addition to those feelings of guilt and shame, she soon found herself having to contend with feelings of rage too. A new arts teacher called Millicent Ferriday (or Millie, as she insisted colleagues call her) had started at Sneyd End High School in the autumn of 1968, fresh out of the teacher training college in Dudley. As well as being as flirty as they came, the bubbly twenty-three-year-old blonde also helped with girls' PE lessons. It was presumably the combination of the youthful Miss Ferriday's forwardness and her ability to look cracking in gym shorts and a vest top that caught the lustful eye of Graham Weston. Suddenly, Ruby found herself dropped like a stone – as if whatever she and Weston had briefly had going had never happened. Having chalked up another notch on the bedpost that was his 'open marriage' the ratchet had been released to begin the task of locking instead upon another victim.

* * * * *

"Is she up to pressure yet?" Jonathan called up, returning along the track from the signal box.

"Not quite," Cledwyn hung out of the cab and assured him.

This was a landmark moment – well, at least for three grown men who'd committed almost as many years of their spare time to stripping down and restoring the beloved old engine. Repainted in her original Great Western Railway livery, '6418' was about to make her maiden voyage upon the restored rural railway that was her new home. Her firebox was aglow (thanks to Brian furiously shovelling coal) and her boiler was working up steam. Meanwhile, here and there wisps of that steam were swirling from around her wheels and pistons – as if to signal her impatience to put on a show for them.

"Everyone aboard!" the cry eventually went up.

Jonathan clambered up the steps to join Brian and Cled on the footplate, along with Jim Plant – the retired locomotive engineer at her controls, who the restoration team had been pleased to welcome to their ranks, along with his invaluable driving skills.

With a tug on her whistle, he watched for the signalman to acknowledge him and to pull the requisite levers to switch points and drop signals. Upon which – after another, longer blast on the whistle – Jim opened the throttle. There followed a crescendo of loud huffs, plumes of smoke issuing from her funnel. Slowly, but then with gathering pace, '6418' began to grind forward under her own steam – literally and metaphorically.

Brian, Jonathan and Cled hugged and congratulated each other tearfully. Out of the engine shed and into the pale winter sunshine the little pannier engine emerged, trundling down the siding and past the signalman, who was waving back at them. Just a few seconds more and she had rattled over the points to head off down the line as it shadowed a silent, swollen River Severn.

"I never thought I'd live to see this moment," Cledwyn sobbed melodramatically above the din of her machinery. With Jonathan taking a turn at shovelling, Brian was able to peer out the cab at '6418' chugging her way over bridges, along embankments, and in and out of tunnels and cuttings. This wonderful old locomotive had come back from the dead.

The analogy left him pondering whether his marriage to Ruby might yet experience a similar joyful resurrection. To be sure, he recognised now the true cost of his obsession with saving the

Sneyd End railway. Furthermore, with the leisure centre well on its way to completion, he'd reluctantly conceded too that his six-year war of attrition to save it had been in vain. Perhaps it was time to accept instead the crumb of comfort that was the salvation of one of the locomotives that had once worked the line. Smiling at his colleagues to mask the pain, he gazed out again at the passing countryside and prayed anew that Ruby could forgive him – as he indeed stood ready to forgive her and put the mistakes of the past behind them.

* * * * *

It appeared that Graham Weston's latest seduction project would require rather less time and patience to wrap up than his last.

Drifting out onto the car park at the end of another long day in the classroom, Ruby found herself confronted by the sight of this cynical love rat opening the door to his little sports car so that Millie Ferriday could hop inside. No less galling was the eyeful of her gorgeous thighs that this mini-skirt-clad floozy was consciously treating him to as she manoeuvred them into the footwell. Complemented by those white, calf-length leather boots she was wearing, no wonder the lads in school would loiter at the foot of stairwells to similarly catch an eyeful whenever she passed on her way to and from lessons. Whatever happened to the dress code for staff, Ruby fumed!

"Off somewhere nice, are we?" she bitchily enquired upon passing by on the way to her own car.

"Just offering a member of staff a lift home," Weston glanced across at her and explained.

The very sight of those bright blue eyes attempting to convey innocence made Ruby quiver – this time in a very different manner to how they'd done not so many weeks back.

"Yes, I suppose it is a bit nippy this afternoon to be waiting about at bus stops," she sneered. "More so when one is wearing an outfit like that!" she observed for Millie's benefit, the blousy young arts teacher returning her contemptuous stare.

"I suppose too that it's the mark of an extremely chivalrous man to *just* offer lifts to a member of staff when *he* lives in

Wolverhampton and *she* lives in Dudley," she added for good measure, retraining her embittered gaze upon her former lover.

Neither of them deigned to respond to such a patently resentful barb. Instead, Weston closed the car door and strode around the other side, staring regretfully at his one-time plaything before jumping in and starting the car up.

Having splendidly made her point, Ruby consoled herself that Graham Weston was no longer worth the waste of her time and breath – if indeed he ever had been.

However, the gleam of satisfaction lasted only until she had jumped into her own car. Watching Weston speed away in the company of his latest prospective *inamorata*, she rested her head onto the steering wheel and began to cry.

* * * * *

"Morning, Constable."

"Morning, Bob. Up bright and early, as usual."

Dawn was bleaching the darkness from the eastern skyline and the streets were deserted – save for Bob the Milkman doing the rounds on his float. Being treated to his usual cheerful greeting was the welcome herald that it was time for a weary PC Jonathan Hunt to head back to the station after a long night shift.

Just then though the tranquillity was broken by a dull crump that echoed off the surrounding buildings, followed by a loud crashing sound.

"That was an explosion," Jonathan cocked his ear instinctively.

Sure enough, the copper turned about to observe that a huge plume of dust was rising to envelop the Tiger Street flats. Meanwhile, Bob had jumped from his float to stare up, appalled.

"Quick! Get in and drive!" Jonathan ordered him, pointing in the direction of the estate and diving into the passenger side of the cab. This Bob did, turning the float around, and hitting the accelerator for all he was worth.

"Victor Control, Victor Control, this is Victor One-Five," the policeman yelled into his two-way radio, "Am proceeding to Tiger Street, where there appears to have been some kind of explosion. Request ambulance and fire brigade support. Over."

"Can't you make this thing go any faster?" he broke to berate the milkman.

"I'm giving it all it's got! It's a bloody milk float!" Bob pleaded as he steered his whining steed down the back streets.

When the little float did eventually reach the scene – by which time that dust cloud had settled – the true extent of what had happened was apparent. Jonathan leapt from the cab, horror-struck that an entire flank of Mayflower House – one of the estate's two colossal tower blocks – had vanished! From beneath his helmet he gazed up at the vista of severed concrete walls and water cascading down that torn flank from ruptured pipes. Whatever had occasioned the explosion had caused every room on that corner of the block to collapse and pancake down to the ground in a mound of twisted debris. Surely no one who'd been asleep in those rooms had stood a chance. Meanwhile, the first dazed survivors of the blast were emerging from the main entrance in their slippers and nightclothes to also gaze in disbelief at what was left of their block.

"Help me! Help me!" he heard a woman's voice shrieking.

Everyone looked up to behold the middle-aged woman in her nightdress, who was balancing on what was left of the floor panel next to an exposed doorway. She was staring down in terror at the forty foot of fresh air that was all that divided her from her fellow residents now gaping up in horror from the street.

"Stay where you are! I'm coming up!" Jonathan yelled – though it was plain that, with only the tiniest platform to balance upon, the petrified woman was going nowhere. That said, with flakes of masonry tumbling from around her every time she shuffled on her perch it was possible she could find herself arriving on the ground before he could reach her.

Jonathan fought his way up the stairwell, past more terrified residents making their way down to safety. Upon reaching the fourth floor, he thought he could detect ominous creaking and groaning noises emanating from the floors above him. Indeed, who could tell whether the force of the explosion might have weakened the structure enough to send what remained of Mayflower House crashing down.

He peered through the letterbox of the flat to observe the dawn sky intruding into what would otherwise have been a darkened hallway. He could only assume that, disorientated by the explosion, the poor woman must have run into the kitchen, not realising that it was no longer there (yet luckily having grabbed hold of something just in time to avoid falling to her death).

Hearing her frantic cries, he tried the handle of the front door. No surprise, it was locked. Bashing unsuccessfully at the door with his shoulder, he took several paces backwards along the corridor and ran at it instead, the heel of his stout, size-ten policeman's shoe impacting hard upon it. A few more such kicks and the door burst open at last. He raced down the corridor to halt at the looming precipice where once the kitchen had been. Staring down at the first fire engine arriving in the street below, he came over all bilious – again. Why did he get to respond to all the incidents that involved working at such giddy heights?

The pitiful state of the woman still balancing on that ledge galvanised his thoughts and banished his phobia – or at least tempered it with an awareness of duty and compassion.

"You're okay, love. Listen, I'm going to stretch out my hand. I want you to take hold of it and allow me to draw you back to where I am," he explained, stepping onto the ledge to reach across to her while gripping the door lintel with his other hand.

"No! I can't!" she sobbed, more bits of masonry descending from the ledge as she clung to the spot, shivering.

"Yes, you can. What's your name?" he enquired, offering her a reassuring smile.

"M-m-mary. Mary P-p-pritchard," she sobbed again, feebly returning that smile.

"Listen, Mary. The firemen are here and will get you down," he replied, pointing to them readying their ladder. "Was there anybody else in the flat with you?" he needed to know.

"M-m-my d-d-daughter, Susan. She was… she…" she stuttered before coming over distraught and tearful again.

"Shhh! Stay calm! Stay calm!"

Hauling himself back along the ledge, he left Mrs Pritchard's rescue to the more experienced hands of the fire crews. Instead, he ducked back inside the flat to fling open every door in the search for her daughter. However, there was no sign of her anywhere – including in the bedroom that was adorned with posters of The Kinks, The Hollies, The Tremeloes, and The Monkees (and which clearly indicated it belonged to a teenager). Perhaps the girl had fled down the stairs already.

He re-emerged through the kitchen door to observe the ladder being swung into place, the fireman at its pinnacle having taken on the task of reassuring the woman. With just enough reach to extend to within a few inches of her, he began the invidious task of coaching her to forsake the dubious safety of that ledge and accept his hand of rescue. After some hesitation, this Mary eventually did – the crowds below letting out an audible collective gasp as she flung herself across the divide and into her rescuer's waiting arms.

* * * * *

"Councillor Bissell, do you have anything to say about…"

"Councillor Bissell, what is the Council's response to…"

As he made his way up the steps to the Council House, the portly leader of Sneyd End Borough Council was assailed by a jostling mob of reporters and cameramen – all of whom knew exactly where to find the man who was suddenly at the apex of a breaking political storm. He also found himself bathed in a myriad of popping flashbulbs. Why, there were even camera crews from national television joining in the scrum.

"Gentleman, gentleman," he cried, gesturing for order. "I am about to meet with the Chief Housing Officer and we will be issuing a statement shortly. In the meantime, my thoughts are with the victims of this terrible tragedy."

"Councillor Bissell, what do you say to angry residents who are blaming the use of poor-quality materials for what happened at Mayflower House?" another hack interjected.

"Look, let's not jump to hasty conclusions. The first indications are that it was a…"

"Councillor Bissell," someone else butted in. "How do you respond to the charge being levelled that you personally received kickbacks from building contractors for awarding…"

"I reject that accusation completely!" the Leader turned and fired the journalist a livid stare, the man jolted back a pace upon receiving an irate finger jabbed in his shoulder. "And if your miserable rag even dares to print such a scurrilous libel then I will sue it for every penny in the bank!"

"Councillor Bissell, what do you say to those people in your own party who are now openly calling for you to quit?" another hack thought he'd have a go.

Horace Bissell had heard enough. Employing his considerable bulk to angrily bulldoze the reporters aside, at last he made it to the doors to the building, though accompanied by more flashbulbs popping. He hastened inside as the curator shoved his press pursuers away to bolt the doors shut behind him. Straightening a hat and coat that were skewwhiff from the mobbing, the Leader stormed up the steps that led to his opulent first floor office.

"Where's the Borough Architect?" he burst through the door to breathlessly harangue his hapless young secretary.

"He's at a conference in London today," she replied, the lump oscillating in her throat a hint that she was readying herself for another of her boss's blistering, volcanic outbursts.

"Then find him!"

"Find him?" she gulped again.

"Yes, you stupid woman! I said find him! I don't care where he is or what he's doing. Get him to a telephone and tell him I want him back up in Sneyd End on the very next train. Tell him we've got a crisis on our hands!"

* * * * *

She'd never realised how much that school and its pupils really meant to her. Taking from the sideboard the large album in which she kept all the final year photographs she'd appeared in, Ruby sat down on the sofa to study it anew.

Some of the faces she picked out as she flicked the pages she could never forget as long as she lived: from the Year of '66 she spotted the bushy mane of Emily Ashmore – swept back over a head full of hopeless dreams, her uncertain smile emblematic of the pain and disappointment of her tragically short life.

Other faces carried more tenuous memories: there was Gary Willetts from the Year of '64 snarling at the camera (as was his doltish sidekick: Wayne Fisher). Was the thuggish skinhead still on the run from police because of his hand in Emily's death? Or had he also somehow fallen victim to whatever (or whoever) was behind this strange and worrying prevalence of premature mortality amongst the youngsters she'd once taught.

Turning the page, for example, there was Kevin Wood staring back at her from the Year of '68. Truth to tell, not the sharpest intellect she'd ever come across. However, beseeching God in His Heaven, she yearned to know what this jovial and good-natured young lad had ever done to suffer the fate of just 'disappearing'. Likewise, Gillian Hickman (Ruby's gaze roaming the press cuttings about her disappearance that she'd filed inside the album). She began to wonder how many more of her pupils might similarly have 'disappeared' when the time came for the Year of '69 to pose for their group leaving photograph!

Meanwhile, the surviving faces in those serried group photographs brought back a wealth of other memories to this teacher who'd tried her best to purvey knowledge and instil self-worth in a large and, at times, unruly secondary school.

There was Mark Randall and Adrian Cooper from the Year of '67 – along with the girl she'd caught them scrapping over that day in the boys' toilets: Deborah Watson. Ruby had lost count of the times she'd had to reprove the flighty young lass for turning around in class and chatting to her mates. At least on the day this leaving photograph had been taken she had made an exception and was facing the front with a proud smile on her face!

By the time she'd moved along the row of girls to pick out a more pertinent face from that year, the front door had opened: Brian had arrived home from work. Hanging up his coat in the hall, he wondered whether today – at last – it might be safe to venture small talk with his distant and resentful wife. Then he noticed her sat on the sofa in the living room, legs tucked under her bottom, sobbing over something that was resting in her lap.

He gently eased himself down beside her, trailing a hand along her neck and shoulders. For once she didn't pull away, permitting him to rest it there. With his other hand, he poked his glasses back up his nose and craned in to see whose face in the photograph album her finger had alighted upon.

"That was Susan Pritchard," she snuffled.

"I know. It's fortunate she was the only victim of the blast – if fortunate is the right word," he apologised, for once remarkably attuned to his wife's sensibilities. "The fire investigators think she must have wandered into the kitchen to make a cup of tea for her mother, lit the stove, and ignited the gas leak. The resulting explosion not only destroyed the kitchen but caused every other kitchen above to collapse down on top of it. Had it not been so early in the morning – with most residents of Mayflower House still in bed – many more people could have lost their lives."

"She was the most wonderful pupil I ever taught," Ruby wept. "She'd set her heart on going to university and becoming a doctor. To think that a girl from a broken home, who lived in a council flat on one of the roughest estates in town, was all set to succeed at such a thing! And now she's dead – and we will never know what she might have achieved with her life. Why does God allow good people to die? Why, oh why, oh why?" she pleaded with her husband, tilting her tearful face against his chest.

The lay preacher had no answer. He could have referred his sorrowful wife to the sermon he'd preached the other day about the Tower of Siloam – a shoddily-built tall building in Jesus's day that had collapsed, also claiming innocent lives for no particular rhyme or reason. Instead, he just held her tight and permitted her to carry on venting her despair.

"Why does God allow such evil things to happen? Why does He allow us to do evil things to each other? Why have *I* done evil things when all I ever wanted to be was a loving wife – and to be an example to the young people I teach?" her plea suddenly became more emphatically personal. "Why have I failed you, Brian; and them; and everyone else who ever looked to me? Why have I betrayed my faith? And rendered both it and me a laughing stock? Why? Why? Why?"

He was trying hard not to cry himself, aware that mourning Susan Pritchard's death was a foil to Ruby for something else that had been tormenting her.

"But you *are* an example to them, Ruby. You're an outstanding teacher," he hugged and assured her.

But not a loving wife? Guilt-stricken by the absence of that reassurance, she sat up straight to implore him.

"Don't you ever just wish you could go back to a more innocent time," she pined. "Maybe even into your mother's womb – some lost idyll before you became conscious of sin? Before you became conscious of *your own sin*? It's why that expression 'innocent children' always makes me laugh," the twenty-eight-year-old teacher hissed scornfully. "I don't ever remember a time as a child when I was truly 'innocent'. In fact, as I grew older I just became more conscious of my sin.

"It's why when I first gave my life to Christ and read St Paul's letter to Timothy – where he tells us *'Christ Jesus came into the world to save sinners, of whom I am the chief'* – I used to think it was religious hyperbole. Surely the man through whom God spoke some of the Bible's most awesome words couldn't be the 'chief sinner'! Likewise, John Bunyan entitling his autobiography *'Grace Abounding To The Chief Of Sinners'*; or when John Wesley preached *'I the chief of sinners am, but Jesus died for me'*; and when his brother Charles, the hymnist, penned *'that Thou such mercies has bestowed on me, the chief of sinners, me!'*. But they are *all* wrong, I wanted to scream: *I* am the 'chief of sinners', Brian! Me! Me! Me!" she wailed.

"Ruby, we are *all* sinners; you, me, your 'innocent' pupils – and your not-so-innocent teaching colleagues too," he dared to point out. "In fact, if we're honest, it's a toss-up who amongst us is the 'chief'! But keep not from sowing because of the birds: we can only do our best in the strength God grants us; trying to overcome evil with good; trying to overcome *our own* innate evil by reflecting His goodness in our lives. You and I have *both* been trying to do that in our own different ways – to make a stand for what is just and right. And we have both made mistakes along the way. Yet we must keep on making a stand for justice and righteousness not because we think we can thereby please God and somehow earn *His* love; but rather because Christ loved us first and, through His atoning sacrifice on the Cross, has forgiven us and set us free from the wrath our mistakes deserve. By His example, He now implores us to forgive others who have made mistakes too – including each other," he insisted, employing a gentle finger to lift her chin so that, encouraged, she might gaze into his moistening eyes.

Noticing the Bible she'd left open on the coffee table, he momentarily eased away from her to reach across and leaf through the Old Testament to a verse in the Book of Joel…

> *"Therefore also now, saith the LORD, turn ye even to Me with all your heart, and with fasting, and with weeping, and with mourning. And rend your heart, and not your garments, and turn unto the LORD your God: for He is gracious and merciful, slow to anger, and of great kindness, and repenteth him of the evil,"*

Granting Ruby a moment to reflect upon those words, he skipped some more pages to read from Paul's Epistle to the Philippians in the New Testament…

> *"But this one thing I do, forgetting those things which are behind, and reaching forth unto those things which are before, I press toward the mark for the prize of the high calling of God in Christ Jesus."*

Ruby managed a faint smile. Perhaps the season for mourning 'those things which are behind' had passed. Perhaps it was time to forgive each other – as Brian had urged. However, before she did there were some words on her own heart that she knew it was incumbent upon her to say out loud in his presence.

"I'm sorry, Brian," she confessed. "I was a fool to believe that the things of this world – no matter how beguiling – can ever satisfy like walking in a right relationship with God. And I was certainly a fool for believing that any man – no matter how superficially charming – could ever love me as much as you do. I don't deserve to be forgiven for thinking that."

It was an allusion to a 'mistake' that even Brian was not so obtuse that he couldn't recognise. Graciously, he smiled – even as he was snuffling apologetically himself.

"Not half as much a fool as I've been," he admitted. "Neither do I deserve to be forgiven for the way I so often assumed you would just fall in line with my campaigning. Therefore, I can understand why, so many times, you must have thought I didn't really love you. That I was more concerned about saving a confounded railway line! However, I do love you, Ruby. So if you can forgive me, then know that I forgive you too."

For a few moments no further words passed between them. With Ruby resting her head against his, they enjoyed the sensation of being reconciled with the other. In due course, they spontaneously stared into the other's eyes, blossoming forgiveness compelling them to fashion their lips for the softest of kisses – a second such kiss progressing into something more passionate. Their lips still searching out each other, together they slipped backwards into the sofa's embrace.

Then, just as she was getting him going, she broke to sit up and look him in the eye again.

"Anyway, what makes you think that I objected to you campaigning?" she offered him a mischievous frown. "If anything, it was rather that I believed there were more worthwhile things that you and I should have championed together."

"You mean like opposing that war in Vietnam?" he surmised, recalling her indignant rants at the nightly television news.

Maybe not: he watched as she glanced away for a moment – as if to ponder her reply.

"No. But as it happens," she faced him again and hinted, "today there is a cause out there that an awful lot of people feel very strongly about – including me. Moreover, it's a cause which is crying out for someone in this town to take up; to stand up for what is 'just and right', as you put it. Now, were you to direct your passion and your eloquence into a cause like that then you *know* you could count on my full and unstinting support."

18

It's the four-yearly ritual that every politician dreads – even if, in the case of the Leader of Sneyd End Borough Council, seeking re-election for his seat on the council was usually a mere formality.

Thus it was that Horace Bissell now found himself sharing a bench with his dutiful wife in the waiting room of the Borough's electoral registration office, having earlier handed in the signed nomination papers that would enable his name to be entered on the ballot to contest the Sneyd Central ward.

Sneyd Central being the safest Labour ward in the Borough (taking in as it did the poorer quarters of town – including those now infamous Tiger Street flats), in any normal year they didn't just weigh Horace Bissell's vote; they searched for his opponent's vote with a magnifying glass! However, 1969 was no normal year. Come polling day on May 1st there was every chance that, as well as Labour losing control of the Council, the 'paper candidate' the Conservative Party had wheeled out in Sneyd Central might make inroads into its leader's vote too.

To be sure, the Wilson government's popularity had yet to recover from the battering it had taken during the humiliating sterling devaluation crisis eighteen months earlier – compounded by a misjudged televised address to the nation in which the Prime Minister had sought to kid voters that it was not 'the pound in their pockets' that had been devalued. The savage public spending cuts that followed had led to a further haemorrhaging of Labour's traditional working-class support.

One consequence of those cuts was to bring an abrupt end to the dash to build yet more blocks of high-rise flats. Indeed, it was pondering anew the political fall-out from the fate of one of them in Sneyd End that caused Horace Bissell to rise to his feet and commence pacing the floor again. He paused only to trawl up his watch from his waistcoat: it was 11:53 am. Seven more minutes and he would know for sure if worrying rumours that had found their way back to him were true or not.

"You know, Mavis, the problem with people in this town is that they can't see the bigger picture; the wood for the trees, as they say," he grunted to his wife – who remained seated on the bench, her handbag in the lap of her mauve twin-set, her hands propped on top of it. "That's why they still need *me* at the helm: someone who can think big; get things done; show them what a bold and ambitious Labour council can really achieve," he paced back and forth, spewing out another angry rodomontade. Not for nothing did Horace Bissell's fellow councillors joke about him that 'there but for the grace of God goes God'!

"I tell you, Mavis: the Tories might look down on me because I left school at fourteen without a qualification to my name; but let it never be said that I lack drive and vision. Twenty years of my life I've dedicated to public service in this town. During that time, I've made lasting improvements to the lives of the people I represent. And as for all this talk amongst my so-called Labour 'comrades' about mounting a challenge to my leadership, well, I tell you again, Mavis: if they seriously think I'm going to just step aside and let those pygmies unravel everything I've done then they are seriously mistaken. I'll fight them all the way."

Mavis Bissell nodded loyally. Her husband had indeed been a bold and visionary city father (if, at times, a headstrong and irascible one – more so of late, his legendary short temper rendered more neuralgic still by those pesky journalists who were poking about in his financial affairs).

The Leader trawled his watch up from his waistcoat one more time: it was 11:57 am. Perhaps he could breathe easy at last – or as easy as a man whose 'drive and ambition' had now alienated the very people it had once dazzled.

He dropped the watch back in his pocket and exhaled volubly – the signal for Mavis too to rise now that his vigil had relented. With just three minutes left to the deadline for submission of nomination papers, it would appear the only person who'd stepped up to contest Horace Bissell's seat was the doddering non-entity who was the Tories' usual 'paper' candidate.

Just then however, the door from the street burst open. Who should race inside to collide headlong into the bulbous leader but the very opponent that he'd most feared.

"Oh… Er... Hello, C-c-councillor B-b-bissell. Fancy s-s-seeing you here," Brian Danks expressed flustered surprise while hastily snatching at the wad of documents he'd been carrying that the impact had scattered hither and thither. Paperwork safely in his grasp again, he bodged back onto his nose those famous outsized spectacles that had also been knocked askew during the collision. He offered Councillor Bissell and his wife a goofy smile.

"Why, you! So it's true: you really do intend to challenge me in my own ward!" he fumed at the gangling Snakeman.

"Of c-c-course, I am. After all, s-s-someone has to m-m-make a st-st-stand for decency and integrity in this town; to expose and root out all these d-d-dodgy d-d-deals and sh-sh-shady p-p-practices that have been going on in high places."

"I hope you're not referring to me, young man!" the leader eyeballed him angrily. Indeed, Mavis Bissell observed her husband angling to throw a punch at his impudent rival.

"Look, if you'll exc-c-cuse me, C-c-councillor, I have precisely n-n-ninety-six s-s-seconds in which to deliver my n-n-nomination papers..." Brian protested, eyeballing instead his own watch dangling from his wrist. Perhaps Ruby was right: he should have set out earlier and allowed himself more time.

"Not so fast!" the leader snarled, spreading out his hands and employing his substantial girth to outflank each attempt by the Snakeman to dodge around him and deliver those precious signed documents.

"May I respectfully remind you, C-c-councillor, that we live in a dem-m-mocracy. You can't st-st-stop me from..."

"Can't I? Then just watch me!"

"Horace! Stop this now! Think of your blood pressure!" Mavis grabbed her husband's arms and pleaded with him.

After a nifty feint to the left and then to the right, the younger and more nibble candidate finally darted around the livid council leader to race up and knock on the oak-panelled door of the electoral registration officer. Wisely foregoing the courtesy of waiting for a reply, the Snakeman stormed through it before his opponent could assail him again, slamming it shut in the leader's face. Thankfully, even as imperious and intimidating a figure as Horace Bissell baulked at barging inside to apprehend him.

"Mark my word! You'll pay for this, Danks!" he raged instead.

* * * * *

It had been three long years since Ruby Danks had last delivered election flyers to the Tiger Street flats. Yet how different was this campaign from the last one her husband had fought. For example, instead of having to rely on just his wife and a gaggle of dogged helpers, this afternoon more than a dozen volunteers had come forward to assist the 'Independent Clean-up Sneyd End' candidate in his fight to take Horace Bissell's seat, appalled by quotidian revelations in the press about the way their local council was run.

Having reached the top floor, she wandered up to that same vented window to gaze out again across the town – at St Stephen's Church (where she and Brian had recently renewed their vows); at the grey, angular lines of the new leisure centre nearing completion on the old station site; and at the traffic on the M6 motorway in the distance. Once again, this spot made for the perfect place to pause from her labours and reflect.

Like a haunting reminder of why Ruby had so readily agreed to support Brian in his bid to become a councillor, intruding into that view too was that gouged-out flank of Mayflower House, the block empty and deserted in readiness for its pending demolition. Until then, this stark vista would stand as a reminder of Susan Pritchard's needless death, as well as a testament to everything that had gone awry with Horace Bissell's pretention that he might transform Sneyd End into 'the Athens of the Midlands'.

Just then, Ruby's contemplation was interrupted by the emergence from her flat of a housewife in curlers and slippers, the jaunty lyrics of The Marmalade's rendition of *'Ob-La-Di, Ob-La-Da'* that was playing on the radio emerging with her. Bending down to collect the bottles that the milkman had left beside her front door, she glanced up and spotted this smartly-attired stranger – yet someone who she thought she recognised.

"Still admiring the view, I see," she said, the penny eventually dropping. *Déjà vu*: straightening up, she sidled up to the window alongside Ruby, clutching the bottles to her bosom.

"Except that it's not such an edifying one now," Ruby suggested, both women staring at the bleak remains of Tiger Street's other, now abandoned tower block.

Unsure what 'edifying' meant, the housewife was blunter.

"That Bissell bloke should be hung, drawn and quartered for allowing the contractors to cut corners when these things were built," she huffed. "Every time I go into the kitchen nowadays I dread what might happen. Meanwhile, the doctor has had to prescribe Valium to Mrs Bates at No. 90 so she can deal with the anxiety. And you know the most appalling thing? All the housing department offered the tenants of Mayflower House were flats in tower blocks on other estates! Like I once said: these politicians am' all the bleedin' same. They promise you the world and give you sweet Fanny Adams! But well, what can yer' do?"

This time Ruby seized her moment. She drew out one of her husband's flyers and presented it to her.

"You can vote for this man instead: Brian Danks – the 'Independent Clean-up Sneyd End' candidate; someone who has pledged to stand up for common sense and decency, as well as for openness and transparency in the Council's dealings."

The woman speed-read both the front and the back of the flyer. Ruby looked on in gathering expectation as she eventually pursed her lips and nodded.

"Yeah. He sounds like a good bloke. I'll vote for him. Let's hope he can sort this mess out. Can I keep this?" she held up the flyer. "To remind me where to put my cross on the voting paper?"

"With his compliments," Ruby beamed.

The woman returned the smile before drifting back to her flat, closing the door behind her.

* * * * *

Jonathan Hunt was wandering the streets of Sneyd End again. Except tonight – rather than doing so as a police officer in uniform – he was once again flitting from house to house like a skulking fugitive. However, like so many people he'd fallen into conversation with these last few weeks while plodding his beat, he too had been left appalled by the stories he'd heard about how corruptly his local council had been run. As he moved swiftly to despatch a flyer through the letterboxes of each of the privately-owned apartments on the Wentworth View estate that image kept haunting him of a terrified Mary Pritchard, coated in dust and clinging precariously to what was left of her fourth-floor flat. Hence why he'd had no hesitation about using his night off to deliver Brian's election leaflets – irrespective of police regulations that expressly forbade it!

That said, his ardour was tempered by concern that no one should spot him doing so. To this end – working alone, and with a slouch hat over his napper and the collar of his gabardine coat drawn up around his neck – it was while returning down the stairwell of this particular block that he was suddenly startled by the sound of a door opening on the landing below. Panicking, he drew back and ducked out of sight.

"… I know you're a busy woman, Pauline; and you know your mother and I love coming over to see you. But do try to visit *us* more often if you can… Here, what's this? Someone has left something in your letterbox." he heard an ominously familiar voice venture to point out.

Déjà vu: the palpitating copper raised his head just enough to be able to peer over the banister and confirm his worst fear. It was Chief Superintendent Trotter – his boss!

"What is it, Cyril?" his wife enquired.

"It looks like it's an election flyer – from this 'independent' candidate who's standing in your ward; who, as well as still harping on about that old railway, is now trying to convince everyone he can 'clean-up' the politics of this town as well."

"Oh, you mean Brian Danks," Jonathan spotted the occupant of the flat note – a not unattractive young lady with a cute, freckled face and a glorious head of bobbed red hair. He knew he was risking discovery, but he simply had to linger to undertake a more detailed examination of her.

"Yes, he's still quite a character," Trotter's wife chuckled, endeavouring to take the edge of her husband's scepticism.

"I know him from those occasions when I take children from my school to the zoo," their daughter piped up. "He's a really nice man – very passionate, yet genuine and witty with it. That's why

I'll be voting for him. His wife's a good friend of mine too. In fact, we work closely together in the teachers' union."

Interesting, Jonathan smiled to himself, unseen: this 'Pauline' woman supports Brian Danks; and is a friend of Ruby's. Meanwhile, though he knew Chief Superintendent Trotter had a daughter of whom he was immensely fond, this was the first time he'd run into her.

"I can see this so-called 'Snakeman of Sneyd End' may have charmed you, my girl. But trust me: the man is a trouble-maker," his boss cautioned. "All that malarkey not so long back when he climbed up that confounded crane! Why, the crazy fool could have got himself killed – along with the poor constable who was trying to talk him down."

Jonathan couldn't resist another wry smile – all the time still covertly admiring this young woman, who he observed don a bewitching wry smile of her own to insist that "I'm sure police officers have suffered worst fates at the hands of protesters than to lose their helmets in the kerfuffle!"

"You might make light of such things, Pauline. However, I'm going to make sure he attempts no more silly stunts like that during this election. I suppose the only thing he has going for him is that, what with all these stories in the newspapers, he might just unseat that insufferable Horace Bissell. I can't stand that man, Margaret," he turned to his wife and gnashed.

Jonathan risked discovery again by peering up to observe Pauline peruse the flyer her father had found in her letterbox (her girlish good looks and adorable figure reminding the bachelor policeman of how long he'd been without female company!).

He remained out of sight while the Trotters bade a final goodnight and headed off down the stairs. However, he surfaced again – this time to admire how their daughter's cute little bottom nestled nicely in that tan suede mini-skirt she was wearing (Pauline having drifted over to the landing window to wave to her parents as their Rover saloon pulled off the car park).

Such admiration having got the better of him, he failed to duck in time when she turned about to head back inside, the amber-crowned teacher spotting him staring down at her from the landing above.

"Who are you?" she clutched at her chest with a start. "And what are you doing there? Look, my father's a senior police officer, I'll have you know!"

"Er... I'm n-n-not... I m-m-mean, I wasn't..." he wittered, racking his brain for a plausible excuse for his voyeurism.

In the end, all he could think to do was to doff his hat and clutch it to his chest in a show of contrition. He also showed her the wad of election flyers that he was gripping in his other hand.

"Wait a minute. I recognise you," she announced. "Aren't you that policeman I see plodding around here now and again?"

Yikes! Cover blown! Once her father got to find out that not only had one of his officers been distributing literature of a political nature but had also been covertly spying on his daughter in her home, then his career in the police force would be over for sure. Meanwhile, he watched anxiously as her lour abated and the curious blue eyes that Pauline Trotter had trained upon him dipped to survey again that flyer in her hand.

"You've been delivering these? For Brian Danks?" she looked up and quizzed him coyly.

He nodded, standing erect so that she might study him in more detail: his boyish, guilt-laden grin; his neat black hair; and a face that bore the residual pitting of the teenage acne he'd once been teased about – even as she herself had endured similar such ribaldry on account of her swathe of freckles.

"You do realise you could get into a lot of trouble for doing that?" she added.

He nodded in remorse.

"And that my father is a senior police officer?"

He nodded again, lowering his gaze as if resigned to being completely at her mercy – as were *his* hopes of ever becoming a 'senior police officer' himself. However – and to his surprise – her mien of faux, schoolmarmish dismay mellowed, to be replaced by the first hints of an alluringly coquettish smile.

"Then it's just as well that your secret is safe with me!" she teased him playfully. "Fancy a coffee?"

* * * * *

The big day had arrived: the culmination of everything Brian and Ruby Danks been working towards these last few weeks. The polls had closed. The people had made their choice. *Déjà vu*: in Sneyd End Town Hall the first ballot boxes were arriving from polling stations around the town, to be emptied and verified by the army of counting clerks who were sat around the tables that ringed the hall's cavernous interior.

Wandering about those tables with his wife, Brian couldn't help but be struck by how different things were this time. A mere six months earlier he'd been alternately dismissed or despised as a busybody – someone given to dramatic, if ultimately futile publicity stunts; a starry-eyed crank whose sentimental attachment to a forgotten railway line threatened to stand in the way of completing a new leisure centre that the town desperately needed. And yet now he was being feted as 'the saviour of Sneyd End'; the man whose superlative oratory about 'cleaning-up' its council had not only filled to overflowing the public meeting he'd held but had even been reported on national television too!

Meanwhile, away from the spotlight of his public persona, six months earlier his marriage had been in crisis, his wife in the sway of another man. Today, however, not only was Ruby by his side once more, proudly holding his hand and returning the smiles the counting agents were beaming at them, but as a couple they were closer than they'd ever been. Indeed, for once, it had not been a case of the indomitable Brian dragging his loyal (if put-upon) spouse around on another of his quixotic campaigns; this time it had been *she* who'd stirred *him* to greater endeavour – his muse, his confidante, his campaign manager, his cheerleader-in-chief, and (once again) his lover and closest friend. Pausing from surveying the count, he turned to marvel at her again.

Looking stylish in the fashionable brown maxi skirt she was wearing, she appeased his childlike doting by reaching up to offer him a discreet peck on the lips. As she did, from out of the corner of her eye she spotted Myrtle Danks admiring them approvingly – Brian's mother gracious enough to concede that her son now had a new cheerleader-in-chief.

Ruby broke to return that smile. For, as well as this heartening turn-around in their matrimonial fortunes, there was one further piece of good news that she was angling to break to both Brian and his mother. However, lest it overshadow the momentous events going on in the Town Hall tonight, she resolved to sit on that news until the morning.

As on the last occasion Brian had been present at an election count, he couldn't escape the looming presence of his corpulent rival. However, that gaudy red rosette pinned to the breast of Councillor Horace Bissell's baggy suit belied a more subdued character. With his name in the papers for all the wrong reasons, and the Labour Party in Sneyd End in open revolt over revelations about his 'lavish' lifestyle (certainly far above his means as a supposedly working-class 'man-of-the-people'), perhaps he sensed that tonight was but the opening chapter in the travails that awaited him now the polls had closed and the people had spoken. Ironically – and as if to rub salt in the wound – completion of the new leisure centre in which he'd invested so much political capital was still behind schedule. With the results declared so far confirming that Labour had lost control of Sneyd End Borough Council, in any event he was going to be denied the prize of officially declaring it open in a few weeks' time. To be sure, Horace Bissell was 'God' no more in the town.

"I, Cedric Buttercroft, being the Returning Officer for the said ward announce the result to be as follows," the voice rang out when the time came to reveal the outcome of the most eagerly awaited contest of the night. Ruby rested a supportive hand upon the shoulder of her diminutive mother-in-law as together they watched the candidates shuffling anxiously on the stage.

"… Atkins, Godfrey Herbert – two hundred and nine votes."

The geriatric Conservative candidate raised his cane and raised a smile for the supporters in the hall who cheered – content with the knowledge that his party had won control of the Council for the first time that even someone as long-in-the-tooth as he could remember.

"… Bissell, Horace Theobald – eight hundred and seventy-seven votes."

The beleaguered leader of the council snorted and stared at his shoes, clearly aggrieved. He – like everyone else looking on to witness this denouement – knew what was coming next.

"… Danks, Brian Matthew – one thousand, eight hundred and ten votes."

He'd done it! His supporters and well-wishers in the hall cheered him to the rafters – as did Ruby and Myrtle Danks too, flinging their arms around each other to dance for joy.

"I w-w-want to s-s-say th-th-thank you to the many p-p-people who have offered their s-s-support to my election campaign," their hero mumbled when the returning officer invited him to step up to the microphone. Reading from the notes he'd made in preparation, he thought to add "…And especially to my wife, Ruby, without whom I would be neither the man nor the candidate I am today... Oh, and I'd like to thank my Mom too!"

Nervous (as he often was) upon addressing a strange new gathering, a touching flurry of amusement accompanied his mother signalling forgiveness for his little oversight. Ruby also returned her husband's fond smile. Fortified with this, it didn't take long for this master wordsmith to step into his stride, the notes in his hand soon superfluous as Brian Danks reiterated his vision for Sneyd End (even as he had yet to work out how he might bring Bill Patterson and the Tory councillors present onboard with it – the real victors of tonight's elections in the Borough).

Yet the most moving part of his acceptance speech came when, at its conclusion, he paid tribute to his slain opponent (who was still staring at his shoes, as if unable to take in the magnitude of his trouncing. The people had indeed spoken – the bastards!).

"Finally, Mr Returning Officer, I know Horace Bissell and I have had our disagreements over the years," he admitted – to further amusement from those in the room who recognised the understatement. For the first time too, Horace Bissell looked up, curious about what his nemesis intended to say.

"However, I would like to applaud him for being a most formidable opponent; a man who knew his own mind and was never afraid to speak up for the things he believed in – even if to do so was often to court controversy. In that respect, I guess, he's taught me well!" the Snakeman unwittingly joked, this time to less subdued hilarity. Why, even the dethroned leader of the council summoned a grudging smile.

"However, once upon a time Horace Bissell offered me another piece of advice about what one man can realistically achieve – no matter how fired up he is with the 'dream' he has, as Martin Luther King might have said. And that is: if you stick at 'the game of politics' long enough you'll discover that half a loaf is better than no loaf at all; that you might not get everything you want; but if you 'play the game' then at least you'll get something. Alas, I regret that compromise, expediency, and 'playing the game' are not necessarily in my nature," he conceded self-effacingly, Ruby at least appreciating the heartache that had often attended such a character trait.

"That said, I fear there has been too much expediency, too much compromise, and too much 'playing the game' going on in this town of late – often to the detriment of the people we politicians are elected to serve."

Cue a mumble of 'hear, hear' from around the Town Hall that was unnerving to those more experienced politicians who had themselves been busy 'playing the game'.

"I believe it's why the people of Sneyd End have warmed to someone who is once again willing to offer them honesty, integrity and principle; someone who, in those timeless words of Abraham Lincoln, will promise to serve 'with malice toward none, with charity for all, and with firmness in the right as God gives us to see the right'; someone whose election I hope will herald a new dawn for politics in this town. Thank you."

Even the counting staff stood to the feet and joined in the applause that greeted the spectacular (and long overdue) admission into the arena of public service of the legendary 'Snakeman of Sneyd End'. Now he would have the opportunity to give practical form to those ideas and aspirations that had for so long floated around unfulfilled in that quiff-topped head of his. Perhaps it really was a 'new dawn' for politics in the town; a time for its political leaders to govern again with 'malice toward none' and 'charity for all'.

However, shrewder heads – Ruby's included – could discern that, behind the façade of polite approbation with which Brian's rousing evocations of Abraham Lincoln and Dr Martin Luther King were greeted, dark clouds were looming. Councillor Bill

Patterson certainly had his own ideas about how the Conservative Party would run Sneyd End from now on.

Meanwhile, though he had been soundly beaten, who could say whether ex-Councillor Horace Bissell might yet possess a final card up his sleeve with which – brooding and humiliated – he could exact revenge upon his nemesis.

19

"So, congratulations are in order, are they not... Councillor."

"Thank you," said Brian, humbled. He clinked his wine glass, first with those of his two dinner guests, then with Ruby's.

It had been a while since The Dankses had entertained folks for dinner. As such, they'd pulled out all the stops to make Jonathan Hunt and Pauline Trotter welcome in their home. Ruby had put her heart and soul into preparing the starters of stuffed asparagus rolls followed by the beef bourguignon main course. Having been banished from the kitchen for meddling with her ingredients, Brian had instead set the table and dropped something onto the turntable of their new stereo system with which to complement the ambience. So it was that wistful strains of American country singer Glen Campbell were playing softly in the background as the new councillor joined his wife and their guests at the table.

"You must be quite chuffed with the turn-around in your political fortunes, mate," Jonathan insisted.

"Yes, it's richly deserved. I've always admired you, Brian: for the way you've faced disparagement and ostracism with such grace and fortitude," added Pauline.

Brian was uncharacteristically modest.

"I can't say there weren't times when I didn't feel like throwing in the towel," he shrugged. "To paraphrase King David in the Bible: I was greatly distressed; for the people spoke of stoning me. But, again, like David," Brian's recounting of his story perked up, "I was encouraged in the Lord my God – First Samuel Chapter Thirty, Verse Six."

Ostensibly, the invitations had been extended as a way of contriving an excuse to bring Jonathan and Pauline together – the Dankses having jointly agreed that their respective best friends had been single for far too long; and that, if introduced, they might just find they had things in common. Little did they know that their friends were already 'acquainted' with each other

following a bizarre encounter during his election campaign –
which Pauline now recounted.

"... The threat of being hauled before my father for delivering
your leaflets had poor Jonathan here trembling in his boots.
Therefore, I took pity on him and invited him in for a coffee
instead! Besides, what my father doesn't know won't hurt him,"
she smiled – the same coquettish smile that had tantalised her new
boyfriend the evening they'd first met.

"Well, I never, Jonathan: it's just as well she fancied you too
then!" Brian maladroitly guffawed.

Ruby unsubtly tapped his foot under the table, having spotted
both guests momentarily blushing. Otherwise, it was fortunate
that Jonathan and Pauline had hit it off sufficiently to appreciate
the comical side of their hosts' thoughtful scheming.

"Here, mate: you should have seen Horace Bissell's face –
when the boys hauled him down the station for questioning about
accepting backhanders in exchange for awarding construction
contracts," Jonathan crowed, imagining the news would occasion
a flush of *schadenfreude* on the part of his old friend.

The Snakeman, however, was more circumspect.

"It's a tragedy," he sighed regretfully. "For the tenants of
Mayflower House, whose lives have been blighted by the corners
that were cut by those contractors; for poor Susan Pritchard, of
course, who lost her life; but also, for Horace Bissell himself."

Jonathan looked mildly askance. Pauline too was curious.
However, Ruby knew where her husband was coming from. She
looked on as he explained this strange willingness to show
magnanimity towards his rebarbative foe.

"For all his objectionable ways – and in no way am I excusing
them – I can't help thinking that once upon a time Horace Bissell
was a young man in a hurry, who entered politics brimming with
idealism – yearning to change the world and make it a better
place. Not unlike me, I suppose," he opined with touching and
uncharacteristic self-awareness.

"And yet somewhere along the way he became addicted to
power. The temptation to wangle a way of rewarding what he
considered to be his genius in making things happen got the better
of him. Power and temptation: the two never make happy

bedfellows. I guess therein lies a lesson for all politicians – including me," he mused, sporting the expression of a man who was humbly (and prayerfully) cognisant of *his own* shortcomings.

It occasioned a moment for each of them to pause and reflect. However, the pensive silence also presented the ideal moment for Ruby to banish despondency and announce another joyous reason why Jonathan and Pauline had been invited round tonight. Glancing briefly at her husband – and unable to contain her excitement – she fired them each a teasing smile.

"Brian and I have some other good news to celebrate," she ventured tentatively, glancing at him a second time before taking the plunge. "I'm pregnant!"

Jonathan was chuffed (in the relaxed manner with which the male of the species often greets such momentous news). Pauline, however, was ecstatic, rising from the table to crane across and present her fellow teacher with a great big girly hug.

"Congratulations. And you've been trying for so long! How far gone are you?" she wanted to know.

"Almost three months."

"And do you want a boy or a girl?"

"Oh, I don't know. I suppose I wouldn't mind a little girl – although I suspect Brian wants a boy," Ruby chuckled, glancing at him again and wondering if he realised that, if so, he might not have that train set in the box room all to himself for much longer.

"I'm not fussed," the prospective father hummed. "*'Lo, children are a heritage of the Lord: and the fruit of the womb is His reward'* – Psalm One Hundred and Twenty-Seven," he assailed them again with his prodigious knowledge of Scripture.

Otherwise, Jonathan had a pressing reason of his own for having seized this chance to get together with his best mate – a matter a world removed from his courtship with his boss's daughter; or the travails of a corrupt town hall boss whose eyes had grown bigger than his legendary, expansive belly; or even the delightful news that Ruby's own belly would soon be expanding (and for the best reason in the world). He waited until the animated chatter about babies had run its course before opening with a seemingly innocent aside

"I popped in to see the local Sikh community the other day."

Intrigued as to what such a seemingly trivial digression might portend, all three of his listeners looked up from their meals.

"They've bought that old, disused church on Park Street and have made it into their place of worship – or Gurdwara, as they call it. After the attacks and abuse they've suffered over the last few years, I thought it would be a nice gesture to reassure them that their local police do take such incidents seriously."

"That's very noble of you, Jonathan," Ruby commended him.

"Yes, I just wish my father was a bit less grudging towards coloured people," Pauline groaned, for her new boyfriend was likely to be ploughing a lone furrow until something changed in the culture and hierarchy of the West Midlands Constabulary.

"It's true that some of my colleague's think I'm wasting my time. But, well, I take people as I find them, no matter what colour their skin; nor the god they worship. The Sikhs are certainly a friendly and welcoming people."

Sensing that his listeners were still no wiser about the relevance of his heart-warming tale of community-spiritedness to the evening's other awesome news, the policeman manoeuvred a little closer to what he was angling to reveal.

"One of the more commendable things about the Sikh religion – or so they've been explaining to me – is the tradition of *langar*. It's their term for what we would call a soup kitchen: somewhere where they can offer hospitality to strangers – especially the local down-and-outs. Usually it consists of a free meal and a cup of tea."

"Yes, Father Allen organises something similar," Ruby noted of their ever-charitable parish priest.

"I got talking to the person who runs it," Jonathan continued. "A guy called Inderjit. You probably know his daughter, Ruby – Parminder. She goes to your school."

Ruby acknowledged the coincidence, recalling the conversation she'd had with her father in the aftermath of Parminder being bullied. However, she – like the others – was still no wiser about its relevance to what they'd been discussing.

"He was telling me about a tramp who used to turn up every week, regular as clockwork: some old bloke called Bert. You may have seen him around the town – pushing his belongings around in a tatty old shopping trolley."

"He must be the one I bumped into a while back dossing down in the old railway tunnel," Brian replied, pulling a tell-tale face to announce that he was trawling his memory for such things.

"Well, a few months ago he stopped coming. Inderjit tells me he hasn't seen him since. It got me thinking: neither have I."

Jonathan offered Brian a poignant stare that took a few seconds to register. Upon which, the Snakeman sat back in his chair and returned it with one of his own.

"You're not suggesting that this old tramp might have been another victim of whatever it is that's been going on in that tunnel, are you?" Ruby intercepted her husband's question.

Jonathan's gaze alighted upon her, then upon a baffled Pauline, and then back again upon Brian.

"I'm certain something out of the ordinary has been going on in there," he announced. "As you mentioned, Bert used to pass the winter nights in there to keep warm – despite British Rail's half-hearted attempt to fence the thing off," he continued.

"It's warm in there alright!" Ruby enlightened Pauline, recalling an excursion she herself had made inside it a few years back, accompanying Brian on one of his many railway rambles. "It's dead spooky too," she shuddered.

"Well, a few days ago when I was off-duty I took the liberty of stepping through the hole in the fence to have a shufty in there myself," he said, having halted from his meal, arms propped on the table for dramatic effect and chin resting on the apex of his interlocked fingers. "Amongst the many items that I found discarded in there just happened to be Bert's old shopping trolley – still containing his worldly possessions."

"I suppose it's possible the kids might have pinched it and dumped it there as a prank," Brian suggested. "The cruel little so-and-sos: they're always poking fun at the poor man,"

"I also found that tattered overcoat he always wore too; the one he never removed – even at the height of summer. Inderjit told me he even declined the Gurdwara's offer to furnish him with a new one. However, there is one thing that *might* have persuaded Bert to remove his overcoat..."

"... The overpowering heat inside that tunnel," Brian finished the sentence and cocked an eye at him. The subtle nodding of Jonathan's head affirmed they were on the same wavelength.

"And a frail old man without his heavy overcoat would have been a considerably easier meal for a python to digest than had he been wearing it."

"Python!" Pauline exclaimed. "But I thought that story about a giant snake was just that: a tale put about to frighten schoolchildren and stop them playing where they shouldn't."

"I'm not so sure," said Jonathan, glancing at her before retraining his policeman's forensic eye upon his friend. "Looking back, most of these missing youngsters were only wearing light summer clothing at the time of their disappearances; except for Kevin Wood. And yet, for some inexplicable reason, the officers who conducted the search for him also found his heavy donkey jacket abandoned inside the tunnel; presumably because he'd removed it."

"But, even if such a huge, man-eating snake did exist, surely someone would have spotted it before now. After all, snakes have to bask in the sun to warm up," Ruby put it to him, availing herself of the passing knowledge that derived from being married to an internationally-renowned herpetologist.

"Well, of course, somebody has," Jonathan interjected. "The trouble is Ernie Baxter was two sheets to the wind when he allegedly spotted that 'giant snake' over Fens Bank. Consequently, no one has ever taken him seriously – including me. But now I'm beginning to wonder if it wasn't the booze talking after all. Added to which, I would hazard a guess there must be a network of drainage shafts criss-crossing from the tunnel to Fens Bank that would enable such a snake to move unseen between the two locations."

Suddenly, the prandial conversation had taken a frightening turn. Ruby and Pauline were both struggling to get their heads around such a fantastical theory. However, calling upon a decade of experience studying and handling such creatures, Brian weighed in with some more deliberative observations of his own.

"Nobody would have seen it because the snake would have little need to venture outside the tunnel. It's warm in there –

certainly warm enough to sustain a large constrictor. There's a readily-available supply of food in the form of all those sizeable rats that have also made the place their home. And even if food gets scarce – during the winter, for example, when it's too cold to venture out and hunt prey – a snake can brumate."

"Brumate?" Pauline sought enlightenment.

"Brumation," he obliged. "It's what reptiles do during cold weather. It's a form of hibernation. The snake's body metabolism will virtually shut down and it will go into a deep sleep, obviating the need to hunt. In fact, a brumating snake can go for months without feeding – especially if it's eaten well during the summer."

"Interestingly, Gillian Hickman disappeared over Fens Bank on a hot summer's day: the sort of day that would have warmed up a cold-blooded reptile quite nicely," Jonathan noted.

"Bertie – the next-door neighbours' pet Labrador – also went missing on a hot summer's day," Ruby recalled.

"No, it can't be," Pauline shook her head defiantly. "Who would ever believe that a giant snake has been devouring our pets? And our children?"

"Certainly not your father," Jonathan turned to his new flame. "He's still convinced that Raymond Morris, the Cannock Chase murderer, is the culprit; and that he's refusing to confess to killing them – just like he is to those other youngsters whose murders we think he's responsible for. Besides, recalling his response on the last occasion when I tried to convince him CID had nabbed the wrong suspect, I don't imagine he's going to be inclined to pay heed to me barging into his office again, this time to warn that there's a huge snake on the loose!" he stared at Brian knowingly.

"If only we had some hard evidence to go on," the Snakeman glanced away and agonised.

Meanwhile, the two women watched as Jonathan stood to his feet and wandered out into the hall to where he'd left a box at the foot of the coat stand his jacket was hanging on. Pauline thought it might have been a gift of some sort to show appreciation for their hosts' hospitality (although she'd omitted to question what it might be or to pry inside).

"You mean like this," he announced upon his return, opening the box to haul out a long piece of flaky something-or-other.

Brian recognised the object straight away, a rictus gape accompanying the sudden popping of his eyes.

"Oh – my – goodness!" he gasped, hurriedly nudging his glasses up his nose and drawing in to take a closer look. "Where did you get hold of this?"

"It's something else I stumbled upon while poking around inside that tunnel," the policeman crowed. "However, before I drop it on the Chief Super's desk I thought I'd show you first – to examine it in your professional capacity."

"Yuk! That's a snake's skin," Pauline grimaced, appalled at the thought of what had been gracing the back seat of her little Hillman Imp on the journey here.

"It's a big one too!" Ruby shuddered.

She turned to her husband, only to discover he'd bounced out of his seat and was bounding over to the bookcase. Walking his fingers to locate a hefty, authoritative tome, he pulled it out and flicked anxiously through its pages. After a moment spent scanning the illustration on the page he'd alighted upon – his lips silently mouthing the words of the accompanying text – he bore the book over to the dining table upon which Jonathan had stretched out his worrying find, there to compare the two.

"I thought so!" he tapped the page, "*Python Reticulatus*: the Reticulated Python. A native of India and South-East Asia, it's the world's longest snake – even though the South American green anaconda is the heaviest. Female reticulated pythons can grow to over twenty-feet in length, although there are rumours of 'retics' in the wild exceeding even that. There have also been several unverified reports over the years of this species of snake attacking and eating humans."

"Oh, please God, no!" Ruby swooned at the thought that her pupils might have ended up inside one.

Pauline manoeuvred around the table to cast a womanly arm of comfort around her. However, while Ruby was weeping against her bosom and the two men were debating theories about how such a beast might have gotten there, a light suddenly came on in Pauline's tangerine-topped head.

"You say this snake was most likely dumped in the tunnel?" she interrupted them to interrogate Brian.

"That's the only possible explanation," he broke to affirm.

"Look, I know this might be a long shot: but a few years back I remember setting one of my classes the task of writing about their pets. I thought it would be interesting to find out who had the most unusual one. It was Friday, November 22nd 1963 – I remember it well because it was the day that President Kennedy was assassinated. They say people will never forget what they were doing on that day," she pointed out.

"As you can imagine," she then proffered an incongruous grin, "there were plenty of tales about dogs, cats, rabbits and budgies. However, there was this one little lad who told me his father owned a snake called Betty. From what he said, it sounded big and scary; a bit like the lad's father, in fact – who I recall was something of a notorious ruffian!

"Well, I remember asking the lad a while later how Betty was doing. It was then that he told me his father had taken her to the local zoo because she'd grown too big to look after. I can't vouch for the veracity of what he told the class that day – you know the tales children sometimes tell," she glanced at Ruby knowingly. "But, assuming he was telling the truth, you don't suppose his father could have... well, you know... simply got rid of Betty somewhere else instead?"

Brian was again trawling his prodigious memory.

"We've never had a reticulated python at the Zoo," his self-interrogating frown morphed into one of disquiet. "In fact, all the time I've been there we've only ever had one python handed in by a member of the public – and that was Maisie, our albino ball python. And she arrived with us on Wednesday, March 27th 1963! I remember that too – it was the day that the Beeching Report on 'The Reshaping of British Railways' was published!"

Jonathan was conscious that all this talk of giant snakes had not only overshadowed Brian and Ruby's big announcement, but that enormous piece of sloughed skin he'd stretched out on their dining table had rather put everybody off the dessert course too.

"I'm sorry to have raised this matter tonight," he explained. "However, someone needs to alert the authorities to the possibility that such a creature might be out there somewhere; and before it has the chance to kill again!"

He had that forensic glint in his eye once more. It took a few seconds before Brian cottoned on to the hint being dropped.

"M-m-meaning m-m-me?" he gabbled.

"You're one of the country's most respected experts on snakes," his friend insisted. "If there's anyone people will listen to, it's you – especially given your new status in the town."

After all the years of ridicule and contempt, and of being brushed off as a deluded fanatic, Ruby knew her husband was quite enjoying his newfound respectability as a local politician. Mindful of this, she ventured to strike a note of caution.

"Suppose nobody listens though. After all, I've never heard of anyone in this country being devoured by a snake. If you're wrong, then by sticking his neck out and going public about this my husband risks becoming a laughing stock again," she insisted.

All eyes lingered on Jonathan. It was true: surely Brian had suffered enough obloquy for saying things that those in authority were loathed to hear. Was it fair to expect him to endure even more? Perhaps the seasoned copper really did need to unearth some more hard evidence about this mysterious 'Betty'.

* * * * *

"A word... if I may."

Graham Weston's discreet purloining of Ruby as she was passing in the corridor was more disconcerting because these last few weeks he'd purposely sought to avoid her, content instead to lavish his oleaginous charm upon that brazen young arts teacher.

Though wary, Ruby followed him to his office as instructed; somewhere safe from wagging ears where he felt more comfortable conversing with her. Stepping inside and closing the door behind her, she watched him casually fold his arms and lean back against his desk – the same convenient flat surface upon which (to her lasting shame) she'd permitted him to ravish her on what had turned out to be the final occasion they'd been intimate with each other. What manner of insanity had gripped her that she'd consented to such a thing? And risked their affair being uncovered in the process?

"A little bird tells me congratulations are in order," he opened, offering her a hearty smile that was curiously at odds with the grave tone in which he'd summoned her.

"Thank you. I was going to tell you; and to sort out the formalities with the office," she assured him awkwardly.

"You should know that nothing stays secret in this place for long," he grinned mischievously. "How far gone are you?"

"Almost four months."

"And do you want a boy or a girl?"

"Oh, I don't know," she snapped impatiently. "Look, is this the only reason you've invited me in here? And before you ask, no: it's not yours! So you can stop panicking!"

He tried not to make it obvious that establishing her child's paternity was indeed a consideration (though, armed with what she'd told him so far, he'd quickly done the maths).

"Well, actually no – it isn't," he glanced away as if to choose his words. "I'm afraid there have been developments, Ruby."

"Developments?" she puzzled.

"Yes. Regarding you and me, and, well... Look," he desisted from beating about the bush to return her anxious stare. "It seems people have been blabbing; and, well... It's got back to the school governors. Or should I say to one governor in particular."

"You mean Horace Bissell?"

Ruby's succinct observation obviated the need for Weston to elaborate. The defeated former leader of the council was wreaking his revenge.

"I often wonder if that obsessive husband of yours realises what an almighty hornets' nest he kicked over by standing against – and then defeating – ex-Councillor Bissell. Now, apprised of what we've been up to, the man is on a mission and won't be content until both of us are out the door."

Though it seemed so unfair that Ruby was being traduced for having succumbed to temptation that she'd otherwise resisted for so long, she'd been only too aware of the reputational damage to the school that dallying with its head teacher would occasion if ever it went public. Now it looked like it was about to – fanned into flame by a vengeful town hall boss who, armed with this knowledge, stood ready to spread the poison.

"The good news is that Horace Bissell is not an unreasonable man. He heard me out when I recounted your good work during the six years you've been at Sneyd End High School, and that our, you know... was all just a rather foolish, well... a fling."

She was visibly irritated – by the inference that the ex-councillor might have a magnanimous bone somewhere in his corpulent body; but more so that, even now, Graham Weston couldn't bring himself to describe what they'd briefly had going as anything that had vaguely involved affection on his part; or, Heaven forbid, love! No, to him it remained 'foolishness': a 'fling' with someone's neglected wife; a 'diversion'; a 'bit of fun on the side' (or on his desk!). Boy, what a sucker she'd been!

"Suffice to say, he's managed to persuade his fellow governors that if you go of your own accord, then nothing will be said; and that you will leave your employment with the school with exemplary references. That said, it appears the good words I put in on your behalf have turned out to be superfluous now that you're with child. I guess you'll be leaving us at the end of the summer anyway – and for the best of reasons, might I add. You'll make an excellent mother, Ruby. After all, I know you and Brian have always wanted a child."

She grinned uneasily, unsure whether those words really were a compliment; or just more patronising drivel intended to sugar what was going to be a very bitter pill to swallow, as it were.

"As for me, I too must now await whatever fate the gods of karma have in store for me," he shrugged philosophically.

If it was a play for sympathy then it fell on stony ground, for to look into those artful blue eyes was to sense that most of the 'good words' he'd put in with those to whom he answered had undoubtedly been on his own account.

"And Millie?" Ruby's resentment oozed out.

"Millie?"

"Well, if I'm being made to walk the plank, it's only right that 'Little Miss Kinky Boots' is made to do likewise."

He frowned – first with feigned innocence and then with contrived offence.

"I can assure you that absolutely no impropriety has taken place between Miss Ferriday and me," he protested – though from the way she stared him out he could tell she didn't believe him.

Yet what did it matter now? 'Little Miss Kinky Boots' would find out soon enough what falling under the spell of the impossibly handsome Graham Weston could do to the career – as well as the self-respect – of a promising young teacher.

20

The 'Pig & Whistle' was normally too lively for Eddie Foster. Therefore, after a day's graft he preferred to unwind in the more laid-back ambience of the 'Miner's Arms' on Sneyd End High Street – a place that was also more conducive to ordering the 'business' that supplemented the twenty quid a week he earned as a warehouseman. Besides, the beer was better!

Consequently, it was here on this quiet Tuesday evening that he was to be found huddled over his pint in readiness to meet a man he was hoping might put a bit more business his way.

Sure enough, there strolled into the smoke room a tall, broad-shouldered character with black, swept-back hair and a shady-looking, pock-marked face who, from the way he was glancing about the room, looked like he might be the man in question.

Fag bobbing between his lips, Eddie glanced at the watch draped over his muscular, tattooed forearm. This guy was eager: he was twenty minutes early! Still: business is business. Eddie sat up straight and feigned to look suitably unfazed when, having ordered himself a pint, his prospective client wandered over.

"Eddie Foster?" the man enquired, placing his glass down on the table and pulling out a chair.

"That's me. Yow' must be Joe then?"

"Well, no," he announced, "Actually, my name's Hunt – PC 2988 Hunt of Sneyd End Police," he informed him, pulling his warrant card from his jacket pocket and flashing it discreetly.

The look of horror that fleetingly passed over Eddie's stubbled face belied the more brazen demeanour he steeled himself to present to this unwanted and unexpected visitor.

"And?" he huffed, locking his eyes onto Jonathan's.

"A word… if I may."

"Worrabout'? I ay' done nuffin'," the object of his enquiry grunted defiantly.

"Now, now. That wouldn't be the guilty conscience talking would it, Eddie?" Jonathan sat back in his chair and folded his arms, observing this small-time crook squirming.

"Like Ar' said: yow' ay' got nuffin' on me."

"I wouldn't be so sure about that. For example, might it have been you who put Harry Parkes in hospital the other day with a broken face – possibly because he knew about a certain profitable little sideline you have trading knock-off goods from that warehouse you work at?"

Jonathan could have added that it was because Harry Parkes was willing to talk to them that Sneyd End CID was one step closer to pouncing on Eddie Foster and closing his criminal enterprise down.

"So yow've come here ter' tell me Ar've bin' a birrova' naughty boy, eh?" Eddie was still brazening it out, confident that the risk of the rest of his body being broken would ensure Harry kept quiet.

"No, I've come about a potentially far more serious matter than the theft of building materials from Millbank's Yard."

Eddie looked genuinely mystified, racking his brain to recall who else he'd put in Casualty lately. Meanwhile, armed with the intelligence Pauline had provided by trawling back through her school's records to pinpoint the name and address of the 'ruffian' father she'd told them about, Jonathan had done the rest of the homework that – along with a bit of off-duty surveillance and a word or two down the station – had led him to the favourite watering hole of one Edward Gordon Foster.

"I believe you once owned a snake," Jonathan put it to him, leaning forward to draw his pint to his lips.

"Yer' wot'?"

"A reticulated python named Betty, to be precise. Rather a dangerous pet to keep, I'd say. But then, you're a dangerous guy, aren't you, Eddie," he glanced at him, alluding to his reputation for violence towards those who crossed him.

"I ay' ever owned no snake," Eddie insisted, recalling the times that the weighty constrictor had come in handy for putting the frighteners on people.

"Of course, Eddie, in return for your help in this matter I can always put in a good word for you should you find your collar being felt for more serious offences – like theft; or handling stolen goods; or GBH; or demanding money with menaces."

Eddie downed what was left of his own pint, stubbed out his fag, and proffered the kind of grudging stare that suggested he might indeed be partial to bartering a lenient sentence.

"Okay," he conceded, "Ar' once owned a snake called Betty. But that wuz' years agoo'. Why d'ya wanna' know?"

"We're anxious to catch up with her. We believe she might be responsible for the disappearance of those missing youngsters."

Eddie grunted again, this time in scorn.

"Doh' tell me yow' believe all that 'giant snake' bollocks! Anyway, I ay' gorr'er now. Ar' sold her on… to a zoo."

"Which zoo?" Jonathan pressed him.

"Oh, Ar' doh' know. Ar' cor' remember. Like Ar' said, it wuz' years agoo'."

"There are only two zoos within a fifty-mile radius of Sneyd End, Eddie. Neither one of them owns, or has ever been gifted with, a reticulated python. Is your memory really that bad?"

"Orright', Ar' sold her ter' some bloke Ar' met in a pub."

"Which bloke? Which pub?"

"Look, Ar' cor' remember."

"Or did you just dispose of Betty by some other means? After all, not everybody wants the responsibility that goes with looking after an aggressive python that's outgrown its pen."

Observing the determined look in the copper's eye, Eddie knew he'd run out of obfuscations, and that he risked losing whatever chance remained of the Old Bill seeing their way clear to taking his multifarious petty crimes into account.

"Okay," he finally admitted. "Ar' dosed 'er up on the missus's sleepin' pills and dumped her down the railway embankment. Her wuz' tied up in a sack. Ar' doubt if her would 'ave survived the night. They need to be kept warm, yer' know, do pythons."

"We have reason to believe she *did* survive the night though – *and* that she found a nice warm place in which to shelter; a place where she would have been able to thrive, and to grow, and to sooner or later start hunting quite substantial prey – like three teenagers and an old tramp, for example! Besides, no one has ever reported coming across a dead python tied up in a sack. But a few days ago, in the old railway tunnel, I did come across a piece of sloughed snake skin that's been positively verified as belonging to a reticulated python – one that could possibly exceed twenty-five feet in length."

The realisation of what his reckless act that night in the cemetery might have occasioned was dawning upon this small-time crook. His eyes widened. Any trace of a swagger was gone.

"Of course, you're not the only person who finds the story about the legendary man-eating snake of Sneyd End a bit far-fetched. I suspect I'll have a difficult job convincing my superiors too. And that's why I'll need your help, Eddie."

"Help?" he glanced up, startled.

"I need you to repeat to them what you've just told me. That way – and armed with the evidence I have so far – I think I can make the case for convincing them the story is true after all."

* * * * *

THE SNEYD END GAZETTE
Thursday, July 10th 1969

TOWN HALL CORRUPTION – ARRESTS MADE
Police have today confirmed that both Horace Bissell, the former leader of Sneyd End Borough Council, and Edward Lawson, its Borough Architect, have been formally charged with receiving gifts and other financial inducements in return for the awarding of building contracts by the Council...

MISSING MAN – APPEAL FOR INFORMATION
The family of Wayne Fisher – the nineteen-year-old man who was reported missing over four weeks ago – have appealed for anyone who may have seen him to get in touch with local police. Wayne, who is five-foot two inches tall and has cropped hair, was last seen wandering over Fens Bank on Wednesday, June 4th..."

APOLLO MISSION – ALL SYSTEMS GO!
Final preparations are being made for the launch next week of the first-ever mission to land a man on the Moon. Apollo 11 is

due to blast off from the Kennedy Space Centre in Florida at 9.32am local time on Wednesday (2.32pm in the United Kingdom). An estimated five hundred million people worldwide are expected to watch live coverage of the launch on television…

* * * * *

PC Jonathan Hunt had decided the time had come for him to make a terrible truth known to his superiors: that there was indeed a giant snake on the loose somewhere in Sneyd End. It was for this purpose that he had finally plucked up the courage to walk up to Chief Superintendent Trotter's office and knock on the door.

"Come in."

Armed with that cardboard box he'd scooped under his arm, Jonathan gripped the handle and crossed the threshold, about to find out whether Pauline having announced to her parents who she was dating would prove an asset or a liability.

"Ah, PC Hunt. To what do I owe the pleasure?" his boss chortled, adding "By the way, excellent work apprehending that burglar you disturbed last night. With light-fingered Dicky Jones in the cells, we should now be able to clear up a whole series of break-ins in the town which we suspect he's behind. I'm minded to put your name forward for a commendation, Hunt."

"Thank you, sir. But that's not why I've come to see you."

The crisp, moustachioed police chief looked up in curiosity, noting the copper's grave expression. And what on Earth was in that box that was under his arm?

"It's about the disappearance of those teenagers whose whereabouts are still unaccounted for," Jonathan swallowed the lump bobbing in his throat and informed him.

"Oh, I see. In which case, you'd better take a seat."

"I'd rather stand, sir… if that's okay."

"As you wish, Constable," Trotter eyed him up and down, intrigued as to what pearl of wisdom Hunt was about to reveal that might solve a mystery that remained a source of acute embarrassment to the force.

"Sir, I believe I may have stumbled upon evidence that will assist us in our ongoing inquiries."

"Go on," his listener bade him, reclining into his chair and folding his arms in a display of wary attentiveness. He watched while Jonathan placed the box on his desk, opened it, and hauled out a strange scaly object.

"It's a piece of shed skin – from a snake, sir," the constable enlightened him.

"I can see that, Constable," Trotter replied, bemused.

"I have it on good authority that it belongs to an extremely large snake – a reticulated python, to be precise, sir."

"And?"

"And that this python could be responsible for the disappearances of Gary Willetts, Gillian Hickman, Kevin Wood, and now Wayne Fisher. It may also be responsible for the disappearance of Bert Duggins – that old tramp with the shopping trolley who hasn't been seen in months."

Unsure whether to be impressed or amused by this bizarre theory, Chief Superintendent Trotter subconsciously flashed his eyebrows, the ripple striating his forehead. CID had certainly never conceived of such a far-fetched possibility.

"So is this the only evidence you have that such a beast might be out there somewhere? After all, Constable, you have to admit: it's not every day that good folk in the Black Country find themselves being eaten by rogue pythons!"

Jonathan picked up on his boss's mildly derisive tone.

"No, sir. I have it on good authority that several years ago just such a python – which had been kept as a pet by its owner – was abandoned on the Sneyd End railway line; and that it could be sheltering in the old tunnel – somewhere warm where it would be able to survive through a British winter."

"And who is this 'good authority', may I ask? You haven't been talking to that 'Snakeman' friend of yours again, have you, Constable?"

"Sir, Brian Danks is one of the world's leading experts on snakes. He's travelled extensively studying these animals. I trust his judgement when he confirms that this piece of skin – which I found in the tunnel – does indeed belong to the world's largest constricting snake. He estimates that the one that shed this skin could possibly exceed twenty-five feet in length."

Trotter huffed in audible disbelief and swivelled impatiently in his chair, rising from it to wander over to the window.

"Hunt, you're a superb copper. But I have to say that there are times when you demonstrate a worrying lack of objectivity – nay, an almost startling naivety – especially when it comes to the tales that zoo-keeping friend of yours imbibes you with. In fact, I'm tempted to say he sends you along to fire his bullets for him."

"Sir?"

"Come on, Hunt. You know Brian Danks is an out-and-out rabble-rouser, who still hasn't got it out of his head that he's going to re-open that blessed railway. For goodness sake, man, this idiot almost got you killed! Did the thought never occur to you that *he* might be the source of all these ridiculous tales that have been put about concerning a giant, man-eating snake; and that *he* might have planted that skin in the tunnel in the hope that someone would find it and come running to the police? After all, he works in the right job to get hold of a piece of this stuff," his boss pointed contemptuously at the trophy on his desk.

"But, sir…"

"No, Hunt, I will not permit you to be a party to fuelling rumours of this nature. This bumbling busybody is already milking this town hall corruption business for all its worth. The last thing we need is for him to be terrifying folk with tall stories about people being devoured by enormous snakes."

"But, sir, I've talked to the man who owned the snake. What's more, it was still alive when he dumped it down the old railway embankment."

"Oh, yes. And who might this character be?" Trotter barked.

The courageous young policeman was aware that his boss was reaching the limits of his patience. Therefore, he took a deep breath and played the only card he had left that might convince him that this claim was not some ridiculous wheeze dreamed up by the assiduous new Councillor Brian Danks.

"Eddie Foster, sir."

Trotter strode back to his desk, his countenance darkening.

"Eddie Foster?" he leered at Jonathan. "Eddie Foster, the small-time racketeer – who CID has been preparing a file on?"

"Yes, sir. He confirmed to me that he once owned, and then abandoned, a reticulated python called Betty. I did ask him if he would come forward and volunteer this information himself, sir; but he declined," said Jonathan regretfully – dismayed that, in the end, this unscrupulous thug preferred to take his chance being nicked for dealing in dodgy copper piping than to face the wrath of British justice for his part in unleashing a creature that might be responsible for the deaths of several young people.

Trotter, meanwhile, had turned rubicund with anger.

"You talked to Eddie Foster – a suspect my officers have spent weeks putting together the evidence to nail? Do you know what you have done, Hunt?" he seethed. "By your reckless act you could have compromised an important criminal investigation. That's a very serious disciplinary matter, man. Have you completely taken leave of your senses?"

Jonathan could only form his mouth to offer mitigation that, in the end, he couldn't bring himself to verbalise. He had indeed gone way out on a limb. He'd risked not only the wrath of his boss, but also that of a formal disciplinary hearing. It left him wondering whether it might be an opportune time to brush up on his former accountancy skills! Trotter, however, wasn't quite finished with him yet.

"Like I said, Hunt, you're a bloody good policeman," he insisted, drifting back to the window, his hands behind his back as he feigned to stare at the street scene outside. Then, his voice having softened, he added "What's more, my daughter seems to have taken a shine to you. But then – for reasons that completely escape me – Pauline is also smitten by that confounded Snakeman and his outlandish causes," he scoffed in a tone that had even so lost its earlier, rabid edge.

"Be that as it may, Margaret was only commenting to me the other day that she seems happier and more settled than we've seen her in a long time. So perhaps you're doing something right, Hunt," he joked (though the copper thought it wise not to laugh).

"Now I'm prepared to overlook this little lapse in diligence on your part," the Chief conceded. "However, I want you to promise me that you will forget all this nonsense about giant snakes; and that you will desist from conversing with a key suspect in a stolen goods inquiry. And finally, for goodness sake – old school chum or not – keep away from Brian Danks. He's a fantasist, Hunt; and a troublemaker. Take it from me: he won't be content until he's got the whole town in uproar. Goodness knows, he's been trying long enough!"

Grateful for the reprieve and touched by his boss's magnanimity, Jonathan nodded. Dating the Chief Super's daughter – his only child and the apple of his eye – did indeed have its advantages.

As for what to do about Betty, he resigned himself to having done his bit. It would now be left to others to unearth the truth about the fearsome creature that he suspected was out there somewhere, waiting to strike again.

* * * * *

"Are you sure we're supposed to go in there?"

The litany of questions that fourteen-year-old Parminder Kaur had been assailing her more intrepid classmate with had become wearisome. Robin Jukes had walked the length of the infamous Sneyd End Tunnel a few times now – including as part of the initiation for new boys attending Sneyd End High School. Therefore, unlike the warier female novice with whom he intended to complete the passage again this afternoon, it held no fear. Or at least that was the impression he was consciously trying to convey for Parminder's benefit.

"It's alright. Loads of people have wandered through there," he endeavoured to reassure her as together they approached its northern entrance on their way home.

"But it's dark in there. There could be hidden dangers. And what about, you know... the snake?"

Robin halted and offered her a look of worldly-wise incredulity for having been taken in by such a tall story.

"Nah, there ay' no snake. Doh' yer' think someone would have caught it by now if there was. Besides, this is Britain, not India: it's too cold for big snakes like that to survive in the wild. Or so the Snakeman once told me."

In common with many youngsters caught up in the excitement of 'the Space Age', Parminder's ambition was to be an astronaut when she left school, exploring space and enabling people to live on the moon – as all sorts of people would soon be doing (or so Mr Evans, the physics teacher, had told them in class). Therefore, to her proudly scientific mind, Robin's observation did indeed seem a logical deduction. Backed up by the assurance of Sneyd End's very own august expert in such matters, it at least put that worry to bed. However, gazing ahead at that fenced-off tunnel mouth reminded her of other dangers that entering within might chance. Still desperately apprehensive about what they were about to do, it was concerning these that Robin's diminutive Indian friend continued to cluck in his ear.

"I really shouldn't be doing this, you know. I've told you before: my father wouldn't approve of... well, you know: me being alone in there... with a boy," she ventured crablike.

Robin was aware that the social and religious mores that attended her faith circumscribed her from doing things her white female classmates took for granted. Keeping the company of a raffish and irreverent young white boy was one of them – notwithstanding that he'd gallantly defended her against periodic racialist gibes doing the rounds in the school. In fact, he'd taken quite a shine to Parminder in the time they'd been friends. There were times when he was tempted to think the feeling was mutual.

"Look, we'm not doin' anyfink' wrong. Trust me. Besides, it looks like it's gonna' rain," her champion pointed out, glancing up at the darkening heavens.

Sure enough it was sensing the pitter-patter of raindrops that finally persuaded the hesitant teenager to follow her companion as he slipped through the missing railing and switched on the powerful torch he'd taken from his satchel. Remembering his grandmother's advice about the importance of chivalry, Robin turned about to assist Parminder as she too picked her way through the gap to step inside the gloomy tunnel, his hand lingering to savour the feel of her soft feminine digits.

It was certainly eerie inside the tunnel. Robin's torch pierced the blackness to illuminate all sort of detritus that had been abandoned in here during the five years since the line had closed:

a discarded mattress here; an old pram or bicycle there; walls that had been daubed with graffiti; evidence of fires that had been lit. Not that there was any need to light fires, aside from to provide illumination for whatever errant teenagers got up to in here. Indeed, Parminder was taken by just how warm it was inside the tunnel. Meanwhile, the beam of Robin's torch was picking out hints of movement too – the colony of rats that inhabited this place, he enlightened her.

She gasped and flinched. Perhaps it was also to keep these chunky rodents at bay that those fires had been lit.

"I d-d-don't like rats," she spluttered nervously. "I sp-sp-spotted one the other day scurrying from the boiler room at school – a really big one, it was. Mrs Danks saw it too. She thinks there might be a nest of them in there; and that it's time Mr Weston called in the pest controllers."

"Better still, why doh' she get her hubby to chuck some of his snakes in there!" Robin guffawed.

Parminder halted and stared at him, unamused.

"Anyway, come on. It should only take fifteen minutes or so to walk to the other end," he endeavoured to reassure her, pointing to the tiny pinprick of daylight visible up ahead.

"Doh' your parents let you go out with boys then?" he enquired by-and-by, hoping that by making conversation he might take Parminder's mind of her nagging anxieties.

"My father would not approve," she repeated that Pavlovian mantra he'd become accustomed to hearing. "Many Sikh parents arrange their children's marriages for them. But first my father wants me to go to university and complete my education. We Sikhs place great importance upon education as a means of improving our lives and that of our families. Then he says he will let me choose my own husband. I would like to marry a nice Sikh boy though. My father tells me it is important that we Sikhs stick together and not forget who we are. Many times in the past we have faced persecution for our faith."

"Yeah, but surely there must be white boys you fancy, like," he harrumphed. "After all, we've got willies too – just like Indian boys have. And you Indian girls have the same thingies as white girls, doh' you. They'm just a different colour, that's all. Oh, and perhaps yours have a bit more hair!" he observed rather bluntly.

In the glow of the torch Parminder caught his eyes roaming the outline of her body. She declined to confirm his assumptions.

"That Christine Bone's got a hairy one, you know. And Elaine Woodward's is ginger! Ar' sid' 'em once when they were in the shower. Me and David Dale ran into the girls' changing area for a loff', like – when they were getting changed after netball. It day' arf' give 'em a fright, it did! Still, it taught us more about what girls' bodies look like than any of them' funny drawings that Mrs Danks handed out in sex education classes! It was even worth gettin' caught by Miss Ferriday!" he guffawed, recalling the dressing down they'd received from her afterwards.

"Yer' doh' really play sport either, do you?" he pointed out in the absence of a response from her.

"I don't like sport. I prefer science subjects," she proffered.

Robin was underwhelmed. He found science hard work – notwithstanding that, thanks to Parminder helping him with his homework, he now possessed a more proficient grasp of it.

"So what kind of music do you like?" he steered the conversation back onto more familiar terrain. However, sensing a response might not be forthcoming on that score either he proceeded to reel off his own preferences instead.

"I like that *'Fire Brigade'* song by The Move. And that *'Lily The Pink'* record by The Scaffold is really funny. I like Desmond Dekker too – you know, that Jamaican geezer who sings *'Get up in di' mahnin', slavin fah' bread, sah', so dat' ev'ry mout' can be fed... Poh', poh', me' Iz-rah-lites'*!" he crooned to her in his best patois, looking to lighten proceedings. It appeared to work. A smile briefly returned to Parminder's cherubic face.

"I don't really listen to Western music. However, we Sikhs do like to sing and to dance. We call it Bhangra. Like your rock-and-roll, it has lots of rhythm and lots of drums. It is the traditional music we play when we are happy and want to celebrate – for example, when the harvest is gathered in."

"Doh' s'pose you've heard of the Rolling Stones then? They'm a rock-and-roll band. They sing *'Paint It Black'* and *'Jumpin'*

Jack Flash'. They were on the telly the other day cuz' their guitarist died in a swimming pool."

"My father would not approve," she fell back on that mantra again, explaining that "Many of these 'pop groups' take drugs, and drink alcohol, and do things that are forbidden by my faith."

Sometimes Robin wondered whether it might have been more profitable had he just latched onto an English girl instead! However, for all that she was hard work, he genuinely liked Parminder. Perhaps Indian girls just required more finesse. Spotting a left-behind sleeper up ahead, he halted to sit down upon it, placing the torch down where it might provide sufficient illumination for him to gesture for her to join him.

"I'd rather keep going," she urged. "This place gives me the creeps. Besides, my father will worry if I am home late."

"Yeah, he's a birrova' worrier, your old man, ay' he," Robin noted with a hint of amusement tinged with despair. "Come on, just a short rest and then we can be on our way."

Aware that her protests must be grating on him, she relented and sat down alongside him. And though she thought she'd left sufficient gap between them for the sake of propriety, somehow Robin contrived to shuffle up to her and close it.

"So I suppose you ay' ever kissed a boy either then?" the interrogation recommenced.

She turned to gaze into eyes that were curious, if a tad mischievous.

"No. I have never kissed a boy," she replied dolefully.

"Oh, well. I ay' ever kissed a girl either. Well, not a proper kiss; like you see people doin' in them' plays on television," Robin confessed in a gesture of pubescent solidarity.

She summoned up a smile. It was the cue for her admirer to lean in and drape his arm around her. Parminder glanced nervously at the hand that had appeared clutching her shoulder.

"I want you to know I'm grateful for your help, Parminder: you know, with my homework, like. I know I ay' as brainy as you. And I doh' s'pose I'll ever be an astronaut, like what you wanna' be. Maybe I'll end up workin' in a foundry – like me' dad and me' grandad. But if I do pass any exams, then I want you to know I woh' forget how you've helped me."

The mischief in that face aglow in the torchlight was indeed radiating his touching gratitude. His smile then straightened and he moved in to steal a peck on her cheek. She blushed and glanced away in embarrassment. Then, before he could properly ready himself, she looked into his sweet grey-blue eyes and it was her turn to move in and steal a kiss – this time a brief and awkward one upon his lips. His belated response was to draw her in closer and hold her possessively.

"So what's yours like then," he was also curious to know.

"I'm sorry?" she replied, perplexed.

"Yer' know: your thingy," he pointed to her lap. "Tell you what: I'll show you mine if you show me yours," he then offered, the mischievous grin having returned.

This time she was genuinely scandalised, unhooking his arm from her shoulder and shuffling along the sleeper.

"That is none of your business. You should not be asking a girl a question like that. And neither do I want to see… yours," she protested in a fluster. "My father would not…"

"Yeah, I know: he wouldn't approve!" Robin grunted.

By now, Parminder had risen to her feet and was motioning to recommence their journey to the tunnel's end. Robin, meanwhile, had dipped his eyes in remorse at his clumsiness. He really didn't know much about girls at all! However, conceiving an alternative wheeze to detain her, he too now rose to his feet.

"Look, I'm sorry. Shall we have another kiss instead; a longer one this time – using our tongues," he suggested excitedly.

"Listen, Robin…!" she abruptly hushed him.

"Okay, I'm sorry again," he pleaded, seizing her hand. "But I do like you, Parminder. You will still be my friend…?"

"No, quiet!" she insisted, pressing her finger to her lips.

All exhortations and explanations ceased. The echoing of their voices tailed off. There was a silence in the tunnel broken only by the vague sound of movement originating somewhere along the shaft behind them.

"What was that?" Parminder whispered timorously.

Robin had heard it too and grabbed the torch to shine its penetrating beam about. However, he couldn't pick anything out.

"It's probably them' rats again. But they woh' hurt you."

"I still say we should not be here," she insisted, grabbing her satchel and seizing his arm so impulsively that it caused him to drop the torch. The battery door jolted. Its contents spilled out. Suddenly, everything was pitch black.

Parminder screamed. Meanwhile, Robin was desperately scrabbling about to locate the batteries and slot them back into the torch the right way around. In between Parminder's fretting, the shuffling sound was growing ever closer.

"Hurry, Robin, hurry!" she squealed, fumbling to grab his arm.

At last, the batteries were all slotted in and the torch powered back into life. Shining it about, when its beam finally picked out the source of the disturbance, both teenagers froze in terror. For there, slithering towards them was the largest snake they had ever seen, the two florid red jewels that were its eyes reflecting the torchlight. However, for some inexplicable reason it then halted, its tongue flicking back and forth warily.

"Wh-wh-what is it?" Parminder's teeth chattered uncontrollably – though the answer was self-evident: the story about a giant snake was true after all.

Betty's opportunistic instinct was meanwhile telling her to grab this unexpected human prey while the chance presented itself. However, the blinding torch beam had momentarily discombobulated the python – not that she relied on sight to hunt in the dark confines of her lair. Instead, by picking out their body heat using pit organs on her head Betty could sense that there were two potential meals in front of her. But which one to go for? The smaller heat source would obviously be easier to overpower and to swallow. However, who could say whether the larger heat source might then retaliate, smiting Betty with a possibly lethal blow to the head. And a snake will protect its vulnerable, defenceless head at all costs.

Truth to tell, Betty had faced a similar dilemma before. On that occasion she'd gone for the larger heat source, neutralising the smaller heat source with a lashing from her powerful body. But would it work again? It was not just the tremulous teenagers who were rooted to the spot with indecision.

"Sl-sl-slowly st-st-step b-b-backwards," Robin ordered her.

After a moment of hesitation during which Parminder stared at Robin with tristful eyes, she obediently tip-toed away from him.

Betty's tongue was flicking again: just one heat source within striking distance this time. Coiling up in readiness, she was confident she could subdue it.

Meanwhile, on that memorable trip to the zoo Robin recalled the Snakeman cautioning the children that snakes are very sensitive to sudden, loud noises. For although they couldn't 'hear' sounds in the sense that humans could, their bodies were able to pick up the vibrations those sounds transmitted. Transferring the torch to his left hand while all the time training it to dazzle their assailant, he crouched down in the dust to grab a discarded metal bar. Rising to his feet again and wielding it in his right hand in the manner of a club, he too now tiptoed backwards.

Betty could detect his retreat by the faint vibrations his footsteps were transferring through the ground. Slowly too, she uncoiled and dragged herself along to keep tabs upon her prey. Like a deadly game of grandmother's footsteps, each time Robin halted, Betty would halt too. Finally, halting again, he began to strike the ground with hefty thuds from the bar in his hand.

Betty flinched. The vibrations she was picking up were brash and vexatious. With the element of surprise lost, maybe this particular prey was going to be more trouble than it was worth.

Robin noticed that the serpent was no longer trailing him. Instead, as if by some miracle of deliverance, his torch picked it out disappearing head first down a drainage shaft, its huge great trunk slithering down after it.

"It looks like it's gone," he called back to Parminder.

"Good. Let's get out of here before it pops up somewhere else," she badgered him.

Both youngsters quickened the pace until, at last, Robin could assist a trembling Parminder to squeeze through the gap in the fence at the southern entrance to the tunnel.

"Phew! That was close!" he panted.

"You idiot! Don't ever bring me here again, do you understand!" Parminder shrieked at him. "Now take me home. Or better still, I will make my own way home."

"Home?" he gasped. "We cor' just goo' home. We need to tell someone what we've just seen. We must tell our parents about this creature; and report it to the police too."

Parents? Police? Parminder froze, gripped by a panic that was almost as palpable as that which had accompanied running into the snake itself.

"No, I forbid you. My father will be very angry with me that I was alone with you in this place. You must promise me you will never say a thing to anyone about us being here."

"But... We cor' just..."

"Promise me, Robin," she insisted.

Then, furtively glancing about to make sure no one was watching, she flung her arms around the shoulders of her clandestine boyfriend and offered him a second kiss – this time of the very sort he'd been so eager to steal from her inside the tunnel. For several long seconds they rather amateurishly sucked on each other's lips and tongues – neither one entirely sure whether they were doing this 'kissing' thing right. Not that Robin was complaining. He pulled her in closer. And when they did finally surface for air, in return for her indulgence those big brown eyes were again demanding from him an assurance.

"Yeah, orright'. I woh' say nuffink'," he conceded.

"Good. This must be our secret. No one else must ever know we were here. And no one must know that we kissed. My father would not approve," she repeated, sealing their pact with one more fleeting kiss before hurrying on her way.

21

Monday July 13th 1969: there was a buzz of the unexpected abroad in the chamber of Sneyd End Council House, the likes of which few of the members gathering to take their seats could remember. All weekend in pubs, in shopping queues, and at bus stops, in the newspapers and on local television, talk had been dominated by the arrest on charges of corruption of not just its former leader, but also of one of its most senior officers too. All of a sudden, it had become apparent just why Horace Bissell – in league with the Borough Architect – had been so keen to scotch opposition to controversial developments like the infamous Tiger Street flats, the town centre's swanky new shopping centre, and the controversial leisure centre that was sat astride the town's former railway line: both men had stood to gain financially from their completion.

Taking his seat too at the head of the Conservative benches, Councillor Bill Patterson would ordinarily have been chafing at the bit to exploit the Labour Group's evident embarrassment. However, the revelation that one of the main characters who'd been bribing its former leader was none other than local building magnate and one-time Conservative parliamentary candidate, Martin de Vere, had at a stroke removed that temptation.

Only just turning up in time for the six o'clock start, Councillor Brian Danks made a hurried and somewhat chaotic entrance into the chamber, colliding with a clerk and scattering the addendum papers the man had been circulating. Apologising noisily and profusely to a line of already-seated councillors as he then manoeuvred his way past to take up his own place in the chamber, upon sitting down and opening his briefcase Brian was forced to apologise again when an uneaten banana and a copy of 'Railway Modeller' magazine tumbled from it into the lap of the demure woman sat next to him.

"Buffoon!" Councillor Patterson could be overheard muttering to his deputy as eyes rolled in despair.

It was not an auspicious start to the meeting of the council at which Brian intended to deliver his maiden speech. However, before he could snatch a moment to re-read his notes (and curious eyes behind him crane over his shoulder to see what they might contain), the aura of expectation was broken by the chamber doors being flung open.

"All be upstanding for the Worshipful Mayor of Sneyd End," the cry went out as the Mayor was ushered in – attired in scarlet, fur-trimmed robes and his chain of office. Preceding him, with the mace that he settled on its plinth at the front of the chamber, was his attendant. Following in his train was the Town Clerk in his wig and black gown, while bringing up the rear was the Mayor's chaplain – Father Allen smiling indulgently at Brian as he breezed past attired in his dog collar and curate's gown.

Brian was new to all this pomp and procedure. As an independent councillor lacking the support of a group of party colleagues, he was conscious that, after all the things that had gone before, the other thirty-five Labour and Conservative members gathered around him were almost certainly willing him to fail; eager to trip him up if it aided the process of intimidating this maverick politician into keeping quiet.

However, keeping quiet was not in Brian Danks's nature. He waited patiently while the Mayor ploughed through his opening announcements, backbench councillors nit-picked over obscure points in the minutes of the previous meeting, and Councillor Patterson and his new Labour opposite number sparred over the main items of business on the agenda. Taking a moment to turn and stare up into the public gallery, the Snakeman spotted and acknowledged familiar faces amongst the reporters taking notes. He spotted Ruby too, there to savour the occasion of that maiden speech – even if a trace of unease about what he was about to say tempered the smile she offered him in return.

Indeed, what exactly did Councillor Brian Danks intend to say? Alas, both councillors and reporters would have to wait a while longer to find out – although the gossip amongst them was unanimous that it had to be some sort of withering condemnation of the dodgy shenanigans that had brought Sneyd End a sudden and dubious infamy in the country at large.

At last, with the usual political knockabout stuff out of the way, it was time to find out. Having done his homework – and using a procedure of the Council that allowed its elected members to question committee chairmen about the decisions of recent committee meetings – the Snakeman raised his hand to indicate that he wished to question an item on the Education Committee minutes: the one concerning safety measures that had been put in place in the Borough's schools in the light of those unsolved disappearances of young people in the town.

There was genuine puzzlement that the 'new boy' had overlooked several potential minute items where he could have highlighted the over-familiarity of certain councillors with the Borough's building contractors. Instead, he was asking a question about safety measures in schools! The Chairman of the Education Committee yawned and sat up ready to swat away the probing of this irksome new member.

"Th-th-thank you, Mr M-m-mayor," Brian rose to his feet and bumbled his way through his opening courtesies. "While it's still thought that the disappearance of these young people might be the work of a serial killer, I have thought long and hard about this matter and would now like put forward another possibility that I believe warrants serious consideration..."

"Mr Mayor, on a point of order, this is most inappropriate," Bill Patterson stood to protest (and with a pained expression that spoke of impatience). "This minute deals with safety measures in our schools. It is not intended to offer Councillor Danks a platform to speculate about ongoing criminal investigations."

"Yes, if he has information, let him tell the police!" a Labour member cried out.

"Councillor Danks, kindly stick to the matter in hand, if you will," the Mayor instructed him wearily. It looked like Brian Danks was going to be one of *those* councillors!

"Yes, Mr M-m-mayor, of course. What I was trying to say is that there is much more that needs to be done to assure the safety of our young people – indeed, of everyone here in Sneyd End. And it has to do with the old railway line..."

Cue groans and more rolling of eyes around the chamber.

"It didn't take him long to jump on his hobby horse," someone hissed.

"Yes, what's that got to do with safety in our schools?" hectored another.

"Mr Mayor, the old railway tunnel – or, more precisely, what I fear may be lurking inside there – provides the clue to…"

"Oh, come on. You done that accursed railway line to death!" the heckling continued.

"Yes, he's supposed to be asking a question, not giving us a lecture," someone reminded the Mayor.

"QUESTION! QUESTION! QUESTION…!" councillors on both sides began to chant in unison – such that it was impossible for Brian to make himself heard. Ruby meanwhile masked her eyes with her hand, unable to bear the spectacle of people once more baying for her husband's blood.

"Order…! Order…! Order…!" the Mayor meanwhile rose to his feet, hammering his gavel to demand decorum. The chamber duly fell silent – aside from a certain councillor still trying to make his point.

"Councillor Danks, when *I* am on my feet you sit down and keep quiet," he bawled again for the Snakeman's benefit.

"Er, yes, Mr M-m-mayor. S-s-sorry, Mr M-m-mayor," Brian twittered sheepishly and sat down.

"Now, I appreciate you're a new councillor and that there are things you want to say," the Mayor indulged him. "However, Committee Questions are just that: a time for questions about the decisions of the Council's various committees. Therefore, please ask the Chairman your question, if you will. No statements; no grandstanding; just a straight-forward question."

For a moment, Brian hesitated. He wanted to offer important background information that would help make sense of what he was about to say and draw upon the expertise he'd acquired during ten years of study and research. However, it was not going to be. Sensing the bristling stares of the councillors around him, he rose charily from his seat and addressed the chamber with as much earnest as he could muster.

"Mr Mayor, I would like to ask the Chairman if he has ever entertained the possibility that certain rumours that have been put about around this town could actually be true? That, as I have good reason to believe, there is indeed a giant snake dwelling in that old railway tunnel…"

This time cue wails of utter disbelief.

"… A reticulated python, to be precise – one that is at least twenty-five feet in length and could weigh in excess of two hundred and fifty pounds…"

"Mr Mayor, this is outrageous…" Bill Patterson stood to his feet and fumed.

"… And that it is this snake that could be responsible for the disappearances of one or more of those missing youngsters."

"What? He's suggesting they've been eaten by a python?" an elderly councillor cupped his ear, checking with a colleague that he'd heard correctly.

"Are you completely insane, man?" another councillor stood and screamed at him.

Shrill abuse and personal accusations were being hurled at him from every direction. However, he had done it: like Stephen the Martyr in the Book of Acts, he had made public something that he knew in his bones to be true. Likewise, he was now receiving a public stoning for having done so (or at least a metaphorical one). He sat down and closed his eyes in prayer, trying to ignore the clamour for the Mayor to censure him for his 'absurd' and 'irresponsible' remarks.

However, the Snakeman was also shrewd enough to know that his ace card, as always, wasn't going to be the predictable, boorish reaction of the town's politicians. While they were busy cawing in indignation, the Snakeman had proved once again that he was a rich source of copy to the reporters in the public gallery, who Ruby observed frantically scribbling down what they'd just heard before racing outside to find a phone box.

* * * * *

"Chief Superintendent, what's your response to…?"
"Chief Superintendent, can I ask you…?"
"Chief Superintendent, do you intend to…?"

"Gentlemen, gentlemen..." Cyril Trotter waved his hands to bring some semblance of decorum to the melee that his press conference had descended into.

With reporters braying questions and photographers and TV cameramen jostling to get the best shots, it was as much as he could do to obtain the calm he needed to address them without interruption, reading from the press release he'd prepared.

"A statement was made at last night's meeting of Sneyd End Council to the effect that there is a snake – possibly a python – at large in this town. No evidence was presented at that meeting to back-up this incredible claim; and to date my officers have received no information from members of the public concerning sightings of this supposed snake; nor any other evidence to indicate that such a creature exists. Therefore, we have no reason to believe there is any veracity in the claim that was made.

"Furthermore, I want to place on record my dismay at the potential of such wild and unsubstantiated remarks to needlessly sow alarm amongst members of the public. I therefore reiterate that we have *no* evidence that this so-called 'giant snake' is anything more than an idle tale that has been put about and which, regrettably, a certain councillor has sought to draw attention to in the interests of his own self-publicity."

Harsh words! However, if Chief Superintendent Trotter imagined that there the matter would rest, he was mistaken. Straight away, questions began to fly at him from all directions.

"But Chief Superintendent, Councillor Danks *has* presented quite compelling evidence that, at the very least, a snake released into the wild might indeed be inhabiting the old railway tunnel," one of the press pack reminded him.

"Well, Councillor Danks hasn't seen fit to permit me to see this 'evidence'," the Chief snapped impatiently.

"Chief Superintendent, can you confirm categorically that this is the first time it's been put to you that a man-eating python might be responsible for the deaths of those missing youngsters?" another reporter jostled forward to call out above the scrum.

A lump visibly bobbed in Cyril Trotter's throat.

"Look, gentleman, I am not prepared to speculate about such matters, and to thereby give this hare-brained story a credence it does not deserve," was all the police chief would say as, flanked by his officers, he pushed past the heaving press pack to exit the conference room.

"Ridiculous little halfwit!" he fumed to those officers once they were safely ensconced within the bowels of the police station. "I've told you all before: that self-styled 'Snakeman' is a clown and a troublemaker. Now he's got the whole town in uproar – again!"

"Yes, he's certainly put the cat amongst the pigeons, sir. Or should that be the snake amongst them!" an underling tried his hand at humour (his boss's caustic stare informing him that he failed to find the joke amusing).

"But what if he is right, sir? What if there *is* a snake slithering along the sewers beneath our feet, ready to pop up and strike at any moment?" another officer fretted, watching for his Chief Super's reaction.

The very thought sent shivers down the spine of Trotter's young secretary as she too followed after him. If it wasn't bad enough having to check before placing her bottom on the toilet seat lest her male colleague had stretched clingfilm over the pan as a prank, this morning when nipping into the ladies' room she'd instead found herself checking to see whether a head with a flicking tongue might have surfaced from the U-bend!

"Anyway, enough of this silliness!" said the Chief, halting and turning about. "Get me PC Hunt," he then barked at her.

"PC Hunt, sir?"

"Yes, PC Hunt! I don't care where he is or what he's doing. I want him back at the station now and reporting to my office. Do you understand, woman?"

"Er, yes, sir," she burbled. "Of course, sir. I'll ask the control room to put out a radio message right away."

Thereupon, her boss stormed inside his office and slammed the door shut behind him.

* * * * *

"... *Guidance is internal... Twelve, eleven, ten, nine... Ignition sequence starts... Six, five, four, three, two, one, zero. All engines running... Lift-off! We have a lift-off! Thirty-two minutes past the hour, lift-off on Apollo 11...*"

Conscious that they were watching history being made, the much-heralded launch had so gripped the pupils of Sneyd End High School that, for once, there was no need for the teaching staff to harry them to pay attention.

Gathering them together in the assembly hall had been Graham Weston's brainwave. What better way to mark the end of term than to wheel in the large television set from the science block so that the entire school could witness the fulfilment of that promise made eight years earlier by the late President Kennedy: that before the decade was out the United States would land a man on the Moon and return him safely to the Earth.

"... Tower cleared... Neil Armstrong reporting a roll-and-pitch programme that puts Apollo 11 on a proper heading..."

Indeed, the Apollo 11 mission looked set to consummate a fascination with science, technology, and especially space exploration that – as much as the music, the fashions, or the social upheavals – had come to define the 1960s. From *'Doctor Who'* and *'Lost In Space'* to *'Thunderbirds'* and *'Star Trek'*, television programmes had enthused young minds with boundless possibilities for travel and adventure in space. If astronauts Neil Armstrong, Michael Collins and Buzz Aldrin really could conquer this 'final frontier' then before long, it was confidently predicted, all kinds of people would be shuttling back and forth to the Moon, which would be no more remarkable than boarding an airplane to Europe.

"...Apollo 11, this is Houston. You are 'go' for staging..."

The school looked on as the colossal engines of the huge Saturn V rocket thrust it through the cloudless Florida sky, jettisoning its various 'stages' as onwards and upwards it soared towards its destination over two hundred and thirty-eight thousand miles away. From her vantage point on a seat on one side of the aisle, Ruby Danks could revel in the sense of awe and wonder abroad amongst even her most hard-bitten students at this triumph of human endeavour. Mr Evans, the physics teacher, even had tears in his eyes!

"...Eight miles down range, twelve miles high... Velocity four thousand feet per second... Stand by for Mode 1-Charlie..."

If nothing else, the excitement that had attended the 'Space Race' had provided a welcome diversion from the decade's dispiriting political dramas – of which the most salient remained the bloody conflict still raging in Vietnam, where over a thousand young Americans each week were being returned home in body bags. While opposition to the war had rent the United States from top to bottom, at least on this day the whole country had come together to celebrate a supremely American achievement.

"... Thrusters 'go' all engines... This is Houston, 'go' all engines, you're looking good..."

To be sure, for two of Ruby's pupils this afternoon's excitement remained overshadowed by a terrible secret to which they were party. Sat next to her, Robin Jukes broke from imbibing those stirring images of the Apollo spacecraft departing Earth's atmosphere to lean forward and gaze at Parminder Kaur, who was seated at the far end of the row. Eventually, she noticed him. When she turned her guilt-laden eyes away, he sat up and glanced at Mrs Danks instead, her hands resting upon the discernible bump in her tummy that was the reason this would be her last week teaching science at Sneyd End High School.

Ruby returned his faltering smile, extending it to Parminder too – who she noticed was also looking at her in that same self-conscious manner.

It was the turn of Ruby's smile to falter. She suspected people had taken to offering her these half-scathing, half-pitying looks because word had gone around that the bump might not be the only reason she would not be returning in September. She was aware of jokes doing the rounds in the staff room concerning what the school's head teacher got up to at (or on!) his desk, as well as gossip that was scurrilously questioning if he might be the father of her child!

"... Houston, be advised the visual is 'go' today... And yeah, they finally gave me a window to look out of...!"

With the Apollo craft by now little more than a glowing dot on the tracking camera, from his place a few rows ahead of her Graham Weston glanced over his shoulder and spotted his one-time lover deep in anguish. Ruby cut dead the brief, non-committal smile he offered. It galled that he'd somehow managed to wangle a way of keeping his job when, to all intents and purposes, she was being forced from hers. Meanwhile, to look away was to instead spy Millie Ferriday re-crossing her legs, Little Miss Kinky Boots surely not oblivious to the fourth-form lads on the row alongside her gawping at the way that teeny suede skirt of hers had ridden up to expose her shapely thighs.

"... One hundred and ninety miles down range now... Seventy-two miles high... Velocity eleven thousand feet per second..."

Of course, of late there was another explanation for those mordant looks that staff and pupils had been giving Ruby: that maybe they'd read the newspapers and were regretting on her behalf that her maverick husband had once again made a fool of himself (and, by implication, of his longsuffering wife also).

However, unlike on previous occasions, this time Ruby was determined to stand by her spouse, confident that he was right to warn that a killer snake was indeed inhabiting that old railway tunnel. All it needed was for other, independent witnesses to come forward and attest that it was true. It was in this spirit of defiance that she offered a more resolute air when she caught Robin and Parminder staring at her in that same manner again.

* * * * *

"... That's one small step for man... One giant leap for mankind..."

It was just coming up to seven o'clock on the morning of Monday, July 21ˢᵗ 1969. PC Jonathan Hunt glanced up at the television set in the canteen of Sneyd End Nick to observe coverage from the previous evening of Neil Armstrong stepping out of the lunar module to become the first human being ever to set foot on the Moon. However, this memorable moment was of only passing interest to the chastened young policeman who was waiting to start his shift (and who was otherwise lazily stirring the mug of tea that had been set before him).

"You know, you are one incredibly lucky copper. Old Trotter has had officers drummed out of the force for lesser things," a colleague attempted to rouse him, placing down his own mug and sliding into the chair across the table. He too took a moment to observe the grainy black-and-white footage on the TV screen.

"Of course, it helps that his daughter has probably put in a good word for you," he then leaned in and observed with a wry smile. "You see, the Chief has quite a soft spot for his precious Pauline. So it was a wise choice on your part: asking her out, like. Or was it Pauline who asked you out?"

The aside finally goaded a grin of sorts from Jonathan. Once Chief Superintendent Trotter's initial fury had waned, he had indeed stayed the imminent suspension from duty that he'd threatened to inflict upon his freelancing officer – Jonathan having truthfully pleaded that he'd had no inkling that his best friend was going to make that bombshell announcement in the council chamber; nor that he would wave in front of incredulous press hacks that huge piece of sloughed snake skin that Jonathan had handed to him for safekeeping.

However, if nothing else, Brian's dramatic public relations stunt had got the town talking; so much so that the Chief could no longer pretend that the existence of such a deadly animal wasn't at least a possibility. However, though paying lip service to the clamour to investigate it, devoting police resources to doing so was another matter. Either Chief Superintendent Trotter had not the slightest clue about how to go about hunting down an escaped python (his pride certainly wouldn't permit him to call in the Black Country's resident 'expert' in such matters!); or he was dragging his feet because he remained unconvinced that it was out there. Either way, he was adamant that PC Jonathan Hunt would be having nothing to do with any such investigation!

"Anyway, one welcome outcome of this business about a giant snake is that it has put an end to folk constantly trespassing over Fens Bank," his colleague noted with relief. "Sergeant Johnson has been patrolling it on the quiet with his dog team – so at least someone in this nick is taking what your mate said seriously. He was telling me his men haven't seen a soul over there all week: no kids riding their new chopper bikes, no illicit anglers, no teenage lovers looking for somewhere quiet for a spot of canoodling! Let's hope it stays that way for the summer."

Jonathan grinned again. Pauline's pull on her doting father's affections indeed meant he was one 'lucky copper'. However, it still left the matter of that snake unresolved. As he sipped on his tea and glanced up at the flickering televised images of those American astronauts bobbing about on the Moon he wondered what would it take to finally convince the head of Sneyd End Police that it warranted far more attention than it had been given so far?

22

It had been an interesting week, to say the least. Thank goodness it was over and the Dankses could look ahead to making final preparations for the arrival of their new baby. For now though, Brian was content to ambush his pregnant wife while she was preparing lunch, nestling up to her to eagerly scrunch those laden boobs while nibbling at her neck – all of which she was rather enjoying when the doorbell suddenly chimed.

"Typical!" she looked up and huffed.

"Ignore it. It's probably another reporter after a quote," Brian insisted in between sucking on her ear lobes.

The doorbell chimed a second time.

"I better see who it is," she moaned again, flinging aside the tea towel in her hand and slipping his lustful grasp.

Into the hall she waddled, there to discern two visitors standing silhouetted by the sunlight that was bursting through the frosted glass pane of the front door. She opened it to discover a pair of familiar faces staring back at her – faces that she hadn't been expecting to see again in a hurry (and certainly not on the first day of the school holidays).

"Robin. Parminder. What are you doing here?" she was intrigued.

"Hello, Mrs Danks. It's your husband we've come to see," Parminder announced, glancing at her companion before adding with characteristic politeness, "That is, if you don't mind."

"Yeah, we looked his address up in the phone book, like," Robin explained with his own inimitable frankness.

However, beneath that unruly mop of blonde hair, his adolescent face was laden with a foreboding that, for once, was in marked contrast to the impish smirk he usually reserved for his erstwhile form mistress. Parminder's doleful eyes meanwhile also foretold culpable anxiety, tempting Ruby to step aside.

"I supposed you better come in then," she bade them, her own curious expression darkening to match.

* * * * *

Though Fens Bank was quieter than normal, Betty was skittish. It was as if that flicking tongue that distilled the air could sense that, for once, it was *she* who might be someone's prey.

As on previous occasions at this time of year, the python had been tempted to desert the sanctuary of that dark, humid tunnel and traverse the drains and gullies that had a few minutes earlier brought it out onto the more extensive hunting grounds of those lukewarm cooling ponds. Slithering silently through the tall grass she could take advantage of her excellent camouflage to seek more varied prey while the hot weather persisted.

Sure enough, she detected the vibration of footsteps heading her way along the bank. Sliding back through the reed bed at the water's edge, she slipped beneath the waters so that just the tip of her head remained visible. That way, unseen, she could observe her intended victims as they wandered past, both man and his dog oblivious to her presence just a few feet away.

Or so she thought. Suddenly, the black-and-tan Alsation halted. Catching the scent of something unusual in the long grass, it turned to face the water, straining at its leash and barking tremulously. Instinctively, Betty's head submerged.

"What is it, Max?" the police officer crouched down to interrogate his dog, eyes also scanning the surface of the opaque, pea-green water.

Though obediently at heel, Max was whining anxiously, his attention gripped by the silent ripple that had spread out upon it.

"Well, whatever it was, it's gone now," the officer consoled his mutt.

Perhaps it was just another one of those rats that had been spooking his dog – the only signs of life either of them had come across all afternoon. Even the horses that grazed these parts had been moved elsewhere. Meanwhile, that 'giant snake' story – allied to these extra police patrols – had at least succeeded in keeping the kids away from this notorious unofficial playground.

* * * * *

'DING-DING!'

Pauline gave the bell on the front desk a hearty thump. As she did, it prompted Ruby to sidle up to her fellow teacher.

"Thank you for coming with me today," she smiled feebly.

"That's okay," Pauline offered her a matey smile of her own.

"Only I suspect that Brian is not exactly flavour of the month at this police station – and certainly not with your father."

"No, maybe not," Pauline conceded with a knowing grin.

Through the frosted glass panel of the back office she watched while a portly figure lazily drifted over to the door, opening it to pop his head around. However, his lassitude vanished the moment he spied the face and the distinctive orange hair.

"Ah, Miss Trotter. To what do we owe the pleasure?" he chortled, unctuously minding his p's-and-q's in the presence of the Chief Superintendent's beloved daughter.

"Sergeant, this is Ruby Danks," she introduced her companion before beckoning in the direction of the teenage boy and girl who were fidgeting on the padded bench by the entrance door.

"And over there is Robin Jukes and Parminder Kaur. They're pupils of Sneyd End High School. And me? I'm just here to offer them a bit of moral support, as you might say."

"Oh. I see," the sergeant tried not to make his bemusement obvious. "Then how can your local police be of assistance to you today?"

"It's about the snake. Robin and Parminder have important information they wish to report," Ruby enlightened him.

"Oh. Right," he hummed, his bemusement deepening. "Well, if you ladies will just wait here I'll see if I can find someone for them to talk to."

Then, as he was about to disappear back into the office, he turned about in the doorway and proffered Ruby a second glance.

"Ruby Danks, you say? You wouldn't happen to be the wife of... you know... Brian Danks... the 'Snakeman'?" he wondered.

"I am," she replied resolutely.

"Oh. Anyway, like I said, an officer will be with you shortly," the sergeant blinked, resuming a more business-like manner.

And with that he was gone, leaving Pauline and Ruby to prop themselves against the desk and await his return. Meanwhile, Robin and Parminder were huddled together on that bench, staring at each other anxiously.

* * * * *

It was certainly one mighty incredible tale. In fact, if true, it promised to change everything. Detective Sergeant Mike Abbey finished scribbling and paused for a moment of reflection – as if to ponder whether he hadn't instead been imagining the last twenty minutes of the interview he'd just conducted.

"Of course, you do realise the seriousness of what you've just told me," he stared the two youngsters out – as if to likewise remove any last scintilla of doubt in his mind before he headed upstairs to break this momentous news to his boss.

Parminder glanced at Robin, then at Ruby, before returning the officer's probing glare.

"I assure you, sir. We are telling the truth."

His eyes continued to dart back and forth between these two unlikely specimens of furtive puppy love. The Indian girl seemed genuine, if abashed. However, the copper remained mistrustful of her English 'boyfriend', the lad's impish face and cocky manner lending the impression that this might be some outlandish prank.

"Honest, mate," Robin read his thoughts, compelled to protest. "We woulda' told you earlier, but… well, Parminder's old man ay' gunna' be happy knowing we wuz' playin' together in the tunnel. We day' get up to nuffink' though," he was most adamant.

The detective's hawkish gaze remained on him for a few moments more before relenting. Gathering his notes together, he tapped them on the desk to straighten them into a wad.

"Wait here," he instructed them, rising, notes in hand, to the scraping of his chair, thereby leaving Ruby and the two witnesses alone together in the interview room.

Their ex-teacher's doe-eyed smile meanwhile offered them the reassurance they needed to know they had done the right thing.

* * * * *

As the Chief Superintendent paced his office, pausing to stare out of the window, DS Abbey thought he could discern his boss's resistance to the prospect yielding. And yet despite the sworn testimony of two eye-witnesses, even now Cyril Trotter couldn't bring himself to accept that there might indeed be an enormous serpent stalking the town it was beholden upon him to protect.

"You have to understand, Detective Sergeant: it's imperative that we keep the lid on this matter. If people out there think we're taking this idiot's scaremongering seriously then there will be panic. And besides, I'm still not convinced this blessed Snakeman and his wife haven't put those two kids up to this? You know what this man's like: he will stop at nothing to further his campaign to save that railway. After all, you did say these two youngsters are pupils at his wife's school. How do we know *she* hasn't encouraged them to make up this tale to dig her husband out of the hole his ridiculous claims have landed him in?"

"Sir, it's my belief that they *are* telling the truth. In particular, the Indian girl appears to have been very reluctant to come here today. I don't believe she would have risked her father finding out about her friendship with her white classmate had she not felt compelled to describe to us what she saw. What they both saw! At the very least don't you think we ought to be talking to Councillor Danks. After all, he is an expert on these matters. If anyone can catch this thing then he can."

"Absolutely not! That man has caused enough trouble for us already. I forbid you or any other officer from having anything to do with him," Trotter insisted, revealing that it was stubborn pride that was now preventing the most senior policeman in Sneyd End from calling upon that expertise.

"So what shall I do, sir? With these statements?" his underling was eager to know, holding up the ream of papers in his hand. "Surely we can't just discount them?"

"File them for now, Abbey. I want further verification before we do anything hasty. I am not prepared to stick my neck out without irrefutable proof that this creature is real. The Chief Constable will chew my arse to shreds if I start pulling my officers off other important tasks – like finding the person who's abducted those missing teenagers – only to discover that I've sent them out on a wild goose chase. What's more, one initiated and stoked up by that blabber-mouthed, self-aggrandising fantasist! I will not do it, Sergeant. I want reliable, independent verification, do you understand!"

"Er, yes, sir. Of course," Abbey twittered resignedly.

Just then, there was a knock on the door.

"Oh, what now! Come in!" Trotter hollered impatiently.

Through the door hurried a WPC from the control room – her radio headset still dangling around her neck, having legged it up the three flights of stairs that led to Trotter's office. Hanging on the door to catch her breath, she fought to get her words out.

"Chief Superintendent, sir... A report has just come in... from PC Appleby..." she panted.

"Well, get on with it, woman!" her boss demanded.

"He was patrolling... over Fens Bank... with Max... that's his dog, sir..."

"Dog? I don't remember giving orders for my officers to go gallivanting over there with dogs!" Trotter's livid stare alighted upon DS Abbey – who fired him a blank look in return.

"He's radioed in, sir... to say... he's just spotted an enormous snake... swimming in one of the Fens Bank cooling ponds... I've taken the liberty of ordering all available officers to attend... If that's alright, sir."

Trotter's anger evaporated that instant, replaced by an expression of utter shock. Though the dutiful WPC awaited confirmation that she'd acted correctly – and Trotter's mouth hung open – it was apparent she wasn't going to receive a reply.

Meanwhile, having performed his duty to apprise his superior of the statements those two teenagers had made, Abbey tucked the papers under his arm and joined the shaken policewoman over by the door.

"Do I take it we now have our 'verification', sir?" he cocked an eye at his ashen-faced boss before heading back downstairs.

* * * * *

"I'm sorry. I didn't mean to disappoint you."

Sometimes apologies are heartfelt; sometimes they're perfunctory. Sometimes they're issued from a sense of obligation; sometimes they're issued because, unsettled by a disapproving silence, the person offering them can think of nothing better to say. Perched on the sofa in the sitting room, her father's silent, penetrating gaze trained upon her, a downcast Parminder Kaur was unsure exactly what she meant by those simple words.

"You know why we are disappointed," Inderjit Singh reminded his daughter again. "Your mother and I are concerned for your welfare. Sometimes there are pleasures in this world that, though they may seem innocent, can lead a girl away from the path of virtue. Alas, meeting up with boys can be one of them."

"But we were doing no harm," Parminder protested as respectfully as she dared. "Robin behaves very kindly towards me. He is a good friend. In fact, he is my best friend."

"But he is a white boy. And he is not a Sikh."

"No, he is not. But what difference does that make, Father? After all, did not Guru Gobind Singh himself remind us: *'manas ki jaat sabey eke pehchanbo'*," she pleaded in her native Punjabi. "*'Consider all mankind to be a single race or caste'*," she then translated in her other, masterfully-acquired tongue.

His daughter's pious recitation admonished him, chipping away at his disapproval. When he once more elected to give voice to paternal concern, it was with a tender and more tractable spirit.

"How did this boy become your 'best friend'? You are the only Indian girl in your class, I know. But are there not English girls who want to be your friends?"

"Yes, there are English girls who I am friends with, Father."

"Then what is so special about this Robin? You accept it is most unusual for a fourteen-year-old Indian girl to have a white boy as her best friend. Besides, there are teenage girls at the Gurdwara. Could not one of them be your best friend?"

Parminder's dolorous eyes were studying every corner of the room except the one in which her father was sat, even though – contrary to her fears – he had yet to raise his voice to her during this solemn dressing down he was treating her to. However, she understood from the way his stern gaze lingered upon her that he expected answers to his questions.

"Robin has protected me from those pupils who bullied me. It is because of him that I am no longer called hurtful names at school. He also helped repair my satchel when the strap broke."

"I see. He has been protecting you; and repairing your satchel. That is very noble. And for that I suppose I should be grateful to him. But he is also a teenage boy – and, by your own admission, he is what English people call 'a bit of a lad'. Therefore, you will understand why your mother and I are worried that his motives may not always be pure. Pray tell me: what favours has this boy been expecting from you in return for his protection?"

Parminder looked up, the sudden popping of her eyes conveying indignation at the casting of such an aspersion.

"Father, he has asked for nothing from me other than my friendship," she was adamant. However, with her father's gaze still unrelenting, that resolution quickly faltered.

"Well, that is not quite true," she eventually confessed, dipping her eyes and fumbling with her hands in her lap. "You see, he asked me to… Well, actually I offered…" she then stalled.

It was the turn of her father's eyes to pop.

"I was reluctant to do it at first because I knew it was wrong. And that you would be angry," her voice then sank with regret, "But, you see, I've been… Well, I mean… we've been…"

Beneath Inderjit's taut blue turban, cogs were angrily grinding away inside his head. They, in turn, worked lips that tightened sternly beneath that flowing black beard. In trepidation, his beloved daughter was on the cusp of owning up to what sounded like a most shameful thing for a Sikh girl to have done.

"I've been helping Robin with his homework," she admitted.

"His homework?" her father blinked, thinking he'd misheard.

"Yes, Robin is not… well, he's not as fortunate as I am to have parents who care about his education," she explained, afraid that her father would be as disapproving of a boy with underwhelming career prospects as he was one who was not of her faith. "So I have been helping him to understand biology, physics and chemistry – subjects I am very good at.

"I was worried that Mrs Danks would find out," she elaborated. "I think she suspected I was, because she wrote on one piece of homework that Robin submitted how 'surprised' she was that he had answered every single question correctly!

"However, it is not all my doing, Father. Robin is a very bright boy who just needed someone to help him unlock his talent. You see, Mrs Danks called him out in front of the class the other day and asked him to describe examples of anaerobic respiration in mammals. And Robin managed to do it all on his own by remembering the things I've taught him," her voice gained a sudden tunefulness upon recalling her 'best friend' flushed with pride that he'd not only mastered the subject but had managed to impress his perennially-suspicious biology teacher as well.

"Mrs Danks was pleased and told Robin that, if his work continues to improve, he should stay on and sit his 'O' levels," she added, emboldened enough to flash one of those adorable smiles that never failed to soften her father's generous heart.

It was with a palpable sense of relief that Inderjit Singh learned that his daughter's remarkable erudition had been the only favour she'd been liberal with. He rose from his chair to wander over to her and tenderly pat her shoulder.

"My daughter, it tells us in the Guru Granth Sahib that a place in God's house can be attained if we do service to others in this world," he consoled her. "As well as helping Robin master these difficult subjects at school, you also found the courage to tell the police about this terrible snake that has been taking lives. By your act of service, you may yet save other lives. That too is very noble. And for that too I suppose I should be grateful to you – and to this Robin boy, who is your best friend."

* * * * *

It had all the compelling, unspoken drama of that moment when opposing generals Ulysses S. Grant and Robert E. Lee famously sat down together at Appomattox Court House to negotiate terms for ending the American Civil War.

As on that occasion too, there was a touching absence of rancour between these two once implacable adversaries. Like General Grant, Brian Danks was graciously reluctant to get to the point of their meeting, bumbling and attempting to make small talk about the continuing fine weather – as if embarrassed by his vindication. Instead (once Trotter's secretary had discreetly delivered the Snakeman a refreshing cup of tea), like General Lee, it fell to the chastened Chief Superintendent to verbalise the reason they'd agreed to meet up.

"It would appear that you were right about that snake," he humbly conceded, sitting back in his swivel chair across the desk from where he'd bidden Brian take a seat. "The question now is: how do we catch the critter? As you would imagine, it's not a task my officers have to perform every day. Therefore, I was rather hoping they could call upon the knowledge of someone more experienced in these matters. I'm told they don't come any more knowledgeable and experienced than you, Councillor."

The generous compliment appeared to work. A smile dawned upon the Snakeman's face as he shoved those bulky black glasses back up his nose and leaned forward, legs crossed, to explain that "It will not be straight-forward. I'm afraid the warm weather may have extended the range that the python can travel considerably: the tunnel; the cooling ponds; as well as the drains and gullies in between. It's even possible that the serpent might have ventured out into the adjacent woodland. And while reticulated pythons are opportunistic feeders that will seize prey whenever they come across it, I suspect this one has been feeding rather well of late. Hence it might not be in any hurry to take whatever bait we put down – especially if it senses danger or feels threatened. They're smart animals, snakes."

Cyril Trotter pondered the sort of prey that this 'smart animal' had implicitly been dining upon. It compounded his remorse that he'd allowed himself to be blinded into thinking that the key to solving the 'disappearances' of those hapless teenagers had lain in coaxing further confessions out of a convicted child murderer.

"Well, unfortunately the weathermen aren't forecasting a cold snap just yet," he laughed nervously out of the side of his mouth. "However, I recall from my service in North Africa during the war that, being cold-blooded creatures, the best time to find a snake is at daybreak, when they crawl out into the open to warm up. Maybe an early start might do the trick."

The smile on Brian's face broadened – even as *he* felt chastened that maybe Sneyd End's police chief wasn't the bone-headed blimp he'd assumed him to be. And lo, he knew a thing or two about snakes too!

"I'd say that would be an excellent idea," he nodded. "That said, reticulated pythons are jungle or swamp-dwelling reptiles. They prefer not to stray too far from a body of water – both to hide in and because, owing to their enormous size, moving through water requires less effort. So while, by all means, we should scour open spaces at sunrise, at some point that search will have to involve examining local watercourses too. And I'm afraid it will have to be done using the painstaking process of wading in and probing for it," he added.

Trotter's comportment subtly changed upon imagining what such a task would entail for his men. However, his eyes widened still further when the Snakeman trawled up another salient fact gleaned from his years of studying these creatures.

"Not to worry you unduly, Chief Superintendent, but I should point out too that these snakes are capable of parthenogenesis."

"Partheno-what?" Trotter frowned. What could he mean?

"Parthenogenesis. If the female – and Betty is a female – can't find a mate then, assuming the climatic conditions are right, she can reproduce without recourse to male insemination."

"Reproduce? You mean there might be more than one of these things out there?" the police chief gulped.

"It can't be discounted. On the bright side though, rarely for a snake, the female reticulated python will incubate the eggs herself by twitching her own body on top of the nest to generate warmth for them. So finding Betty might also lead us to her youngsters too – assuming she has any, of course."

Heartening though it was to know that this learned, if slightly-awkward individual was indeed a boundless fount of knowledge about this killer the Chief Superintendent had tasked himself with finding, he sure had a way of unsettling his listener.

"Well, I guess we'll just have to cross that bridge when we come to it," Trotter puffed. "I will place a team of my officers at your disposal. They'll provide the brawn to assist you in whatever way you need to track this beast down – and, if necessary, its offspring! I take it you will want to bring other snake experts in from around the country to help you?"

"No, just my assistant. She works with me at the zoo," Brian enthused, rubbing his hands together and re-crossing his legs.

"She?" the wary chief cocked an eye.

"Yes, I know: there aren't many female snake handlers out there. But don't worry: like me, Julie is quite looking forward to finding Betty," he assured the startled policeman. "Neither will she have a problem working with your men, Chief Superintendent. In fact, don't tell her I said so," he chuckled, shielding his mouth with his hand, "but she's 'a bit of a lad' herself!"

Pauline was right: this Snakeman friend of hers was certainly a character. Working with such an oddball individual – not to mention whoever this tomboyish understudy was that he was intending to bring along with him – was certainly going to be a challenge. However, the apprehensive police chief hadn't heard the best of it yet.

"There is one other small favour I have to ask in return for helping you to catch this snake," Brian chortled with a mixture of presumption and embarrassment.

"Favour?"

"Yes, if possible I want to capture Betty alive."

"Alive?" Trotter gasped, this time feeling the need to temper his indulgence. "Are you crazy, man! If what you've said is correct, then this snake could be responsible for the deaths of several people in this town. This is not another one of your jungle safari japes; this is a hunt for a highly dangerous animal that is resident – and quite possibly breeding – in a populated urban area. If my men *do* locate it, then I assure you it will be killed on sight. We simply cannot risk it escaping to kill again."

"But to capture and study a python of this size would be a once-in-a-lifetime opportunity. It could advance our knowledge of these animals considerably."

"No!" Trotter put his foot down, sitting up straight at his desk.

"Then I'm afraid I might have to reconsider…"

"Reconsider? Councillor Danks, may I respectfully remind you that this is your public duty we are talking about. You owe it to your fellow citizens to…"

"At least give me a chance," Brian pleaded, "If I can successfully capture her alive, then Betty is mine to study. If not, then your men can do to her as they see fit."

Maybe it was the childlike sincerity in eyes that twinkled behind those gawky glasses; or maybe it was the rare willingness of Trotter's erstwhile antagonist to entertain a compromise. However – slowly, but surely – the Chief Superintendent's angry glare mellowed. He sat back in his chair again.

"Okay," he availed himself of a deep breath. "You will have one chance – and one chance only – of taking this creature alive. If you fail, then I will expect you to assist my officers in dealing with it once and for all – even upon pain of its demise. Do I make myself clear?"

Brian also sat back in his chair as if to briefly think about it – a face-saving way of masking his self-consciousness when striving to drive a hard bargain.

"Deal!" he agreed, leaning forward to offer the Chief Superintendent a limp handshake with which to thereby solemnise their accord.

23

"Rather them than me!" the policeman opined thankfully, taking a moment to remove his helmet and mop his brow.

The cooling ponds of Fens Bank had already been trawled the previous year by police divers searching for Gillian Hickman. On this hot August afternoon, they were being trawled again, this time to uncover a snake. Suffice to say, given what they now knew, it was with far greater trepidation that the army of frogmen was tentatively probing their murky depths today.

Despite Brian assuring the copper by his side that, were Betty to attack, there was sufficient manpower to hand to rapidly overpower her, still he was unconvinced. It was not for nothing that the guys who'd been tasked to undertake this onerous duty were sticking closer together than normal!

"Can't we just lob a stick or two of dynamite in there?" the copper frowned, only partly in jest. As he said it, he thought he detected a crack appear in the Snakeman's earnest demeanour.

"Of course, if Betty is lurking in there she would have had to surface by now. A reticulated python of her size can stay submerged for thirty minutes; maybe forty-five at a push," he folded his arms and explained matter-of-factly. "Betty is an air-breathing animal. She can't stay underwater forever."

'Betty'! 'A python of her size'! The officer blinked unnoticed, unsure whether to be amused that this freak of nature had a name; or daunted that, by all accounts, he and his colleagues were hunting a veritable monster. In due course, he broke from observing the ongoing exploration to catch the Black Country's leading herpetologist unfold his arms, prop his hands on his hips, and tilt his fleshy snout skywards as if to sniff the air.

"Is it me? Or does it seem quiet today?" he enquired, employing a different sense as it happened.

"That snake has scared all the kids away, that's why," the policeman scoffed.

"No, Constable. I don't mean in the sense of people coming and going. I mean the Alcock & Robbins steel works," he pointed to the huge plant in the distance. "Normally, you can hear it humming away. But today it's strangely silent."

"That's because British Steel have shut the plant down to undertake maintenance work on the blast furnaces. The company's given the workforce the month of August off – my brother included, who works there. The jammy devil! I can just picture him now, sunning himself in the back garden as we speak," the policeman grinned with misty-eyed envy, "fag in one hand and a pint from the outdoor in the other."

"Hmmn," the Snakeman mused, directing his gaze instead at the frogmen labouring in the cooling pond, "I guess that explains why the water temperature is cooler than I was expecting."

* * * * *

It was hot and exhausting work. PC Jonathan Hunt was convinced it was punishment for him showing Pauline's father up to be a bone-headed blimp who'd been unwilling to listen.

To be sure (and to Jonathan's relief), Chief Superintendent Trotter *was* now listening. Furthermore (to his surprise and delight), Trotter had relented and permitted him to join in the hunt for the snake he'd warned about. However, the fact that he'd today been ordered to don a set of chest-high rubber waders and trudge through the fetid mud of the abandoned and overgrown Sneyd End Canal suggested he had yet to be forgiven.

Lest Betty might be hiding beneath it, he was slowly and methodically probing the glutinous black mire with a long pole, working alongside a detail of his colleagues from the station who were similarly clad. Quite how they would react if one of them perchance bodged and aroused the snake had been a topic of wary debate all afternoon. All they had by way of reassurance on that score was the presence of the shy, if hoydenish young lady who was directing them (and who, they'd been assured, knew a thing or two about handling large snakes).

Jonathan had met Julie Newington once or twice socially (Brian having introduced her as the assistant keeper at the zoo's reptile house). A chubby, if not unattractive twenty-five-year-old with chestnut hair that was tied up in a functional pony-tail, this unlikely snake handler was otherwise a woman of few words. Meanwhile, her uncoy manner, as well as her reluctance to assuage their light-hearted banter about whether she had a boyfriend, had prompted his colleagues to mutter amongst themselves that perhaps boys were not her thing.

However, if there was one male of the species with whom she did share a touching chemistry it was her boss. In no wise manner a sexual chemistry (from what little she'd shared about herself it seemed that Julie was as obsessive about motorbikes as Brian Danks was about trains – and as both of them were about snakes!), on those occasions when Jonathan had observed them huddled together to discuss strategies and tactics, he'd picked up on this strange bond of respect and admiration that existed between them. It was as if the Snakeman and his unconventional assistant really were ready to trust each other with their lives.

"Uh-oh!" one of the officers suddenly piped up.

All probing ceased. All eyes looked up.

"What is it, Dave?" said Jonathan, though from the way his colleague had turned white as a sheet he could guess the answer.

Straight away, Julie abandoned her own probing and, grabbing a spade from the bank, waded through the squelching sludge to arrive alongside the horror-struck copper.

"It's there," he gestured to her, pressing his pole against the spot. "I distinctly felt it move when I touched it."

With barely a trace of trepidation, Julie began to gently dig the mud away to examine whatever it was he'd struck. Her steadfast demeanour presented a marked contrast with the police detail, the blokes subconsciously edging away from their hapless colleague.

"Whoah! I felt it move again!" Dave cried, closing his eyes and clenching his teeth as if he was about to present them all with a bowel movement.

"I think I can see it," Julie calmly announced, squatting down to examine the dark, mottled trunk. "Now all I need to do is to establish which end is the head and which end is the tail."

"Can't you just whack the bloody thing with that shovel?" Dave urged her, only partly in jest.

Julie ignored his tremulous plea. Like Brian, she had a professional interest in capturing this fascinating serpent alive if possible. What's more, she might just have beaten him to it!

"If I can get a hold on the head, then I want you guys to quickly grab the trunk," she glanced up and instructed them, adding "And remember: this one could be a big 'un!"

The disbelieving looks she received in return told her that, given a choice, these bobbies would rather be helping children cross the road; or maybe even chasing bank robbers! However, looking to each other, they drew breaths and began crouching down in readiness to seize the snake.

Meanwhile, Julie bore an ominous frown – as if unable to establish which end of the snake was which. She took a chance and gently placed her hands on the trunk, gripping it and slowly drawing it out of the mud. The officers looked on aghast as the pace of that withdrawal quickened. Suddenly, the entire trunk sprang out and was flailing about wildly, only to eventually crash down on the terrified team member who'd first located it.

Dave's infantile wailing – as well as his colleagues' similarly pathetic bleats – quickly abated though when he looked up in amazement; then with relief accompanied by nervous laughter. It was a length of twelve-inch diameter rubber hose that had been dumped in the canal and laid buried in the silt. ·

Jonathan immediately removed the rubber gloves from his hands and began thrashing them hard against Dave's shoulders.

"Don't you do that to us again, you stupid pillock!" he fumed.

While he was swishing at his confrère, he failed to notice Julie break into a rare grin. Having worked out his nervous tension, by the time Jonathan had pulled the gloves back on his hands her quiet resolve had returned. She chucked the shovel back onto the bank and took up her probe again, the signal for her more excitable co-workers to resume the search.

* * * * *

One week into the hunt to capture Betty – on yet another sweltering summer day above ground – the team of police officers assigned to comb the half-a-mile of abandoned Sneyd End Tunnel had finally completed their search of the various drain shafts that lined it. Unsurprisingly, it was as hot and humid as ever in here.

It had been a thankless task. The men had had to laboriously probe around inside each one, aware that at any minute they might incur the wrath of the fearsome snake. Meanwhile, armed with a head torch and his trusty snake hook, Brian Danks had also been inside the tunnel all morning on the look-out for evidence of Betty's whereabouts. So far all he'd turned up was a trail or two of chalky-looking turds – which his experienced eye for such things knew to be snake poo. Rather worryingly though, he had failed to come across any fresh droppings.

However, at least Brian could report back to Chief Superintendent Trotter that, to date, he'd found no trace of any nesting activity on the part of their quarry, either in the tunnel or the surrounding countryside. Fingers crossed, it appeared Betty had yet to experience the joys of motherhood!

"Looks like we're done then, sir," chirped the sergeant in charge as he and his officers prepared to head back towards that welcome glimmer of daylight.

"Yes, thank you, Sergeant. Please convey to your men my gratitude and admiration."

"I will, sir, Thank you for your kind words."

Though the Snakeman's familiar spectacles were reflecting the glare from the powerful arc lights the men had been working beneath, the sergeant could discern a pensive glint that had appeared in his beady eyes.

"But no python?" Brian brooded aloud, stroking his chin.

"No, sir. Plenty of rats. But no python, I'm afraid."

* * * * *

"Warra' bleedin' palaver," the stouter of the two middle-aged women huffed, indignantly folding her arms in such a way that her substantial bosom heaved upwards.

"Arr. Yow'd 'ave thought after almost a fortnight of huntin' high and low for the thing they'd 'ave found it by now," her friend who was draped in a head scarf agreed.

"It's a disgrace they cor' tell folk whether they'm any nearer to findin' it. It's mekin' me ill. Ar' cor' sleep at night."

When Ruby Danks had sat down next to these plumpish dames on the bench in Sneyd End's new shopping centre it had been to rest after hauling her heavily-pregnant self around Fine Fare. Draping her arms upon her sizeable 'bump', the conversation underway further along the bench sounded like a repeat of one she'd overheard while queuing at the check-out. There was no denying that the increasingly drawn-out saga of the escaped python was a source of mounting frustration to the citizens of Sneyd End – as it was to her husband, who'd so far failed to snare it (the only consolation for Brian being that, with the huge snake still on the loose, his vexatious mother-in-law had cancelled plans to come up and visit them over the summer!)

Otherwise, Ruby smiled politely before feigning to stare up in marvel at the glass atrium of this futuristic temple to modern consumerism, squinting in the sunlight that was streaming through it. Meanwhile, the chuckling water feature and potted palm trees beneath it permitted shoppers to believe they really had escaped the dreariness of this otherwise unremarkable industrial town – if only for a morning.

What's more, the free parking in the adjacent multi-storey car park had obviated the need for shoppers to circuit the town centre searching for a space. It prompted Ruby to ponder that maybe not all Horace Bissell's grandiose regeneration projects were ill-conceived. She just hoped they'd used better quality concrete in its construction than they had in the Tiger Street flats! Meanwhile, as if in anticipation of Brian badgering them about the role of public transport in the urban realm, the planners had even thought to construct a brand-new bus station next door to it.

"Of course, Ar' blame that Councillor What's-His-Name – yer' know, that bleedin' 'Snakeman'. It's him who's bin' scarin' folk with all this talk about this giant worreva'-it-is!" the buxom dame sat next to her meanwhile scoffed.

"Arr'. The bloke's yampy! That's the last time Ar' vote fer' him, Ar' con' tell yer'… 'Ere, yow' orright', love?"

Ruby smiled politely again upon noticing the two women surveying with concern her obvious discomfort. However, this time she feigned to grimace at a twinge she thought might mask the real reason why she'd suddenly come over all self-conscious: namely, that her husband once more risked becoming a source of discord and derision in the town.

* * * * *

Respite at last – and in the most unlikely of places. Having probed a large pipe that seemed promising, Betty had eventually swum her way into a place that would normally have been a hive of human activity. Today however, there was none of the loud noise (and correspondingly angry vibrations) that had perhaps deterred her from venturing into this place until now.

Indeed, human beings seemed to be strangely absent. Not that Betty was fazed. At least it meant there was nobody about to report that thirty-feet of reticulated python was lazily exploring the depths of the manmade pool she'd discovered, unfazed too by the presence of the various chemicals that had been added to treat the tepid water she was swimming in. It all made for the perfect sanctuary for a weary snake. Indeed, the only thing missing was something to eat. However, that could wait. Something would turn up sooner or later. It always did.

* * * * *

"So, it would appear that this 'Betty' doesn't want to be found," Chief Superintendent Trotter sighed in exasperation.

Sat in his office again – across that same desk from him – for a moment the Snakeman was at a loss for something to say to the frustrated police chief. Conscious of how much effort it had taken to persuade Trotter that the snake in question actually existed, he was loathed to be the bearer of such discouraging news. However, despite two weeks of searching all the known boltholes where a python might hang out he had yet to even catch sight of the serpent, let alone capture it.

"I can only put it down to the weather," he explained rather limply. "In particular, it's been quite warm at night. This means she will have been able to stay active for longer and consequently venture further from the tunnel than she has before perhaps. In fact, the evidence I've turned up so far suggests she may not have been back to the tunnel for some time."

"Presumably she's through with dining on rats then!" Trotter snorted cynically.

It was not supposed to be like this. If snakes had a psychology, then Brian Danks prided himself on being able to read it. And yet it was almost as if Betty instinctively knew the game had changed and that, for once, it was she who was being stalked. As such, perhaps she'd decided to lie low for a while – and in a place where her human pursuers might never think to look for her. Or, indeed, where she might have a better prospect of dining on the kind of human prey Brian feared she'd developed a taste for.

"In which case, we might have to widen the net," he thought he'd better warn his listener. "For instance, perhaps it's time to undertake a more thorough search of the network of sewers that runs beneath the town."

"The sewers?" Trotter raised an eyebrow.

"Yes, pythons are adaptable animals. And although, in this country, pet snakes that escape into sewers seldom survive for long, the possibility that Betty might have entered one cannot be ruled out – especially if it's being fed by a source of warm water."

Trotter interlocked his fingers together to fashion a ball, which he then pressed to his lips, as if in contemplation – all the time eyeing the Snakeman up while gently swivelling in his chair.

"You do realise that if my officers start hauling up drains along the High Street then we could have real difficulty managing the public reaction to all this? We could provoke panic. I mean, I've already had Councillor Patterson on the phone to me complaining that numbers are down in that new swimming baths – despite the hot weather. Apparently, rumours have been doing the rounds that this snake might have somehow gotten into its pipework; and that it might thereby enter the pool itself. Fanciful, I know. But the trouble is, the longer we go on drawing a blank the more inclined people are to believe these kinds of scare stories.

"I should tell you as well, Councillor, I've had a television crew from *'ATV Today'* up here this morning, wanting to know why it's taking so long to catch this snake. It was all rather embarrassing, to say the least, that I had nothing to tell them. The only consolation has been that they've agreed to include an appeal for information on *'Police 5'* about that armed robbery that took place the other week."

"Ah, 'keep 'em peeled'!" Brian tapped an eyebrow in a weedy attempt at humour. However, Shaw Taylor he was not. And neither was Chief Superintendent Trotter amused.

"More worrying still," he instead leaned forward to address him, "is that other voices are suggesting that this 'giant snake' business is just one big hoax; and that you're fuelling these rumours for the purpose of deterring any further development on that old railway line. If that is the case, then I have to say it appears to be working," he sniffed, perhaps not wholly impervious to the farcical side of this snake-hunt. "It's certainly put a dent in the takings of the leisure centre – so much so that yesterday the Council took the decision to close the pool for a week to undertake some remedial work to it."

Brian sat up and shook his head.

"I assure you, Chief Superintendent: that is most definitely not the case," he twittered. "After all, don't just take my word for it. You have Constable Appleby's testimony that this colossal snake is real. That's why it's most imperative that there be no let-up in the hunt to track it down."

Trotter was swivelling from side to side in his chair again, his interlocked fingers once more pressed to his lips as he continued to stare intently at the Snakeman. Then – reluctant to gainsay the eye-witness testimony of one of his best officers – he fleetingly nodded. His men would indeed have to start lifting the drains.

24

"Oh, wow! I don't believe it!" she swooned.

Suddenly, the hands that seventeen-year-old Deborah Watson had been ordered to cover her eyes with she now rushed instead to muffle the gasp that was escaping past her gaping mouth.

To be sure, she thought her new boyfriend had been kidding her when he'd let slip that promotion at work would come with a company car. Yet, lo! Here it was – pulled up right in front of her big, fluttering, awestruck eyes.

To say Vince Fullard was chuffed with this latest nugget of good fortune was an understatement. Just gone twenty-two years-old, already his career with Albert Header & Son (Midlands) Ltd – manufacturer of quality brackets, wall ties, and architectural ironmongery – was progressing nicely, having impressed the boss with his initiative and enthusiasm. Rewarded with elevation to the position of sales executive to the company's customers in Wales and the West Country (for which this brand-new flame red Ford Capri 1600 GT XL would come in very handy), with a bit of luck he might also have impressed his latest attractive, curvy, and (supposedly) virginal new bird sufficiently for him to get his end away with her.

Rather less impressed was Deborah's mother, whose crabby features he noticed twitching from behind the net curtain while he was showing off this superlative motor car. Wary of this flash and arrogant young man's intentions towards her daughter, it would take more than ostentatious displays of career success to convince the cavillous old bat that he wasn't just out to sow his oats before moving on to his next conquest.

That said, young Vince was loathed to settle down just yet. He was tall; he was good-looking; and he was going places. Life was good. Why would he want to tie himself down by accompanying some bird on a visit to the building society?

"So d'ya fancy a spin in it?" he grinned.

"Can do," Deborah's eyes fluttered again coyly.

"Hop in then," he urged, opening the passenger door for her. "I thought we could maybe go for a drive somewhere. After all, it's a nice evening," he remarked, squinting at the westerly sun.

"I better tell Mum first," she begged, trotting back up the front path as spritely as her wedge heels would permit.

"And mek' sure y'am back by eleven o'clock," her boyfriend heard Mrs Watson instruct her daughter.

Vince Fullard rolled his eyes. Perish the thought of having the pernickety Mrs Watson as a mother-in-law!

* * * * *

"Good evening. It's ten o'clock on Friday, August 15th and here is the news.

"Londonderry is reported to be quiet tonight after three days of rioting. In what's being called the 'Battle of the Bogside', over three hundred-and-fifty policemen have been injured during violent clashes that have taken place in the city's nationalist quarter.

"With the Irish government warning that it 'could not stand by' in the face of further attacks upon the Catholic community in the north, the Prime Minister yesterday ordered British troops to be deployed to restore order – a move that has been generally welcomed by nationalist leaders..."

Munching on his sandwiches while lazily flicking the pages of a smutty magazine, Billy Slater stared up at the Bakelite radio on the filing cabinet and cussed. Like most people on the mainland, he remained mystified by Northern Ireland, its warring tribes, and its unfathomable religious hatreds.

It was set to be another long shift. These last few nights had been made more tedious still by the fact that there was hardly anybody about in the sprawling Alcock & Robbins steel works. With the furnaces out of commission, there were no night shifts on duty in the rolling mills and hence none of the usual familiar faces with whom he could stop and chat while doing the rounds patrolling the plant. And titillating though the voluptuous wench was who was parading herself in the *'Readers' Wives'* section, she was a poor substitute for real human company.

Meanwhile, those rounds had to be done. Polishing off his supper, he snapped the lid back on his Tupperware box, rising to his feet to slip both it and magazine back inside his duffle bag.

> *"... Finally, tens of thousands of young people have been converging on upstate New York for this weekend's Woodstock Festival. Billed as 'Three Days of Peace, Love and Music', folk singer Joan Baez is headlining this evening's performance. Further acts lined up to perform over the next two days include Jefferson Airplane, Janis Joplin, Grateful Dead, and Crosby, Stills, Nash & Young.*
>
> *"Meanwhile, with heavy rain forecast, concern has been expressed about the organisers' ability to cope with the expected two hundred thousand people who are believed to be heading for the Festival..."*

Switching off the radio, Billy placed his cap on his head and picked up his torch and a hefty bunch of keys. Whistling a tune as he made his way out of the gate house, he paused to light a cigarette and to gaze up at the star-spangled sky.

* * * * *

"Strewth! This thing doh' arf' move!" Deborah noted, momentarily pinned in her seat as Vince slotted the car through the gears and hit the accelerator. Both windows were down and the Rolling Stones' *'Honky Tonk Woman'* was playing on the radio.

"Eighty-two brake horse power, to be precise. It'll deliver a top speed of ninety-six miles an hour," Vince crowed, taking a moment in the glow of passing headlights to admire how the lime green mini skirt and matching blouse she was wearing complimented her gorgeous figure.

Deborah herself was not remotely interested in the technical specifications that her boyfriend was reeling off. It was enough to know that being seen in the Capri was sure to have her mates dripping with envy – a small price to pay for its owner's tendency, at times, to get a bit too touchy-feely with her.

"How's your job then?" he deigned to enquire of her day, sensing that maybe she was tiring of hearing him boast incessantly about his own excellent career prospects.

"Boring. But it's job, ay' it," she glanced away from him and huffed. "It's why I cor' wait for the weekend to come around. And then when it does I get to play out again," she offered him a childhood analogy, as well as a coquettish smile.

The smile lingered as she savoured her 'boring' job (or, more precisely, the modest pay packet she picked up each Thursday, which enabled her to go fashion shopping up Birmingham on Saturdays, invariably returning home with an armful of bags from the likes of Biba and Bus Stop). To think, in the end high school had been a waste of four years of her life – including all that useless biology that Mrs Danks had tried to cram into her head.

Clearly intrigued by the way the contents of those shopping bags showcased the vacuous teenager's shapely legs and perked-up bosom, for the manager who'd interviewed her it was sufficient that she could type a letter, answer a telephone, and make cups of tea for his clients. The rest, he'd lustfully assured her, she could perfect on the secretarial course at night school that he'd enrolled her for on Monday evenings.

It spoke of a truism that she (like countless teenage girls before her) had learned and learned well: namely that she possessed something that men were interested in and were often prepared to jump through all manner of hoops to get their hands on. Play her cards right and this, rather than her education (or the paucity of it), would be the key to getting on in this world.

And yet, as her mother had lectured her, it was beholden upon 'a good girl' like her to keep her legs shut and hold that metaphorical 'something' in reserve for the young man who was willing to place a ring on her finger. It was advice that Deborah had resolved to heed… well, she'd try.

* * * * *

The deserted steel plant was positively ghostly. With just a handful of contractors working around the clock to re-line the blast furnaces in time to be fired back up in September, it was turning out to be a lonely night shift indeed. There was nobody in the drop forge, nobody in the machine shops, and nobody in those cavernous rolling mills either. Whistling to himself as much for company as entertainment, Billy Slater felt like he was roaming the decks of the *'Mary Celeste'*.

By and by, he noticed that the gate to the settling pond was open. Wondering over, he inspected the lock to establish that someone had failed to secure it properly when the plant had shut down. However, before closing it he shone his torch into the pond itself. The size of an Olympic swimming pool, the water was clear enough for the beam to illuminate right to the bottom.

However, the very stillness of the place gave him the creeps. A man could have drowned in that pool and nobody would ever have known. Pondering that morbid thought, he closed the gate and locked it, rattling the padlock just to be sure. He then carried on his way, a bright albino moon looking down on him.

* * * * *

"Yer' sure we woh' be disturbed 'ere?" she nagged him again.

He resurfaced from feasting on her slender neck to sit up straight in his seat.

"Of course, we woh'," he pacified her, a hint of impatience in his tone. "Have yer' sid' anybody else come down here yet?"

Indeed, now that the parcels depot that had served the adjacent railway line had closed vehicles seldom ventured down the dark, lonely lane that ran alongside the Alcock & Robbins steel works. Having reconnoitred this place on his bike as a teenager, Vince Fullard was aware that, in the absence of somewhere more salubrious, it was as good a place as any to explore the delights that dwelt beneath Deborah's trendy outfit. What he hadn't counted on were the jitters of a teenage girl who – when she wasn't dropping hints about getting engaged and getting married – was fretting that this forlorn spot was maybe just a bit too lonely. Why even the huge floodlit steel plant behind that perimeter fence was silent and deserted.

"'Ere, watch where y'am puttin' yer' hands, will ya'," she shuffled again.

"Uh! I thought you liked your men to be adventurous," Vince resurfaced once more, this time to behold the buttons of the blouse he'd just fumbled with being hastily done up again.

"Who told yer' that?" she glared at him indignantly, reaching up to flick on the interior light.

"How about Adrian Cooper? His brother's a mate of mine. He said he came home one evening to find you and young Adrian gooin' at it like a pair of rabbits on his parent's settee."

"That's a lie! I ay' never done it... not with Adrian Cooper," she protested, a tad unconvincingly.

"Mind you, then again Adrian Cooper never took you out in one of these things, did he," Vince cooed, nestling up and easing her back into the embrace of the passenger seat, subtly reaching a hand up to extinguish the interior light.

The reminder seemed to do the trick. As well as permitting his slobbering mandibles to progress down her neck, this time she was partial to that wandering right hand exploring the more southerly aspects of her anatomy. The jaunt in the Capri might just have done the trick after all.

"Vince," she suddenly shoved him aside to sit bolt upright, popping the light on again.

"What now?" he hissed through gritted teeth that had been compelled to abandon nibbling on a nipple he'd exposed (and which she hastily popped back inside her bra).

"Can you close your window?" he observed a pair of winsome eyes implore from beneath her side fringe.

"But it's hot in here!" he insisted.

"Please. It's just that... it's spooky out there."

Obligingly, he wound up the driver's window so that just the narrowest slit remained open. Then, having further placated her with a munching French kiss, he extinguished the light and eased her back into the seat again, this time to hopefully plant his flag of conquest within the most luscious southerly haunt of all.

* * * * *

It was indeed a sultry night. Having forsaken the sanctuary of the settling pond, Betty had slithered across the railway sidings and found her way out through a rabbit hole beneath the perimeter fence. All the time, she was alive to the hues of activity that her finely-tuned infra-red sensor pits were picking up.

Lumbering out onto a tarmac surface that was still warm from the hot afternoon sun, those sensors were able to pick out an even more brilliant smorgasbord of hues: the fiery glows from a hot engine and exhaust pipe. Meanwhile, the heat sources within that parked-up car seemed to be in motion, indicating the presence of more animate (and perhaps edible) objects. Inching herself closer to the vehicle, she extended her sleek, phallus-shaped head upwards, as if to peer inside its windows. Unseen by the car's necking occupants, she slithered silently up and across the warm bonnet, her tongue flicking as she went.

Indeed, Betty wasn't the only snake being aroused. Her head probing at the narrow slit of that open window, those sensory pits were able to more fully map out the infra-red glow of sexual frenzy. However, try as she might, Betty was unable to insert herself through such a miniscule gap. Eventually, in frustration, the snake allowed itself to slink to the ground. There was nothing for it but to abandon these amorous humans to their nocturnal passion. She slithered away to find more amenable prey.

* * * * *

Billy Slater was about to head back to the gatehouse when he spotted something curious. Some sort of track appeared to have been gouged into the dusty ground across from the railway sidings. Examining it in more detail, it was about the width of a lorry tyre, and with a course not unlike that of a motorbike that had swerved this way and that on an erratic journey over to the perimeter fence. Except that, unlike a motorbike, it had fashioned only one groove in the dust.

Intrigued, he followed that course as it shadowed the fence before terminating at a rabbit hole that had been dug beneath it. There it disappeared into the undergrowth.

Strange, he muttered to himself. However, it was then – to his shock and disbelief – that he spotted it!

The shiny new Ford Capri had been parked up in the quiet lane that led to the old parcels depot. Much as Billy admired the sleek sporty coupé, what was going on inside the car was of far greater thrill. Through its windows he could make out that the driver had lumbered his way over to the passenger seat and was astride the woman who was in the car with him!

Suddenly, all thought of that mysterious track in the dust departed his head – to be replaced instead by sexual arousal that left him quivering with excitement. He edged closer to the fence to observe this guy giving it to his bird for all he was worth. What's more, judging by the voluble panting emanating from inside the car, she was not averse to it being given!

From behind the cover of a blackberry bush in full fruit, Billy had a ringside seat for the action – and with that full moon enabling him to make out her nakedness! Even so, he craned for a better view. Indeed, so absorbed was the randy night watchman in this unexpected love fest that he failed to notice that the couple were far from being alone in this desolate spot. From within that blackberry bush there were vague stirrings of which they – and their titillated voyeur – remained blissfully unaware.

* * * * *

"What was that?" she sprang up in the seat with a start, brusquely shoving aside his sweaty torso.

"What was what?" Vince gnashed. Would this stupid wench ever stop mithering about stuff and just relax!

"I thought I heard summat'. A scream, like."

"Oh, bloody hell, Deb. It's probably just a fox or something."

"Yer' doh' s'pose it's that giant snake that everyone's bin' gooin' on about, do yer'?"

"Doh' be daft! Snakes cor' scream!" he sneered, peering through her window. However, all he could make out was that same blackberry bush that they'd been parked up next to for the last half-hour, as well as the floodlit steel works beyond it.

She craned forward to locate her panties in the jumble of garments in the footwell. Slipping them on, she flicked on the interior light to glance at the tiny watch around her wrist – one of the few items of attire that was still in its usual place.

"We berra' be gerrin' back," she urged him.

"Nah, we've got plenty of time yet," he insisted.

With the aid of a few softly spoken words (as well as the planting of further incisor marks on her neck), he managed to ease Deborah back into the embrace of the fully-reclined seat again.

* * * * *

Billy Slater never saw the monster that sank its fangs into his leg. And though he cried out in terror, the python quickly looped enough of its colossal trunk around him that his cries ceased.

In vain he clawed at those massive coils, his fingernails scraping into the creature's scales. Yet each time he expended breath, the snake further tightened its grip. Billy cried out a final time. However, though his mouth gaped, no sound was emitted.

Ominously, his entire life now flashed before him. What a way to depart this mortal coil! Too late now to say sorry for the things he'd done wrong. Too late to wish he'd instead done more things right. Too late to apologise to his wife for gratifying the opportunistic sexual temptation that had brought him to this denouement. Too late to say sorry to his beloved children and grandchildren, who he was about to leave behind.

Betty could perceive none of this belated remorse. What she could perceive though was that the massive constriction she was applying had finally shut down the circulation of blood to her victim's heart and head. Billy Slater was dead. Releasing her grip and distending her jaws in readiness, there now commenced the fraught task of swallowing him.

* * * * *

The flag of conquest had been planted at last – even if Vince Fullard was still smarting from the annoying interruptions that had attended it. Meanwhile, cleaning herself up, Deborah wondered if that was why he was reluctant to engage in post-coital tenderness with her. Instead, he jumped back into the driver's seat, racing his trousers up over his knees and zipping them up. He wound down the window again for some welcome fresh air before finally deigning to glance across at her.

"Try not to mek' a mess of the seat," he grunted. "This thing's only just left the showroom, like."

"Yeah, well. It ay' all my mess, is it," she snapped irately as she endeavoured to identify and sort her own discarded garments.

While she did, her boyfriend spotted headlights approaching in the distance. Deborah spotted them too, hastening to zip up her skirt. Then – to their horror – as the car drew near a set of flashing blue lights lit up the night sky.

"Bloody 'ell! Mum'll kill me!" she squealed, hurriedly poking her arms into her blouse – only to remove them again upon realising that she'd yet to slot them into her bra.

* * * * *

Like amorous humans, feeding snakes abhor disturbance. The scrunching of gravel chips as the police car drew to a halt jolted the enormous snake. Having with effort hooked those enormous jaws around its victim, the choice was stark: trust that the dense blackberry bush would afford her the concealment she needed to wait out the disturbance until it had passed; or abort this latest meal and make good her escape while she still possessed the vigour to do so. Meanwhile, she picked up more vibrations – this time of a human being alighting from the arriving car and resolutely grinding its stout size ten shoes into the tarmac.

"Evening, sir... miss. Any particular reason why you're parked in this spot?" PC Jonathan Hunt squatted down and shone his torch through the open window of the Capri – as if the answer wasn't blindingly self-evident!

"Just chatting, officer," its driver twittered with a smile.

"Then it appears to have been rather an animated conversation, if I may say so," the policeman noted, illuminating the girl to observe the dishevelment of her chestnut locks. She smiled back at him as if butter wouldn't melt in a mouth that was glistening with smudged lipstick. He lowered the torch to permit her to puff those locks back into place and reapply her make-up.

"This is a bit of a smart motor for a young man like you to be driving, sir," Jonathan observed instead, rising to his feet to pace around it, admiring its lines – as well as the peculiar dusty trail that had been deposited across the bonnet. Perhaps not all the 'chatting' they'd engaged in had taken place *inside* the car.

"Yours?" he enquired, returning to the driver's window.

"Yes. I picked it up today. Well, I say mine. Actually it's a company car. I'm a sales representative: for Albert Header & Son (Midlands) Ltd – manufacturer of quality brackets, wall ties, and architectural ironmongery," the young man chortled proudly.

"Really? Then sir is a very fortunate young man," Jonathan observed, squatting back down to address him, as well as to admire again the pretty young thing in the passenger seat who'd meanwhile made herself more presentable.

"Of course, I trust sir is not unaware that there's a dangerous snake at large somewhere in this town," he continued. "Therefore, coming across you all by yourselves in this lonely spot, you'll appreciate we're anxious you don't become its next meal."

"Thank you for your concern, officer," the driver shrugged, as if to mask the enormity of his ingratitude.

"So maybe it's time to take this young lady home," Jonathan suggested, glancing at the teenager one final time, "… before her parents become anxious for her welfare too."

The grinning young man took the hint, slotting the key into the ignition so that the throaty Capri could execute a hasty three-point turn before pulling away.

However, before re-joining his bemused colleague in their panda car, Jonathan drifted over to the perimeter fence of the steel plant to stare across at the parched scrubland that separated this lonely lane from the railway sidings, peering over the blackberry bush that had sprouted through it. Having failed to catch up with that elusive snake, he glanced up at the big, bright moon above and wondered when and where Betty's next victim would turn up.

* * * * *

Having received the call, Brian and Julie had made their way to the scene as fast as they could. Alighting from Julie's motorbike, they hurried over to the police cordon, inside of which an incident tent had been erected.

"I'm afraid he's not a pretty sight," Detective Inspector Grayson explained as he escorted them over to the ambulance being loaded up. "We received the call just after midday. His wife was concerned that he hadn't come home. A search of the plant was conducted; and his body was discovered over by that fence."

With a nod from Grayson, one of his men lifted the cover from the face of the victim. Both Brian and Julie had seen the regurgitated remains of aborted python kills before. Neither, however, had ever come face-to-face with a regurgitated human corpse – notwithstanding that those powerful stomach acids had barely had time to begin their work of dissolving it.

"Yes, Inspector. I'm afraid that's Betty's handiwork alright," Brian confirmed.

Another nod from Grayson and that melted face was covered over again. Thereupon, he led the two snake experts inside the cordon and over to the fence, where the evidence of the animal's passage could be observed from the grooves that had been gouged in the dry and dusty terrain.

"His name's William Slater. He was a fifty-five-year-old security guard," he meanwhile reeled off the victim's particulars. "We presume he was doing his rounds when the snake pounced. Judging by these trails, it's possible the creature has been on walkabout around the plant while it's been shut – or slither-about; or whatever snakes do when they go exploring."

"Drat!" Brian cursed, turning to his assistant and demonstratively smacking his forehead. "The steel plant was the one place we never thought to look. I should have known that, with the cooling water pumps switched off, Betty might attempt to swim or crawl back through the outlet pipes."

"There's a further twist to this latest attack," Grayson noted, staring through the fence. "Last night, a panda car was patrolling down this lane when its officers came across a courting couple getting frisky inside their car. Your friend PC Hunt made a cursory search of the area around the fence; but didn't spot the snake. However, he did recall seeing similar marks to these on the bonnet of their car. We suspect one or both of those young lovers might have been the python's intended victim."

"Lucky pair!" said Julie, also peering through the fence at the juxtaposition of slither marks and tyre tracks.

"Then your patrol must have disturbed Betty and spooked her into regurgitating Mr Slater," Brian began to piece the story together. "You see, snakes are at their most vulnerable immediately after swallowing a large prey. Betty would have been virtually immobile. And to think: Jonathan was unaware that he was probably stood right next to her," the Snakeman shook his head in frustration. A priceless opportunity to corner their quarry had been missed.

"The question is: where has the snake disappeared to in the meantime? PC Hunt reported patrolling here at eleven o'clock last night," Grayson informed them, glancing at his watch. "That means it's had a sixteen-hour head start on us. How far can a python travel in sixteen hours?" he asked rhetorically.

"Far enough, I fear, Inspector," Brian agonised, his brow furrowing as he studied the skyline of his home town in the distance.

* * * * *

Following a fraught press conference during which Chief Superintendent Trotter had regretfully announced that his men had discovered the remains of Betty's latest victim, panic had indeed gripped Sneyd End – just as its chief of police had feared. Press and television people suddenly descended upon this small, unsung town from all over the country. Indeed, Pauline had switched on the television news to discover her father being put on the spot by an ABC News reporter from Australia!

Meanwhile, those TV news bulletins were brimming with tales of how normal life in the town had ceased. For example, one housewife described pouring the entire contents of a bottle of bleach down her loo after each flush in the hope of deterring the snake from visiting her abode (supplemented by the heavy slabs that her husband placed on the toilet lid at night just to be sure). Otherwise, gardens and allotments went untended; dogs went unwalked; parents no longer took their children to the park; and workmen refused to venture down manholes.

So serious had the crisis become that by the end of the third week of August the matter had been taken out of Trotter's hands. In response to the public outcry, it was announced that the army would be brought in to lead an enhanced operation to track down the elusive snake. It also ended any hope that Brian Danks had been entertaining of capturing it alive. With at least one confirmed death to her name now, the new man in charge of finding her was adamant: this 'Betty' would be relentlessly hunted, cornered, and killed.

25

'Operation Lemon' it was to be called: the mission to hunt down the giant snake that was terrorising a Midlands town. Notwithstanding that one of the American reporters present reminded the gathering that, in his country, a 'lemon' was the term used to describe a dodgy automobile, the new man in charge dismissed the observation by reminding those present that – as was British military custom – the codename had been picked entirely at random. Besides, he folded his arms and charged bluntly: British cars were made of sterner stuff (which was startling news to those press hacks who'd earlier in the week been filing reports from the picket lines of one of the West Midlands' strike-prone motor factories).

With his rigid bearing, craggy, weathered features, and assured, no-nonsense delivery, Colonel Peter Urquhart was the very personification of a British army officer. Having been wounded during the evacuation of Dunkirk in 1940, he'd gone on to serve his country with distinction in a military career spanning almost thirty years. However, when another journalist cynically enquired what particular qualifications he possessed for leading a snake-hunt, to the man's surprise 'Urk' (as the men under his command were known to affectionately refer to him) explained that, having fought the Japanese in the Far East and led post-war counter-insurgency operations in the jungles of Malaya and Borneo, he'd come across the odd snake or two in his time – including, he joked, a twelve foot Burmese python that he'd returned from patrol one night to find had taken up residence in his bivouac! The flurry of amusement the remark occasioned was the first signal that his audience was warming to him.

Observing proceedings from the back of the room, Julie Newington had also initially shared the prejudices of the assembled press corps about this ostensibly haughty and self-important figure in khaki. However, as the conference wore on and the fifty-two-year-old infantry commander opened up about himself and fielded further questions from the excited press corps – often with similarly dry and witty ripostes – she could better appreciate mutterings she'd overheard amongst the more astute journalists about why this tenacious, if unorthodox soldier's career had progressed no further. If keeping Protestants and Catholics from each other's throats in Northern Ireland required a military commander who possessed tact and diplomacy, then the powers-that-be in the Ministry of Defence had presumably deemed the task of hunting a large snake better suited to one with more unconventional soldiering qualities.

Furthermore, having fully expected her boss to be cashiered on account of his high-profile role in the unsuccessful pursuit of the python so far, Julie was as surprised as the rest of the reporters present to hear the Colonel boldly announce that he would be retaining the services of Brian Danks (and by implication her services too), generously describing him as a world-renowned (if undoubtedly colourful) herpetologist who, because he also possessed extensive knowledge of the local area, would remain invaluable to the mission. It was yet another signal that – for all his clichéd military mannerisms (and not unlike her boss) – Colonel Urquhart was indisputably a maverick.

* * * * *

Brian Danks had never before looked down on his home town from above. As the army helicopter flew low over Sneyd End, it was possible to make out all its familiar landmarks: the eye-catching new shopping centre in the town centre; the tall spire of St Stephen's Church; and running alongside it the abandoned railway line – one end leading to the southern end of the tunnel that once carried it beneath the town, the other bisected by the new leisure centre where once the town's station had stood.

Banking sharply, the pilot overflew the northern end of the tunnel, the remains of the overgrown track bed still visible as it shadowed the silted-up Sneyd End Canal. Up ahead was the giant Alcock & Robbins steel works; while perched on higher ground on the other side of the Wednesbury Road loomed the town's large secondary school.

Meanwhile, everywhere below the drab olive outfits of soldiers could be made out – peering down drains, combing back gardens, probing watercourses, and raking through undergrowth. With over three hundred troops at his disposal, Colonel Urquhart certainly had the manpower he needed to flush Betty out.

"Of course, now the weather's cooled it should make our task a lot easier. At least that blessed snake won't be so fond of roaming above ground," the Colonel announced above the throbbing of the helicopter's rotors, speaking into his intercom headset while his sharp blue eyes scanned the terrain below.

"She may have already made her way back to the tunnel," Brian advised. "However, if not, it's possible she's been caught out by the sharp drop in temperature over the last day or two. In which case, she will have had to find some other warm place in which to shelter – and in a hurry too. Our task is to locate where that place might be."

"Well, I've instructed my men to be pretty systematic in their combing of the town – including all the likely boltholes. Where ever your python's hiding, Councillor, they will find it."

It was heartening to know. As well as this determined, can-do spirit that the Colonel had brought to the search, his penchant for boldness and decisiveness, seasoned (as always) by an irreverent and disarming wit, had stirred something within the Snakeman. It was no exaggeration to say that, despite their vastly differing backgrounds, a touching, if intangible symbiosis was developing between the bumbling zoo keeper and the bluff senior officer. And although Brian was very much the junior partner in this mission, most graciously the soldier never allowed the civilian to think for one minute that he regarded him as anything other than a valued equal. It was with this in mind that the Colonel glanced across at him with a matey glint in his eye.

"I'm sure I don't need to tell you, of all people, Brian: but ordinarily snakes will avoid human contact, the noise we make when we tramp through their habitats invariably sending them hurrying for cover. However, one of the key tactics that the jungle soldier possesses in his pursuit of the enemy is stealth: the ability to move silently and unseen through often dense, forested terrain. As such, more than most people, sooner or later the jungle soldier will make contact with a snake – usually to both parties' horror and surprise! It happened to me on several occasions.

"I don't mind confessing that the first time you run into one it scares you shitless," he laughed self-effacingly. Then the eyes that were still surveying the town beneath them curled and that can-do spirit welled up.

"However, you soon learn to overcome your fear. What's more, the snake quickly perceives that you're no longer afraid of it. Don't ask me how, but it subtly alters its mindset. From that moment on, you have the upper hand in the encounter. I want to instil that mindset in this snake too: to make Betty conscious that – no matter how big and brassy she is – we are not afraid of her."

* * * * *

It was far from ideal. However, it was warm; and it was quiet. More importantly, its complex of buildings was strangely devoid of humans – or so it had seemed.

However, wandering inside for a few minutes to inspect the plant and machinery – as well as to set the boiler ready for when the place reopened in a few days' time – the caretaker failed to spot that a massive snake had curled itself up tightly in a cavity behind it. Neither had Betty seen fit to announce her presence. Instead, she'd allowed the visitor to come and go unmolested.

She knew she might be holed up here for some time. With the weather having turned colder, there was now no chance of finding her way back to the warmth and succour of the tunnel in which she'd thrived. Therefore, it was just as well that this place too had a ready, if somewhat less well-stocked source of food. Back to a diet of rats again! Otherwise, this sudden interruption aside, the snake slumbered on undisturbed.

* * * * *

The problem of where to billet three hundred squaddies who were working tirelessly to flush out a giant snake had been solved by packing camp beds into the cavernous sports hall of the new leisure centre. Meanwhile – and in one of the jollier outcomes of

'The Snake-Hunt of Sneyd End' (as the newspapers were dubbing it) – both the 'Pig & Whistle' and 'The Miners' Arms' reported a surge in takings as this influx of military personnel sought somewhere conducive to while away their off-duty moments.

Unsurprisingly, the officers assigned to 'Operation Lemon' expected a more upmarket standard of accommodation to be placed at their disposal – as well as a better class of relaxation to look forward to at the end of the day than a game of darts played over a pint and a bag of pork scratchings.

As its commanding officer, Colonel Urquhart could have commandeered the best room in Sneyd End's only hotel. However, in a remarkable and endearing display of unstuffiness, he'd instead taken up a kind offer from Brian Danks to stay with him and his wife at their modern, semi-detached abode on Sneyd Park estate. Notwithstanding the mobile hanging from the ceiling, the battered, old teddy bear with the eye missing on the dresser, and the cute little cartoons of ducks and fishes embossed on the drapes, the bedroom to which Ruby had shown him was a good deal homelier than those in the draughty flea pit that was the 'King's Head' on the Tipton Road! Suffice to say, Ruby's anticipated new arrival wouldn't be requiring it for another few weeks yet – by which time, Betty would hopefully be history.

"It really is most kind of you both to make me welcome," Urk thanked them as Brian volubly urged him to tuck into another of the lady-of-the-house's sumptuous, exotic recipes.

"Our pleasure, Colonel. As the Good Book admonishes us: *'Be not forgetful to entertain strangers: for thereby some have entertained angels unawares',*" the lay reader riposted, quick as a flash. "Hebrews Chapter Thirteen, Verse Two."

"An angel, you say, eh? You flatter me, old chap. Though hopefully I'm no longer a stranger!" the Colonel guffawed.

"Of course not, Colonel. You're most welcome," Ruby replied, rather less excitably. "Besides, my mother always told me the British army fights better on a full stomach," she joked.

"It does indeed! And hunts snakes better on one too!" Urk guffawed again, complimenting Ruby on her lamb curry. Truly this hospitable couple had taken him to their hearts.

In between mouthfuls, Ruby noticed how the gaze of their lodger had drifted to that black-and-white photograph that was sat atop the sideboard – the one of Arthur and Myrtle Danks on their wedding day in 1939 (with war imminent, Brian's father already in uniform). Brian too had noticed Urk studying it on a previous occasion, only to have the telephone ring and his recounting of the story behind the photograph interrupted before it had properly begun. The Snakeman was about to try again when the Colonel trained his eyes upon his wife instead.

"Brian tells me you're a teacher, Ruby," he remarked.

"That's right. Well, I was – until this little bundle of joy took up residence," she explained, glancing down at the 'bump' that was pressing against the lip of the dining table.

"I mention it because I was chatting to the headmaster of that big secondary school on the Wednesbury Road today," Urk then informed them. "Mr Weston, is it?"

So enticing were the chunks of diced lamb that the Colonel was chasing around his plate that he failed to notice Brian and Ruby glance up at each other. Ruby dipped her eyes awkwardly. How could she explain to their esteemed guest the circumstances that had made her *persona non grata* at a place that held so many memories for her – good and bad?

"Some of the town's primary schools have decided to remain closed until we catch up with this confounded snake," he continued, "to give the kiddies an extended summer holiday, as it were. However, Mr Weston was seeking my opinion about whether it wasn't better to have his pupils *in* school, where he can keep an eye on them, rather than roaming the streets getting up to goodness knows what mischief. Therefore, he's announced he will re-open his school as normal on Tuesday. It's a move I've wholeheartedly endorsed."

"A wise decision," Ruby noted plaintively.

"What I did say to him is that either you or I, Brian, are going to have to sit the youngsters down in assembly first thing on Tuesday morning and explain to them in no uncertain terms the danger that's still out there; and why they must make their way to and from school quickly and safely. No deviating from main roads; no larking about over Fens Bank; and certainly no disappearing inside that old railway tunnel – which Mr Weston told me has become something of a short cut home for the more adventurous of his little darlings."

Brian raised a smile: after what Robin and Parminder had reported encountering he was amazed that anybody in Sneyd End would be insane enough to want to venture inside the tunnel now. Meanwhile, as the jolly banter continued, Ruby raised a smile too – this time accompanied by a quiet prayer of thanksgiving for the easy-going rapport that her husband had established with the man who was now in charge of the snake-hunt. It made a refreshing change from the more tenuous relationship he'd had with Chief Superintendent Trotter – who, though he'd come to grudgingly respect the Snakeman, had never quite shaken off his residual suspicion of him.

Once the meal was consumed, from the kitchen Ruby could observe both men studying Lizzie (who was probing her way around her glass tank in the living room) while discussing plans for apprehending her much larger cousin. With his comical eccentricities and his awkwardness in social situations, Ruby accepted that her husband wasn't always the easiest of characters to get along with. Bizarrely however, this decorated soldier seemed to have genuinely taken to him – almost as a doting father would a son.

What's more, the feeling was clearly mutual. As if to underline this strange endearment, she marvelled too that the Colonel must be the first visitor they'd entertained who, instead of permitting Brian to proudly show off his model railway out of a sense of polite obligation, had positively enthused over that intricate lay-out in the spare room – recounting his own boyhood passion for trains as he did. Why, her faith tempted her to believe that it was almost as if God had placed Colonel Peter Urquhart across Brian Danks's path for a reason.

* * * * *

"Right, you men," the boyish lieutenant addressed the troops gathered around him, "this young lady here is Julie Newington. She will be working with you today to make sure this tunnel is thoroughly searched *and* sealed so that the python can no longer return to it. If any of you spot anything suspicious, summon her immediately and she will supervise its investigation; and – if it is the snake we're looking for – then its extermination as well."

It was not quite what Julie wanted to hear. Like Brian, she'd not entirely given up hope of capturing Betty alive. Neither was she wholly encouraged by the bemused looks of these teenage squaddies that it was a *woman* who would be overseeing that 'extermination' (and 'a meaty bird' at that, she'd overheard them joking amongst themselves). The implication: what could *a woman* possibly know about grappling with a large snake? However, with Brian elsewhere, it had fallen to his tomboyish assistant to oversee the important task of making sure Betty was denied access to this crucial hide-out.

Once dismissed, one-by-one the forty-strong detail stepped through the gap in the railings at the entrance of Sneyd End Tunnel to trudge off into a blackness pierced by the beams of the powerful searchlights they wielded – and which, as they progressed, they would shine to assist this *woman* as she knelt down and inspected inside its drainage shafts with her trusty snake hook. Satisfied each one was devoid of serpents, she would rise to her feet and signal for it to be sealed off with the sandbags that had meanwhile been unloaded from a truck at the tunnel entrance, there to be passed along the chain of men that had formed up inside.

"Crikey! It's hot in 'ere!" was the common complaint she was meanwhile overhearing.

Eventually ordered to take five from their exertions, someone gathered together enough bits of timber for a fire to be lit in an old brazier they'd come across along the way. The lads were thus able to brew some char – which they sat down on some old sleepers to slurp from tin mugs. One of the corporals gestured for their female overseer to break from probing and share a mug with them. Accepting their kind offer, Julie found herself invited to listen in to the expletive-laden banter with which they were endeavouring to see the funny side of 'Operation Lemon'.

"'Ere, how come you're into handlin' snakes then?" their beefy sergeant commenced a probing of his own, glancing across at her. "After all, it ain't yer' normal occupation for a woman, is it... If yer' know what I mean."

"I'm not your 'normal' woman," she ventured cagily. Recalling her experience searching the canal with those police officers, she could sense where this line of enquiry was leading.

"Yer' can certainly say that again, love," he snickered, to the amusement of his men. "Most girls I know would run a mile from a snake – especially one they say could be anything up to thirty-feet long! But you give the impression of wantin' to pat the thing on the head and read it a bedtime story."

Maintaining a straight face, the object of his derision stared at the Cockney trooper over the top of her tin mug. In the absence of a response, her interrogator delved a little deeper.

"So, this 'Snakeman' geezer: is he yer' boyfriend then?" he feigned to idly enquire.

"No. He's not. Brian Danks is happily-married," she assured him. "His wife is expecting their first child. And me? Well, I'm not in a relationship at present... with a man, that is."

Looking her up and down in the flickering hues from the fire, the inquisitive NCO read between the lines, surmising from her grudging and ambiguous reply that she would not welcome further snooping into her personal life.

"Anyway, where is the organ grinder this mornin'?" he eyed her again, trying a different tack. "And how come we've ended up with the monkey instead?"

There were further embarrassed sniggers.

"He's over at the secondary school," she enlightened him, pointedly refusing to be riled by such condescension. "He's addressing the pupils on their first day back at school. Brian likes working with young people. He's eager to explain to them that, while we should always respect snakes, we shouldn't harbour an irrational fear of them either. Like all God's creatures, they have their place in this world. Most of the problems that we humans encounter with snakes occur when we invade their habitat and fail to treat them with proper respect."

She could see the hard-bitten serviceman was unimpressed.

"Yeah, well. The sooner this one gets a bullet in the head the better," he grunted contemptuously, taking a final swig of tea before tossing the dregs aside. He then stood to his feet, flexing himself before addressing the blokes around him.

"Anyway, you lot. Any of you fancy an arm-wrestle?" he enquired, pointing to one of the recesses of the tunnel in which workmen had once sheltered from passing trains – and in which he'd spotted an old packing crate had been dumped. "The usual stuff? Ten bob on the side; a quid to the winner?

"Oh, come on, Sarge. You've already cleaned me out this week," one of the other NCOs groaned, speaking for his pals.

"Yer' bunch of poofters! Do none of yer' wanna' win yer' money back then?" he crowed. However, there were no takers.

"I'll challenge you."

Everybody looked up, surprised that a feminine voice had thrown down the gauntlet. They watched Julie toss away the dregs of her own tea and demonstrably rise to her feet. At first, their muscular sergeant was taken aback; then mildly amused.

"Go on, Sarge. You've never lost a match yet," one of his men reminded him, supplemented by the chivvying of his mates. Meanwhile, the burly NCO stared at each of them in turn before training a wary eye upon Julie.

"Okay. You're on," he nodded, still eyeing her up and down as he snapped his fingers for a private to drag the packing crate over. What better way to wipe that smirk from the face of this contemptible fat dyke.

Kneeling in the dust, both champion and upstart challenger rested their right elbows upon the chest, locking hands and staring into the other's eyes. With a corporal counting them down, the tournament commenced.

"Come on, Sarge! You can do it!" the cries quickly went up.

However, there was an element amongst the detail who Julie noticed had declined to cheer. Instead they were looking on with an air of *schadenfreude*, amused that their sergeant's opening surge had failed to tip the lass's hand. And although he was inching her arm over, the Snakeman's taciturn assistant was fighting back for all she was worth. There was muscle in that arm the 'meaty bird' had bared.

Teeth clenched and adrenalin flowing, both contestants were pumping every ounce of strength they possessed into those tensed and juddering forearms. However, at first imperceptibly, then with a series of jolts the NCO found his own hand being forced backwards. Then, at last, the back of that hand impacted upon the rough wooden crate and he gnashed in shame.

"Bloody 'ell! She's beaten him!" a private marvelled.

"I say up there: how are things going, Sergeant?" the detail suddenly caught the lieutenant's clipped tones echoing along the tunnel, the flames from the brazier illuminating his approach.

Everyone snapped to attention – as did their sergeant, standing to his feet and levering a throbbing hand to his forehead in salute.

"I was about to order the men back to work again, sir," he replied. "Meanwhile, Miss Newington here has been explaining all about snakes and how we should show them more respect."

"Jolly good, Sergeant. In which case, I shall expect the men to be fully *au fait* about this python we're looking for. Hopefully by the time we're finished in this godforsaken tunnel it'll be one less place where the blighter can hide."

* * * * *

The travails of young love! It was as quiet a place as they could find. Having seen next to nothing of her over the school holidays, Robin was now desperate to meet up with Parminder again. And not because he still needed her help with his homework! In receipt of the note he'd passed her in class this morning she'd agreed to rendezvous with him on the steps that led down to the boiler room, where hopefully no one would spot them. Even better, to his surprise Robin had tried the door to it and found it had been left unlocked.

"You know that my father has forbidden me from meeting you in this way," she explained as he bundled her inside.

"I know. But I just wanted to tell you that, you know… well… I've missed you," he offered her a sorrowful smile.

"I've missed you too," it pained her to admit. "But you have to understand that I cannot go against my family. So perhaps it's best if we stop seeing each other. Besides, after what Mr Danks told us in assembly, from tomorrow my uncle will be giving me a lift to and from school in his car – at least until they catch this snake. Therefore, I will no longer need you to walk me home. In which case, perhaps it's better if we agree to end things now."

"So this is it then?" he surmised, a tear visible in his eye. Reluctantly, Parminder nodded.

"Yes, but please understand, I will always be grateful to you," she was anxious to make clear. "And I will always look upon you as a friend – a very good friend. Who knows: one day – when we're older, and should we meet again in different circumstances – then maybe we can be more than just friends."

A tear fled her eye too – for she had spoken those touching words as much in prayer as in consolation for the boy she was hurting by doing this – such a gentle soul who'd shattered every stereotype of how a working-class white boy would behave towards a brown-skinned girl from a distant continent. She hoped that one day Robin would look back on the friendship they'd briefly enjoyed with the same fondness that she would.

Meanwhile, he motioned to offer her a parting peck on the cheek. However, she forestalled it. Instead, she offered him her delicate hand. With a heavy heart, he looked down at it before finally slipping his own around it to gently shake it.

"And don't worry about your homework," she assured him with a smile. "You will be just fine. You're a smart lad, Robin. So instead of dreaming about me, you dream about those 'O' levels and 'A' levels – and about going to university once you've passed them. You have a great future ahead of you."

And with that, she slipped out of the dimly-lit boiler room. After a moment spent dabbing away further tears for the love he'd lost, he gazed around at the machinery humming away behind him. Such an incongruous place for two people to say goodbye, he snuffled. Then he too stepped back out into the sunlight above, shutting the door to this secluded place behind him.

Yet this secluded place was not so secluded after all. Unseen behind a wall cavity, Betty was stirred by the scent of human sexual longing that these two furtive teenagers had left lingering in the air (and which her sensitive tongue had picked up on). With the building above now warmed up nicely, perhaps it was time to go exploring again.

* * * * *

There was something in there, but no one was sure what. Too big to be a fox's den or a badger's set, yet too small for even someone as wiry as Brian Danks to crawl inside, there was only one thing for it. Reluctantly, the Snakeman stepped back from the mouth of the hollow that the platoon assigned to comb this part of Sneyd Woods had discovered. Clambering down the bracken-clad bank – employing his snake hook to steady himself – clambering up and passing him was a corporal with two large tanks strapped to his back and a most peculiar weapon in his hands.

Training it at the mouth of the hollow, the soldier glanced down at his subaltern, who gave the nod. He then squeezed the trigger – igniting a flaming stream of gelled petroleum that flooded it, instantly cremating whatever creature was unlucky enough to have been sheltering inside.

Brian winced. He'd seen TV footage of flame-throwers being used to wipe out Viet Cong guerrillas in their tunnel lairs. However, to feel the lash of heat on his face and sniff the scent of (what he assumed to be) burning flesh was truly sobering. Employing such summary means had been a rare point of disagreement between him and the man in overall charge of 'Operation Lemon'.

"No point in getting sentimental, Brian old chap," Colonel Urquhart consoled him on the journey back to Operational HQ (aka St Stephen's church hall, which Father Allen had generously placed at the army's disposal – much to the annoyance of the Mothers' Union, who traditionally met there on Tuesday afternoons). "Poking about in such a place is simply not worth the risk. It's a bitter lesson we learned at Imphal in '44. So look upon that snake as no different to a Jap sniper holed up in a jungle cave!" he nudged him.

"Except we don't know for certain if Betty was in there," Brian rather inconveniently pointed out.

"Right now, we don't. But once that hollow has cooled, I've ordered it to be dug out. Then we'll know for sure. That said, my gut instinct is that Betty has taken shelter somewhere indoors. Now that my men have completed their search of these woods, I intend that they redouble the searching of buildings instead – starting with a raking over of that steel plant again. Trust me, Brian: we'll catch up with this snake yet."

"Talking of the war, I see from the resumé of your career that you were injured at Dunkirk," Brian noted matter-of-factly once their Land Rover had re-joined the main road.

"I was indeed," Urk replied. "Shrapnel wounds – from being caught up in a Stuka attack on the beach. Ordinarily, sand is pretty good at absorbing the impact of exploding ordnance. However, this particular bomb landed within a few yards of my platoon. Several men were killed. I was lucky to survive at all."

"My father was killed at Dunkirk," the Snakeman noted.

"I know he was, Brian."

Amused that it was not just a love of trains and some hair-raising encounters with snakes that the two men had in common, at first the import of those words didn't register. When the penny did finally drop, Brian Danks turned to witness the Colonel glance at him with a dolent glimmer in his eye.

"Your father was with me on that beach," he calmly elaborated. "In fact, I was his commanding officer."

"And my f-f-father was one of those m-m-men who was killed by that b-b-bomb?" Brian mumbled in sudden trepidation.

The Colonel nodded regretfully. Spying the approach of a bus lay-by, he pulled over and extinguished the engine. Thereupon he could relax his hold on the steering wheel and properly recount the final moments of Arthur Danks to his visibly dumbfounded only son – the boy he never lived to see grow up.

"He wasn't killed instantly – even though he took the full force of the shrapnel that should have ripped into me. You could therefore say I owe my own life to your father.

"We managed to transport him to a field hospital, although there wasn't much they could do for him. However, during his final moments he clung to my hand and told me about the baby boy that his wife had given birth to; and who he had been looking forward to holding in his arms for the first time – had he made it off that beach and back to England."

Brian had never been told the full story of his father's final day on this Earth. To hear it now, after all these years – and from the very last person to have spoken with him – was truly sobering. He brushed away a stray tear.

"Your father knew he was dying. With his closing breath, he begged me to one day search out his son and to tell him how much he was loved; and how his father had wanted the best for him. And that maybe one day – through my eyes, as it were – he might get to behold the man the boy would become."

Suddenly, Brian was conscious that an 'angel across his path' had spoken – an 'angel' he'd been entertaining in his home, no less. Observing tears seeping from behind those chunky black spectacles, Urk reached over to grip his shoulder.

"Forgive me, old chap: but war intervened, postings came and went, and somehow I never did get the chance to seek you out – though I've often thought about your father's dying words ever since. However, when I was assigned to this mission and came across your name on the briefing notes, and then saw your face on television, I confess thinking to myself: 'Was it possible? Could it be?' Then, when I saw that photograph of your father on your sideboard, I knew it was.

"So here I am, Brian. If you like, imagine it's your father now addressing you – through me. Imagine that it's him – and not me – who is now telling you how proud I am of you: how proud I am of the work that you've done to advance mankind's knowledge of reptiles; how proud I am that you're working tirelessly to protect your town from one of its more rogue specimens; and even how proud I am of what you've tried to do to save a railway line that I know means so much to you. Who knows, maybe one day your campaign to reopen it will not have been in vain after all."

Brian Danks often struggled to show emotion. Seldom too was he given to crying in front of others. However, for the first time in years the repressed anguish that he felt that his father had been so cruelly taken from him now gushed from his eyes. Meanwhile, Urk employed that outstretched hand to grip him again in manly consolation.

"Come on, Brian. Take heart. I just sense that sometime this week we will finally catch up with this snake that you and I have been searching for. And when we do – and the people of Sneyd End can again sleep peacefully in their beds – I want all the accolades to go to you. This will be your achievement, your triumph. This mission could not have succeeded without your expert knowledge and input. It's not for nothing that people call you 'The Snakeman of Sneyd End', you know! And I believe it will be by that endearing name too that future generations in this town will also gratefully remember you."

26

They were encounters about which she was decidedly uneasy. Not content with seducing her at her cluttered lodgings when her landlady wasn't about – as well as at his more opulent marital pad when his wife wasn't either – these last few days Graham Weston had schemed to detain Millie Ferriday after school so that he could ravish her in his office too.

It was in the aftermath of one such hurried encounter that she found herself glancing his way while slipping on her panties. He spotted her uncertain countenance.

"Something wrong?" he enquired, tucking his shirt in his trousers.

"Don't you think what we're doing is terribly risky?" she fretted aloud. "I mean anyone could have just walked in. Being discovered could cost us both our jobs."

The *flambeur* emitted an abrupt, dismissive snigger.

"Maybe. But isn't that what makes these trysts exciting?"

Maybe it was. However, she couldn't mask her unease, having come to the dispiriting conclusion that it was the daring that attended their sexual liaisons – as opposed to any romantic feelings he might harbour towards her – that had become the thrill to which Graham Weston was addicted. Did he behave this way towards women because some closet misogyny compelled him to? Or simply because his urbane charm and demonstrative good looks enabled him to?

"Of course, if you prefer we can go back to my place. Virginia doesn't mind me seeing you. She has a lover too somewhere, I'm sure." he explained – as if such a blasé and surreal revelation was supposed to make her feel better.

Instead, it further fuelled that disillusionment, the long school holidays having afforded her the time and space to reflect upon this insane affair she'd embarked upon. Was it really worth jeopardising the career she loved just to wind up the plaything of an emotionally-fickle man? Yes, the sex was undeniably exhilarating. However, only reluctantly did she offer the handsome head teacher her usual kittenish grin in return.

"You look less than convinced," he pressed her as she poured her suppressed anger into straightening out her bra straps.

"Let's just say I'm beginning to sympathise with Ruby Danks. I suppose you've had her on that desk too – before I came along, that is," she sneered, unruffling her sweater and swishing her long blonde hair around her shoulders.

"I wouldn't worry about Ruby," he scoffed. "She's happy at last. Any day now she'll have a baby to cuddle – though God alone knows what she sees in its father! All I did was to kindly instruct her in what was missing from her marriage."

"In which case, it's just a shame that your act of kindness led to her being hounded from her job" Millie replied, glaring at him before grabbing her jacket and handbag and making for the door.

"Don't you want a lift home?" he asked with an assumption in his tone that belied irritation at this sudden bumptiousness.

"No," she replied abruptly, pausing with the door handle in her grasp. "I thought I'd catch the bus... for a change."

Graham Weston could detect the sound of scales falling from previously awestruck eyes. But then they always did in the end. Maybe the time had come to set this racy young thing free lest (like Ruby) she become possessive and demanding. Shame: she possessed such a cracking body too! Though resolved to seek out a fresh priapic diversion, he drifted over to savour that body again. Lifting her hand from the door handle, he gazed into her eyes and drew her forward to demand a parting kiss.

Though it felt sordid and wrong, she indulged him this liberty. Eyes closed, her tongue shadowed his. However, when his hand lifted her skirt and began pawing at her bottom she signalled that the time for taking that sort of liberty was over. Brushing his hand away, she reached for the door handle.

"You know, one thing intrigues me," she opined, releasing it and turning to face him again. "How come you managed to save your skin when Ruby ended up being thrown to the wolves? I mean, by all accounts it's not as though she exactly flung herself at you," she added tartly.

He again offered her that smirk that so grated.

"Let's just say she – or rather that imbecilic husband of hers – crossed swords once too often with the man who, until recently, was the chairman of governors of this school. The final straw was when Brian Danks unseated Horace Bissell and turfed him off the Council. Catching wind that the Snakeman's wife had been rather a naughty girl, I guess he was gleeful to have stumbled upon the perfect means for exacting his revenge."

Imbecile? Having met Ruby's husband for the first time earlier in the week when he'd addressed the school assembly, Millie thought he'd come across as quite a lively and knowledgeable character – and refreshingly genuine with it. The students had certainly warmed to his witty and informative presentation. Okay, Brian Danks was a bit quirky; and he was undoubtedly passionate. But he was far from being the malign and inept character that his more vocal critics had been eager to imply – including this man who'd cynically screwed his wife.

"However, as we now know, it looks like the former leader of the council has been a rather naughty boy himself – all these stories about him accepting backhanders from council building contractors. I guess it explains the shoddy workmanship that went into the construction of this school, for example.

"Of course," he couldn't resist adding, "I already knew he'd been stitching up dodgy deals to the detriment of the ratepayers of Sneyd End – and from a well-placed source at that. That's because, before you came along, I'd been instructing Horace Bissell's secretary in what was missing from *her* marriage too!"

If the smug and vainglorious school head had hoped to impress the naïve young arts teacher with how he had his finger on the pulse of what was going on in Sneyd End – in its bedrooms, as well as its corridors of power – he was mistaken. Though Millie listened without comment, the admission that he'd been seducing one man's wife at the same time he'd been sleeping with another was the cue for more scales to tumble from those angry eyes.

"Therefore, let's just say that what she confided in me afforded me a degree of bargaining power when confronting my scabrous chairman of governors. Hence Horace Bissell and I did a 'dodgy deal' of our own: that the price of my silence – and of keeping *my* job – was that Ruby Danks would unfortunately lose hers."

Millie shook her head, appalled. This man really was utterly shameless! It left her with dwindling confidence about her own fate should word of *their* affair similarly come to the attention of the school's governing body – especially when Weston's eyes tightened as if to remind her that he would no more hesitate to jettison her than he had her hapless predecessor.

"Not that it matters now anyway," his glare softened as he attempted to explain away this act of expedience. "Horace Bissell is staring at a spell in jail; Ruby's going to be a mummy; and that dimwit husband of hers is basking in all the publicity he could ever have hoped for now that this wretched snake business is all over the newspapers and television."

Millie Ferriday's patience finally snapped.

"Dimwit?" she spat scornfully. "Uh! Brian Danks is a better man than *you* will ever be."

"Look, enough of this tiresome petulance. Are you sure you don't want a lift?" he repeated, willing to overlook the slight in return for a final, valedictory quickie. "We can maybe stop off somewhere for a drink; then maybe for something else afterwards!" he lustfully licked his lips, playing on the one thing he'd convinced himself would guarantee her obeisance.

To which she stared up at him in visible disbelief.

"I wouldn't accept another lift from you if the alternative was walking home in a hailstorm!" she shook her head.

And with that the handle was this time depressed and the door flung open.

"Millie!" he cried.

"Drop dead!" she gnashed in reply, slamming it behind her with such force as to this time leave him in no doubt that her contempt for him was real.

However, he'd barely begun to reflect upon her summary instruction when his ears resounded instead to the sound of her screaming hysterically.

He rushed to open the door and behold the heart-stopping sight. For there, in front of his very eyes, was that huge snake – the trunk of which was spread along the corridor. What's more, it had reared up, hissing loudly and ready to strike.

"Get inside!" he cried to her.

However, gripped with sheer terror, Millie was pinned to the wall, her rictus gaze locked upon the baying serpent.

Weston grabbed her arm and yanked her back into his office. Upon which, the snake lunged. That gaping mouth sank its needle-sharp teeth into one of her leather boots, latching onto it. However, the slamming of the door behind them impacted hard against the serpent's jaw, causing it to recoil and let go.

Once back inside, she collapsed into his arms, wailing uncontrollably. However, he abruptly shoved her aside, instead picking up the telephone on his desk. Poking a finger into the '9' on the dial, he twisted it thrice.

"Hello... Operator...? Yes. Police... This is the head teacher of Sneyd End High School here. I've just found that snake everyone's been looking for. Or rather, it's found me!"

* * * * *

The results were impressive. With the additional manpower at his disposal, Colonel Peter Urquhart could now boast that whole swathes of Sneyd End (and certainly the most obvious hiding places) had been searched and secured. All that remained was to conduct a second, precautionary sweep of such sensitive locations as the town's new leisure centre and its large secondary school – which the man in charge of 'Operation Lemon' proudly assured his listeners would be completed by tomorrow.

All this progress was graphically illustrated on the large map that had been mounted on the stage of St Stephen's church hall, the Colonel indicating the places in question by tapping at it with his baton.

"But still no snake?" some hack rather annoyingly pointed out.

No, still no snake; the Colonel conceded – although putting his usual brusque and reassuring gloss on this embarrassing omission. However, while the assembled reporters were scoffing and scribbling, a young subaltern hurried onto the stage to whisper something in his commanding officer's ear.

Glancing up from the back of the hall, both Brian Danks and Julie Newington observed the Colonel's countenance darken before a tell-tale grin then flashed across his face. It could only mean one thing: Betty had finally blown her cover!

"You will forgive me, gentlemen," Urk called out to the excited press corps, "But there's something I need to attend to immediately. In my absence, Captain Tongue here will finish the briefing and answer any further questions you may have."

"Probably the Prime Minister on the phone wanting to know why he hasn't found that bloody snake yet!" another journalist meanwhile snickered to a colleague.

With this hastily-summoned stand-in struggling to regain the attention of the press ensemble, Julie nudged Brian, a nod in the direction of the door doing the talking. Together they sloped off unseen to catch up with the Colonel on the car park outside.

"Ah, Brian. Marvellous news – we've found the snake!" he turned and enthused. "Though not such great news for the person who's just run into it – the head teacher of that school where your wife worked. Apparently, it has him and a young female teacher who's with him trapped inside his office. A call to the police came through a few moments ago."

There was a split second during which, in his emotional transparency, Brian Danks was beaming from ear to ear with wicked delight – though neither Urk nor Julie could have guessed the ulterior reason. However, the pressing need to rise to a professional challenge quickly erased the mien from his face. Instead, the Colonel urged both the Snakeman and his assistant to join him aboard the canvas-backed military Land Rover that drew up alongside. The junior officer who was in the driving seat was already on the radio rustling up a company of his men to rendezvous with them at the school.

Hurriedly diving into the back of it, it was fortuitous that it was the same Land Rover that had borne Brian and Julie to the press conference following an afternoon spent combing the steel works. As such, in amongst the jumble of items on the floor were the very things they would need to apprehend a large snake: namely those metal snake hooks and a sizeable hessian sack in which to secure it. As the military convoy set off at speed across the town Brian Danks was beaming with wicked delight once more – as was his assistant.

* * * * *

"I knew it was a bad idea to keep seeing each other," Millie wept – petrified by that massive reptile that was lurking, like divine judgement, on the other side of that flimsy plywood door

"Oh, shut up, woman!" Graham Weston finally snapped, having been listening at it for signs of movement.

"Look. I'm sorry," he then sighed, drifting over to her. However, his belated show of concern caused her to angrily shove him away.

Over and above her sobbing however, he thought he could hear vehicles making their way up the driveway to the school. He rushed to the window to observe that a Land Rover and two trucks brimming with armed soldiers had pulled up on the car park outside the staff room.

"Here! We're up here!" he swung the window open and called down, spotting Colonel Urquhart alight from the lead vehicle. Jumping from the back of it too was Brian Danks – as well as some chubby, butch-looking woman in trousers who tumbled out of it gripping a huge sack and a pair of metal poles.

"The snake is on the corridor outside my office on the second floor – or at least I think it still is," he cautioned them.

"Then sit tight. We're coming up to deal with it," Urk instructed him, thereupon ordering the two dozen or more soldiers to fan out and secure the building.

As the sound of clumping boots echoed around the schoolyard – as did the ominous clicking of the safety catches on their rifles – Weston lingered to observe the contempt with which the Snakeman was staring up at him. His assistant having handed him his snake hook, eventually Brian Danks wrenched himself away and hurried after her as she stormed inside the main entrance.

* * * * *

"Whoah! Not so fast. Where do you think you're going with that?" Urk halted Julie as she was about to climb the stairwell, pointing to the large sack she was carrying. Catching wind of the rebuke, Brian turned on the stairs.

"Colonel, there's a chance Julie and I might be able to capture Betty alive. Please, at least let us try," he called down.

"Are you joking, man?" the officer roared. "Two weeks we've been hunting for this animal. So now we have it there will be no messing about. My men have orders to shoot this thing on sight."

Just then their divergence of views was interrupted by the sound of a woman in distress heading their way from the floor above. They looked up to witness the terrified young teacher stumble down the stairs as if in a waking nightmare. With one of the soldiers grabbing her, steadying her, and quietening her, everyone raced up the stairs and into Graham Weston's office.

"It was massive!" he was attempting to explain to the soldiers who'd already piled inside, spanning his arms apart to demonstrate what he meant.

"Yes, well. Wherever it was, it's gone now," the Colonel cursed, breezing inside in the company of Brian and Julie.

"I was discussing work with a member of my staff when the snake just appeared outside," the tremulous head teacher explained, rushing a hand through his rich dark mane.

"'Discussing work' with her, you say? Alone in your office? After school?" Brian strode up and quizzed him sardonically. "*Quelle surprise!* Or should the French term be: *plus ça change?*" he then grunted, angrily shoving those familiar black spectacles back up his nose. For one terrible moment, Graham Weston feared the 'dimwit' he'd cuckolded was about to wrap that snake hook around his neck.

"Colonel, sir!" the moment of reckoning was interrupted by a soldier yelling from the corridor outside. Everyone raced out to witness the trooper pointing to a large rectangular vent that had been forced from the wall.

"That's almost certainly where the snake emerged from," Brian surmised, kneeling and peering inside. "And where it's disappeared back into, I'm afraid."

"The school's heated by warm air circulated through those ducts. They run the length of the building; and on every floor,"

Julie piped up, having been present on the first occasion the school had been searched a few weeks back.

"I'd say that duct is wide enough for a python to crawl along," the Colonel noted, also stooping to peer inside.

"But it's a sealed system. How on Earth did this creature manage to get inside?" Weston scratched his head, appalled.

"While these grills can be forced from the inside, sir, they can't be opened from the outside. Not unless this Betty is a dab hand with a screwdriver!" an NCO pointed out, examining how it had been mounted to the wall.

"Which means somewhere in this building there must be another vent that's missing and through which she was able to gain access to the duct network – possibly because it wasn't screwed back on right when this place was searched the first time," Julie piped up again.

"In which case, if we can locate and seal that missing vent hole before Betty can find it again we've got her trapped!" Brian rose to his feet and brushed a hand through his own wavy quiff.

The call went out for the search teams to check every single vent on every single floor, the school echoing to clumping boots racing up and down stairwells and along deserted corridors. Brian himself was hurrying along the passage that led to the assembly hall when he spotted something. For there, mounted on the wall, was a large, framed black-and-white photograph that had captured a familiar face. *'Annual Sports Day – 1966. Winner of the 100-metre race...'* read the inscription. And there, proudly clutching the trophy, was none other than *'... Emily Ashmore'*.

The Snakeman swallowed hard. Beholding the teenager's Mona Lisa smile and dark, bushy hair (swept into a ponytail) brought so many memories flooding back. It also brought him down to Earth with a jolt. This heady chase that he was caught up in – and which had consumed his every waking moment for the last six weeks – was no longer the quest of a world-renowned herpetologist to secure the ultimate professional acclaim. No, the hunt for this particular snake was personal!

* * * * *

Found it at last. Clambering down the basement steps into an electrical plant room, they could observe that access into the duct network had indeed been the result of someone not refitting a vent to the wall, the offending grill hanging limply by a solitary screw. However, no less ominously, a sapper who'd joined them was glowering with alarm as he hovered his hand over those humming fuse boards – questioning why the architect who'd designed this school had routed a vent to the room in the first place when, if anything, it required cooling rather than heating! Was there no end to how lazy contractors had put lives in Sneyd End at risk by exploiting the venality of its most senior politician!

Otherwise, having calculated in his head how far the bulky python could have slithered from the corridor outside Graham Weston's office, Brian Danks knelt down with a torch to inspect inside the exposed duct. Doing so confirmed a hunch.

"Gentlemen," he rose to his feet to confidently announce, "Betty is still in the duct system somewhere!"

Though her pursuers had yet to catch sight of her, there was an audible sigh of collective rejoicing that she'd been cornered.

"I guess the only question now is how we winkle her out of there, Colonel, sir," a boyish lieutenant pointed out.

"Sir, there's a stock of tear gas canisters back at the leisure centre. I can get on the radio and have the quartermaster despatch them right away," a burly sergeant informed him.

It sounded only marginally less drastic than poking a flame thrower inside! Indeed, Brian was not entirely convinced that raiding the military's traditional arsenal of such weapons was the right solution to the problem. In this vein, he offered his own considered opinion on the matter.

"Colonel, tear gas will immobilise the snake. It may even kill it. However, it will not deal with the problem of extracting it from the duct network. And if the snake does expire, then ask yourself: do you really want this school out of action for weeks on end while the entire system is taken apart to locate its decomposing corpse? All thirty feet of it!"

Colonel Urquhart pondered the dilemma under the guise of stroking his chin. Meanwhile, the sergeant glanced first at Brian and then at his CO, impatient to give the word.

"What's *your* plan then?" Urk pressed the Snakeman.

"Force Betty out. Ramp the heating up so high that she'll be compelled to flee the ducts on pain of being cooked alive."

"So that you can then *capture* her alive?" the Colonel curled an eyebrow, shrewd enough to have worked out his little game.

Brian sighed imploringly.

"One chance – that's all I ask," he insisted, glancing at Julie for moral support.

The crusty commander pondered it for a moment.

"Okay, have the caretaker turn the boiler up to the maximum. We'll turn this school into a sauna if we have too," he announced.

"Oh, and Corporal," he added, turning to the anxious sapper still examining those shimmering fuse boards.

"Sir?"

"I said a sauna, not an inferno. Make sure the heating is diverted from this particular vent before you do," he ordered.

"Yes, sir."

"In the meantime, I just hope you two know what you're doing," he said, fixing an eye upon Brian and Julie in turn. "But just in case, while you and the young lady here are waiting for Betty to re-emerge from that missing vent," he said, pointing to it, "I'm ordering that an armed guard be posted on every other potential egress point from the duct network."

"Er, I'd rather we not, Colonel," Urk was surprised to hear his order being gainsaid. "Wait down here, that is."

"It's elementary science," Brian clarified his remark. "You see, heat rises. Therefore, as the temperature inside the ducts increases so the snake will seek relief by climbing higher up the network. That said though, my guess is that Betty will try to find her way back to that broken vent outside the headmaster's office. So if you don't mind, Colonel, that's where my assistant and I will be waiting for her," he insisted, glancing again at Julie.

27

Julie Newington couldn't fail to notice how that wolfish head teacher held some sort of morbid fascination for her boss. While she'd been sat on her haunches in the corridor, looking out for a python about to pop its head from an exposed heating duct, Brian Danks had been roaming Graham Weston's office, perusing his books and studying his photographs – like an envying victor venturing to catalogue a slain opponent's treasure.

She'd noticed too that there was one particular photograph that he kept returning to. It was taken at a Christmas party and featured this smug charmer posing with his arm around Brian's wife. She was of a mind to ask after its significance. However, her boss had made a point of never prying into her private life and she had never pried into his. It was an unspoken rule that had enabled these two enigmatic, chalk-and-cheese individuals to form such an effective professional partnership at the zoo.

He broke from studying it to unhook it from the wall and contemptuously toss it in the waste paper basket beside Weston's desk. Thereafter, he emerged to pace about the corridor instead, demonstratively inspecting the exposed vent – as if conscious that he might have drawn attention to whatever pain or hurt was bound up in that haunting image.

"Phew! It's getting mighty hot," he huffed.

"Boss, I'm beginning to wonder whether your big idea won't drive *us* out of the building long before it does Betty!" Julie quipped, blowing hard and taking a handkerchief to the perspiration beneath the collar of her open-necked shirt.

"They're not healthy, you know – these warm air heating systems. They circulate dust and germs and goodness knows what. They can even make people sick. It's something I feel quite strongly about. Not that anybody ever listens when I try telling them. In fact, people never listen to me when I try telling them things," he chuntered.

Julie beamed him an indulgent smile. Sick buildings: yet another hopeless cause by which this comically-outspoken man had sought to kick against perceived wisdom.

"I never liked school, you know," he continued his random musing, changing the subject. "Well, not strictly true. I loved the subjects – especially history, which Mr Davies taught. He was my favourite teacher. Oh, and I liked animal biology too, of course – which is what I eventually graduated in. It was at university that I met Ruby. We both studied biology together. Meanwhile, had I not specialised in herpetology I might never have met you," he turned to Julie and chuckled with touching innocence.

She had the sense that Brian Danks was angling to unburden himself of something that was both personal and profound. To this end maybe, he sat back down on the floor beside her, removing a handkerchief from his pocket to mop his own perspiring brow. She settled back against the wall to listen.

"I guess it was because I was always different to other boys," he recommenced his expansive monologue. "They were rugged and handsome and spoke with confidence. I was the skinny geek with the large specs who stuttered. They were into adventure and sport – and into girls as well. Meanwhile, I had my head in books and spotted trains. It was because I was different that the other kids at school sometimes picked on me.

"I did like girls though," he let slip (though with the same semi-contrite self-effacement with which he'd confessed to spotting trains!). "Well, I did as I got older. Girls never liked me though – probably because I wasn't very clued up about them. Even when I summoned up the courage to ask them out, I got the words all wrong. Therefore, they shunned me at school – and at university too; that's when they weren't taunting me or looking down their noses at me. But then I'm afraid I've never been very good at understanding people," he admitted with sad eyes that spoke more eloquently than his words.

Countering such despondency, Julie offered him an empathetic smile that spoke with similar eloquence. She felt his pain. She too had been despised and taunted at school: because of her weight; because of her quiet manner; because of her unladylike choice of hobbies and career aspirations; and not least because, likewise, she too was never very clued up about the opposite sex (notwithstanding that she could invariably beat them at arm-wrestling!). Yes, life can be hard when one is 'different'.

"That was until Ruby came along, of course. As if by some miracle of insight, she was able to reach out and connect with me. She's been my rock amidst the storms that have so frequently assailed me. They say a stubborn ass needs a stubborn driver: I would be a different person today had I not met her. More introspective maybe; more consumed by my own obsessions; more resentful of the fact that no one ever listens to me. Once there was a time when I came close to losing her. But, well…" he was on the verge of being candid. "Thank God in His mercy that I didn't," he sighed after a pause, drawing back.

Along with that photograph he'd binned, this partial opening of his heart enabled Julie to deduce to whom this complex man had very nearly 'lost' his wife.

"But people *are* listening to you now, Brian," she consoled him. "And, who knows: one day they might even re-open that old railway line again!" she chuckled, squeezing his hand.

"I hope so," he shrugged, grateful for her kind words.

"You know, Ruby once told me you might not get to choose who you fall in love with – that soppy, fairy tale kind of love that people write and sing about. However, you *do* make a choice whether to carry on loving them – even when it hurts; even when it seems hopeless," he recalled wistfully.

"In which case, it's just as well there's a God in Heaven; and that He decreed that Ruby should 'choose' me to love over all other boys; and that He has graciously granted her the strength to *carry on* loving me too – even when it must have hurt; and even when, at times, it must have seemed hopeless."

Julie nodded obligingly. Whereupon there ensued a silence between them as they both sat staring at that exposed vent and contemplating this alternately exhilarating and infuriating thing they call love. Then he rested one of his hands upon hers, his eyes first dipping in awkwardness before he eventually willed himself to stare into her own.

"I want to thank you, Julie," he spoke with the utmost sincerity, "for also being so patient and understanding with me during the time we've worked together. I guess it can't always have been easy. I'm a bit of a strange character, aren't I! And yet, like Ruby, you have graciously accepted me for who I am. For that I shall always be grateful."

She was humbled.

"It's been a pleasure and a privilege, boss. Thank you for accepting me for who *I* am too," she said, "and for teaching me so much – about snakes and reptiles; about kindness and consideration; and about myself too. For that I too shall always be grateful," she smiled again, her free hand making a fist that reached over to playfully punch his upper arm.

* * * * *

The soft roar of the warm air heating, combined with the heat it was forcing out and the weariness induced by a long day, had enticed both Brian and Julie to commit the cardinal sin of snake watching: they'd briefly nodded off!

Brief enough for Betty to avail herself of the tranquillity that had befallen the corridor to slip silently out of that open heating vent, desperate to cool down. Slowly and hesitantly she lumbered up to the somnolent couple, tongue flicking and with her colossal girth trailing behind her.

Julie awoke first, eyes wide in terror, transfixed by the enormous python. She nudged Brian as discreetly as she dared, praying he wouldn't wake with a start. He too now flashed his eyes wide, though summoning the presence of mind to remain perfectly still lest the python instinctively strike in self-defence. However, huddled sufficiently close together for Betty to maybe mistake them for one animal that was too large for even a snake of her unprecedented size to overpower and swallow, he could only pray that the serpent would therefore retreat.

However, like her pursuers, Betty was nothing if not a maverick. Rather than skulk away, she sought to investigate this conjoined heat source. Drawing up to taste the air, she then proceeded to slither her huge bulk across Brian's legs so that her tongue was able to flit across the features of his face.

Never in ten years of working with these animals had *he* experienced such terror. What's more, with that sensitive tongue able to detect the pheromones emitted by that much-vaunted 'smell of fear', he was desperate for it not to show. Julie, meanwhile, was silently cursing that, though within reach of being able to grab Betty by the throat, she would not be able to do so without provoking a strike. And a snake bite to the face – even from a non-venomous one – is an extremely dangerous thing.

All they could do was watch and pray while Betty's probing tongue continue to flit across their faces. To make matters worse, the sheer weight of her trunk upon them was becoming unbearable. Sooner or later, one of them was going to flinch.

At last, curiosity assuaged, the massive python turned away to slither down the empty corridor. Slowly and silently too, Brian and Julie rose to their feet. His snake hook in his hand, Brian felt confident enough to gently take hold of Betty's tail. Able to stare almost directly along her trunk, he was taken aback: the sheer size of this animal was breath-taking! Experience told him they would need extra pairs of hands if they were to successfully grapple with her. However, such caution was cast aside in the sheer exhilaration of being just one step away from capturing alive the largest snake the world had ever seen.

No less mind-blowing was Betty's power too. She reared up – aware that something was going on behind her. Then thirty-foot (and four hundred pounds) of solid muscle tried to haul itself forward again, running up against the resistance offered by six-foot (and one hundred-and-seventy pounds) of somewhat punier human being. It was as much as Brian could do to prevent himself being dragged along the varnished wooden floor.

By now though, he had vexed the wanderer. In its annoyance, the huge snake turned about almost to its full body length to investigate the impediment. Spotting its assailant, it hissed loudly, instinctively lunging at Brian. Instinctively too, he leapt out of the way – aided by the fact that, though aggressive, the snake's weight rendered it relatively slow to strike.

By now, Julie was engaging with the snake too, attempting to distract its attention. Betty lunged at her too. However, in stepping backwards she stumbled. In an instant, the serpent had locked its gaping jaw onto her forearm. She gnashed with pain as she felt those needle-like teeth puncture her skin – cursing that she had committed her second careless mistake that day.

And yet, try as she might, Betty simply couldn't close that mouth around her opponent (thereby to manoeuvre and tighten her coils around her). While her upper jaw had Julie's arm snagged tight, the teeth of her bottom jaw had snared upon the flare of her trousers.

It presented Brian with the opportunity he needed to seize the snake by the head and prise that upper jaw from his assistant's arm. Panting and clutching at her blooded limb, Julie slid herself along the floor, out of Betty's way.

However, with his assistant *hors de combat* the Snakeman found himself facing the wrath of the mighty beast alone. Though gripping Betty's throat for all he was worth, with both his hands occupied he could do little to prevent the snake from wrapping her powerful coils around him. Forced to the floor, in no time at all Betty had a second one wrapped around him also. Suddenly, he was at the serpent's mercy. The 'Snakeman of Sneyd End' was literally having the life throttled out of him.

In desperation Julie launched herself at the beast, determined she would not desert her colleague in his moment of peril. However, with her arm too badly mauled to be able to delve inside that seething mass of scaly flesh and locate the head – let alone retrieve it – it was useless. With her good arm, she thumped the animal's thick, rippling trunk again and again in frustration.

"Help…! Help…!" she croaked, her voice echoing down the corridor, her copious blood dappling both floor and snake.

"Tell Ruby I love her… And… tell my child… I love him too… Or her…!" Brian was gasping with what breath he had left.

"No!" Julie wailed. "Hang on in, boss. I will not let this happen. You *will* live to hold your child! I promise!"

She cried for help again – though the commotion had already alerted her rescuers. A trio of soldiers rushed up to the monstrous animal to take aim with their rifles.

"Hold your fire!" the Colonel also raced up and barked, recognising that it would be impossible for his men to shoot the snake dead without also hitting its prospective meal.

Instead he ran over and plunged his own hands inside those constricting coils until – with his foot pressed again them to gain leverage – he located the snake's head and could yank it free. Eyeball to eyeball (and gritting his teeth), Colonel Peter Urquhart could behold at last the fearsome creature he'd vowed to kill.

"Bayonet…! I said bayonet, man!" he hollered at one of the soldiers who still had Betty in his sights.

The young squaddie rose to his feet, drew out his regulation issue bayonet and warily stepped up to the struggling python.

"Now cut!" the Colonel ordered, holding Betty's neck aloft.

The soldier's Adam's apple bobbed in his throat.

"Cut, man, I said!"

Basic training had never prepared the lad for this. However, he took the knife and began to slice through tissue and bone. At once, the snake began to writhe, releasing its grip upon Brian as it raged against its undoing. With the beast in its death throes – and without waiting for orders – the other soldiers set aside their weapons and rushed in to grab those thrashing coils – flailing that continued even after its head had been severed from its body.

Tossing that head aside in disgust, the Colonel watched in horror as it too continued to flex – those jaws snapping impotently. Meanwhile, the attention of his men shifted to reviving the Snakeman's crumpled and motionless form.

* * * * *

Having been tipped off by Jonathan Hunt that the giant snake had been discovered stalking her old school, Ruby had been pacing the living room so anxiously in prayer this last hour that she'd almost worn a groove in the piles of their new fitted carpet.

Tempted to forego the agony of waiting around for news by jumping in the car and driving there – even though, nearing her due date, it would be as much as she could do to squeeze herself behind the steering wheel – her torment was eventually cut short by the glow of headlights. A police panda car had pulled up outside No. 14 Churchill Avenue.

Clutching the small of her back and tearfully hurrying to the front door, she intercepted the chime of the doorbell just as Jonathan pressed it.

"It's Brian, isn't it," she just knew before either he or the policewoman at his side had said a word.

"It's best if we come in, Ruby," the ashen-faced policeman insisted, solemnly removing his cap.

"He's dead, isn't he," she starkly rephrased her plea, by now so overcome with dread that Jonathan feared he might be called upon to demonstrate a policeman's legendary *ad hoc* midwifery skills on that well-trodden carpet. His WPC companion bade Ruby sit down on the sofa to head off that distressing eventuality, sitting down beside her and calming her twitching hands.

"He's not dead, Ruby. But he is very poorly," she explained. "So please – for the sake of your baby – try not to worry."

Blubbering relief coursed through the pregnant teacher, whereupon the policewoman's hand of comfort alighted upon her shoulder and squeezed it reassuringly.

"WPC Clements is right, Ruby. The doctors think Brian will pull through. We can take you to see him at the hospital. That's if you feel up to it."

For the first time all evening, Ruby Danks permitted her smile to escape. Dabbing at her eyes, she nodded her consent.

"Remember," said Jonathan, as he rose to his feet and draped her coat around her, "the 'Snakeman of Sneyd End' is nothing if not a fighter – whether it's saving old railways, battling town hall corruption, or hunting down giant snakes. Goodness knows, you and I – of all people – can testify to that!"

28

Rhabdomyolysis was the medical term for it. A common occurrence in the aftermath of traumatic crush injuries (and, ironically, snake bites!), its symptom include nausea, muscle ache and swelling, and heavy bleeding – as well as kidney malfunction that can result in passing urine the colour of neat whisky.

Councillor Brian Danks would experience all these things as the medical teams battled to stabilise his condition following his near-fatal encounter with Betty, the killer python. Though he would be hospitalised for the best part of a month, he would eventually make a full recovery. During that time, he took comfort from the outpouring of gratitude with which the people of Sneyd End greeted news that the colossal snake that had been terrorising their town had finally been slain.

Heartened as he was by this acclaim, by far the greater joy was to be able to hold in his arms his new-born son – Jonathan Arthur Danks – born in that same hospital where he was recovering on Friday, September 26th 1969 and weighing in at eight pounds eight ounces. It was the same day that The Beatles would release *'Abbey Road'* – the last album the Fab Four would record together before they would announce the end of an incredible creative partnership that, as much as anything else, had come to define a remarkable decade.

On that same day too, former councillor Horace Bissell would be convicted of corruption in public office and sentenced to serve six years in prison. The jury at Birmingham Crown Court would hear how the man with a vision to make his town 'the Athens of the Midlands' had pocketed over £150,000 in kickbacks from contractors during his six years at the helm of Sneyd End Borough Council. In his summing up, the presiding judge would tell the corpulent municipal leader that he had "tarnished the reputation of local government."

Friday, September 26th 1969 would also be the day that Graham Weston would be formally suspended from his post as head teacher of Sneyd End High School pending investigations into his dalliances with teaching staff at the school. Alas, he would not hang around to await his governing body's deliberations. Resigning his headship, he subsequently moved to France, where he would set up his own business offering translation services. Perhaps having decided that there was no longer any benefit to be derived from her sojourn with this man, his wife would decline to join him and would instead file for divorce. After all, 'the snake that cannot cast its skin perishes'.

Away from the limelight, Julie Newington would also make a full recovery (though with a permanent reminder of her ordeal in the form of a scar on her right arm). She would be present when the autopsy was conducted on Betty – though it would prove exceedingly difficult to identify precisely what (or rather who) the python had been dining on during the five years it had spent stalking Sneyd End. However, amongst the paucity of items that were retrieved from her innards was the tag from a dog's collar that read *'Bertie – 12 Churchill Avenue, Sneyd End'*.

The pathologist also discovered traces of human hair and fingernails – the keratin they're fashioned from one of the few substances that the snake's powerful stomach acids could not break down. Alas, a quarter of a century would pass before the advent of DNA profiling would enable West Midlands Police to confirm at last that, amongst the snake's victims, had been the missing youngsters of Sneyd End.

* * * * *

"'Ere, boyo! Turn that bloody radio down, will you. I can't hear myself think, I can't."

Over in a corner of the cavernous engine shed a long-haired student broke from sweeping the floor. Observing the Welshman's expostulating scowl, he grudgingly drifted over to the work bench to tweak the volume knob as instructed.

With the jaunty strains of Mungo Jerry's *'In The Summertime'* duly silenced, at last Cledwyn Davies could puff on his pipe and savour the sound of a steam locomotive hissing and chuntering in readiness. Stepping out into the sunshine, he strode over towards the rake of brown-and-cream carriages that the fully-restored Great Western Railway pannier locomotive had been coupled up to. It was Saturday, June 20th 1970 and '6418' was about to depart with the first passenger train to run on this newly-opened preserved railway since the line had closed seven years earlier.

It was a mere two days after the country's Labour government had gone down to a surprise General Election defeat; and a week following England crashing out of the World Cup in Mexico following the team's 3-2 quarter final defeat to West Germany (an ill omen that Harold Wilson would blame for his own defeat).

And so the 'Swinging Sixties' had passed into history, there to become a jumble of memories – the music; the fashions; the 'white heat' of technology that had given the country computers, colour television and Concorde. Jaded too was the hippies' dream of a communal utopia seasoned by mind-bending drugs and free love. Even the 'Space Race' had become passé following the dramatic aborting of the ill-fated Apollo 13 mission. Everywhere, the hope and optimism of the 1960s had given way to the ennui that would attend a more uncertain decade.

However, such solicitude was far from the thoughts of the crowds that had gathered today on the station of this sleepy Shropshire market town, as well as thronging the carriages to ride on this inaugural departure. Sprinkled amongst them were plenty of delighted railway buffs all jostling with their cameras to record this historic day.

"You know, it's a pity Jim Plant couldn't be here to witness this moment," Cledwyn scowled upon mounting the cab, where Brian was busy shovelling coal into '6418's glowing firebox.

"Yes, shame. He'll be off his feet for weeks while his broken leg heals," noted Jonathan, who'd also joined them.

"I know the feeling!" Brian chuckled, halting from his labour to study the locomotive's gauges.

To which Jonathan tossed aside the rag he was wiping his hands on to place one of them upon Brian's shoulder and offer his best friend a thankful smile.

"I do hope his replacement takes care of this old girl," their former history teacher was meanwhile clucking, glancing at Brian in between leaning out of the cab and staring down the platform, perchance to catch sight of the man in question.

"Don't worry. He's got years of experience under his belt. I assure you, you won't find a finer locomotive engineer in the entire United Kingdom," Brian confidently proclaimed.

"Mind you," he added, "I can't take all the credit for finding him. Like you, I was in a right panic when I heard what Jim had done. However, *Jehovah Jireh – 'the Lord will provide,' –* Genesis, Chapter Twenty-Two, Verse Eleven," the Snakeman chortled, employing his customary penchant for alighting upon a handy and instructive passage from Scripture.

"You see, it just so happened that Ruby was ear-wigging my telephone conversation with Jonathan – the one in which *he* was panicking about where we would find another engine driver; and at such short notice too. It was when I put the phone down that she smiled at me and said: 'I think I know where'."

"Good job too. It would have been terrible to have had to disappoint all these people, it would. Anyway, where's he got to – this 'locomotive engineer' friend of your wife's?" Cledwyn was becoming agitated, studying his watch and again staring down the platform heaving with expectant well-wishers.

As if on cue, out of the gents' toilets there strode a swarthy gentleman of noble bearing and proud, determined gait, who now thrust a passage through the excited crowds – instantly standing apart from them on account of the bright saffron-coloured turban from which his wiry black beard emerged.

"Ah, Inderjit. The old girl's up to steam. All she requires is a steady hand on the throttle," Brian enthused as he welcomed the latest member of '6418's preservation team into the cab.

"Thank you most kindly, sir," he humbly implored. "This is a very special day for me. You have no idea how full of joy I am to be driving your railway engine," the grateful Sikh was most insistent, clasping his hands in gratitude.

After a moment or two spent casting a professional eye over those gauges, Inderjit perched himself on the flip-down seat and savoured the thrill of being behind the controls of a passenger train for the first time in over twenty years. Ahead of them, the signal arm tipped. Behind them, the guard stood ready with a green flag in his hand and a whistle betwixt his lips. However, at that precise moment onto the platform there raced a quintet of anxious last-minute passengers – one of whom was carrying a bonny babe in her arms.

"Hold the train!" Pauline Trotter cried.

Upon which, Ruby's father hurriedly opened a carriage door so that she, as well as Brian's mother and his less-than-enamoured mother-in-law could hurry aboard (Mrs Leadbetter tarrying to dust off a fleck of soot from the jacket of her twin-set – only to be impatiently bundled into the carriage by her husband!).

Ruby meanwhile lingered just long enough to wave to her husband, who'd spied her from the cab of the locomotive, a big, bright smile upon his face. He waved back heartily. Ruby then took hold of their baby's tiny hand and waved it too at his proud father before also disappearing inside the carriage.

With all its passengers safely aboard, Inderjit let out a deafening blast on the locomotive's whistle. With the crowds waving and cheering wildly, Brian released the brake and '6418' chuffed its way out of the station, hauling its clattering rake of carriages behind it. From the road bridge that it ducked beneath, enthusiasts were also waving, cheering, and snapping with their little cameras – notwithstanding the belching plume of thick black smoke that momentarily enveloped them.

The joys of steam railways!

* * * * *

With the restoration of '6418' complete, at least one small piece of Sneyd End's railway history would live on, bringing joy and happy memories to the thousands of tourists and railway enthusiasts who flocked each year to ride aboard her trains.

Alas elsewhere, the early 1970s would witness British Rail complete the 'Beeching' programme of closing unprofitable lines and stations. In March 1972, Birmingham's magnificent Snow Hill Station would also close – by now a ghostly, weed-strewn relic served only by an infrequent railcar service to Wolverhampton. Thereafter – ignominy of ignominies – it would be used as a car park before being demolished five years later.

Vanished too seemed any hope of trains ever returning to the branch line to Sneyd End. The tunnel beneath the town that had witnessed such drama would this time be bricked-up completely, while the line on either side of it would be abandoned to creeping foliage. As Brian Danks had feared, the motor car had won. The only consolation for the people of his town (if not for the Snakeman himself) was that – with the redeveloping of the old station where once he had indulged his passion for trains – at least they had acquired a modern, new leisure centre!

"No conurbation in Britain has as high a proportion of commuters who travel to work by car as the West Midlands. Thus, the area provides the nearest British approach to the car dominance reached in, say, Los Angeles...

"Traffic congestion in urban areas is one of the most serious and urgent problems of the day. The restriction of movement brought about by the increasing use of cars becomes more severe year by year and threatens to strangle the commercial life of town and city centres.

"Fortunately, there is now an increased awareness of the problem and the urgent need of a solution."

'A Passenger Transport Development Plan For The West Midlands' – published by the West Midlands Passenger Transport Executive

November 1972

"The provision of an effective public transport system is seen as essential to the regeneration of the West Midlands; and the potential for a light rail system – known as Midland Metro – to act as a catalyst for such regeneration was identified in the West Midlands Structure Plan...

"The West Midlands Passenger Transport Authority has decided that a disused rail formation between Wolverhampton and Birmingham, and passing through the Black Country, should be the subject of the first bill before Parliament, and work is in hand to present that bill.

"This however is only a part of the initial network, and it is intended that a subsequent bill will give the power to provide a tram network sufficient to encompass the wider benefits that Midland Metro can bring in reducing road congestion."

'The West Midlands Passenger Transport Executive Three Year Plan' – published by the West Midlands Passenger Transport Executive

June 1988

"Following the success of Midland Metro Line One (Wolverhampton City Centre to Birmingham Snow Hill), Centro is investing in more much-needed tram routes to create an integrated network.

"As a light rail system, Metro is the key to the success of public transport in the West Midlands. It offers value-for-money, operates at a frequency of every eight minutes, has an enviable reputation for reliability and punctuality, and is easily accessible for customers with disabilities and those with pushchairs or heavy shopping.

"Electrically powered, Metro is clean, quiet and environmentally responsible."

'Better Public Transport'
– published by Centro (the trading name of the West Midlands Passenger Transport Executive)

January 2004

POSTSCRIPT

Friday, October 12th 2018,
Sneyd End, West Midlands

'The past is a foreign country; they do things differently there' goes the old saying. All morning he'd been rehearsing his speech in his head, pondering what to include and what to leave out. Conscious that most of the people gathered here today weren't even born when the man of whom he would be speaking had been in his prime, he was eager to strike just the right note for a day that was intended to be both a commemoration and a celebration.

To be sure, one thing Jon Danks had inherited from his father was a flair for public speaking. It had helped make him a successful and much-loved presenter of television wildlife documentaries (a passion for the natural world being something else he'd inherited from his father). And yet a further touching trait he'd inherited was an initial wariness of strange gatherings. Today, it was briefly discernible to perspicacious eyes amongst the crowd that had assembled for this important event – amongst whose number he could gaze out and spy familiar faces.

There was retired Chief Superintendent Jonathan Hunt and his wife, Pauline – herself a retired local head teacher. Elsewhere he spotted Councillor Parminder Jukes – Sneyd End's member on the Transport Delivery Committee of the West Midlands Combined Authority, which was charged with overseeing public transport schemes in the conurbation (and next to her, her husband, Robin – a senior project manager who'd delivered many of those schemes). Somewhere in the crowd too he spotted Julie Newington, who'd been his boss at the local safari park when – as a trainee reptile keeper fresh out of university – Jon himself had taken the first steps upon the remarkable journey that was his own successful career.

Meanwhile, gazing on at the head of the throng was Jon's younger sister, Emily (the principal of Sneyd End's new secondary school academy), as well as his mother, Ruby (the wizened one-time biology teacher beaming with pride at the achievements of both her children and her former pupils).

Many more of those faces in the crowd had turned out to hear their town's most famous son – Jon Danks having made a name for himself (like his father before him, only more so). Before they did though, they listened politely while the Mayor of the West Midlands delivered a speech of his own, in which he enthused about how this new Metro line would make travelling across the Black Country faster and more convenient (and on which the immaculate, blue-liveried tram they were all gathered around would operate). So it was that, upon the round of applause that followed, Jonathan Arthur Danks – naturalist, author, lecturer, and broadcaster – snapped out of his fleeting daydream and, at the Mayor's bidding, stepped up to the microphone.

"Mr Mayor, honoured guests, ladies and gentlemen," he opened, nudging his thin-rimmed spectacles up his nose.

"I confess that, when I first heard that this most fitting tribute was being planned for my father, I was both moved and humbled. For those who knew him, Brian Danks was a man of many passions; one of which was a belief that investing in public transport was the key to parrying an over-dependence upon the private motor car that was both short-sighted and unwise.

"It was what drove him to campaign firstly to prevent the railway that ran through his home town from being closed; and then, when that endeavour failed, to prevent the track bed from being sold off and redeveloped. Indeed, as a borough councillor for Sneyd End during the 1970s, his finest hour was undoubtedly his successful lobbying of both British Rail and the West Midlands Passenger Transport Authority to retain the track bed of the Sneyd End branch line until such time that a new generation of politicians and transport planners could bring forth a scheme to reopen it for passenger service again. Sadly, it was to be Brian Danks's last great crusade before his untimely death from leukaemia in 1979, at the age of just thirty-nine."

Both Ruby and Emily blanched, the daughter laying a hand of comfort upon the mother's shoulder. For many years afterwards the cruel and seemingly pointless loss of such a promising life had rankled. Why Brian? Why such a loving husband and father? Why my husband? Why my father? However, the One Hundred and Thirty-Eighth Psalm reminds us that the Lord *will* fulfil His purposes in the life of the believer; or 'cometh the hour, cometh the man' – as a worldly aphorism has it.

Mindful of this and of the purpose for which they had gathered today, Emily and her mother hugged each other and gave thanks for the life and times of Brian Danks. They gave thanks too that (unlike his own father before him) at least he'd been granted the joy of holding his own children in his arms – even if, for reasons that they would never know (well, at least not this side of eternity), it had been for just a few short, yet precious years; time enough to instil in them all the noblest qualities of the father. Today's keynote speaker reminded everyone gathered that it had been time enough too for this wacky, yet remarkable man to perform a service on this Earth for which, with hindsight, he had been uniquely gifted by the Almighty.

"Ladies and gentlemen, I believe that new era for public transport in Sneyd End that Brian Danks was looking forward to has dawned at last. This new Walsall-Dudley Metro line will not only provide a fast, frequent tram service through the town, but – thanks to an interchange at Wednesbury – will enable passengers to connect with similar fast and frequent trams to Birmingham and Wolverhampton. It means that a passenger boarding a tram at the Metro stop upon which we're standing will be able to arrive in Birmingham city centre just over half-an-hour later – not far off the twenty-minute journey time aboard the last 'Sneyd End Shuttle' train that departed this very spot in June 1964. That once there that passenger will also be able to connect with trains to London from the city's re-opened Snow Hill Station is another milestone in the restoration of the region's historic transport links – of which, had he lived to see it, I know my father would have been immensely proud.

"Of course, Brian Danks was no stranger to a life lived in the public eye – or should that be to controversy and notoriety," his son admitted, to a frisson of laughter amongst those who remembered the man well. "Not for nothing did he earn the nickname 'The Snakeman of Sneyd End'. It hints not only at the study and conservation of reptiles that was his other lifelong passion, but of a fateful summer almost half-a-century ago when the people of this town had a more pressing reason to be grateful to my father. The events of that summer have been told and retold ever since. For the sake of brevity – and because it looks like it's about to rain – I will not recount them now," he informed his listeners, glancing up at the clouds and prompting further, more subdued humour.

"Therefore, as much as this day is ostensibly a remembrance of a slightly awkward, slightly eccentric man who was into snakes and steam trains, I know my father would want it to be a remembrance too of others – of those who lost their lives to that chimeric creature for which our town regrettably remains infamous; and of those people who worked tirelessly throughout that summer to end its reign of terror.

"So, it's not just in honour of its namesake," Jon insisted, turning to face the set of tiny velvet curtains that had been velcroed to the tram, "but for all those people that I consider it a great privilege to formally name this tram *'Brian Danks'*."

Whereupon, a round of hearty and spontaneous applause broke out as he hauled aside the drapes to reveal the eponymous nameplate that had been affixed to Tram No. 22.

With the naming ceremony concluded (and those clouds growing darker by the minute), it was time for the Mayor, the celebrity speaker, and the invited guests to be ushered aboard the first ever tram to depart from Sneyd End's new Metro stop. Into its airy, concertinaed carriages they huddled, the stragglers having to make do with strap-hanging in the aisles. Then its warning bell clanged, its doors effortlessly slid shut, and the tram glided out of the platform at the very moment that the heavens opened.

Poignantly, its first manoeuvre was to trundle across the site of the town's former leisure centre, now redeveloped to include a park-and-ride car park, as well as a piazza of wine bars and bistros to complete the ambience of the Black Country's newest transport hub. With the maintenance costs of Horace Bissell's final, jerry-built bequest to the town rising – capped off by the discovery that it was riddled with asbestos – in 2005 the local council had reluctantly taken the decision to demolish it. Hence the opportunity had unexpectedly presented itself for Sneyd End's abandoned railway line to be connected to the region's expanding Metro network – its old station site included.

However, it was as the tram picked up speed that the remembrance of which Jon Danks had so eloquently spoken became almost tangible to those passengers aboard who could recall the events of that distant summer – to Jonathan and Pauline; to Robin and Parminder; to Ruby and to Julie. With a wail of its siren, the interior lights came on and suddenly the hammering of the rain was replaced by the roar of warm, rushing air as it plunged into the nine hundred yard-long Sneyd End Tunnel.

And then, no sooner had the tram entered the tunnel than it was out of it again, shadowing the restored Sneyd End Canal as it traversed the Fens Bank nature reserve, those disused cooling ponds in the distance reflecting the canvas of dramatic, leaden clouds pierced by a brief and welcoming shaft of bright sunlight. In no time at all, Tram No. 22 *'Brian Danks'* was trundling into the mammoth shopping mall that now sat atop where once a steel works had stood. Alongside this gleaming temple to twenty-first century retail therapy, the tram now decelerated to dock with perfect precision at the platform of its dedicated Metro stop.

Could it really be that it had taken just under ten uneventful seconds to pass through the obsidian shaft that had once been the lair of a giant python called Betty? Was it really so long ago that – in the school on the hill that overlooked it – such a terrifying creature had met its match in a gawky, larger-than-life character called Brian Danks?

Truly, the past is another country.

I do hope you have enjoyed reading *'The Snakeman Of Sneyd End'*. If so, then can I beg one final indulgence: that you very kindly leave a review of this book on the Amazon site you purchased it from:-

United Kingdom/Ireland – amazon.co.uk
United States – amazon.com
Canada – amazon.ca
Australia/New Zealand – amazon.com.au

Reviews greatly assist authors to promote their books as widely as possible. A review needn't be a long essay. Even a simple 'I enjoyed this book' will suffice.

Thank you, and God bless.

Ray Burston

If you have enjoyed reading *THE SNAKEMAN OF SNEYD END*, why not search out another tense thriller set on the railways of the West Midlands...

"We've been quite crafty: we tried finding out who won that massive lottery pay-out the other week, but the Editor got cold feet..." Jill chuckled to herself, thereby not noticing an eye pop open before hastily closing again as she turned to address him once more, sighing "... I say good luck to the guy, whoever he is. I just wish he'd share out a few of his millions with me!"

"M-m-m-more lemonade?" Paul burbled self-consciously, offering her a swig of the next best thing.

****

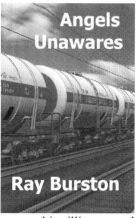

Angels Unawares

Ray Burston

Take one bumbling railway booking clerk. Take one multi-million pound "rollover" Lottery prize. Put the two together and that shy individual's otherwise ordinary life need never be ordinary again.

Will he splash out on all the material goodies that life has to offer to those with spare cash? Will he dispose of his winnings on fast cars, holidays or big houses? Or even indulge his hobby of riding around on trains? Or is there a much more radical and heart-warming way of spending the nation's biggest gambling prize ever?

Take one heinous and sickening murder. Take one wealthy, bumbling philanthropist with a desire to see justice done. Introduce him to an individual only too willing to assist him – at a price! An individual who is meanwhile nursing a grudge against the British political establishment and who will stop at nothing to be avenged for other perceived wrongs.

Then, all of a sudden, the prize of a lifetime has become a most terrible curse; and instead our taciturn train-spotter finds himself riding the "train from hell".

ABOUT THE AUTHOR...

Ray Burston was born and lives in the English Midlands and has so far published eleven novels.

In 'ANGELS UNAWARES', a well-meaning recluse wins a huge lottery prize and, through misplaced altruism, ends up becoming roped into a violent terrorist plot.

'OPERATION SPREAD EAGLE' follows the eventful story of an aid convoy put together by British volunteers to repair and re-equip a maternity hospital in impoverished southern Albania, and is based on his own experiences as a member of just such a mission in 1993.

Shadowing his own experiences as a politician, 'THE MAKING OF THE MEMBER' follows the turbulent careers of two ambitious parliamentary candidates set against the backdrop of British political life during the 1980s. The sequel – 'THE MAKING OF THE MINISTER' – follows them into parliament and takes the story up to 2010. A final book in the trilogy is planned for after the next General Election!

'ACT OF ATONEMENT' is an intimate study of friendship, love and betrayal set against the backdrop of the bitter war that France fought in Algeria between 1954 and 1962.

Waged across three oceans, two continents and one desert, 'THE SOUGHING OF THE WIND' chronicles the final fateful voyage of Admiral Graf von Spee's German cruiser squadron at the outset of the First World War (and has been knitted together from true accounts of this incredible story).

'TO REACH FOR THE STARS' tells the enchanting and often harrowing tale of a young woman who breaks out of a claustrophobic home environment to enlist in Britain's Women's Auxiliary Air Force (and is based around the story of his own late mother's wartime service with RAF Bomber Command).

Confronting every woman's worst nightmare, 'THE BLACK COUNTRY GIGOLO' is a gripping psychological thriller in which a strikingly handsome young man captivates three very different women, only to confront them again with a truly shocking event from their pasts.

Set on the Isle of Wight during Britain's most memorable long, hot summer, 'THE SUMMER OF '76' is a tale of two young people from different sides of a big, wide ocean uncovering dark secrets about their families' pasts.

Set in Ray's native Black Country during the 1960s, in 'THE SNAKEMAN OF SNEYD END' an eccentric local campaigner unearths the truth about the mysterious disappearance of young people in the town, and which takes place against the backdrop of the controversial closure of its railway.

Ray's latest novel – 'MR SMITH & MISS PATEL' recounts how a an ambitious and successful divorcee winds up a castaway on a remote uninhabited island, his perilous exile given an unexpected twist when he discovers he's sharing it with a most unusual and illuminating companion.

Ray's reasons for becoming a writer are many, but one is that he has always been fascinated by history - and in particular by how ordinary people can find themselves caught up in the sweep of its happenstance. The story of mankind has often hinged on the deeds of such people – "whose names are found inscribed on war memorials, but not in history books" (as the French novelist Jean Lartéguy once observed). Most of Ray's novels echo this theme of ordinary people shaping larger events.

YOU CAN FOLLOW RAY ON FACEBOOK BY SEARCHING FOR 'RAY BURSTON - AUTHOR'.

Printed in Poland
by Amazon Fulfillment
Poland Sp. z o.o., Wrocław

49941707R00214